Ultimatum

By

Vladimir Fleurisma

Table of Contents

Dedication

To my family

Chapter 1

This is Thomas. Thomas will be dead in forty-eight minutes, twenty-six seconds, but for now he's just tired. His job's stressful.

Dr. Phillips couldn't have felt like this all those decades; it was his job.

It takes Thomas five minutes to get out of bed. No one likes being up at 5:45 on a Sunday morning. His wife's probably with Benny downstairs. For some reason that kid is always up early on weekends; not weekdays when he should be, damn infants. Now 6:00 a.m., Thomas' toiletries are finished. 6:10 he's dressed for work. He smiles at his son's baby talk as Kelly lifts her head from the refrigerator with a bottle but no smile or kiss. She's been like that lately.

"Come on, Kel," he says, but she's not acknowledging him. "Are you going to be like this every day?" She's still ignoring him. "Goddammit, woman, what the fuck is your problem?" he asks, slamming the stovetop.

The loud bang startles Benny.

"See what you did?" says Kelley, lifting Benny. "It's ok. Daddy didn't mean it. He'd tell you himself, but he has to work today," she adds spitefully.

"That's not fair," says Thomas as she and Benny pass him on their way upstairs.

Kelly doesn't understand and Thomas can't worry about her feelings. She should be happy he's not on the front lines fighting the Coalition. Twelve years of war, and she's living a comfortable life. Why the complaints? Thomas won't bother with Kelley's confusing ways now; he has responsibilities. At 6:19, he's channel surfing with a bowl of cereal. There's a re-airing of a political discussion. It's election season after all.

#

"Because President Wallace lied," says Cliff. "The Coalition will surrender by the end of my first term. We're in the same place we were fifteen years ago and fifty before that."

Rob, Cliff's colleague, is sighing at his friend's clear misinterpretation of the facts.

"First of all," begins Rob. "He set conditions for how that would happen, but we have to deal in facts. The neutrals finally have to make a decision. And we have more of everything."

"What are you—what?" says Cliff.

"Oh please just stop, Cliff. Please just stop with *the It's too hard; no end in sight*. It's a tired argument that never manages to answer anything."

"Classic Rob—change the subject when you're losing. Ignore basic human behavior when it doesn't fit your point. While in the throes of your nonsense, add a fact that completely misrepresents its origin. You know-"

"Hold on, Cliff," interrupts Claire, the show host. "Rob, does he have a point; times are tough everywhere, and by every economic standard we're doing better than the Coalition. Isn't that a strong argument?"

"No," says Cliff. Let's state some facts. "Regular people don't read economic reports and most don't care. When you're dying of starvation, you go to where the food is closest. More than likely that'll be where the security is also. Is there anyone in the thirty-eight that's found it to be different? Has that fact of human nature changed, or did you finally wake up Rob?"

"Rob?" asks Claire.

"This is crap," says Rob. "Pardon my language, but let's state the actual facts. There was just a survey put out by tretus.com showing we've taken 59.8 square miles since recommencing. None of those people seem terribly upset about that fact do they, Cliff? But oh wait, I know what's coming, 4.65 billion people in the world, but of course, we must be inhaling too much oxygen. We literally make food for others to eat so of course our friends owe us nothing."

"I swear sometimes you sound like an accountant. The Coalition's territory is 9,078 square miles, so who cares you pompous——. Why don't you shove a rock up your ass so we can see a steam engine?"

"Gentlemen, we're getting off track here," shouts Claire.

#

There is a knock at the door. Will is letting himself in as always.

"Hey, we're gonna miss the shuttle if you don't hurry up," says Will.

Its 6:28 so Will is right again, the jerk, and Thomas just remembers he forgot his briefcase upstairs. He pauses at the sound of Benny. The little boy laid another bomb in his diapers, didn't he? Kelley is changing him. What can Thomas say? A poop joke? No, those suck. I love you? No, too cheesy.

"We'll talk tonight, ok?" says Thomas.

Kelly snaps her head around. "I want a divorce," she says.

Thomas feels as if an electric current is liquefying his bowels. Did he hear that right? Yes, he heard perfectly. Should he-what the fuck? He slams the door and storms outside before he does something he'll regret as Kelly stands, holding in her emotions. If she cries Benny will and—and what is it with this boy's stomach? Then the tears roll out.

Will's confused by Thomas' sudden change in demeanor and leaving the TV on. Who does that?

#

"Just admit it," says Rob.

"I'll admit you're a chronic fear-monger," says Cliff. "Everyone's desperate. Show me a stat on crazy behavior algorithms."

"Now who sounds like an accountant?"

#

Thomas is flooring the pedal while Will takes in the majestic view of the smog-infused blue morning.

"If you're having trouble with Kelley maybe she should come to work with you, to see what you're doing," says Will.

"No," Thomas says flatly, veering onto the highway.

"Hey, you were working last night right? Did you see anything weird?" Thomas shakes his head. "Someone added a new security program to the bottom level. The tech guys are trying to scrub it, cause you know new programs could have backdoors, but they keep getting locked out."

"Secretary's going to be pissed; he's been real excited lately."

"Yeah, he has. I bet you're getting another promotion out of this," says Will, nudging Thomas who shakes his head. "Well, he's coming today. And so is Daniel." Will air quotes the name in clear dislike. "Both via video conference."

"Really, this is a big day then. Try not to embarrass me."

"No promises," says Will, catching something through the haze. "What is that?"

A blackish object is streaking across the sky.

Six 240-megaton nuclear warheads have just struck the greater Pennsylvania area.

Chapter 2

No, D thinks as the crackling fills the tunnels. *Get control of yourself. A fucking nuke couldn't kill you; these ugly bastards won't either.*

He takes a deep, ragged breath. Normally he'd be running as fast, as far, and for as long as possible, but like an idiot, he was sleeping. Sleeping?

The one fucking time I didn't want any, my goddamn eyes close, and now everyone's dead. Well, what's done is done.

Get up marine. You've got a mission. Get up.

As D pushes himself off the rusted tunnel wall, it crumbles, letting in freezing black sludge like the sound of scrabbling rats.

Shit.

The uglies don't see, but they can hear very well. However, a maze of metal sound can be a bit unreliable. He can do this. *Find a map. Well, use the uglies to navigate away from their general location, find an exit, then find a map of the tunnel system. Things here aren't matching his records. It's only been a year and a half. It couldn't have changed that much. There's a pattern. Find it, or you're dead.*

"Shit," he says aloud in his new husky voice, courtesy of the puckered four-inch check mark scar on the right of his neck.

He's up and running in one fluid motion. A loud squeaky crackle comes; it's the type of sound that tickles the inner ear, causing involuntary shivers. D's as used to the sound as anyone can be, and it's as if the pygmies are close, hopping like some absurd pack of blistered, overgrown softballs. D keeps to the side of the ribbed tunnel, using the up-slope to gauge his distance from the side. He keeps to a steady trot. Only a fool runs full speed in pitch black over unknown territory. Of course, if he didn't let one of the brutes break his flashlight, that wouldn't be a problem either.

Forget about it. Either go topside or find shelter.

He has nineteen thirty-caliber bullets in his rifle and the knives in his boots. That's it. No food or medicine, and he needs to clean the filter in his suit's CO_2 converter soon. He's still got his skin. He skinned that sniffer months ago, and it's still useful, so that helps with the cold. He might have to lighten his satchel to move faster. He feels the irregularity under his feet and sniffs. It's the telltale sign of a fork in the road. He's reached an intersection point of four paths, not knowing where to go.

He's not on his game today. If his sister were here, she'd be reminding him of that right now. It'd be something about preparation topping instinct or some useless shit.

"Make a decision before the enemy makes one for you." That's what General used to say when D was a boy.

He goes straight, barely pausing as he clears the intersection point. It was a good choice, he realizes, as he stops to hear. There's hissing and grunting. He goes back to the steady trot, telling himself to stop every ten seconds and listen. He's in a larger tunnel now. Its diameter is twice his seven-foot wingspan, which means if he's caught in here, flanking will be very easy and a stepladder might pass right by him without him noticing.

It's unlikely; he's noticed that virtually all stepladders are on the righthand side of tunnels, but some freight elevators sit to the left in a few states. He hasn't been here long enough to know if construction tendencies work that way or not. Those could be great places to hide for a few hours. He could zigzag so he doesn't miss it, but that's stupid. It would slow him down for one. All the uglies are more agile than people and the sludge might have something on it the sniffers could pick up on.

"One problem at a time marine. Don't get excited. You're you for a reason."

The uglies are still hissing. D's doing all right, but there's still no stepladder. D's known he's been lost since his flashlight broke, but this isn't right. There's supposed to be landmarks down here.

This tunnel must not be finished. That means there are routes for construction workers to use for lunch breaks and end of shifts. Those could be at any point in the tunnel, but they always lead up. Find one.

It's a few minutes more of twists and turns before D's at a tunnel too tight to get through without crawling. He'll have to double back. Just as he's doubling back, there's grunting. It's coming directly ahead but sounds far enough off. The intersection point is an L shape and detours left.

Can I make it in time?

"You better make it in time," D tells himself.

He keeps to the right of the tunnel, his left now, and sprints. It's a deep crackling coming towards him. The way he came is only eight feet in diameter, so this could be a good thing. The brute might be carrying some of the pygmies until they get in a good position to ambush. D can use that. He feels in his bag.

There's nine grenades and adhesive. In a place this tight, with unknown air quality, either air pressure or chemicals could kill D with the uglies. That would defeat the purpose.

So what else?

D has four seconds before he reaches the intersection. What to do? He tosses up the grenade as he heads down the righthand tunnel. He's fairly certain he placed it right. He passed the place twice, and nothing's wrong with his sense of touch. He sprints ahead as the grunting turns to unbearable crackling. His suit is open, letting the biting cold seep in. When he's five seconds from the intersection, he turns, eye to the scope. Yes, it's useless when there's no light, but it's muscle memory. His right ear will hear the brute coming.

The unnatural thing comes, gagging it sounds like. D estimates and tilts his gun up one mil-dot. He fires. The tracer round gives a brief flash, silhouetting a hulking shape vomiting two dozen small things and the grenade above, just three inches off. D fires again, and a large orange and black cloud engulfs the tunnel, raging forward after D. He blankets himself as the searing air and flames roll over him.

D's groaning as he lifts the skin off himself. He folded the four-meter-wide skin evenly before covering himself so half of it's still useful. He feels his russet brown skin and square jaw for burns. Nothing hurts and nothing feels out of place. Fire hurts. There's a bright pocket of flame coming from the uglies and little wicks around the tunnel. It looks like he burned everything close to him. He can't hear the crackling only the pops of bodily fluid from the beasts.

A quick pat down of the skin smothers the flames. He steps closer to the horde and finds a line of corpses about two hundred yards long. He nods to himself. That was a damn good shot. One problem down. Now, find the exit before more come. The ambient light will make things easier for a few hundred yards until he realizes what's wrong. His industrial green suit doesn't have any cuts or scratches, but the black sludge running down his leg makes the problem clear. The tunnel's falling apart, and he just let off a bomb.

There's more hairline fractures on the top of the tunnel than D can count. Parts of the metal are melted in spots, which only means that larger slabs of rust and steel will fall when it does collapse.

He wishes he had a better sense of how far the flames went. He'd know how far to run then. There is a way. D was going to replace the skin, but the air's still warm. He'll just leave it open until the cold returns.

It's not a perfect plan. It's about negative thirty degrees topside, but he shouldn't need more than ten minutes to find an exit. D's wrong. There's a creaking like metal snapping. The skin's wrapping around his torso as he speed walks down the righthand side of the tunnel. For most things that involve speed in confined spaces, being six foot three isn't an advantage, but D's supremely agile for any height, and if the roof falls, the skin can stop most penetration. Crushing, on the other hand, is a problem.

Something falls. The soundwaves ricochet from all directions, so D keeps his current heading. Spikes of metal are easier to navigate with the flames still behind him. He runs this way and that, keeping to the places with the most light. There's still no exit; then a gust of wind pushes him forward with the sound of screeching rusted metal. The thump of ten thousand pounds of metal and rock block the light.

"Shit."

D goes back to his steady trot, keeping slightly to the right. The ten-minute mark passed about seven minutes ago, and D's having a silent cursing tirade. He passed three intersections and is hearing another tremble. It feels like it's coming from this tunnel.

I can't see shit. This is very fucking annoying.

He's positive he missed the exit, but there's not a chance he's doubling back. A four-foot thick slab of rock smashes down just behind him, and D's running. It's foolish, yes, and he learns why as his foot catches the raised lip of the tunnel floor. He doesn't fall, but his flailing to keep his balance sends him into the side, crumbling the wall and causing more shaking.

"Dammit. Oh shit," he says aloud. It's the designated word of the day.

The floor just tried to buck him. Now he has to keep a steady pace. No one's running through this type of terrain. He tries hopping over a bulging patch of ground, but it rises with him then promptly fractures as he tries pushing off it, sending him sliding back. Another piece of roof crashes down, causing his landing spot to compress and peak like the world's smallest mountain. He's over the faultline just as it shivers and falls, taking everything above it. D's deeply concerned; he turns back and must wait a full three seconds before he hears the rock crash to the bottom.

The entire tunnel's a jumbled mess now. D can't trot like he wants but carefully step over and around the rock and crumpled steel. He's only got one suit, and it only blocks radiation.

"How did you let that big bastard break your flashlight, you idiot?" D asks himself.

D's feeling his way to a new problem. At first, he thought the tunnel got blocked off, but the tunnel broke in half, and this part has sunken to knee level. D thinks about shooting a tracer round to see just how bad it is, but letting off shots in a structure proven to be architecturally unsound is stupid. So, he's crouching, now hoping the bottom didn't fall off like the one a few minutes ago. It's a tight fit, but D's on a strict starvation and rations diet, so he's through and lets go of the ledge.

It only took half a second, but it felt like an hour to hit bottom. It's as jumbled as the other side of the tunnel but stable...until it starts shaking.

Fuck.

He's still doing his careful step around routine but a bit quicker. There's no exit down here. He's coming to face that fact. He'll have to find a flat, sturdy piece of tunnel to sit in until he can find his way out again.

Maybe I can make myself a torch. Yeah, maybe a pitchfork too, something real classy and nostal—

"Fuck!" he growls.

A piece of the tunnel has landed on his hand. He tugs and tugs, but his hand's not moving.

"Don't panic. Don't panic," he tells himself, heart nearly bursting from his chest.

Adrenaline's numbed his hand, so D doesn't notice or hear the popping sound from his fingers as he twists his hand to escape with the now too familiar rumbling sound of fragile infrastructure. The rock won't move. It only takes a moment. D hoped from the moment this happened he wouldn't have to do this, but he won't waste time trying to talk himself out of it. D's rifle's off his back, aiming at his left hand. As he shoots, the ground shifts, tilting him forward, sending the shot deep into the black.

His hand is free, but the floor around the sixty-foot column of rock is fracturing like quicksand. D's up running forward, like a drunken man not caring about a careful pace as the uneven surface makes him flail and slip. Fifteen bullets left. He shoots ahead and finds his bullet slam right into a wall. D shoots again, hoping he can...uh...shoot through the wall. He should've aimed for the hinges.

D's not one for overt facial expressions, but no one can see, so his eyes bulge in shock. He slaps the door, looking for a way in. He won't attempt shooting; this is a military-grade door. There's no way in without a key. The composite metal's too strong. This doesn't stop D banging on it as the crashing sounds fill his ear. More rock and steel fall behind him, coming closer with each crash. D's pushing against the door, now grunting with effort. He shoots the hinges and watches the bullet ping harmlessly to the roof, the roof that's now breaking, dropping pebbles over him as he keeps pushing.

The tunnel's screaming now. Its sides are folding in on itself as bolts and rivets spurt out. The door is shaking now, humming like an enraged metal dragon. D's face is red with desperation as he punches the door, demanding it to open. The door bows out, pushing D back. He shoots it again.

I'll unload my entire magazine on this fucking door. I'm not leaving without a fight.

The muzzle flash highlights something. Rock is sliding right onto the door. Slowly, the column is forcing its way through the door. These new doors are meant to stop Coalition bunker bombs, but what can stop twenty thousand pounds of irresistible earth? The door snaps against the pressure, sending a waterfall of dirt down into the deep. D doesn't wait for it to end. Another tracer round shows a slab has fallen to make a right angle inside the room. He leaps in, angling himself to reach the slab, and is trotting along this five-foot-tall hallway. A tracer round shows him steps leading up. They're only a hundred feet away, and the slab is shifting, letting dust fall on D's helmet.

The slab groans like volcanoes erupting. It falls, but D doesn't see it. He's skipping steps on his way up eight flights. The tunnels continue their scream, but D is out on level ground. *Not like the temperamental bitch below.* He's almost about to laugh. He hasn't done that in a while. He's at a door, the same composite material but open—wide; welcoming D with soft white light. D would say hello, but the pain's here.

He's broken bones before, and he doesn't need to check if his left pinky and ring finger are cracked and dislocated. He'll live. He's got painkillers, though he's not going to use them, and he can find a stick to make himself a splint. Right now, he needs rest and food. As he walks over the congealed path leading out the door, he wonders if the dead man lying against the wall would care if he stripped him naked.

D can see the self-inflicted bullet wound through the mouth and out the top of the skull. The man has the long, jagged bite mark of an ugly on his arm. He was dead either way. Well, D's found one at least, and this dead man's got a gun and a great suit.

Chapter 3

Jamie, looks up at a sky that looks back with supreme indifference. It's Monday. Seventy-nine weeks. A week starts on Sunday, but Jamie's one of those people who doesn't consider Sunday the start of the week. If work weeks start on Monday, then Monday's when it starts. Her watch says 8:38 a.m., but it might as well be midnight. She throws a middle finger at the sky again then checks to make sure no one saw. First Lieutenant Varnum's got to maintain decorum at all public times.

The ship lurches, and she grabs the railing, padded combat gloves aiding her grip. That doesn't stop the toxic water from splashing her faceplate.

Disrespectful water thinks it's got the right to wash my camouflaged hazmat suit without my permission. Well, fuck it too.

That's when Andre coughs. Jamie turns, ready to punch something. *I said that last bit out loud, didn't I?*

"Sergeant Greer?" she asks sternly.

Andre knows better than to laugh at her, in public anyway.

"It's half past eight," he begins. "You wanted me to bring the civvies up." He points behind him.

Thirty-seven people are stepping on deck. Zach, as always, is first. Her new right eye makes it easier to see some things, but not others. She can see posture for instance, but their faces are blurred. The doctor said the other things would take time to develop.

My sight did come back. He couldn't have been full of complete shit.

"You know, Lancaster County was so damned expensive five years ago. I wanted a house here, but Adina didn't," says Zach.

Jamie winces. She apologized for that. Well, the captain did on her behalf.

"Decorum," says Captain Tiller. "Glaring every time someone asks a question won't help anything, Lieutenant."

Jamie doesn't answer. It's one of the few times Tiller's right about something. Andre slaps one of the civvies upside the helmet. Pat tried to take off his helmet. *What's wrong with him?* PFC's Jo Carbolo and Paul Anastasio follow the last ones topside, gripping Tim. He and Craig were fighting again. So that makes seventy-four. No suicides. That makes today a good day so far.

"Patti looks a bit twitchy," says Captain.

"She was complaining about wanting real air last night. What's that even mean?" says Jamie.

The Captain smiles, shaking his head while Andre yells at Tim and Craig.

"Today's a big day, Jamie. Wanna get your routine in?" asks Captain.

"You know, I don't," says Jamie. "Just glad we're back home. It's been a long time."

"Well, that's complete bullshit. I expect my second in command to be honest with me. Why are you worried?"

Jamie stares up at the six-foot six captain. A question like that can mean anything given the day. She looks out at the darkness and comes out with it just as the mini-replica Statue of Liberty smashes to the deck, sending everyone scattering. Now she owes Andre half a peach-flavor ration pack. *The bitch couldn't wait two days, could she?* Andre's smiling his white teeth from across the deck. His chocolate skin would be blushing if it could. That's four straight wins. First were the amphibious wheels, then the two propeller blades, the ship cracks, and now the lady. *He's good at this.*

Jo and Paul look sick as they report no strays in the lower compartments. There are only eighty-three people on the ship. Andre already counted, but the young guys need to feel helpful and judging by those eyes, he's won another bet.

"Help us shine these lights," the sergeant says.

The floodlights shine on both sides of the ship. Twenty-eight ambushes and fifty-four dead. They don't overlook things like water-born flanks from desperate people. Where the land isn't white, it's twisted metal and rock sprinkled with cars and furniture.

"I really hate you fucking people," says Lilly.

It's been a few days, so it's no shock. Thinks Jamie.

"Are you going to lie again to keep us quiet?" Lilly asks Jamie. "Come on, say there's still a government, please just be patient. Well where the fuck is it?" she screams.

Jamie's jaw clenches. Captain's standing there waiting, doing nothing. Jamie's not going to answer; she points her rifle at Lilly. Lilly stops then turns to cry on her husband, Matt's, shoulder. She screams again after her helmet bumps into his. Jamie smiles; the gun always shuts Lilly up.

"I really don't like her," says Lilly.

It's not the first time Jamie wonders if she made a mistake taking these people off boats, screaming, dehydrated, *clueless.*

I hate civvies, she thinks, turning to a smirking Captain.

"Your duty is to protect, not like, Lieutenant," says Captain as the ship's helmsman informs them of a blockage ahead.

A fallen bridge has closed off too much of the Susquehanna River to wade across. If they want to reach this signal, they'll have to disembark now. It's too much to ask for a dock, so the helmsman's looking for the shortest place to extend the ramp. He, three of the officers, and twenty civvies will stay with the ship as always. Captain wanted to bring everyone, but Jamie insisted against that. They compromised on leaving some of the civvies with the ship.

Jamie organizes the fifty-five people into something respectable. This routine is old hat by now, but on days like today, the civvies can be difficult. She's already used the rifle. *Maybe I'll threaten to shank someone. That'll get a laugh.* A cocoon of military people surrounds the civvies as the ship anchors. Andre does another headcount while Jamie speaks to Captain as the others pretend they can't see.

"Sir, our last order was to stay clear of any large land bodies," says Jamie.

"As I said last week, that was fourteen months ago, Lieutenant," says Captain.

"I know, sir, but Pennsylvania was a population center. And...well, I don't believe you've thoroughly thought this out. With all due respect."

"Speak plainly, Jamie," says Captain. "No one's listening."

"This stinks like a trap, and you know it. This signal sounds legit, sure, but I think you're letting hope get in the way of good sense. You didn't want to hear my objection over coming here, fine, but not letting me take a scouting team? Bringing yourself and civvies along into for all we know is still a war zone is dangerous and—" Jamie pauses as Captain waits. "You're being stupid, and I don't know if I can fix this for you."

Captain leans over the five-foot-nine Jamie. "Do you know why I put up with you?"

Because I run the ship, handle logistics, and have too much respect for your position to start a mutiny to remove you from command. Jamie shakes her head.

"Because you're smart, innovative, and determined. But sometimes you think you know every damn thing, and other times you're a two-bit psych doc. Look at our situation. The civvies can handle themselves. They've been at this long enough. Stop treating them like children. We have cracks in the ship, three days' worth of food, no medication, not much ammo, no support, and some of us are showing signs of radiation sickness. Now Jamie, I respect your ideas—you know nine out of ten I'd agree with, but right now, you're wrong. We're going to Three Mile so get over it."

"Yes, sir," she says stiffly. If this doesn't work, I'll have to speak with Andre about chains of command.

After lowering the ramp, Andre repeats the rules. "If you see something, say something and stay close, dammit. We don't want to lose any more of you. Oh, if you lose your weapons, that's on you. You're not getting a spare."

The civvies nod, knowing the words by heart. Suddenly Greer, while watching jury-rigged flashlights, sunken bloodshot eyes, hunched postures, and premature wrinkles, finds an overwhelming lack of optimism. He and Jamie need to have a real talk later. For now, he'll take in the recycled air of his CO_2 converter and lead the survivors down the ramp.

#

Hours into their forage, they reach an affluent shopping district where a contorted skyscraper's 180 floors fill the lobby of six nearby buildings. For a half-mile, this seems to be the pattern. If they could scan above the buildings, they'd see the starburst pattern of bombs, but what they can see explains clearly enough. Charred faces expressing bemusement, car frames melted to asphalt, pets and wildlife alike now, one with power cables, while light poles and rebar embrace over rotted remains.

"We're crossing this to get to a nuke dump?" says Patti.

"Shut up," says Andre as they approach a narrowing passage.

The passage is a nightmare for maneuverability. Aside from looking like what a place would if a building vomited, there's ice shielding, sharpening and compacting everything into subtle shades of black and gray ice. Greer wants to find another way.

Jamie agrees and volunteers Jo and Paul to find an alternate route while Andre does another headcount. The corporals resent grunt work. They've been with these people since the beginning and earned respect. Keeping within arm's length of each other, they scan the area.

"We're not going to find anything here either," says Jo.

"Probably not, but at least it gets us out of that boat. And anything's better than hearing you talk about women's armpit hair all day," says Paul.

"It's disgusting, I mean, I have to look at you too."

The lieutenant flashes her pocket light in the set pattern of Morse code from a distance. "You remembered to do that every thirty paces so we know where you are, right?" she sends.

"Yes, ma'am," sends Paul, having completely forgotten to do that. "The lieutenant scares me," he whispers.

"Yeah, too much muscle. I like 'em soft," says Jo.

The corporals laugh then remember where they are. They don't want to be away from the group any longer, so they don't do a thorough check of the area as they should. Instead, it is a quick glance that finds nothing before heading back. Then Jo turns, claiming he heard something, but only finds snow drift.

#

Jamie and the Captain are the last to squeeze into the roofless, eight-storied mall plaza. Craig stumbles over a shriveled forearm before angrily kicking it in protest of everything—scavenging, the hazmat suits, these dead people, his ruined home, and whatever else he can't think of now.

"Get back in line," says Andre, disgusted by the whining.

A few civvies share a laugh at Craig's expense.

"The hell with all of you," says Craig, staring at the still giggling Patti. "You're still fat. Remember that woman."

Patti lost fifty pounds over these months, but it's still a sensitive issue for her. She balls her fist, but Zach, Pat, and Timmy step in to keep the two apart. At the back of the group, Jamie is calling for quiet; her flashlight tints red for rage. The five civvies quiet quickly.

"Did you see that?" Zach whispers to Pat, spotting movement.

"No, I can't see a damn thing out here," says Pat.

"Is that you asking questions again, Zach?" asks Jamie.

The civilians keep silent as they push through a crushed ice cream parlor, preserving mangled bodies in a sweetened selection of milkshakes. They're now at an uprooted parking lot with office desks somehow finding homes on top of vehicles with crushed employees between. The sight is not unexpected but still unsettling.

The group reaches a fork. Andre points the party left but as they pass, Jo calls for a stop, feeling his helmet. He's sure a rock or something struck him. The others are skeptical; it wouldn't be the first time Jo faked something to get back to the ship.

"I know I felt something," says Jo.

"Yeah, I'm sure. Can we go now?" asks Paul.

After a few rude gestures and a warning from Jamie, they pass the plaza into a row of blown out storefronts.

"There, I saw it again," says Zach.

"Saw what?" asks Greer, signaling for a stop.

Pat slides away as Zach gulps air. He timidly points left along a row of debris mounds.

"It looked like the silhouette of a four-legged animal, a big dog."

This makes no sense, but Andre tells two PFCs to investigate.

Other than a corpse half-buried by a file cabinet, they see nothing.

"Sir, I think we should head back, search somewhere else," says Jamie, clutching her rifle.

"There is nowhere else. We're gonna keep going until we get to this damn island," says Captain.

The group turns up the road to where the damage is less. As they trek past hollowed novelty shops, the left side of their cocoon breaks. There are loud cracks of body armor and flailing lights and a crackle.

"What happened?" asks Captain.

Two soldiers lie insensate, one having a large impact crater at the ribcage, the other a collapsed skull.

"Did you see what hit them?" asks Jamie.

"I think I saw gray fur," says Paul.

"We're going back," says Captain.

As they turn, something unidentifiable flanks their right. Another soldier's head now faces 180 degrees from its proper position, causing Timmy to constrict his throat muscles to bellow out his fear. The nearest soldier smacks him upside the head as the ordered seal of protection begins pulsating. Some are cursing, but there have been firefights before, so no one panics yet.

"Where do we go, sir?" asks Jamie. "Just as someone yells "Contact," she fires blindly in all directions, causing what those in the trade call contagious firing.

"I don't know. Just start shooting," shouts Captain, eyes wide.

"Where?"

"Wherever. Just shoot dammit," says Captain, checking his magazine.

No one's paying attention to Timmy, so he seizes his chance. Breaking away from the group, he climbs over a debris mound before sliding down the other side. However, he hasn't asked himself where the attackers are. There is a crackle, not like fire, but an unnerving sort that tickles the inner ear. Timmy never sees what breaks his spinal cord, and thankfully, he can't feel himself rip into halves that fling at the bulk of the survivors. Tumult is easy to find when people are scared, and Timmy flying from the black and landing in two places makes it simple to see why.

"I can't get a good look," yells Andre as blackness takes another.

What Greer can't see are the nebulous attackers breaking the survivors into smaller pockets of fodder. Jamie, Captain, and four officers are speeding towards the ship's relative direction, while five civvies, Patti, Pat, Zach, Lilly, and Matt head the opposite way. Patti is losing her footing. Falling, she grabs at the feet of Zach, who is able to kick her off.

"Wait," she says as Zach keeps running.

"You son of a fucker." yells Patti.

"I can't. I can't," says Zach without turning.

Jamie, now far ahead of Captain and the others, slows down.

"I can't tell where I'm going, sir."

"It doesn't matter," says Captain as various body parts of Jo flop in front of them.

Jamie can't begin to tell how far that throw was but flashes her pocket light at its flight path. Her brother could usually come up with something crazy to get them out of this.

"Captain." Captain isn't here. If we get out of this, I am deposing that son of a— The Captain's head explodes right onto her facial plate. Something broke through the helmet and forehead of Captain and out the back. Her pocket light finds the PFCs shooting a wall of blistered skin. She runs.

Flashlights sheathed in fluid are giving the buffet a haunting red glow in the sea of frozen black. Craig is one of the unlucky few not too scared to understand what is happening. They're eating. They're eating people and throwing them at other people. It's too much. Craig's been feeling sick lately. He throws up. The vomit bounces off the facial plate and back onto his face. He gags and rips off the helmet, taking in the noxious air. He coughs hearing the gnawing of flesh, fracturing bone, and slitting tendons as a shiver-inducing crackle fills his hearing just before his sockets tear off.

The now foursome of civvies is maintaining speed as members of the shaded horde trample Patti. A barrier of wreckage halts their route, looking for a path around; rebar slices Matt's calf, leading him head first into a jagged metal beam. Lilly, preoccupied with being third behind Zach and Pat, is unaware of her husband's fate. Zach reaches the opening and waits for Pat when the head of Patti smacks Pat as he makes his turn. Pat falls to the ground with massive skull breakage. Lilly hurdles Pat to a zigzagging Zach.

"Shit, shit, shit, shit, shit, shit, shit," says Zach with Lilly closing in.

Jamie is some distance away from the two remaining PFCs when she realizes she's lost all sense of direction. She wipes at her facial plate again, annoyed at the gore clinging stubbornly. Her mind's ignoring the fact that the temperature is so low Captain's gray matter has frozen onto her helmet.

The aggressors are close. That damned crackling is causing involuntary shivering. Her flight instincts are overwhelming training. Then there's an explosion.

A yellow glow shows dozens of things rushing towards the fire just as wind from the blast flies debris into her face, adding more sediment to her gore glazed facial plate. These aren't human, that's clear. Something about them is distorted. The frozen blood on her facial plate isn't helping either. They're going for her people. *Someone of my team had a grenade maybe and decided to take as many down as possible. Enough wondering.* Jamie's training forces her to control her shock and duck a swing before falling into a depression. Rolling over, her lights catch a dark, silver coat leaping over her, followed by the congenial sound of a military issued M-70 automatic assault rifle fire.

The lieutenant climbs her way over the depression and sees Greer across the way, surrounded. She smiles just before a mammoth limb breaks Greer's back. She doesn't hear his scream but sees claws carve a path left to right. Jamie's never seen someone literally taken apart like this. She is shocked still. Then Greer flies at her, smashing into her ribs, breaking bone. The force of the blow lifts her from the depression onto the ice where she skids, rolling end over end into and out of a nearby car, rusted metal tearing her suit before she slides to an abrupt stop on the outer wall of a fallen building.

Jamie doesn't lose consciousness but needs a painful breath to regain her senses. Her pocket light's gone, but her rifle is still strapped to her arm. She sees nothing but a sheet of black.

"Come on, you motherfuckers," she yells, straitening her now cracked facial plate. Still nothing.

She decides to increase her rifle's light intensity. Attackers who were rushing towards the still-burning feast stop as the heat of the light touches their hides. Several pause, focusing on its origin. *Did I make a mistake?* The quickness of these things is something to note. She shines her light to the far left as the attacker stops its slow creep towards her. She fires where her instincts tell her the creature is most likely to move. A soft pat and grunt makes her smile.

She shines the light to the far right and sees it. The top of a blood-covered blackish-gray figure sprinting towards her, not caring for where the light lands. There are no justifiable words to describe the inartistic shape. The image burns into her as the muzzle flash sends the abnormal creature into a charging frenzy. She aims center mass and lets a burst fill the thing's middle, causing it to spasm lifelessly. The lieutenant's shooting causes the other ill-favored incarnations to turn their attention to her. She fires again, aiming center mass once more, crumpling another. So whatever these things are *I can kill them.*

Progress.

A plum of something ejects from the back of one attacker, and the rest sprint away. Jamie's at a loss. *Have I scared them off?* Now there's scratching like that of metal. The car she fell through is coming into sight. She turns, looking for something, and finds the opened window of a corner office. She crawls in just as the car smashes into the wall.

The creatures are crackling more while ripping the car away with Jamie swimming over jumbled furniture, seeking the hallway. More objections are packing the office while Jamie uses debris and the doorframe as leverage to reach the hallway. The sides of the downed building start to tremble as Jamie searches for an escape as her gun light fails. Crackles are forcing her down the shaking hall with the involuntary flash of defensive rounds to keep the things back. *Stupid, why didn't I think of that before?* Another burst of bullets. At her twelve, there is a manhole. She is scrambling for this hope as the creatures tear into the hallway, causing a collapse.

\#

Zach, close to exasperation, looks back because he hasn't heard footsteps for several paces. He never looked back to see who was trailing him, but Lilly is now silent. He looks around, seeing a floating light high in the moonless sky, arching closer to him, now two, three. Zach drops to the ground as Lilly's limp form flops over him. His adrenaline reserves magically refill, and Zach continues his run to nowhere. However, a sharp squeezing pain is riding up his calf, over his back, onto the crown of his helmet. Zach is trying to wrestle off the petite demon as its high-pitched hiss works like a homing beacon for its fellows.

Zach's earlobes feel as if about to rupture while the tiny attacker tugs at his helmet. In the midst of his battle, a force knocks Zach to the ground, obliterating the top half of the aggressor.

"Come on," says a towering figure, pulling him to his feet.

Zach asks no questions, just runs. The figure moves remarkably well for not having a visible external light source. Zach has trouble keeping up. The figure is leading Zach to a subway station, over the turnstiles, down steps, and onto train tracks. Seeing Zach drag his feet has the figure, in a raspy voice, curses Zach into an overturned train car. The creatures explode through the turnstiles and quickly onto the train tracks. Zach follows the speeding figure through train cars as a shard of glass cuts his left arm below the shoulder.

At the third to last car, the man stops, lifting a carbon block covering. He pushes Zachariah in with creatures closing in. From the bottom of a stepladder, Zach sees the figure shoot three times before climbing down closing the opening as a large explosion sends shockwaves down the ladder. The man quickly and smoothly wastes no time, pushing Zachariah down a long tunnel to an incomplete, miles-long subterranean construction site with six paths leading any number of places.

"Second to the left," says the figure.

As they reach the tunnel, the man tells Zachariah to help lift a manhole. He pushes Zachariah in before tossing a half-dozen more grenades at the other paths and closing the covering.

#

There's no sound in this unlit room. Zach taps along the wall before reaching the figure.

"Get off my leg," he says in a husky voice. Zach is sure it's a he.

"What are you doing?" asks Zach.

"Shut up."

After a minute or so, the man steps off the ladder with a click, revealing in soft white light, three beds positioned at the center of a hut, and to the right, a shot-open safe, pouring out military rations topped by a dented box. Left of that is a large brown chest, and at the far wall is a second escape hatch. Behind Zach are four residential CO_2 converters, the devices that purify air. In addition, to his immediate left is his rescuer, standing six-foot three-inches tall, dressed in an all-black combat uniform, holding an assault rifle, two combat knives on the inside of either boot, and a satchel. The pants of the uniform fit loosely as with the sleeves and padded gloves of the same quality, implying stealth and versatility, connected to an armored vest with four pockets, two to each side. They lead to a loose neck fiber attaching to a helmet, seventy percent of which is a reflective material crested at a groove running along the top and down through the back of the helmet. The man presses into his palms, folding the helmet into the groove down the back and around the top of the vest, showing russet brown skin, steel and calculating dark brown eyes, a bald head with a clean-shaven face, impeccable teeth, a strong chin, and a deep-penetrating scar curving up the right of his neck.

"I'm Zach," says Zach, extending his hand.

"Were you bitten?" asks the man, referring to Zach's bloodied left shoulder.

"I don't know."

The man fires a shot into said shoulder.

"Owe!" Zachariah screams, backing away.

"Are you itchy?"

"Wait."

The man aims at Zachariah's head. "Is your mouth dry?"

"No dammit. Stop, please."

"I'll find out soon enough." The man lowers his rifle to the chest of Zachariah, motioning to the bed furthest from the rifle. "What were you doing top—" the man begins, then backs away as Zach vomits.

"You son of a bitch," says the man, jumping back.

Zach is face first in his own retch as the man walks over to poke him with the gun barrel. Zach is not moving. The man sucks his teeth, contemplating his next decision. *Killing him would be simple, but where there is one, there are two; I may be able to find resources, and infected people do not vomit.* He needs to know what Zach knows before discarding him.

Chapter 4

Zach awakes to nineteenth-century French opera. The man has taken off the top half of his uniform, leaving a stitched thermal sweater to cover an impressive musculature.

"You're finally up," says the man, sifting through papers.

"What happened?" asks Zach.

"You threw up, and I had to clean that shit."

Zach looks over at the cauterized spew while feeling his bandaged arm. "Why'd you shoot me?"

"Can't be too safe."

Zach finds the lack of contrition annoying. "How long was I out?"

"Four and a half hours," the man says as Zach starts to massage his temples. "You still queasy?"

"No."

"You had radiation sickness. That was my last anti-rad vial so don't get sick again."

"What happened?"

"Didn't I just tell you?"

"I mean—this morning I was on a boat. We stopped here 'cause we needed supplies, and there was a signal. Now—"

"Supplies? Here? You'd have had better luck drinking your own piss."

"Look man, what happened?"

"Are you retarded or something?" Zach drops his head into his hands, and the man asks, "What do you know?"

"I know everything blew up a year and a half ago. I know I was on a business trip when it happened. I know while it was happening, our host and his crew left us. I know, after that, everyone on the ship went crazy trying to figure out what to do because all the electronics went dead. I know a week later, a military ship came to collect people. I know Captain told us we were under attack, and they were ordered to stay off the continents and that the last transmission was over a year ago, repeating the same order, then nothing.

"It's like the world cut us off. Then a couple months ago, we start running low on food and medicine, so we started looking for places with anything. We went to small islands, but since the floods, most of those places are dead. So, that leaves the coasts in violation of standing orders or whatever. Then a few weeks ago, Captain tells us we're heading back to America, tracking a signal, then those things pop out. What are they?"

"Ugly."

"What are they doing?"

"Trying to eat you and making babies." The music switches to nineties heavy metal. The man immediately grabs the music source, a gray, quarter-inch thick multimedia device to play sixties rhythm and blues. "What kind of ship were you on?" the man asks.

"It was uh—it looked new. It travels on land too, but something broke a wheel axis a while back. It had the Statue of Liberty on top of it."

"It was amphibious with the Statue of Liberty? That's one of the newer U.S.S. destroyer models. Those should be able to last up to two years without maintenance," mumbles the man.

"Well, it didn't." Zach leans in, unsure to whom the man is speaking.

The man reaches into his satchel for a bar of soap and a sharpened mirror edge. With a blade from his left boot and the satchel and rifle, the man walks to the leftmost CO_2 converter, keeping Zachariah in his line of sight.

"You ever shot a gun?"

"The military people didn't trust us with guns."

"That means no." The man nods. "Look, I'm going to make this as clear as possible. If I feel that you're putting me in danger, I will shoot you. If you're useful, I won't."

"My name's Zachariah, by the way. Most people call me Zach." The man sits, foaming the soap to lather over his face. "What do you go by?"

"D," says the man.

Zach sits, searching for a way to continue this talk. He moves closer, but D's off hand has the rifle pointing at Zach's chest, forcing him back to the bed. A few minutes pass, and Zach has another question.

"Where did those things come from?"

"I don't know. The first ones started popping up around thirteen months ago. You said you got orders right after this whole thing started, so they must be what the orders were about. I thought it was rough before. Those ugly bastards ate everyone," says D, running the blade along his cheek.

"How many of them are there?"

"A lot. They're fast too, agile, really strong, especially the big ones, all smart. They know how to work together. What am I saying? You just saw it."

"What do you mean?"

"Tactics. How to adjust to situations quickly. They usually outflank you with overwhelming numbers. Identify weak points then pounce. Their skin is interesting too."

"What do you mean?"

"What?" asks D as if realizing Zach is still in the room.

"I'm sorry man, but help me out. How do we fight them?"

"If you ever see one of them, hope it doesn't see you, or smell I mean, and run away, hide, do whatever you have to, just don't get caught because if they don't kill you, whatever they're carrying will."

"That's why you shot me?"

"More so because you didn't answer my question."

"Well, what is it?"

"What is what?"

"Whatever they have?"

"A virus. Kills in ten days. Irritates the skin, gives you cotton mouth. Not always at the same time. Then it invades your brain. Makes you go crazy. The last stage makes you lose control of all motor functions. Your organs start to overwork themselves then either your heart bursts or your brain fries. It looks painful."

"How long does it take for the symptoms to show?"

"You really don't know this?"

"No, I don't. Please man."

"As quick as a few hours. The latest I've seen is thirty-six."

"So how do you fight them?"

"I just told you. Run away, unless you have enough firepower. It's like they're made of Kevlar or something. If you don't hit the right spot, it takes a whole clip to bring one down. Of course, by that time, it's got a hundred of its buddies running after you."

"What was the one you shot?"

"The small ones are soft. Quick little bastards, though. They usually do the scouting. If you want to kill them, getting them to stay still is the challenge. The basics are: use fire or certain gases to throw off their scent."

D whips away the excess soap before moving his grooming kit to the bed, separating him from Zach.

"How did you get here?" asks Zach.

"You said you were on a military ship?" asks D, ignoring the question. Zach nods. "If that's true, they were just identifying and eliminating the biggest threats first. That's why it was so easy to get away."

"What?"

"Uh—you're caught up now right?"

"Hey how did you-" D stops Zach.

"I thought after I answered your damn questions you'd stop asking them."

"Sorry, I just figured since we're stuck together you wouldn't mind the conversation."

"Who said we're stuck together?" says D stonily.

Zach quiets as D pulls out a collection of diagrams and blueprints. Fifteen minutes pass, and Zach cannot help but ask what D is looking at. D answers by upping the music volume. After five minutes, a break comes where Zach asks how D came to live in this place. D sucks his teeth before stopping himself. He has a solution. The music stops and papers shuffle into one stack at the middle bed. Zach's going to help D dot and scan the pages onto his device.

D holds out a pen. "You won't win," he says perfectly flat into Zach's eyes before handing over the pen.

Zach's going to dot every three to six inches along an already pre-lined path before D scans each. There are squiggly lines that veer off at random angles; Zach doesn't get it, but D's already handing him papers. Every three pages, Zach can say whatever's on his mind. D will answer as best he wishes. Zach agrees grudgingly, but it's clear D already said yes for both. It's nice to be useful on the other hand. The other civvies didn't do much past cleaning and running. Zach can tell he's rambling aloud when D looks at him and he stops.

Three pages scan as a loud rumbling thump comes. Both pause. Then after a moment, D is back to scanning. Zach still has that lost panic face. D hates seeing it on civvies, so he answers the unsaid question.

"If it was them they'd keep at it. They're very persistent," D says, motioning for the next pages.

"How long have you lived here?" asks Zach.

"No one lives anywhere anymore," says D.

"So you found this then? How?"

"I looked."

Zach clenches his jaw and almost spies a smirk from D but probably not.

"Two exits," D continues. "Thick walls. If you can't find that look for anywhere with a good vantage point. Never set up camp topside. And stay two days, three days max. Next."

"You from Pennsylvania?"

"No. Next."

"Well, where are you—"

"Three mile. That's where I'm going. Yes, most likely the same transmission you heard. Next."

"How long did it take you to get here?"

D won't answer this on the grounds of grating assholeness.

"We're switching to every four pages."

Normally Zach would ask what the fucking problem is, but D looks like a man who can beat his ass quite easily, so Zach is quiet, then his stomach growls. D looks at Zach then points to the safe and its brown blocks of tasteless nutrition. The packs read four thousand calories per serving.

"This has—" D stops Zach. They're on two pages. "Do you have any water?"

D hands him a sealed water-conversion bottle from his bag.

"You're not getting another one so don't drink all of it," D adds as Zach, with one gulp, takes in nearly half its contents.

"That's a nice suit," says Zach. "I've never seen anything like it. What's it made of?"

D isn't answering that one either, so Zach has to wait four pages. Zach has nothing. D glances at Zach, hoping the message got through, but Zach opens his mouth again. Zach used to be a man of considerable wealth. As the head of Neostat, a once respected tech giant and inventor of the mass storage device, Consumption Unique Banding Elements, known commonly as C.U.B.E.s. He was very well known.

"Neostat?" says D as Zach nods. "Didn't that company go bankrupt. Something about cubes having backdoors for the company to access personal information, the exact opposite of the marketing pitch—then I think the CEO left because he owed a lot of people money?"

"Those assholes tried to ruin me," Zach says loudly.

"How much did you owe?"

"Over three million, but the deal I had lined up in the Mediterranean was going to clear that away."

"I bet you're glad those credit bureaus don't work anymore," says D, giving what might be mistaken as a grin.

Before Zach can ask, however, he must wait four pages.

"This looks like a safe spot you found," says Zach.

"I was lucky. And this isn't safe. Always prepare to leave within five minutes."

"How long have you been here?"

"Well, because my kind heart got the best of me, today is day three. I'll need to make back time tomorrow."

D is still saying I as if Zach is furniture or something.

"Are we—" asks Zach as D raises four fingers.

"Will we reach Three Mile tomorrow?"

"No. It's way too far. There's supposed to be a bunker along the way. I want to stop there. Reload on supplies hopefully. The raucous you and your friends caused should make the path easier."

"I had a wife, Adina," says Zach for no reason D can fathom. "Beautiful woman. A natural brunette, but dyed her hair blonde for the last six years of our marriage. That woman stayed with me through my financial troubles. I was convinced she'd divorce me when that audit came. Most would. But she stayed. We went on a trip to the Mediterranean."

D doesn't ask what happened, but Zach tells anyway.

"She could deal with temporary bankruptcy, but the new reality was too much for her. Two months after all the lights went off, she—mentally retired. That's what Captain called it. I guess he thought it would sound better than she went crazy. Asshole. The pitch-black days and that damned radioactive haze everywhere. I think it was more so that she couldn't feel the air. She told me that's why she wanted to come with me. Then not knowing where her family was. She never complained about it. I think 'cause of my situation. Then came her first attempt. The standard wrist slicing. I got there in time to save her.

"The second was death by drowning, throwing herself in that ocean sludge. Crewmembers pulled her to safety before she got too far away. The last was clever. She just did nothing. She didn't eat or drink. On day two, I tried to use a funnel to force food down her throat. She just threw up later. The third day, she told the lieutenant what I did. I was ordered to stay away from my wife. The fourth day I got an apology.

"Next page," says the dispassionate D.

"Is there anything you miss from your old life?"

"No—well, women and cake."

"The first is understandable but cake?"

"What's wrong with cake?" asks D, reading Zach's face.

"Nothing." Zach shrugs. "I'm just a pie man."

D gives a snort and Zach chuckles.

Progress, thinks Zach. *Progress.*

Zach is thinking up something else to talk about, while D thinks up ways to occupy Zach's time as the last pages are scanned.

"You're a Marine, aren't you?" asks Zach. D nods. "I can tell. Half of the military people on the ship were Marines. You guys have a look about you." D stares expressionlessly at Zach. "You're in really good shape. How are you still looking healthy out here?"

As Zach continues his verbal ambush, D sits undecided on the matter of clubbing Zach over the head with his boot.

"You're special forces? Probably spent twelve years training then you finally got accepted. Now you're passing through trying to survive. I'm right, aren't I?" says Zach.

D walks to the safe and hand's Zach the dented box. Inside are four damaged cubes and a flattop, circled key with spiral grooves to the inside.

"You said you're good with tech, right? Well, let's see how full of shit you are. Fix these four cubes."

These aren't Zach's brand of cubes, but all are based on his design. D tosses him a cloth and vintage Appleseed liquor.

"What's on these cubes?" asks Zach.

D shrugs. "Fix them, and we'll find out together."

It is quiet for the next twenty minutes, as Zach focuses on cleaning the cubes, and D compares this second copy of diagrams to a sewer map from out of state, nodding as he checks points.

"I'm not just good at software, you know," says Zach for no reason again. "I've been a bit obsessed with tech since I was a kid. First, it was video games, then trains, but I settled on software for financial reasons."

D looks him back to the cubes. A half an hour passes before Zach's asking of what D's specialty was in the Marines.

"When'd I say I was-" says D before stopping himself. "It is scout sniper."

"How old do you have to be to be a Marine sniper?"

"Scout," corrects D. "There's no subjective age limit except for eighteen. If you're a good shot, in supreme physical shape, and can survive the fourteen-week course, you can join the team."

"Since we're on age, how old are you?"

"Thirty, you?" asks D.

"Thirty-one," responds Zach.

Zach doesn't look thirty-one. He looks ten years older at least. Zach doesn't have a good reason to lie so D guesses that money troubles are what make Zach so stressed, well that and malnutrition. Zach can see what D is thinking and laughs.

"It's been rough out here," says Zach.

"Tell me about it."

Zach tried his best to fix all the cubes. He points to the inch long motherboard he's taken from each and shows D the fused chips on Cubes 2 and 3 and the partial fixes to Cubes 1 and 4. D nods as if he already knows before tapping his datapad.

"What do you miss most about women?" asks Zach.

"They smell nice and the ass." says D.

"I'm a breast man."

"You're wrong. If strip clubs ever come back, you'll need to go to one."

Zach snorts. "I'm not. You're just lactose intolerant."

D raises a brow at that and nods at Zach, then the music returns.

"What's on that?" asks Zach.

"Lots of things. I haven't been able to look through the entire library yet. A million and a half songs, over twenty thousand movies, some of the pornos give me good ideas, but the sound is the best part. It gets boring when you're out here for weeks by yourself."

This last statement is slightly confusing to Zach. He shouldn't be shocked. *Weeks by himself? How would I be after that much time?*

Zach looks around, stopping at the rifle barrel, trigger box, thirty-round magazine, and other pieces he can't name before seeing a handgun pointing at his forehead.

"Any time," says D, eyes blazing.

"Sorry, it just—forget it." An hour passes, and Zach's tired. D sees the signs and tells him they leave in four hours before turning the datapad so Zach can see the time.

"We leave at half past four in the morning?" Zach asks in shock.

"That's a relative term now."

"You gonna have that on all night?" Zach asks as the music turns to fifties blues.

"Yes," says D as he begins to reassemble his rifle.

Zach stares. D stares right back as if daring Zach to try something. Zach turns his head. In moments, Zach drifts into REM as D hums lyrics through the night.

Chapter 5

Japanese folk music has Zach rising from his bed while D rummages through his bag with his vest sitting beside him,
showing Zach something revolting.

"What the hell is that?" asks Zach.

D turns to the vest. It's the blistered, blackish-gray skin of one of Zach's new friends. "Two of them were fighting. One lost. Took me an hour to skin it and cut out the meat."

"What?"

"Yeah, these things are interesting," D mumbles to himself. "I'm still trying to figure out how they're able to breathe up there with no problem, but I know this skin helps, and it feels nice."

Of what little emotion he shows, he now leaks curiosity and admiration for these creatures, which is concerning to Zach. Suddenly, Zach is rising in a panic; his hazmat suit is ruined. *What'll I do? What'll I do?* D is already walking to the chest to unveil an industrial green hazmat suit, complete with its own standard CO_2 valve, which from an angle looks like a lumped pouch.

"Oh come on, you don't have anything that looks like yours?" asks Zach.

D raises a brow. He's worn this suit for months; its only drawbacks are not being bulletproof or bite-proof or self-repairing, but it blocks radiation. No one can say that's not important. Zach slugs to his bed, with fifteen minutes to fully dress. D wraps the skin around his torso then over his shoulders before putting on the jacket and taking two dental tablets for teeth cleaning. These are the same kind that cleaned Zach's vomit, so Zach declines D's offer but will take a flashlight and a second satchel filled with half the calorie bars of the safe. Zach has a *what the hell for* look on his face.

"I told you, you need to make yourself useful," says D. "About that, you run well enough but you were sick, so take two of the calorie bars now to keep your stamina."

"This is kinda heavy," says Zach, holding the bag.

"Whining gets you shit from me. We're leaving."

The datapad plays an early twenty-first-century hit. *I still love you, baby.* D knows this artist as being famous for suicide twenty years ago; he hums the lyrics. At 4:25 a.m., the music turns off, and the helmet reforms to D's head. Tapping and circling the temples, he tints the facial plate to his liking. Zach's finally ready. With a deep breath, D shuts the lights off. Zach immediately loses all sense of reference as the hatch gives a creaking turn.

"Are you coming?" asks D from somewhere to Zach's right.

Zach follows the voice into a long crawlspace leading to a wall of pipe entrances. Zach clicks on his flashlight to see D pointing to the nine-foot diameter pipe, opening at the top of the dwarfing wall. D is easily scaling up it, using the natural foot holdings of the wall and smart grooves of his boots while Zach is simply managing. D extends a hand for Zach's last step into the pipe. Zach is cautiously lighting each step while D easily makes his way, continually tapping the side of his helmet.

"Do you need the light?" asks Zach.

"I gave it to you, didn't I? Watch your step," says D as Zach stumbles over the sharp edge of the rusted pipeline.

D takes out his datapad in concern. The device shows the pipeline going for a ways, but he's not convinced it's correct. He rubs eroded metal framing between his fingers and decides to find an exit. He says nothing to Zach, of course, so Zach must hurry to keep pace with D as he trots to a door leading down and away from the pipe. Zach belatedly reaches the door as D kicks it open. D taps his helmet as he makes his way down two flights of steps to a solid wall. D stares blankly at a brick wall then begins patting various spots. The ground beneath him disappears with a splash. Zach panics.

How the fuck am I getting out of here now?

"Down here," says D as Zach lowers his light over a cesspool D now finds himself floating in. "Keep the light there; I'll be back."

Zach doesn't like this alone stuff. There's nothing but absolute black, and the flashlight doesn't give much ambient light, so Zach, as opposed to when on the ship with its regenerating lights and people, for the first time keeps back the dark feels and the stifling hardness of the unknown. D can't return soon enough. A full minute or hour, Zach's nerves can't tell, and D's back with news. There's an opening at the bottom of the submerged staircase.

Zach needs to jump in.

"Did you hear me? Get down here," says D.

"I can't swim," says Zach.

"Weren't you just on a boat?"

"I didn't have to swim to get to it."

"Well, that's too bad. Get in."

Zach won't come. D throws multiple four-letter jabs, but Zach's still not moving. D's losing patience quickly and thinks if it's worth convincing Zach to come or leaving the idiot as a loud crashing sound echoes.

"It's them," says D.

Zach jumps feet first into sewage, not stopping to think, as D pulls him through brown chunks, past two ruined doors, up to a manhole. D attempts to push the covering up but can't. He produces a mini explosive from his bag to open the manhole. He sets a five-second fuse before pushing Zach away. The explosion ripples into a cascading white, out towards the men then up and out forming a geyser sucking D then Zach through.

D lands harder than expected on a large cross-section of train tracks. D's still catching his breath as a screaming Zach spurts out to land where D just was. D rises, adjusting his jacket, surprised at the hurt he feels. Zach scrambles to his feet, asking where they will go and why D isn't rushing. D checks to see his unbroken datapad as Zach asks again. D has no idea what Zach's talking about then remembers.

"I wouldn't worry about them. Not now anyway," says D.

Zach stops analyzing the situation. "Real funny, jackass."

"Keep your voice down," says D, observing the area.

Behind them is the collapsed roofing of the subway. It appears as if it was a deliberate explosion from beneath, judging by the star-shaped fall pattern. It's too cold to see temperature variants, but it must have happened within the last few days.

"It should be a straight shot from here," says D.

Ninety minutes pass when the two make it to a rubble suppressed train. D steps to the ledge where the decaying flesh of the conductor, fogging the glass of the exit door, elicits no reaction. The door is stuck on something. With two hard tugs, a half-dozen steaming bodies spill out onto the tracks.

"Try not to touch them. And keep on my six," says D, using the handrails to push himself over the bodies.

Moisture is forming on D's suit as he tip-toes over bodies so desiccated it's not possible to tell genders. Zach remains close, trying to keep clear of the bodies lining the car when D notes how thankful both should be that they are not taking in what must be a colossal stench. Zach's again unsure of D's words and wonders if it sounded like optimism or sarcasm. D doesn't strike Zach as an optimistic person. *What does D mean by keep on my six?*

"Six means back or behind me. So six, twelve, nine, three. Back, front, left, right, get it?" says D to a completely dumbfounded Zach. "I hate civvies," D mumbles continuing on.

Some of the passengers show crush injuries, others, signs of cannibalism. The next train car is lying sideways, keeping all corpses to the bottom, or left as it were. D will have to use the sidebars to swing across. He shows excellent upper-body strength, effortlessly gliding to the next exit where he awaits a depressingly slow Zach, who predictably slips into a lifeless pit. Zach is frantically searching for his flashlight while pushing back desiccated limbs, only managing to make him more entangled. D swoops in to pull Zach up and over the carcasses after a moment of watching.

"I told you not to touch them," says D, handing Zach the flashlight.

D pauses at a glint caught by the flashlight. He jostles with a corpse, probably a woman judging by the skirt, and after a moment, the body falls apart, releasing its death grip along with multicolored fluids. Zach gears to throw up as D turns to him.

"Don't throw up in my suit."

They're now in the second to last car. Zach's having more trouble keeping up, stumbling five consecutive times, making D lash out. He throws Zach against the window, causing a crack.

"Don't fuck with me," says D. "It wouldn't be that hard to snap your neck."

Zach nods, feeling just how much stronger D is than himself. They reach the last car where they find no passengers other than a one-eyed, nine-fingered man, holding a crushed fifty-caliber handgun, blocking the one opened exit. The man's white and black urban combat uniform says he is not of the piles of deceased commuters. He's been dead for weeks. The hole in his skull tells his story simply enough. What crushed that gun of his, barehanded no less, is more important.

D carefully moves the man to an upright position outside the train where he takes the handgun's clip, which somehow melded with the skin of his palm. After peeling the skin off and flicking the handgun back to the one-eyed man, D tells Zach how scavenging is the exception to the rule. D continues on his way as Zach asks to stop. He needs a break.

"These acrobatics are taking it out of me."

D remembers how threatening Zach made him a temporary acrobatic master, but whatever, he knows tech; they'll stop and eat. D turns over an uprooted seat while telling Zach to take only half a ration. Resources fade fast for the greedy. Zach asks why D took such care with the dead man. D doesn't answer. On that note, D checks his new taser.

"Need help?" asks Zach.

"No," says D before taking the rifle off his shoulder. It was under water. D taps the side of his helmet again before opening the facial plate.

"The air's not poisonous here," says D.

Zach waits to see D breathe a few times then takes off his helmet to taste the stuffed, faintly repulsive air while D stands another four-inch flashlight between the two. Satisfied the light won't tip over, D reaches into his satchel, pulling out his cleaning kit of frayed cloth and liquor. He'll use the cloth to dry all the pieces and the liquor to clean his hands when he is finished. Water is for drinking only. Watching D strip down his rifle compels Zach to ask if what he is seeing is as complex as it appears.

"Anything is easier with knowledge and practice," says D.

Zach continues watching D reconfigure the rifle into two guns, a handgun and a shorter barreled rifle.

"I had no idea you could do that."

"Get a grip," says D. "And before you ask, no, you can't do this with most guns. This is a specialized rifle built to take any type of ammunition. The trick is knowing the best ammunition for maximum efficiency. Nine-millimeter is usually best for handguns, but this rifle only has seven point six two ammo, and this new clip has fifty caliber bullets—way too loud. So I want to use the excess parts to make a silencer. The downside is the rifle loses accuracy, which this particular one doesn't have much of anyway, but fifty-cals are quite effective against the uglies."

Zach nods along clearly having no clue what he heard. *Seven point six two what?*

D grunts and keeps cleaning.

"Does that tapping give you a virtual map of the area?" asks Zach.

"Left is air quality and temperature," says D. "Right gives a detailed picture of the land. How detailed depends on your preference. It uses infrared or sound waves. The number of taps determines the accuracy and definition of the image. I like sound waves myself. Infrared hurts the eyes."

"So you are special forces? Is there still a government?"

"If we get trapped, I'll kill both of us. You first since you're a civvie."

"If we—wait kill?" sputters Zach. "You're not a happy person are you?"

"Is that a question?"

"Is that sarcasm?"

D goes back to cleaning the rifle.

"You know if you're worried about a trap, me having a gun might help keep us out of one. You could at least tell me how to stop those things."

"No, I don't trust you, and aim for the middle," says D. "It'd be the sternum on most things. A small soft area that underlines the breastplate or what would be the breastplate for humans. For the bigger ones, anyway. The small ones just get a hit, and they fall apart."

Zach nods with a sip of water. As he's about to throw the bottle away, D stares at him.

Seriously is D one of those green vs gray pollution freaks?

"Those bottles are valuable. They can convert urine to water," says D. "Don't throw it away."

Zach blinks dumbly then stares accusatorily. "Did I just drink piss?"

D stares back completely unfazed. "Was the bottle sealed?"

Zach can't remember. A grin forms on D's face. Zach's about to toss the bottle when D's eyes lock onto his own. The bottle goes back into Zach's bag.

"Jackass," Zach mumbles.

"It's time to go," says D, checking the datapad.

As they leave the train, Zach asks if the water at the other end will be a problem. D thinks based on the amount of water, the fragile state of these tunnels, most likely and soon, but what can they do? Zach's about to ask if they should leave their helmets be, but D still has his open so he doesn't ask. They walk and walk. D has a weird habit of mumbling while blinking rapidly. It makes Zach wonder how long D's really been alone. Why is he checking his bag all the time? What's in it?

"Why are you staring so goddamn hard?" asks D suddenly.

Zach stammers.

"Watch your step," says D.

Zach promptly slips and falls. D shakes his head. Everything around them is black, but Zach manages to slip over a white pile of shit.

"What is this?" demands Zach.

"What? You thought those ugly bastards use bathrooms?" says D. "Don't worry. That looks two days old."

"When can I have a gun?"

"No."

They continue walking. Zach thinks of trying something. D keeps ahead two arm's length from Zach, slightly off to his right. In fact, as Zach gives it more thought, D has had Zach to his right their entire trip, even last night when running, always to the right. Zach steps left. D who has his back to Zach steps left before Zach's step is complete. There's only so much room before D can't go left anymore. Zach moves left again and again. Closer to the wall D turns. In a flash, D has an enormous knife to Zach's neck.

Zach yelps. He didn't think D was that quick. *Where'd that knife come from? Why's there no ground?* Zach glances at a ditch hovering beneath him. *When did that get there?* D has cold eyes.

In this gloom, they match the atmosphere.

"I wasn't—" Zach begins.

"Shut up," says D. "You take the lead."

"I don't know—"

"I'll tell you when to turn." D cuts him off.

They continue like that, nearly as straight as an arrow until they reach a manhole forty-five minutes later.

"Step back fifteen feet," says D before pulling out his mini torch.

Zach stays in his line of sight as D cuts. This is very uncomfortable for Zach. He shines his light and sees black, rubble, and more black.

"Where were you when shit hit the fan?" asks Zach, voice shaking.

"Wisconsin on leave," says D.

"What kind of leave?"

"The forced kind."

D answered? Zach wasn't expecting that. He has to know more.

"Before you ask," says D. "I was awaiting a court martial for breaking a commanding officer's jaw in seven places."

"Why?"

"He was a jackass. He wanted my team to do something I'm pretty sure was illegal. He insisted, and I lost my head. My trial was supposed to begin eight days after the nukes, so yay I guess."

Zach was sure of D's sarcasm this time.

"I thought snipers worked alone."

"Of course I don't."

This is all D says as Zach waits for more. From the little emotion, Zach can tell something about this subject bothers D.

"So—" Zach begins.

"I'm through. Get in."

Black also describes this next subsection of tunnel. It's a two track level with a raised platform. The exit has collapsed on itself, but an opening wide as the station is just ahead.

"What was your rank?" asks Zach.

"What?" D stops to look at Zach. He's noticed Zach talks more when he's nervous. It's better to have a calm civvie than a scared one.

"I'm still a major," says D.

"Still?"

"You ever heard of a battlefield demotion?"

"No."

"Me neither, especially not in noncombat scenarios." D shakes his head. "Second lieutenant," he mutters under his breath.

Chapter 6

Three hours pass before Zach begins dragging his feet. He's talking about Texas while D half-listens. Zach's sure he saw a rodent scurry in the opposite direction. D saw it too, but he'll worry if a pack of them come.

"So where'd you grow up?" asks Zach.

"We're close," says D.

"Wereclos? Where's that?"

"We're here, dammit."

D tells Zach to move ten feet away and to keep his light pointed down the tunnel. The mini-torch is out again; pressurized oxygen was heating the frozen manhole to a fiery red. His helmet reseals as cutting recommences. Halfway through finishing, gravel in the distance disturbs the silence. The annoying squeak of rodents is back, and D's doubling his cutting speed as Zach asks what is going on. D tells him to be quiet before hearing more gravel movement.

"Hurry up," says Zach.

"Shut up," replies D, completing the cutting.

D throws Zach into ankle-high water before hoping in and attempting a quick weld of the manhole. D's pushing Zach down the flooding path, and seconds later a loud bang and splashing ensues.

"Run," D tells Zach as the water begins to rise.

D jerks back in a creature's grip. He feels a pop then a shot sounds, followed by a second and third.

"Get off me."

Zach hears the yell before dropping into deeper water. He swings his light in all directions as a fourth shot rings out and then an unnerving crackle. Zach turns his light to a reflective object moving towards him. The object ducks beneath the water before Zach feels a vice grip on his leg taking him down. It's D using the railing of the swamped stairway to reach a doorframe at the bottom. After pushing Zach into the next flooded hall, D fiddles with a grenade before floating it up to twenty pulsating red orbs swimming at him. Seconds later, there's a shock of whitewater engulfing D and Zach, ripping them away from each other before settling as if nothing happened.

Zach somehow muddles his way to the surface, eyes watery and jutting in every direction; all the more unsettling is the flashlight's flickering. Zach's eyes slow and focus just as a ringing in his ear fades with the only shaft of light. He feels the still rippling water and sees black again.

How the hell am I getting out of this?

Something grabs his leg again, making him swat at the water and yell involuntarily.

"It's me," says D. "Why didn't you go that way?"

Zach follows D to his left where his light shines on a deformed walkway that curves into the wall.

"I thought we were going around them?" asks Zach.

"Yeah, me too. Stay close."

As they leave the water, Zach asks how many of the creatures D can see.

"If you see one think thirty," warns D.

"Well, how many did you see?"

D ignores the question while telling Zach to speed up. Zach's still a bit wobbly, but D's keeping a fast walking pace with periodic stops to turn his head and listen. D's facial plate is lighter, so he can see more.

"There's supposed to be a stepladder seventy yards down," says D. "We'll have to go topside for a bit and try to double back. Hope it's not windy."

"You didn't get all of them?"

"I saw six hundred at that party of yours yesterday—"

D stops, snapping his head around. Somewhere in the black an unnatural is grunting and hissing with some type of liquid bursting out its back. Zach's already in full sprint as D slings the waterlogged rifle before pulling out the handgun and sprinting after Zach. D runs, wincing every other step as the creatures begin crackling.

They'll catch us before we are able to reach the stepladder unless I can do something.

Without turning, a grenade flies. There's a muffled burst and fire but nothing like D was expecting. Then there's more hissing and tearing. D knows he hears a body being ripped apart. Bones are snapping as the crackle comes tickling D's inner ear. One of the uglies swallowed the grenade, and its friends are eating him. *Uglies don't usually do cannibalism.*

Zach glances back, seeing D poking a grenade. He bounces into the sides of the tunnel because he has no light to keep him going in a straight line. Two more explosions send a wave of light past Zach, and a wall of heat and wind follows.

"There it is," shouts D.

The ten-step ladder stands welded into the wall, beautiful and black as onyx. Zach leaps onto the ladder, punching at the frozen manhole. D orders Zach to move his head between the rungs before he fires three shots. The manhole falls apart at Zach's touch, showering him with rust. A strong wind is the only indication that they are topside. D flings two more grenades before heading up the steps. A field of isotopes and swirling snow greets the men while blistered fiends hiss beneath. D looks for Zach, who is stumbling feet ahead. D lifts him then sees it.

"There." He pulls Zach to a flicker of light in the distance.

"What is that?" asks Zach as the light now splits into two.

"Hurry up, dammit," says D as the uglies burst from the tunnel.

D's blindly firing behind himself while Zach churns his legs towards the lights growing further apart. The second light also splits into two before an orange ball of flame arks high in the sky, landing in the midst of abnormals, scattering them. This second light bobs forward, taking on a tall man's shape, pointing them to a mound where the first light stands. D quickly puts several strides between himself and Zach, as the first light motions him along.

D notices that one light is shorter and seems a bit more feminine. One light waits for the tall man and Zach to reach them before typing into a keypad at the side of the circular door. A green light blinks. The first light pulls the door up but misses an unnatural leaping up twenty feet aiming for her back. Without thinking, D aims center mass, and five shots have the beast convulsing, its bulk slamming atop the hatch, shutting it.

"Help me," says the feminine voice of the first light.

The men are pushing the unnatural just enough to clear the frame. Three more figures sprint in from the opposite way. One discharges a yellow fog as another shoots twenty explosives around the hatch. The last light shoots a mammoth cannon ten yards ahead of the farthest explosive. Snow and steam fade and ripple before freezing as the swirls reach far enough away from the field of flames.

Chapter 7

The seven hold still with the last light still perched atop the stepladder. Five minutes pass with the joyful sound of silence. A disinfecting shower sprays as lights three, four, and five raise their guns, startled at the two strangers made invisible during the dark commotion. D raises his gun in response. Lights three and five are the same height as D, with the fourth noticeably thicker but shorter. The tall man tells everyone to lower their weapons as the shower stops, and a door opens into a large hall. D takes a moment to adjust to the brightness as over four dozen people fill the hallway.

"You're outgunned, asshole," says the third light.

"Have fun, you're not getting through this suit," says D.

The tall man raises his voice, telling the others to lower their weapons. Zach hides behind D, whispering something about bulletproof. D lowers his weapon. The tall man takes this moment to step between the parties for an introduction.

"Hi, I'm Hank," he says, extending his hand.

D glances at it to make sure there's no weapon but has his eyes back on light three. *Explosives guy has a big fucking mouth.* All of them have black and white urban camouflaged suits.

"I thought we had a deal here?" says Hank.

D glances at Hank again and steps back. He's outmatched in this position. He takes in Hank now. He looks to be in his late fifties at about six feet, eight inches, Caucasian, graying black hair, gray eyes, and bone-deep scar leading from the bottom right eyelid to the middle of his chin. First light takes off her helmet. It might be the fact that he hasn't seen anyone—let alone a woman— in so long but he thinks that she's very pretty. Standing five-feet nine-inches, with long, flowing black hair, luscious lips, slanted gray eyes, and ochre brown skin, she's shaking her head.

"This is my daughter, Jade," says Hank.

Zach picks his jaw off the floor to introduce himself.

"I'm Zach."

Jade rolls her eyes, scowling before light four puts a protective hand around her waist. He's handsome with green eyes, a chiseled chin, and brown hair that turns blond two inches from the top of his head.

"So this is why you're back early," says a woman, who also looks about fifty with mid-length black hair, slanted brown eyes, and mahogany brown skin. She's attractive for her advanced age. D realizes he really does miss women.

"This is my Betty," says Hank. "The one with Jade is Colt." He points to light four perched on the step ladder. "This is Bruce." He nods to the thick one standing five-feet eleven-inches. "That's Rita. You'll meet everyone else later. For now, I need to know you. Without the guns. Walk with me."

D hands both over to Bruce as a small, dark-honey child leaps into the arms of Hank. "Oh, this is Saffire. Her grandmother's around here somewhere."

D logs all the new faces and dimensions as Hank leads the way with Bruce trailing. They walk down the thirty-foot staircase to a vast dining hall painted white with a large chestnut dining table in the middle and numerous chairs stacked along the walls. Four doors, the one they came through and three at the back wall, left, center, and right, lit by five chandeliers swaying twenty feet above the hall. Door 4 is set into the left-side wall, leading to the lower levels, which totals to fourteen doors, thirteen numbered, seven to the right, even, seven to the left, odd. Door 7 is splintered and missing the top of its three hinges with the unnumbered bathroom directly across the way. A sienna-skinned woman steps out of the bathroom, long, curly black hair covering her face.

D must really be desperate for women. The tight jeans on her hips and legs are something else. At the end of the hall, nearly ninety yards from the exit, is a kitchen and a game room housing seventeen twentieth-century arcade machines.

The kitchen looks freshly renovated, beautiful cabinets stretching along the top and bottom. There is a state-of-the-art refrigerator, a new fold-screen sixty-inch television, a large counter fit for a five-star chef, and a family-size breakfast table for thirty sitting in the middle. Hank asks the two men to sit with him at the head of the table as Betty walks to the refrigerator. She puts a bowl of fruit before D, and he stares in monotone shock. He feels them. It's real fruit, pears, apples, grapes, and more inside the refrigerator. D takes off his gloves to squeeze an orange, taking in its texture as Zach smells a peach. The men eat.

"I hope you don't mind the bright lights. We adjust the intensity depending on the time of day. It helps keep everyone from going crazy," says Hank.

"What were you doing topside?" asks Colt.

"I guess we were looking for you guys," says D, stuffing seeds into a cloth from his bag.

"Where you guys from?" asks Hank.

"Texas," says Zach.

"West," says D, spitting more seeds into the cloth.

"Well, I have to say, I didn't think anyone else was still alive out there before you two showed up. None of us thought there were still people outside. Colt and Bruce came ten months ago. They didn't see anyone either; so how'd you two do it?"

Zach, always ready to share, gives a brief summation of the events leading to now, ending with being saved by the man to his left. Hank nods. He'll need to hear the whole story later. It's clear to D that he doesn't believe them.

"Sorry for my manner but you two smell like you just got out of a sewer."

Jade walks in right after Hank says this. She walks back out, nose wrinkling. Zach takes a very long look as she passes.

"Something wrong with your eyes?" asks Colt.

Zach turns away red-faced. D's annoyed Zach backed down. *I'll have to talk to him about showing weakness to strangers later when I'm not so tired.* Another man steps into the room with a serious face. He eyes the two and comes closer.

"This is Rick," says Hank as D eyes the new man.

Rick looks to be as old as Hank and Betty but with ambiguous racial features. Black hair losing its battle with silver, a cleft chin, and dark brown eyes with smile lines.

"No fighting, no stealing, and unless given explicit permission, you are not to touch anything on anyone," says Rick. "You violate any of these rules, and we'll boot your ass out of here, understand?"

Zach nods quickly, but Rick's only paying attention to D. It seems they've dismissed Zach as a threat already. A tug has D kicking away from the table while pulling out his combat knife. Hank and the others are up as Zach crouches below. D looks down to see Saffire staring at him.

"A bit jumpy, are we?" asks Bruce, pointing D's own rifle at him.

"How about you put that on the table," says Colt, gun cocked at the kitchen entrance.

"Fuck you," says D, not knowing how he missed Colt standing there.

"Everyone keep their triggers pegged for the sake of the child," says Betty. D's eyeing everyone, thinking of how he can get his guns back, coming up blank. Hank motions for D to put his knife down.

D sucks his teeth and slowly puts both on the table. Hank takes both by the handle as D sees a handgun shift in the folds under the table. Hank motions for Betty to take Saffire as the others keep guns on D. Betty is scolding the child out the room, and Hank smirks.

"Saffire's seven," says Hank. "They're curious at the age. Sorry about that."

"Stabbing goes under no fighting," says Rick.

"Rick, I'm getting really old. How'd I miss two-foot-long meat cleavers in this guy's boots?" Hank says, still looking at D.

"You are old, Hank, but that's a good question. Who's in charge of this young man's weapons?" asks Rick.

"I missed them, sir," says Bruce. "It won't happen again."

Hank nods, and with a lazy wave, everyone lowers their weapons, but no one holsters them. D keeps an eye on his weapon in the hands of Bruce. Hank coughs, and D turns to him.

"Are we gonna have a problem?" asks Hank.

Usually, D would give this old bastard quite a few problems, but Zach's shaking his head. Hank nods, smiling just before Betty comes back. She looks at Hank who nods back to her.

"You two stink," she says before motioning them to follow.

"Bruce, Colt," says Hank, and Bruce slides in behind D and Zach as Colt walks behind Betty, guiding them to their room.

"What do you think?" asks Hank.

"Too early," says Rick.

D should've guessed their sleeping quarters would be the splintered door seven. Betty tells them she'll be back with towels as they take in the bullet-riddled walls, overturned and smashed dressers, and wrinkled, burned clothes and bed sheets under the only light swinging over two undamaged beds spaced meters away from each other. Colt and Bruce stand still, sizing up the newcomers.

"Don't try anything," says Colt.

"Or what?" asks D.

Colt steps closer as Betty returns with bars of soap. "We have hot water and a few extra clothes if you want. Oh, and we recycle everything, so please finish that fruit you were eating," Betty says before leaving.

"Nice suit." Bruce smiles to Zach before he and Colt turn to follow Betty.

"What do you think happened here?" asks Zach.

"I think we need to be careful," says D, removing his vest and creature skin. D triggers the helmet to reshape itself for observation.

The underwater explosion scrambled all the sight functions. The suit's made to self-repair, but it's not healing as quickly as it should.

"What's wrong? I can probably help," asks Zach.

"No," says D, feeling for cracks.

Passively informing the men to use the bathroom, Betty returns.

"You two smell like a sewer. Shower. No one's going to touch your stuff. But if you're more comfortable, bring everything with you. Whatever it is, you're taking a shower."

The two sniff themselves as she leaves and decides she's right. Fourteen people doing a bad job hiding weapons stop conversations to eye the two men as they enter the bathroom. It is a large unisex bathroom, fifty-five showerheads spaced evenly around a double row of thirty sinks to form a u-shape are separated by a line of curtains cutting down the middle of the room. The edge of the left-side sinks are painted blue, and the right-side one's pink. To the far left and right are the toilets. The men shower as far from each other as bathroom gender rules allow. D wafts himself and the soap to judge smell. The bar has a pleasant flowery smell, which makes D want to throw it away. Those things topside love distinct smells, but this new place is another battlefield he has to blend into. He uses the soap.

Zach sings praises for hot water as the soap suds multiply. D shakes his head while placing his satchel on the nearest sink. He takes five minutes to make sure the smell is gone. *Zach's been at it for ten fucking minutes. What's the deal?* D pulls out his grooming kit and a second shirt and underwear as Zach asks if the bunker's as big as D imagined.

"The blueprint of this place was bigger. And I wanna see the armory."

Zach doesn't comment on D palming the shard of glass and sliding into his sleeve or the large, jagged scar leading from his left wrist to just past his elbow, let alone the six dozen other bite, stab, and scratch marks, but he needs a razor. D produces a Swiss Army knife. He nicks the edge of the sink to show how keen the edge is, then waits another twelve minutes before prima donna Zach finishes his primping.

"It's been a while," says Zach, smacking his smooth cheeks while observing his reflection. "I feel ten years younger."

"You're done?" asks D, frowning.

"You got those dental tablets?"

D reaches in his satchel for the tablets as a dog tag inadvertently falls out, showing the name Dorian. D has it in his hand before Zach sees a last name. D eyes Zach until he turns away and puts the tag back in the satchel.

They re-enter the hall, twenty-four people now stopping conversation as the two men walk to their room. Zach's grin fades to a flat expression as they take in the room again with cleaner faces. There's blood on the beds. Zach holds the pocketknife out but D waves it away.

Two women walk in. One named Dede, a blonde with a distractingly large cup size, and the other Elle, a redhead with a mousey face. These two aren't great beauties, so maybe D's not really desperate to see women anymore.

"Hi guys," says Dede. "We're the official bunker welcome committee. Would you like a tour? The only fee we require is the protection of two very brave and handsome men."

D sits, telling himself not to fall asleep while Zach has a silly grin on his face as he stares at Dede's breasts, happily accepting her offer. They look at D falling victim to his brain's demands.

"Can you give us a moment to look presentable?" asks Zach.

Zach's giddy. "A blonde and a redhead. What could be better? This place is three for three."

"Three for four. The butch, remember?" says D as Zach nods.

"But what do you think?"

"I don't know yet. You go with them. Tell me how it is. I have to update a few things."

As Zach closes the door, D slowly lifts his left leg, revealing a swelling shin. He curses, letting out his discomfort. Leg injuries are a problem in the best of times. *I need to fix this now.* The leg rests on Zach's bed for examination. A bottle of liquor's dousing a bandage. He wraps it around the shin with a knot and tries standing on it as a sharp pain sits him back down.

"You'll be fine in a few hours, get up," D says to himself.

Betty knocks again, and D's back to a normal sitting position instantly.

"Just wanted to let you know it's two o'clock now, and we have dinner at half past six." D nods with no trace of a grimace, hoping she'll close the door. "Where's your friend?"

"He's on the committee tour," says D.

"Dede tried that on Colt and Bruce too." she laughs.

Betty smiles before finally closing the door, allowing D to raise his leg again. This is an unfamiliar place; he has to keep himself awake. He'll check his other knives before tackling the taser. Distraction usually works.

Another knife from his bag slides into his sleeve. The beds move to a sixty-five-degree angle behind the door. He taps his leg while walking to the dresser. He turns it right-side up, one foot from the doorknob. A grenade hides in his pant leg pocket. He walks to the wall juxtaposed from the door and carves a bullseye. He takes several practice throws, using both hands, sticking the knives dead center. He slaps his cheeks and begins fixing his taser.

Chapter 8

D awakes to the flickering light swaying above a bed, bucking D off. A child, seven years old, stands, smiling with serrated fangs before charging D. Just as D's about to smack the child, more come bubbling up from the other beds to smother him. D swings wildly, hitting one child clawing at his neck, as two others take his legs. Dozens more are on him, tearing at his arms and chest. Water beads down the walls as the room fills with children.

He gathers his strength with a battle cry, forcing the minors off. The youngest, only three, charges, and D connects, shattering the child's face as it dissolves into a puddle. The eldest, sixteen, has a pipe. The boy runs, splashing water as more children dive at D's legs. D feels for one and takes hold, squeezing her as she slaps his forearms. D's eyes open to Zach feverishly slapping at his forearms while hands crush Zach's voice box.

D lets go, and Zach gasps and coughs.

"What the hell was that?" demands Zach.

"Why didn't you knock?" asks D, turning to his jumbled taser.

"I did."

"Everything ok?" asks Betty at the door.

Was she there the whole time?

"Fine," says D, as Zach massages his throat.

"We start in twenty," she says neutrally, as D kneels to poke the dry floor.

"And why'd you put the dresser in front of the door like that?" asks Zach. "The damn thing knocked the door right back to me."

"That's the point," says D, mastering himself. "She was talking about dinner right?" Zach nods. "It's been four hours already?"

Zach has an indignant look as he nods. *What's his problem?* D frowns, pulling up sheets then remembers, *Fat Face has my guns.* He sighs and puts the charge box of the taser in his pocket.

"You still have my knife, right?" D asks.

Zach nods.

"Lead the way."

Zach stares angrily. D stares back.

"Knock next time," says D.

"Asshole," mutters Zach.

D's face relaxes into a slight smirk.

"There you go. I knew your balls were still in there."

Zach turns back, mouth opening and closing.

"We're getting to know each other, Zach," says D, patting his shoulder. "What'd you learn?"

Zach snorts before walking into the dimmed hallway.

"I think they're leaving soon," says Zach. "And there used to be more people here."

"I couldn't nail down Dede but speaking of women, there's one upstairs who looks fucking perfect. You need to see her."

D raises a brow and walks quicker. The dining hall has a half dozen social pockets scattered randomly. Zach nods to Dede and Elle fraternizing near the dining table and notices Jade sitting at a chair to the left of the head of the table with Colt's arm wrapped around her. He seems upset about something, and she rolls her eyes. Bruce stands with Rita in the largest gathering where the sienna-skinned woman briefly turns away from the two before D can get a good look. Zach nods at her with a smile before guiding him to their voluntary tour guides.

D doesn't hear them, but someone taps his left shoulder. He moves his arm up to block the hand while simultaneously palming his glass shard. Most don't notice, but the ones that look like military spaced evenly around the room eye him and Zach. So that's who I need to watch out for.

"Sorry, I was calling you," says Betty. "You didn't hear me?"

D shakes his head.

"Walk with me," she says with a smile.

Half of the soldiers move to keep D in their line of sight, while the others move closer to Zach. Betty leads D to Wanda.

"So Zach says your name's D," says Betty. "Is that D-E-E or is D short for something?"

"It's just D."

"I know your mother didn't name you a letter. What's your—"

"The name's D lady." D eyes Betty squarely.

"Ok," she says, raising her hand before sharing a look with Wanda. "This is D."

"You look tired," says Wanda, who is near seventy with prominent wrinkles on her pale skin, gray hair, and dark-blue nearly black eyes.

"I'm fine," says D, keeping a question to himself.

"See, I told you he was handsome," says Betty.

"Saffy, can't stop talking about you. She thinks you're a super soldier who's angry about something. Is that true or do you just like not smiling?"

D shrugs.

"Word of advice, you're alive. Things could be worse. Smile."

D remains stone-faced. "I get it; girls love the lonely warrior routine. Keep it. It works for you."

"Is that a fact?"

"Are you coming on to me, young man?"

"Is it working?" For a millisecond, the women have gotten what they will consider a smirk.

"Look at that, Betty. He's got charm. What happened here?" asks Wanda, reaching for his curved neck scar. D's out of reach before she can touch it, glancing at his new shadows before covering the scar with his collar.

"You're jumpy." says Wanda.

"I think that's enough," says Betty guiding D away. "Don't worry about that. Wanda was a political strategist; she's used to people swinging at her."

D nods.

"You know, I couldn't help but notice your wake up routine. That happens often?"

"He just shocked me was all."

"Like shell-shocked?"

"Hey look—" says D, stepping back.

"My apologies. I'm trained to notice these things. Force of habit." D looks for Zach, who is smiling with Dede and Elle. "Jade tells me you dropped a brog that was coming for her."

"A what?"

"Brogs. It's the name the guys came up with. Anyway, I have something to ask you. I know there is no way you could have lasted out there, with those things, without being very smart. We're leaving in a few days, and I think you can help."

Hank dings the side of his glass to call everyone to dinner. Four bottles of wine are spaced evenly at the table covered by three long, overlapping white table sheets, which are laced at the end. D sits with Betty and a grinning Elle opposite Jade and Colt with Dede and Zach while Hank sits at the head of the table. Zach nods to a seat to his left. It's the woman he spoke of with her head turned away from D yet again. With all seated, Hank asks the newcomers to rise and introduce themselves. D and Zach look to see who will go first. Zach stands.

"Hello. My name is Zachariah, but you can call me Zach, and it is very nice to meet all of you." Zach sits as Hank looks to D.

D stands. "I'm D." D sits.

"Well um—ok, let me introduce everyone to you."

Hank starts from his left with Jade, Colt, Dede, (skipping Zach) Rita, and the mysterious woman, Cella. D has seen a lot of women in a lot of countries, but Cella is by far the most gorgeous woman he has ever seen. Sienna skin so flawless it glows, dimples accenting a sumptuous mouth made for calming smiles, and brown-hazelnut eyes that shine like stars on a cloudless night. She smirks before turning back to Bruce. D rejoins Hank at the opposite end of the table, pretending to hear the rest of the names being called. D veers back to Cella, still turned away from him.

"Saffire, Wanda, Elle, and my wife Betty," finishes Hank.

"Where's the food?" yells Rick.

Betty advises D to use salt. "Tonight's cook hates spices."

Coren, the cook, comes with a cart of food—two plates of various sliced fruits and the centerpiece of the meal, a vitamin fortified beef-flavored meat substitute shaped in the likeness of a bull's head. Rick and two others, Kellen and Rita, take the largest portions, while Elle asks what part D wants. D remembers she is there. Compared with Cella, Elle's flat and ugly, but he nods and eyes the horn.

This has to be better than months of military rations.

Betty fills her plate with fruit as most other's do. D finds this strange, but after seeing Rick and others inhale the meat, D looks at Zach to decide who will go first. D owes Zach for the choking thing, so with a knife and fork, he takes the plunge.

His face scrunches, his jaw clenches, the veins in his neck swell, and his eyes redden. D spits the food into a napkin before slamming on the plate in disgust. It's worse than rations. Betty begins to laugh aloud, while Elle hides her face. Zach sits with the greatest look of disappointment on his face as D tries wiping away the lingering taste.

"It's an acquired taste," says Betty.

"It requires no taste buds," says D as Betty laughs louder.

"You just came on the wrong day. Wanda cooks tomorrow," says Elle, handing him an orange and glass of wine.

D doesn't drink, but he needs something to wash the taste away. He looks to Saffire, motioning for her juice. She shakes her head, pulling the pitcher closer. D narrows his eye at the brat then rips the orange open. The fruit ends up being a really good masking agent. Zach is on the second of what will be many glasses of wine. He decides not to touch his plate of meat.

It's an hour into the meal, and most people are full of fruit and talking. Elle and D are conversing about body hair.

"They're military people here too," says Elle. "Is this like a principle? No hair equals virginity or something?"

"No, I just don't like it. You rub against her and you get static shock. It'll throw you off."

"What?" she snorts.

"It's dangerous."

"Oh, so they study this in war college? Protecting against the art of kinetic energy."

"We're taught to train for all potential attacks. I'm just saying it's a possibility. Part of being a good marine is assessing all dangers. I have to know what I'm getting myself into."

"That is bullshit." She smiles.

"You letting me eat this food is bullshit."

Elle howls.

"What the hell are you two talking about?" asks a passing Rick.

"Mind your business," says Elle.

The two try continuing their talk with Rick hovering.

"Do you mind?" asks Elle.

"You gonna eat that?" asks Rick, eyeing D's plate.

D quickly hands Rick the plate. The two delve deeper into D's aversion, while Rick cleans the plate. They look back at Rick, who's shaking his head at Elle while muttering something about *not even a day* before placing the cleaned plate in front of D and slowly moving away.

Across the table, Dede and Zach are talking about positions.

"I haven't tried that one," says Zach.

"It's easy," says Dede.

"But I still don't get the need for the bat."

"It's easy. I'll show you."

Coren comes up from the lower level to mock applause pressured by Hank. D and Zach refuse to join in; the food is a betrayal. The smiling Coren, seeing D's empty plate, asks for his opinion.

"It was unique. I respect the—it was unique," says D.

Coren turns to Zach's plate, which is untouched.

"It was very filling," says Zach as Dede keeps her face behind her hands.

"I taught myself," says Coren.

"Why?" blurts Zach. "Sorry," he adds, clearing his throat.

Before turning away, Hank tells Coren to clean the dishes. Coren curses, but Hank turns back as if he hasn't heard. The dinner breaks back into its original social groups with the exception of D, Elle, Dede, and Zach.

Rick, again passing D, turns back with a question.

"Marines right?"

D nods.

"Yeah, you guys always look like you want to kick a baby or something."

"Well, what'd the baby do?" asks D. His expressionless face makes it difficult to tell if he's joking or not. Rick nervously chooses to grin then frowns. He walks away and then comes back.

"We're Green Berets. Me and Hank," says Rick, showing his mechanically repaired bicep and tattoo. D can't tell it's fake until he peers close enough to see the unnatural skin.

"You mind if I sit?" asks Rick.

"Yes, we do," says Elle.

"Hey Hank, come here." Rick sits ignoring Elle. "The new guys owe us a story."

Elle bites her lips in frustration as Hank, Betty, and a few others from the forty-plus pocket come closer. Elle apologizes for Rick, while D feels the unblinking hazelnut eyes of Cella turning back to Bruce as he looks at her. Rick now calls Zach to the dining table.

"The damned winter makes news hard to come by. I was hoping you two newbies could update the bunker," Rick starts.

"What'd you wanna know?" asks D.

"Zach told Dede you were out there for eighteen months," says Rick.

D glances at a sheepish Zach before nodding and sitting back as if waiting for an answer. Rick smiles a false smile after a moment.

"All right, I'll bite," says Rick. "How'd you and Zach meet?"

D tells the story easily enough as if it were an accident, his shot from 450 yards away on the run hitting a foot-wide target dead center.

"It was luck really." says D.

"Oh please, don't give me that," says Hank. "You're a hero; you should take a bow."

D doesn't but seeing as Saffire's not near her pitcher, he motions Hank for it.

"Where were you when this all started?" asks Rick.

D repeats his answer to Zach.

"How were the early days in the heartland?"

D stops himself from rolling his eyes at this old guy with all his damn questions. It's not like D can't see what he's doing. The questions are just open-ended enough to let the answerer fill in the blanks without thinking they said anything of real detail that can be recalled later if there's an inconsistency with an answer.

Good luck with that.

"Was it as bad in Wisconsin as the news said?" asks Rick.

"What'd the news say?" asks D.

Rick's jaw tightens as his fake smile fades. Hank laughs.

"Let me try," says the tall man. "What's your rank sold... marine?"

"Second lieutenant."

"That looks a bit junior for your age. What are you twenty-seven, twenty-eight?"

"Tell me about it," D says, vaguely staring right at Hank.

Hank's not smiling. His frown deepens to a puckering that scares Betty. She puts a hand on his arm.

"What my darling husband really wants to know," says Betty, "is if there are any other settlements like this one. What did you see when there were more people, and when did you first notice the brogs?"

"I think I can help with some of that," says D. "Why didn't you just ask?" he says to Hank and Rick.

"Why don't you start with where you were?" asks Betty.

"All I know is it got dark all the sudden," says D. "I'm microwaving a leftover sandwich, and it stops working. The lights too. Even the clocks."

"Coalition has EMPs with a seven-hundred-mile range," says Hank.

"Had. Bastards," says Rick.

They look back to D as if expecting him to continue. Well, *I have to give them something. So he begins.*

"The standard procedure for all military branches is to prepare for Coalition invasion, so this is what the base commander tells his men." As the soldiers empty the armory, some of the local town's folk come wanting information, but no one knows anything. Later, the base commander, urged by ranking officers, decides to send eight men to the city for intelligence gathering while the remaining soldiers fortify positions in the six hours it takes to walk to and from the city. They come back with talk of smoldering buildings, burned and blind victims, some swearing they saw a flash. No one there knows anything either.

"This is only what the outskirts teach. Marines, fully armed, move through burning townships frantically. In fact, people start shooting, forcing the men back. After this, the base commander refuses to send anyone else to the city."

"The next sunrise isn't as brilliant as the day before. An unfamiliar film blots the sun's light. It is not radioactive, thankfully, but it is enough to cause alarm for the Marines and civilians gathered at the front gate asking for information."

"The base commander can't share resources. He doesn't have enough. A shipment was supposed to come the day before. Some want to help the people, but for all they know, this is the first step of an invasion. Who are they helping if they starve to death? The base commander orders the civvies turned away. They need to fortify the base. There's plenty of ammo to do that at least. The next morning, about five hundred civilians are asking for food and information. Half look like they just came from a war zone. They all get the same answer."

"That night, six hundred are shouting over the sand walls, demanding information. Thirty warning shots overhead send the civvies racing home. I have no idea these many people know a base is here. They never act as if they care, but soon as they need something, they're running to the nearest guy in camouflage. All things considered though, I wonder where the hell everyone is. No choppers, the hand-cranked radios don't work, not even Morse code. It's like everyone disappeared. It worries me, so I keep my go bag on my bed just in case."

"The next day comes with fifteen hundred civvies complaining about spoiled food. I wonder why no one is giving them information. It's fair, but I still don't like the looks they're giving. They're not pleading looks but demanding defiant looks. I start counting how many marines are on the base. The lights are off, and I hope that they come back on soon."

"That night, more than six thousand civilians, armed with hunting rifles and gardening tools, smash through the perimeter. Most marines will kill foreigners, but they're not going to shoot their own—no matter what a base commander says. At twenty to one, it is a complete massacre. Looking back on it, most of the people really didn't have the heart to kill, but the loudest ones did, and the rest just rode the wave."

"They took everything, picture frames, furniture, even my hog's tooth. The base commander has a big hole from sternum to scrotum; garden hoses and pickaxes strangle and impale some, and the rest is bullets. The marines do fight back but not until it is too late. At least two hundred civvies are laid across the second level staircase with probably more upstairs, but I won't look. I can't. Someone tries to cut my head off."

"Maybe those bastards think I'm dead after that shovel connects. I thought I was. It's five of them. I don't kill civvies, but they killed, or tried to kill, everyone. No one's there by morning light. I have a throbbing, persistent pain in my neck and ribs. There's a lot of blood, loose skin, and five fractured ribs. I had to do something about that. They took my bug out bag, which is no surprise, so I have to find something in the streets. The sky has a thick haze to it. I can almost taste the fires drifting closer. I don't know what'll kill me first, my injuries or the air itself."

"You guys see anything like that?" asks D.

Hank and Rick shake their heads.

"We waited for intel on what happened, and when nothing came, we made a decision. Betty and I have a retirement home three hundred miles west of here. Rick came to wish us a happy forty-third anniversary. Jade was of course there. A few neighbors like Wanda and her granddaughter were also there. Most everyone else we picked up along the way. When you've got the only working vehicles, a loving wife doesn't complain about faraday cages and paranoia anymore does she?"

Betty gives a tight-lipped smile to that and says, "Hank's rank gave him privileged information like where emergency defense bunkers might be located. They've been around for years." D nods knowingly. He continues his story.

"I need medical attention. In hours, I find an inebriated fellow, bumbling his way up the street. I think, a drunk's got to have alcohol. I don't want to hurt a civvie, but after last night, I'm a bit upset. I punch the reprobate so hard he falls stock still. I never check if he's dead. The punch spurts some blood in the air, and a bottle falls. It's liquor like the type you'd get from a fine liquor store, vintage Appleseed bottles."

"That's good liquor," says Rick.

"Ricky, shut up," says Betty.

"With clean wounds, I turn to using the fading light to find suitable shelter in the nearby upper-class town, but a roving band of thugs is looting all houses for blocks. One house stands out as having a family of three bludgeoned and mutilated on its front lawn. A scene this perverse would scare most anyone away, making it an ideal resting area. The beds have no sheets, the walls are smeared with blood, most doorways only have hinges, but the carpet in the child's room is soft, so that's something."

"Despite my best efforts, I'm up late the next morning, stiff, groggy, and sore as the gang comes my way, setting fire to every house. I curse for being an idiot. I need a change of bandages and find new rags made from a child's torn clothes scattered around the house. After that, I make a run for it. The smell of death is overwhelming as I enter the living room. Outside, I find that the family is missing. I can't dwell on it. The thugs are close. I can't win a fight, and I'm really hungry."

"Did you eat bugs?" asks Rick.

"Not yet," responds D. "I've had quite a bit of experience looking for food, and when people want to hide things, they always put it where they wouldn't want anyone looking. It's a constant thing with civvies. Who would look under my bed? Who would check behind the TV? They'll never look in my bra. They never seem to get that desperate people don't lose brain power; they gain tenaciousness. The roving gang found everything. I hurry in the opposite direction of the gang for an hour and find an emptied storefront. Stores always have stocks hidden, either in a back room or basement."

"There's a trap door already propped open with a crowbar leading to pitch black. There's no one here, but I am careful. I take the crowbar and break what's left of the door into the black. It bangs off steps before sliding to a stop. It sounds like an eight-foot-tall basement, and no one yelps. I deem it safe. I use the ambient light to guide my steps.

"In the basement is spoiled fruit and bread. I almost smile, spoiled fruit. I go Egyptian style and put the moldy bread on my neck. Under a collapsed freezer tray is a jar of second-stage peach-flavored baby food and a plastic bag to store materials. I can eat and I have penicillin. I can't do anything about the weather so the rag and gas mask combo has to stay."

"I lick the jar five seconds after realizing I've eaten all of it. I'm not even near full when a familiar hunger pang from childhood hits, and I'm suddenly back in my element. Something crashes outside, refocusing my attention. The basement's a bad spot. I think the gang's caught up and is setting fire to the store. Carefully, I walk to the first floor. It's coming from outside. A back way leads to two men taking turns humping what looks like a battered woman. One sees me. The man's half-naked from the waist down, shaking as if detoxing and carrying a bat."

"He yells, sprinting at me. The bat misses as I lean to the side and let the man run into my extended leg. I smash him into the wall as the second man jumps up, syringe in hand, charging. I'm already dodging the first stab before giving the second man a cupped smack to the ear, ruining the man's equilibrium. Quickly, I have the bat in hand as the first man rises, clutching a broken nose, still twitching. I aim for the temple as the man charges. One hits all it takes to cave in the man's skull."

"The second is trying to will himself up, even as blood drips from his ear. I waste no time. Two hits, one to the temple and another to the base of the skull to be sure."

"Wait, what happened to the woman?" asks Elle.

"Oh, she was already dead," says D.

Elle doesn't have the stomach to stay. Wanda takes that moment to get Saffire to bed, even though the girl's shouting about not being tired.

"I'm hesitant to enter the city; I spend the next day deciding if I should. From another looted home, I watch urban fires wave to me. It's in that house that I make a very pleasant discovery. Needing to relieve myself, I use the bathroom. It's useless, yes, but I still have manners. The bathroom doesn't have a toilet. I suspect someone stole that along with the sink, but under the cracked tiles is a safe holding nearly forty million in currency and artifacts, the most useful of which is a set of gold-plated combat knives, the same ones Hank took earlier."

"The next morning or what is probably morning, the sky's getting thick in a disturbing way. I enter the city armed with Appleseed, a bat, and a sealed collection of combat knives. Within minutes of arriving, I duck a stray bullet. The city, despite not having the sun's natural light, is still bright due to its myriad of fires. The streets are loud. Dogs are chasing pedestrians through the avenues, rooftops throw off a helpless few, and a strangely well-kept supermarket stands with six men patrolling its roof. At the market's front entrance is a large sign reading, *Stay the fuck away from this property. We will defend ourselves.* As I stop to read, the men aim high-powered hunting rifles at me, forcing me to walk quickly."

"I find myself in an unusual position: too hungry to be hurt, yet too hurt to be hungry. The city shows, deeper into itself, electric poles turned execution posts. Some of the people hanging there look like they came from Coalition countries, either by phenotype or clothing. Past that, a most disturbing sight. A father and daughter keep safe behind a gated apartment complex as a band of tyrants chase them. Rather than accept the inevitable, the man turns the gun on his child then himself. The tyrants jump the barrier, stripping both naked."

"I eventually stop. I'm tired and my ribs hurt. While recuperating, three dogs bark after me. They're too close to outrun, but I find an idle tire while looking for high ground. As I reach the roof of a nearby car, the dogs leap and clear the car before knocking into me with their front paws. I flip onto my back, still with the tire, as the dogs try tearing into me. My rubber shield has no real effect on the feral dogs. The long-toothed mongrels bite their way to my forearms. I lose my bat somehow, but I find a glass shard from the car and stab it into one dog's jugular vein. Then a great big round man sporting an industrial green suit decapitates the other two before motioning me to shelter."

"The round man has food, clean water, and medicine. He injects me with anti-radiation medication and a rabies vaccination I don't ask for. The round man's larger in the light. He's retired Army with a buzz cut and a twenty-gauge shotgun to match. Pictures of a family plaster all four walls. The round man didn't want to help me, but the military fatigues told him I might be useful, even if I was a Marine. He makes clear that he won't tolerate shenanigans. If I wish to pair up, I'll have to accept the round man as leader. I also can't touch anything without permission. Being injured limits my practical choices. I accept the man's proposition and afterward, canned food and water from a nearby cooler. Hunger being the best seasoning, it ranks cold beans above the most talented chef."

"Hours later, there's a loud thud on the escape hatch. The round man rushes up to it, trying to push it up, but nothing happens no matter how much he strains. It's the only exit, so we are stuck. I wanted to ask why there's only one exit, but I decide against it. During this time, the round man exclaims conspiracy theories of how the Coalition moles planned the attack but is puzzled as to why they haven't invaded. I chime in with explanations that only serve to rile the round man. His family's a calming subject whenever his blood pressure rises too high. I mention a picture."

"I'm watching the round man. He's very agile for his size. There was clear definition in his arms when he tried pushing that hatch open. When he believes me to be asleep, he talks to someone, maybe his wife, Teagen, or one of the children. There are no personal effects. It's only guns, food, and pictures. I don't know if his family is alive or separated. His knuckles go white when he turns to the largest photo of a woman in a flowing white wedding dress, holding a bouquet. I wonder why and when he converted a wine cellar into a prepper's bunker."

"The Coalition was always in control, weren't they?" says the round man the next day while cleaning his shotgun. 'They just decided to steal loved ones to keep everyone in line, didn't they?'

"I say nothing while eating his beans. He doesn't sleep for two nights. On the third day, I go for a can of beans and bump into the round man's shotgun side. I step back as the round man's face goes red. My collection of knives are dull as it turns out, and the round man won't let me near the wet stones."

"While I eat the beans, the round man starts laughing uncontrollably. I'm not really eating and stop pretending. The round man stops laughing with the ghost of a smile on his lips and fires. The gun jams. I charge, throwing the shotgun pin at the round man's eyes and follow with an uppercut. The bulk of the round man muffles the impact. He shoves me back. Using a chair, the round man lifts his jiggling frame into the air and onto my sensitive ribs. Punching at the round man's side only proves to anger him further. He shifts his weight to pin my arms. I force him off. After a knee to the groin, I'm up."

"The round man charges. I throw a stack of canned fruit then water bottles and lastly picture frames. The round man is incensed at my desecration. I don't expect such a hefty man to move this fast, but the round man is bullying his way through everything. I won't make it easy. I reach for his set of combat knives, but he has me in a flash. He slams me against all four walls."

"I smack the man upside the head with the picture frames to no effect; I squeeze into the man's neck fat to no effect. I finally poke his eye, freeing myself. I run, only to be pulled back for a body slam. Pinned again, the round man won't allow me to pinch, by pinning my wrists. I spit in the round man's eye, loosening an arm. Still trapped beneath the girth, I find many broken pieces of glass littering the floor."

"I rub a handful of the shards into the round man's side. He responds with a double ax handle to my face before rising due to bleeding. I blink the glaze out of my eyes and find a long glass shard. The round man's heaving while pulling glass from his side as I stab him from behind repeatedly. The piece breaks into his neck. I use my hands to rub the piece in deeper. The round man's screaming, trying to knock me off by slamming his back against the wall but I won't let go."

"I can't feel the piece, so my fingers dig into the man's neck to pull muscle fibers. The round man is still pinning me between the wall and his back fat. I move towards a rigid column. I grip the column, freezing the round man, and dislocate his spine."

"He just seized up?" asks Rick.

"We start tussling, and he yells grabbing his chest. He looks at me like I'm gonna help him. I watch him fall and wait five minutes. Then I know. Fat bastard."

"I push the man off then wipe blood from my face. I take a moment to recuperate then look for a way out. No one wants to be stuck near a dead body. I can't use the glass to cut my way out, and the shotgun won't help. I search in the empty food cans and behind the picture frames, but nothing useful is here. I've always had a knack for thinking my way out of a trap, but I'm tired. That round man hit hard. I open the cooler for something to eat and find dry ice."

"I almost smile, almost. About two teaspoons of the ice go into a bottle cap filled with water. I throw it and hear a nice pop. I find a measuring cup and redo the experiment using a quarter cup, half a cup, and so on. It's not that I'm in a hurry, but dead bodies decay fast. I'm certain there's enough to make a decent blast for a two-liter bottle. There's more than enough to repeat ten times, and what am I going to do with dry ice topside anyway?"

"I take two satchels, the man's hazmat suit, as many cans, water, and medication as my weakened body can carry, a watch, a flashlight, the shotgun with sixty shells, and my set of combat knives. The cooler is propped on a stack of chairs positioned just beneath the escape hatch so that the blast and all its energy pushes into the hinges. The dry ice explodes slightly, breaking but not opening the exit. I fire ten slugs into the most damaged areas then set another stack of ice and water up—this time twice as large at the hatch. The cooler is lumpy and leaking, but some adhesive and more wood lodged in certain leaks hold it."

"The explosion is powerful. I'm covered with water and dirt before I know it, and a biting cold is already numbing my fingers. But none of that matters because the hatch is open. I stack some broken chairs onto one another to exit. I literally can't see anything. I'm outside; the wind says that much. It's oppressively cold, and there aren't any lights anywhere. The city's black and quiet now. I give the cellar a long look, but the choice is easy. I'm leaving the city as soon as I can find some landmarks to orient myself. Once or twice I trip over bodies I think are snow mounds. Eventually, I'm back at the supermarket to find it and its six guards not there anymore. The next three months are nothing but scavenging and bartering through the country until they come." "Did you hear about any of those city shelters?" asks Hank.

"I heard a lot of things. There's ten or fifty all across the country. That's where the senators and president went. No one knew anything. They just said things to keep themselves going." "Do you know where they came from?" asks Jade.

"I was in Oklahoma when they came up from the south; I'm sure of it. I met some people later who swore they came from the northwest. This guy I teamed up with, Fernando, said he heard something about a legend from the forest, South America. He was a good guy too. He agreed with me. Anyway, so far as I can tell they're everywhere now, and there are a lot fewer people after they came to town. Fourteen months later I see Zach running for his life, so I decide to help him."

"Have you seen a hierarchical relationship?" asks Cella.

D snaps his head to the voice. "They work in groups, but I can't say I've seen any leadership. It's more situational. It's hard to explain, but they don't work like regular animals do, no."

"Have you seen the disease's full course?" Cella leans forward, looking excited.

"Yes, more times than I want to remember. Ten days of that is more than anyone deserves."

"Ten days?" says Cella in confusion.

"Ok," says Hank. "I think that's enough storytelling for one night. Go to bed."

The troop rises for bed. Cella repeats her surprise of hearing ten days. Rick holds D for a moment.

"Damn brogs know how to make a bad day worse, don't they?"

"Yeah, what the hell is a brog anyway?" asks D.

"Burnt dogs? That's what Colt said they looked like."

"I saw one up close; it didn't look like any goddam dog I've ever seen."

"Well what the fuck did it look like?" asks Colt from afar.

"I can't really explain it. I know what I saw, but it's not anything I've ever seen."

"Makes perfect sense," says Colt.

"Kiss my ass. I know what I saw."

"Quit it," says Hank. "Colt, you've got night watch."

As D and Zach head to their room, Cella's moving Dede's hand away before calling to D.

"Any hypothesis on how the creatures survive in the dead atmosphere?" she asks, batting her eyes.

D thinks she's even prettier close up. Her eyes make it hard for him to remember the question. He can't answer the question, so it doesn't matter, but he finds himself again thinking about her beauty. D's more certain the more he looks at Cella that she resembles a fitness model.

"It's not all dead up there," he says. "There's still oxygen. The weather's probably better south of the equator, which would mean more food for them, but they're still up here."

How sweet do those lips taste? He thankfully doesn't say that last sentence aloud.

"They have three extra lungs," he continues. "If that's not it, I have no idea," he quickly adds before he starts rambling.

"You think we could talk about your ideas tomorrow?" asks Cella.

D keeps a stony expression as they make a deal. D doesn't notice the glare Elle's giving Cella as everyone heads to their rooms. Dede blows Zach a kiss before several other ladies crowd into Room 9.

Zach leans against the door, smirking as D asks if he's going to move. Inside, Zach has nothing but praise for D's smooth talking.

"Cella's the type of woman that'll cause fights and end wars."

D nods. "Women who look that good can rearrange priorities quickly."

"What about Elle?" asks Zach.

"Did you see Cella?" says D.

Both nod. "You don't expect a word like 'hierarchical' from a cutie like that. She's interesting." continues D.

Both pause, thinking.

"You're not off the hook. You seem pretty friendly with our big breasted friend."

"I have no idea what you're talking about," says Zach, looking away. "Oh did Betty ask you about leaving? Dede said she might."

"I don't know," says D.

Chapter 9

What do you think?" asks Betty, pulling back bed sheets.

"Which one?" asks Hank.

"D, the muscular one."

"You been looking I see," says Hank. Betty blows him a kiss. "I don't know, you?"

"Well, the girls seem to like him. And he did save Jade so that's a winner in my book."

"That was more a mutual thing. I just don't know enough. He says he's military but anyone could learn to shoot."

"He saved Zach too."

"So they say."

"What about the suit?"

"He could have stolen it from someone else."

"You are determined to find something, aren't you?"

"We don't know him," Hank says gruffly.

"You didn't know Colt either, but you warmed up."

"Jade had more to do with that than anything else."

"That's daddy's little girl, all right."

"It's just—I had time to come to terms with Colt."

"Are you saying you still don't trust Colt?"

"No, I'm just—dammit, Betty, stop it. You know what I mean. We're leaving and I have to be able to trust my people."

"Do you trust my judgment?"

"Yes."

"Good, because I remember a time when you were the unknown and had to prove yourself."

"That was different."

"No, it wasn't. He reminds me of you. He's a bit jittery, but I think I know why that is. He's handsome, confident, and he's survived this long; he has to be smart to do that."

"He's an unknown. You want to take a chance like that now?"

"I did."

"Yeah and look what that got you."

Betty throws a pillow at Hank before telling him to get into bed.

#

Now 12:30 a.m., Colt is on his fifth patrol around the bunker and hears one of his favorite songs through door seven. He knocks and enters to a knife pointing at his temple. Colt jumps back as the knife lowers.

"Your music's too loud," says Colt, half-scared half-angry.

D lowers the sound, waiting for Colt to leave before sharpening his knife more.

Walking back up to the dining area, Colt hears a door lock click. He turns his light to a glare blocking Jade.

"What are you doing?" he asks aggressively.

"I thought you might want some company," she says, frowning.

Colt smiles while motioning her over. As they walk hand in hand up the steps, he hums the lyrics to the song.

"You love that stupid song," says Jade.

"It's a classic," says Colt, now singing the words.

"Stop, please."

"Your father's a good man, but sometimes he can be very stubborn."

Jade laughs at Colt's look of crossness.

"Ah come on. He listens to you, but thinking Dax is alive and recruiting is farfetched, honey. That story's full of holes. Eighteen months in these conditions outside? You saw how ragged I was when I got here. And two strung out hobo's running away, please."

"Are you mad I almost got hurt today?"

"I'm not. You weren't—and seeing you safe is my dream."

"You are so full of shit," she says, smiling.

The chairs are neatly stacked along the wall. The positioning of Colt's flashlights gives the spacious hall proper atmosphere. "Shall we dance?" he asks with a kiss.

Jade accepts, offering her hand and blushing. They glide left to right, front to back, and repeat.

"You have no clue what you're doing," says Jade, chuckling.

"I'm learning," says Colt.

"No you're not," she says as Colt steps on her toe.

"Ow." she pushes away. Colt pulls out a chair. "You did that on purpose," she says, rubbing her toe.

"Aw stop whining. Give me your foot."

He slips off her sandal to gently massage the affected area, working his way from the toe to the ball of the foot then the heel and back up in small circles.

"You didn't tell me what you thought," says Colt.

"Are you serious?" says Jade, pulling her foot away.

"You never want to give me a straight answer."

"That's because this isn't about me. It's about your male ego." Colt grunts in frustration.

"Look at me. You are the most wonderful man I have ever met. You don't have to worry about anyone else, ok?" She pulls his chin to hers.

"But you said he saved your life. And you were smiling and winking at Cella, who likes playing games. You never talk to each other. I don't know what to think."

She sucks her teeth readying to leave.

"Wait. Ok. Does your foot still hurt?"

Her foot lies back across his lap. "You wonder what happened to the others?" she asks.

"No, they made their choice." He tickles her arch. Jade playfully warns Colt to stop. "You think that D fella saw them?"

She throws up her hands. "I didn't get out of my comfortable bed to talk about someone else. Now you have all of me to yourself. Do you want it to stay that way?"

Colt nods.

"Then shut up."

Colt goes quiet, motioning her back for more massaging. Jade pinches his cheek while taking in his light-green iris. Colt's hands move further up her leg. She smirks at him.

This wouldn't be that bad every day, would it? she thinks.

Aloud she says, "You remember your question?"

Colt freezes then looks at her.

"Yes."

Colt's numb for a moment. *The answer only took a full week. This should be a good thing, right?*

"Woman, you better not be playing with me. I can't take that shit."

She pulls him close for a sweet embrace. "You heard me."

Colt lifts her off the chair, swinging her around the hall chanting,

"Yes, yes, yes." Jade laughs, trying to shush him before he wakes everyone. "Look, I know I don't have a ring, but I promise-"

She presses her finger to his lips. "That's not important." They kiss again. "But since you mentioned it."

They laugh again before Colt's nibbling her neck.

"We need to plan our announcement."

"Dinner tomorrow night," he says.

"Really?" she says worriedly. "That's like really soon though."

"When the hell else are we gonna tell them? We're leaving. Don't you want a real party?"

Jade doesn't know what to say so starts kissing him again. Clothes come off, and both are naked on the dining table before they know it. The rest of the night patrol happens on the full length of the table.

Chapter 10

Thank you, Thank you, please be seated. *The former colonies have finally claimed their birthright.* That is what our foes peddle as justification for unwarranted aggression. They say we do not have the right to fight for a reasonable share. They say that as pseudo chiefs of enfranchisement, they and their children alone have the right to thought. They say they are the only ones fit to have a bearable living. They say simply that they are better than us. I cannot say that I am surprised. Such boastful yet basic words from men of basic yet boastful minds leave little to the imagination. To be clear, I have never seen such caustic and flagrant degradation of humanity. They use words like strong and powerful, loud and encompassing. No, no, lonely and meager."

"From the far lands in spectacle to the Americas of velvet, this putrid infantile ghost shows itself. I say ghost to show this Coalition for what it truly is, a falsehood, an image imprinted on a screen, which has remained static for too long. Complacency has allowed this farce to continue. Lack of due diligence has maintained this lie."

"The Coalition exists only as we allow it to. It tortures, maims, and murders only as we allow it to. It is a motif of misery expressed the world over only as we allow it to be. I have decided we will no longer allow it. The genesis of this malcontent is not as some say congealed in the hills of distant mountains six-plus decades past nor concocted in the deep resentment of developed nations from those underdeveloped. To say such things is to allow reason for the irrational."

"If you don't mind, I need to go back to my roots as a scientist. Have you ever seen a wasp's reproduction process? See a wasp does not cultivate its future generation as other species would. Instead, it finds another to do its bidding, namely a caterpillar. See a wasp is not capable of the commitment necessary to feeding and nourishing its own. It must find a surrogate. The genius in this is that the caterpillar, though it fights, slowly becomes infected and succumbs to the wasps bidding. It doesn't realize that the wasp's progeny is eating it from the inside out. As it nourishes the offspring, it also aids in its own destruction."

"Isn't this familiar? The invasion of a foreign organism perverting the mind to the point that its sole purpose is the want of its infection. Once the wasp progeny conclude incubation, it will eliminate any trace of its surrogate, freeing itself to spread elsewhere. Isn't this the tale of countless citizens in countless townships in dozens of countries? These people are infected with a strain of ageless oppression, and it is highly contagious. It transmits through gunpowder and fear tactics and will quickly destroy everything. Unless our vaccine is administered, this wasp will bring itself to our borders. I promise you."

"I said a year ago that we don't yet have what is needed to end this self-imposed isolationism yet. So as such, we should find it. Our forbearers were wise to stop our fight against this parasite while natural forces were harassing our country, but our foe has metastasized into what we have now. We must now ask you, the people, to support our military and stop this parasite."

The screen suddenly blinks off.

"Hey, what happened?" asks Rick, running to the screen.

Hank looks under the breakfast table for the remote. "Where the hell is it?"

"I told you, no politics at the table," says Betty, holding the remote.

"He was getting to the best part," says Rick.

"I don't care."

"Give me the damn remote woman," shouts Hank.

Betty sucks her teeth before tucking the remote into her pocket as she opens the refrigerator door. D and Zach walk in and stop as they feel the tense atmosphere.

"You two gonna sit down?" asks Hank.

Zach moves to the chair vacated by Rick before being told to take the next one while giving Betty an angry stare. Betty points D to a third chair down from Hank.

"You always up this early?" asks Hank.

"Time spent sleeping is time lost," says D. "Something my drill instructor used to tell us."

"Smart man, what was his name?"

"Sergeant Hackett Nicondro. First and last Scandinavian I ever met. He was mean. Brilliant, but mean."

Betty brushes past Hank while putting fruit on the table. "You two hungry?" After the two nod, she leaves the kitchen.

Hank is up from his seat, searching in all the cabinets. "She took it with her," he says, throwing his trivia book.

"What are you talking about?" asks Zach.

"President Alvarez's re-declaration of war," says Rick.

Rick scowls, going for the trivia book as Hank throws a napkin at him.

"Leave it," says Hank, reopening a cabinet in vain.

"You agree?" says Rick, looking at D and Zach.

"What?" asks Zach.

"Hank thinks Alvarez waited too long to declare war. I say he had to let the country restock on materials before getting back out there again."

"I was three when this speech happened," says D. "The next guy had to call a stop in the middle of his second term. Seems Alvarez went too quickly."

Hank scoffs. "Pick a side will you?"

"He did," says Rick. "Alvarez should've waited. Which means I'm right."

Hank grunts and waves dismissively at Rick.

"I was thinking about that fat man in your story," Hank begins. "Why he couldn't understand why the Coalition hadn't started an invasion yet."

D nods.

"Rick and I have had an ongoing bet about why. He says the brogs were eating everyone over there until they ran out of things to eat. Then they swam to the Americas. He says we were actually winning, and the brogs are some feral dogs turned savage by their ecosystem. The Coalition simply panicked and attacked. No one's actually had a good look at one, so who's to say?

"I think the Coalition planned a sneak attack but were countered by our own nuke blitz. The brogs are the Coalitions pet project that got loose right after we hit them with bombs. Then there's a third theory, that the brogs are some manifestation that caught both sides off guard. Thus, we attacked each other thinking one had something to do with it when it's really nature's fault. Cella keeps trying to knock down that one but most of us like it. You?"

"I remember when I was a kid," says Zach before D can answer. "My science teacher always came to class upset. She was a big fan of the 'Green vs. Gray' people. She'd tell us adaptation is the key. You can't change without time. That's what's happening with the dogs. They're dying because we took their adaptability away. Green adapts; gray can't. After yesterday, I'm with the third theory."

Rick chuckles. "Cella will really like that."

"I don't care," says D. "Sure I guess it's good to know where this started, but it's everywhere now. Anyone like to read?"

All three men nod.

"When they first appeared, I had to keep telling myself this isn't an alien invasion. Then, after the initial shock, I got some biology books to figure out what to do. I'm not an expert on animals, but I know enough to know things aren't normal. They pick up on things, work stuff out, not like dogs or the big cats. I mean they really know things they shouldn't. I don't know if it's passed down or learned, but they can do things like us."

"What do you mean?" asks Rick.

"Have you ever seen those wild animal documentaries? When the predators hunt, they pick out the weak ones, work out what to do, then pounce, right? These things go for the strong ones first. And they scout locations to set traps and blockades a day or sometimes weeks in advance. Most books say animals aren't able to think that far ahead. They just don't have the cognition. These bastards can do that, and they're making babies. There's more of them now than when they first came. They have to eat, so where's the extra food? I think I just convinced myself to go with the third theory."

Rick frowns at D while Hank silently ponders.

"How the hell could you know how many there are?" Rick asks.

"How long have you been scouting?" asks D.

"What the hell does that matter?"

"How long?"

"Since we came."

"There weren't a lot of people in this general area before right? It's a hidden military base; there wouldn't be, would there?"

"Let's assume that's right."

"I've personally counted twelve hundred uglies in this seventy mile radius. If you know anything about predator-prey relationships, you know those numbers are completely out of whack. There's not enough food here. I've seen the brutes eat a full grown man in three bites. And I'm pretty sure they're warm-blooded. So why are so many here?"

"This is your horse; you pull it." says Hank.

"They're either expanding because food's running short, or they're expanding because the newbies want better hunting grounds. That also might be the reason you want to leave. They're getting close to finding this spot, and you're afraid they'll break in somehow."

Hank and Rick glance at each other.

"Even if any of what you said was accurate," says Hank, "you know how big this country is. To need to expand that widely would mean millions of brogs."

"Would it?" says D.

"When the hell did you do all this observing?" asks Rick.

"It's my job."

"What is your job?"

"Didn't I just say?"

"Will you just answer a goddamn—"

Betty returns with Jade, Colt, Dede, Cella, Bruce, Elle, and two others, Domelvo and Bode, along with a bag of bacon-flavored meat substitute. The bag label has Zach thinking up a good long stomach-flu excuse. Betty laughs at his expression.

"It's not the food," she says. "It's the cook."

Zach and D glance at each other, saying nothing, as the others take their seats. Cella outmaneuvers Elle to find her place near D. She raises a brow to Elle who angrily takes an open seat five chairs down. Colt graciously slides out the chair directly opposite Hank for Jade, positioning his chair closer to her as the two giggle. The last member, Kellen, belatedly rushes in to find no available chairs.

"You should have gotten here earlier," says Domelvo.

Everyone's stealing glances at Cella as she wraps a bandana around her hair while pouting her lips before stretching her elegant neck. Jade sucks all the attention by stretching her back muscles in a way that naturally enhances her bra size through an old Army shirt of Colt's. Colt's mock cough tells the men to look elsewhere as he smiles, tugging her chair closer. Cella has on one of those genuine fake smiles women are so good at. D's missing something but knows better than to ask anything.

"Hey," she says, turning a real smile to D. "You didn't forget our meeting later, did you?"

"Of course not," says D, making an effort not to notice how toned her legs are through thin black leggings or those dimples as she smiles or the tight abs hiding under her white crop top with the word *sweetness* written across her chest in bold gold lettering.

"What's a seven-letter word for marriage?" asks Hank.

"Divorce," says Rick, causing a laugh from all excluding D and Cella. Betty turns back to Rick, raising an eyebrow.

"Really, what is it?" asks Hank.

"Wedding," say D and Betty.

"Yeah that fits," says Hank, writing in the answer.

"So where are you from?" asks Cella in a low voice.

"You know," says D. "It'd be a lot easier to pay attention to what you're asking if you didn't purse those lips at me."

"Yeah?" Cella smiles, fluttering her eyelashes. "A little thing like me is distracting a big strong guy like you?"

"Of course not. I know exactly what I wanna do."

D's gaze is locked onto Cella who has on even more of a smirk while sliding closer. *This is good. I hate those pretend prudish types.*

"All right, when was marijuana legalized?" asks Hank.

"The year 2038," says Rick.

"You would know, wouldn't you?" says Hank as Rick smiles.

"Look here, mister," states Cella. "You will not be flirting with me without a formal introduction. And flowers. I like flowers."

"That's good for you," says D. "What the hell's that got to do with me?"

"All right," she says, nudging him. "I was afraid you'd wet yourself when I started smiling. This is good."

Someone snorts, and D's frowning.

"Wait," D begins.

"It's a long story." she laughs.

"Bacon's ready," says Betty.

Cella turns all her focus to the plate moving slowly to the table. Domelvo tries to get his huge hands on the strips first, but with a sad look from Cella, he sighs and gives her first dibs.

"You don't want any?" asks Cella, putting three on D's plate.

"I thought you'd get a salad or something," says D.

Cella sucks her teeth. "Maybe if Coren was cooking," she whispers.

He finds himself captivated by this woman's hazelnut eyes. He's thinking of some very nasty things and positions he could put her in. Could she handle it? *She's flirty sure, but I've broken plenty of women like that. It's been months, over a year actually, since I've had sex.*

"I'm going to guess something about you. Tell me if I'm right," says D. "You're the type of woman who gets whatever she damn well asks for."

Cella smirks. "Who says I have to ask?"

"Ok, say you did. What would that be?"

"Are you offering?"

"I don't have to. Offers come to me." He winks.

Cella has on a full smile now. She bites the bacon aggressively.

D almost smiles.

"I saw that," she says.

D shakes his head, but Cella keeps staring so D looks at his bacon. It looks tasty. He looks at Zach. Zach looks at him. It's Zach's turn. The others stop to see Zach slowly lift the strip, open his mouth, and bite down. The flavor supercharges his taste buds. He smiles, chews, then sighs a few times in a row. He nods to D who trepidatiously bites into the bacon. His experience gives a sensation so unbelievable it is upsetting.

Betty smiles; of course she's a great cook. She sits, pinching Hank's face for no particular reason. Hank flicks her hand away, shaking his head. Cella's smiling pleasantly at D before reaching for one of D's strips. He slaps her hand away while his offhand wipes drool into a napkin. Cella opens her mouth in mock outrage before going for seconds, muttering something about gentlemen.

"Who's running today's workout session?" asks Hank.

It's Bruce, and as Jade says it, Cella stiffens, refusing to look her way.

"I think he's adding target practice today," adds Jade. "You remember him willing to help after you asked him, crying and all that?"

"I was not crying to, in front, or about anyone," states Cella, now looking at Jade, smiling tightly. "But I do recall someone's wet bedsheets after the first night they saw Creighton."

Jade's face flushes, eyes blazing, and suddenly everyone's looking for something to do or speed walking out of the kitchen. D's feeling for his knife, ready for whatever while Zach is protecting the bacon. Colt is whispering something to Jade, trying to will her to blink again. Betty's up and between the two, and Cella finally breathes. Colt has a firm grip of Jade's arm and walks her out of the kitchen. Cella coughs, delicately straightens her shirt, then leaves. Hank grunts something about women, while Rick nods, eating strips from the plate while Zach frowns at him.

"Everyone goes to our workouts, no exceptions," says Hank before leaving. "Oh, you're doing the dishes. Both of you," he says as Rick finishes the last strip before following.

Unbeknownst to anyone, Saffire's hiding beneath the table, smiling with an open sketchbook.

"Do you know what the sun looks like?" she asks as D curses, looking down at her. "I tried drawing it, but I can't remember." She shows pages of well-drawn solar panels.

"No one has ever asked me that question before," D says, flipping through the pages. "Your name's spelled with two F's?"

"Uhm, Grandma says the hospital people are stupid, and she doesn't know why mom was trying to be unique. Grandma wanted to change it, but it costs extra to change the name after one's already down. She says she loves me all the same. What was she talking about?"

"You drew these?" D asks, ignoring the question.

"Yeah. Do you draw?"

"I used to but not as much now."

"You should; then you could help me draw gardens. You need sunlight for that. It's called photosynthesis. Cella taught me that. Uncle Rick told me it looked like a big lemon, but my book says the sun is—let me find it." She flips through the pages. "The sun is a luminous celestial body, consisting of mainly hydrogen and helium, around which the earth and the other seven planets revolve and receive heat from, a mean distance of ninety-three million miles or a hundred and fifty million kilometers from earth."

"That's just what I was about to say," says D. "That's in a children's book?"

"No, my coloring book was the only one I had when Uncle Hank and Rick brought us here so grandma makes me read all of Cella's science books. Is it true you killed a brog yesterday? Bruce says he killed a lot but no one believes him."

Just as the girl finishes, Wanda rushes in, eyes wide with concern then fury. "Ok, little girl, leave the young man alone."

Saffire groans. "But he was just about to teach me how to draw a lemon," she whines.

"What?" says Wanda.

D's about to say something as the girl flips to images of brogs with noses all over their bodies.

"I like this one," she says.

"Where did you get that idea from?" asks D.

She shrugs. "Colt said they don't look like anything really but he thinks he saw this."

Dede's rushing into the kitchen annoyed.

"She's not hiding in the war room. She might be playing with Cella's makeup again. I'll—"

She stops as Saffire looks up, smiling.

"Do you know what a psychopath is?" Saffire asks D. "Bruce and Colt keep saying that's what they think you are. Oh and Dede wants to know if you killed a thousand people, no two thousand."

Wanda rushes to yank Saffire by the ear as Dede stares at D horrified before walking away. Zach has a big grin on his face that almost has D laughing.

"We should get these dishes done," says D.

"You wash. I'll dry," says Zach.

A teary-eyed Saffire is back minutes later as the men are working stubborn streaks out of the bacon plate.

"I'm sorry for spreading rumors about you," the girl says head down. "I do not know you, so I should think about your feelings when I decide to make unfounded statements."

"No problem," says D.

"Now," whispers Wanda, "you get to apologize to Bruce and Colt. Then Betty for stealing that fruit." She tugs Saffire.

"This place isn't horrible," says D.

"I told you," says Zach. After a moment, he continues. "So what's your game plan?" D stares at him blankly. "For Cella."

"I'll let my good nature win her over. That's if she's not playing some game. You always have to be careful with women that beautiful. Now, what about you and big titties?"

Zach smiles. "She wants me. I'll get some before we leave here." Both nod before turning to the plate's downright obtuse grease stain.

"Wanna switch?" asks D.

"Nope," says Zach.

Chapter 11

After cleaning the last dish, Zach offers to show D the gaming room. Rita and Domelvo are playing a round of the vintage fighting game Deathstrike, which D happens to love.

"Oh, I've been waiting for you," says Rita.

"Yeah, we gonna have to teach you a lesson," says Domelvo.

Zach smiles, thinking back to yesterday's thorough trouncing of Rita. Now she's brought reinforcements.

"Well there's only one thing to say. Bring it on."

Domelvo reintroduces himself as Dom. He has very dark skin, almost sable, and the whitest teeth D's ever seen. "So you know how to play?"

"A little bit," says D.

"Well step on up then," says Dom.

D cracks his knuckles as Zach purposes the four tag team, him and D versus Dom and Rita. An hour into the game, D and Zach are leading thirty-seven rounds to eleven, with D and Zach in the midst of a nine round win streak as D finishes Dom using a simple four-hit combo. Dom slams the control deck. It's Rita's turn, but she doesn't feel like playing anymore. Zach snorts while Dom scowls.

"There's going to be a tournament tomorrow," says Dom. "If you two think you're so damn good, stop by. I'll be ready then."

It's eleven when an innocent-looking Cella struts in with a fresh coat of strawberry lip gloss and workout clothes, hot pink yoga pants with white lettering down the side, sandals showing off a pedicure, and a cute gray tank top revealing toned arms.

"This is where you were?" says Cella. "We're going to be doing some target practice today so since I hear you're a good shot, I was hoping you'd be my partner."

"You heard that, did you?" says D, not even trying to maintain eye contact but slowly moving his eyes over her beautiful hourglass frame.

It's not fair for a woman to have that face and that type of body. How's anyone supposed to get anything done when she walks into a room?

"A gentleman is supposed to pretend they're not looking," she says, putting her hands on her hips.

"Well, I've never been accused of that," says D. "So you'll just have to deal with my total lack of respect. Do you have a matching set?" He motions to her pants.

"Of course I do. But I like variety. You?"

"One at a time. It's not fair to have one waiting while you wear out the other."

Now D looks her in the eye, and Cella subconsciously steps closer.

"You aren't shy at all are you?"

"Is there something to be scared of, shorty?"

Cella grins broadly. "You gonna be my partner or not?" D waits a moment. Cella fidgets but knows she can't say anything less she look desperate. D slowly nods.

"Great," she says, narrowing her eyes and nudging his arm. "Oh, I want to talk with you about your story." As she turns, D sets his eyes on her firm ass. Zach whispers something into his left ear, but D's lost as his eyes try looping around the doorway.

"Was he looking?" Cella asks Dede as they move from earshot.

"He's a guy, of course he was. Did you feel his arms?"

"Yeah, it's where it needs to be."

"How big do you think he is?"

"You are so nasty," says Cella as the two enter Room 10.

"The self-imposed dry spell is over," says Dede as Elle walks in behind them.

#

"You lucky son of a bitch," says Dom. "Her and Jade got something extra about them." The men nod before Rita groans loudly and leaves. No one notices.

"Glad to see some of the pretty ones made it," says Zach.

"He's got Elle interested too," says Zach.

"Elle, damn quick work," says Dom as D shakes his head.

"Isn't Cella with that fat-face guy?" asks D.

"Bruce? No. Doesn't stop him from trying though," says Dom as Bode, Kellen, Mark, Emmett, and Kellan walk in.

"How about Dede?" asks Zach.

Dom raises an eyebrow. He used to date Dede.

"She's fantastic in bed. She's probably better now that everyone's doing Green Beret workout drills. Amateurs need not apply."

"Where's Rita?" asks Bode.

#

"They're in there right now talking about you," says Rita to Cella. "Dickheads."

"See, I told you; new blood is good," says Dede as Elle shakes her head.

"He didn't say anything about me?" Elle asks.

"Dom was doing the talking," says Rita. "I have to go."

"I don't understand. Bruce has been chasing you for months, but this new guy comes in, and you can't take your eyes off him," says Dede.

"I thought we were friends," says Elle.

"What's your problem?" asks Cella.

"Dede told you I called dibs, bitch," says Elle furiously as the others laugh.

Cella stares, mouth agape. How can Elle seriously think she has a shot with a man who looks like D? Seriously?

"All right," says Jade. "Back to business. He's interested, right? Knows how to talk to women?"

Dede nods, nudging Cella who's still staring confusedly at Elle.

"So then," says Jade. "Are you doing this or not?"

Cella sighs. "How did I get talked into this?"

Dede is beaming while putting a patronizing arm around Cella.

"Do you want to die dry?" she asks.

The ladies are laughing, but Dede is serious. She's been rereading old lifestyle magazines and has found a truth. Celibacy is evil. The ladies laugh again, but Dede has facts.

"Now, Cella, you like that science crap right?" asks Dede. Cella doesn't bother nodding as Dede plows on. "Is it not true that women with healthy sex lives are happier than premature granny's who have never had orgasms?"

"That's social science. I studied biochemistry, virology, and—"

"Sperm is biochemistry," interrupts Dede. "The point is, I'm right. Denying yourself something ingrained in our nature because of some other idiot's mistakes is stupid. And six months is really ridiculous. Where's the harm?"

#

"I like a nice shape—when everything complements everything else," says Dom.

"I like a nice ass," says D. "I like a flat stomach, but without the booty, it's incomplete."

Kellen and Coren nod.

"So ugly is ok as long as there's a booty?" asks Bode before shaking his head. "I can't live like that."

"I didn't say that. A cute face is always appreciated but an ass to go with that is a perfect pairing."

"Titties dammit," says Zach as Bode and Dom nod. "They come with milk and their own cups."

The men laugh before Dom comments. "Just say you like fat chicks man," says Dom.

"Yeah, I've been meaning to ask about that," says Zach.

"We're leaving soon. And Three-Mile Island is a long way away. We gotta be in good running shape," says Dom. "And food rationing."

"If anything over a size three you consider fat, then yeah, I like fat," says D, raising his voice. "I like a proportional waist. If you're athletic, I know you can keep up with me."

#

"You're over Creighton, right?" asks Dede. "And you've never had a problem being friendly, so what's the problem?"

"Dede," says Jade admonishingly. "Cella's got a conscience so long as they're attractive. She's getting up there you know. Maybe she's losing her edge," she finishes with a patronizing smile.

"You're not gonna bait me into this," says Cella calmly.

"I'm sorry, but we're worried about you," says Dede. "You need to get out of that dungeon. All you do is make perfume and that, um, that—"

"I'm calling it an epinephrine aerosol secretor. Or adrenaline and pheromone spray. I'm not sure yet," says Cella.

"Yeah, that shit's got to stop," says Dede. "If you wanna win, none of this big brain shit. He looks like an alpha male type; that's a turn off for them."

"I didn't say I was doing it," says Cella.

"Oh please," says Dede. "Look, this isn't a criticism, but sometimes you come off a bit standoffish." Cella's mouth opens in shock. "I didn't say it was true, but that's a perception and quite frankly its annoying to see the guys look disappointed whenever you skip out on dinner to what is it, 'hypothesize on brog behavior based on secondhand accounts of body type.'" Dede air quotes the sentence as Cella's jaw clenches in annoyance.

"Look," says Jade. "My dad had us doing military training for three months. We need to have fun. You need to have fun. This will be fun. So stop being selfish and have a little fun."

#

"I had a chance to get Jade," says Dom. "It was all set up. She was waiting for me, but I caught a case of the runs after breakfast. You can't talk to a woman when you have to use the bathroom. The next day, Colt's laughing and giggling with her. Bastard."

"Is Dede really that good?" asks Zach.

"I got her more times than she got me."

#

"No, no Cella. You've got it all wrong. All guys want pussy. That's not that hard to give if you're offering. You need to think of this as an intel operation. If you succeed, it's better for all parties, see?" says Jade. "And he's cute."

"Don't let Colt hear you," says Dede.

"Colt won't do a damn thing," says Jade, giving a middle finger. "Think about it, Cella; you like a challenge.

"Why do you care so much?" asks Cella.

"Because I need Dede's edible panties collection."

"What are you putting up?" asks Cella.

"The Jasmine perfume bottle you gave Mom," says Jade sheepishly before plowing on. "I can't bring it with me, and sexy lingerie is more practical for our last night."

"Hold on, you gave Betty one of your perfumes?" asks Elle.

"It was her birthday," says Cella. "And she asked."

"You're not my sparring partner anymore."

"Let's not get off track here," yells Dede. "You've got three days, or I win."

"I could be figuring out how brogs communicate or their mortality rate. How their brain cavities look. Why their soft spot is their soft spot—"

"All things you won't know till we go outside," interrupts Jade. "And no talking about radioactive half-life. No fancy words like deoxyribose, acciaccatura, and craniosacral."

"What's the one that made Rick piss himself?" asks Dede.

"Protactinium?" offers Cella. "We're in a nuclear winter. Knowing what actinium's uranium decays into is important."

"No," says Jade. "None of that. We're probably gonna be dead in a few days. No one cares. No one."

#

"Large breasts are a sign of fertility," says Zach.

"So are hips," says D.

"I need titties," says Zach as Bode, Emmett, and Dom applaud.

"Look, guys. You're wrong. You need a firm foundation," says Coren.

"The back's where it's at," adds D.

"Fuck you, chubby chaser," says Dom.

#

"D has really nice teeth," says Dede as the ladies nod.

"Can we cut the shit?" says Jade. "We all know how you are. Now is it that you'll have the spotlight on you, or that we'll be expecting the usual fawning?"

"You really need to get over being sloppy seconds," says Cella. "I didn't want Colt, and he seems to like you plenty. What's with the jealousy?"

"Bitch, please."

"Please don't curse at me."

"Fuck you."

Dede clears her throat loudly. "When you lose, I want the lilac scent too," says Dede.

"No," says Cella, turning from Jade. "When did I agree to this?"

Jade has an impudent smile on.

"Fine," says Cella. "And I want some of the edibles too."

"Be careful; psychopaths like to chop people up too," says Jade, causing a big laugh that makes Cella flush with anger.

Everyone stops as yelling comes from down the hall. Wanda's screaming about Bruce and Colt. She does this from time to time, but there is the off chance she could be yelling about something important, so everyone's out to check.

"She came down and wanted to know what we were doing so we showed her. What's the big deal?" asks Colt.

"Yeah, she's a natural," says Bruce.

"She's a child. And I'll be damned if she turns into you two," says Wanda.

"What's wrong with us?" asks Colt, scrunching his face.

"Take a guess, ass," says Wanda, eyes bulging with balled fists.

The others are smiling now. It's fun seeing Wanda swell up like this. Wanda, Bruce, and Colt continue arguing. That implies Colt and Bruce are also talking. Wanda is screaming about letting children be children as the crowd swells with mostly hiding smiles. D stands back a discreet distance, watching these people, making character assessments by the minute. Most of the smiles show more relief than happiness. D shakes himself. *Why should I care if they're relieved? Most of these people will be dead by the week's end, and I've got a mission.*

"I thought the boat was volatile," whispers Zach.

Chapter 12

Wanda's raucous has everyone ready an hour before they need to be. Zach and D, being the new guys, are left out of whatever conversations the others are having, so instead of waiting like good little puppies, D's flinging knives at the far wall of their room as Zach asks what materials make up D's suit.

"Dragline," says D, but Zach seems to be confused. "The spider silk. It's combined with a half-dozen other metals to make an armor. The jacket is the most important part, so it has the most armor. It's really light too. If I didn't have to use the helmet, I'd forget I had it on. Your turn," he says, handing Zach the knives.

Moments later, Elle knocks. She's volunteered to round up anyone not willing to participate in training. She ducks knives, breaking the bull's eye carving in the back wall.

"We're about to start," she says, turning to D's carving. "I don't think you can do that."

"No one said we couldn't," says D.

"You see this room. Who can tell the difference?" says Zach.

D makes one last throw that hits direct center and turns to Elle. Elle stifles a grin before guiding both to Door 3. Down a stairwell is the bullet-riddled door of the sparring class, shoddily painted over. To the left, a burned women's clothing room, to the right, a splintered men's clothing room where Dom, Bode, and Kellen sit. All three are stretching in preparation. D thinks Elle said bye before leaving, but he can't remember. Cella is going to be sweating in a few minutes. He's watching that.

"You could try to pretend with her, you know?" says Zach.

"What?" says D, his eyes truly blank as the others snort.

Dom has a broad grin as he shows the men a wide variety of workout clothes. Shirts, shorts, sweaters, and sweatpants, all either light gray, dark gray, or black. Zach takes a light gray shirt and shorts while D takes a black sweater and sweatpants. Dom and the others choose shirts and shorts that will help the women's imagination. They tell D he should wear less.

"The fighting sessions can get intense." says Dom.

D waves them off.

Dom glances at Bode, and Kellen shrugs. There's a slide-away door cracked with bullet holes leading to an expansive exercise facility, which is covered in blue padding and is encircled by a five-lane track. At the far right are elliptical and cycling machines, where Betty and Wanda sit, next to a weightlifting station. At the center of the gymnasium are Greco-Roman wrestling mats where the majority of the troop stand. Spaced from them is a boxing ring opposite the cycling wall. The men take their time passing the observing women. Most are disappointed in D's choice of clothing and equally so for Zach's clear need for vitamin D.

Bode's whispering about the form-fitting shirts and short shorts some women are wearing. Some look nice, but Cella by far looks the best. There is a hierarchy D didn't notice before. Some of these women are real warriors. D can see it in their bearing.

Ok, so maybe some of them do have a shot.

The troop breaks into teams of two when the men decide to stretch their muscles in clear view of the smiling women. Jade's with Colt because of several mishaps leading to broken noses, ribs, and in Sabrina's case, a torn rotator cuff. Cella's frantically searching for a partner, but no one's willing to help except Rita.

"Oh dammit, Cella, she's not gonna kill you," shouts Rick.

Vladimir Fleurisma

The military girls laugh as Cella crosses the invisible line to their section. D and Zach first think to team with each other until Hank and Rick say differently. Saffire rushes in with water and her own workout shorts. She once tried dressing like Cella, but Wanda nearly had a conniption. Class starts with Bruce coming to observe the new tweaks in the teams.

"All right, we don't have time to get the new guys caught up, so they'll just have to catch up," says Bruce. "Move six, nine."

"Wait," says D as a left uppercut sends his chin to the ceiling.

Next comes a right cross, leading to a fireman's carry. As Hank offers a hand, a surprised D slaps it away.

"Good. Again," says Bruce before Rick calls for a halt. Zach looks broken.

After a moment, Zach's moving again, and Bruce calls for the next combo set. Hank throws a right cross and a right knee followed by a suplex. D pops up immediately, not quite angry but annoyed enough to want to break something. Zach's begging for a timeout, but Bruce is suddenly blind. Hank has D in an armbar, transitions to a side slam, and ends in a sleeper hold. D breaks free by thumbing Hank's eye and adding a spinning elbow square to the jaw, finishing with a crumpling kick to the chest.

"Good counter," gasps Hank.

Rick's asking for time while reviving Zach. "Never mind, he's coming back," he says pleasantly.

A seething D pulls his sleeves elbow high for the next attack.

"Hold up, dammit," says Zach. "What the hell is this? You're supposed to tell us what we're doing first."

"Oh, I was under the impression Rick would show you, is he not?" asks Bruce. Zach is silent. "Ok, let's keep going."

Hank lifts D by the arm to bury him shoulder first into the mat.

"I've been doing this a long time, young buck," whispers Hank. D finding himself completely immobilized, uses the only counter available. He tickles Hank's belly button. "Hey, what the hell are you doing?" Hank pushes himself off.

D answers with a kick to the gut and a punch to the face. Hank gathers himself before a pinpoint right cross drops the six-foot-eight man flat. The warm-up is over. Now comes Bruce's favorite part, real-world application. One will play attacker, the other, defender, switching every two times.

Hank offers a handshake before pulling D in for a spear. Rick laughingly toys with an already tapping Zach. Bruce yells for Dom and Bode to take the session seriously, as the two watch the women fight. The military women look like they know what they're doing, but the civilians are coming along. Cella looks like her rotator cuff is about to tear. She's trying to scream for help, but a croak is all that's coming out. Dede and Elle aren't even trying to hit one another as they wait for the time to wind down.

Colt and Jade appear to be working in perfect harmony. Aggressor Colt locks Jade into an armbar, and Jade counters into one of her own. Colt uses his strength to escape before taking a knee to the stomach, doubling over.

"We should try this position," says Jade as she lets go.

"Not in this lifetime, woman," says Colt.

As the sparring goes into full swing, Betty probes Wanda on her recent outburst. Wanda doesn't like all these guns near Saffy.

Zach does a big girlish yelp before Betty ups her bike speed.

"So this has nothing to do with her father?" asks Betty.

"What?" snaps Wanda, upping her bike speed as well. "What— what did I say? Did I even bring that deadbeat up?"

"You mean besides the time Rick tried to teach you some tricks, and you turned volcanic?"

"I did not," yells Wanda, turning down the bike speed. She's too old for this.

"You threw peroxide at him and tried to light a match," says Betty, upping the speed once more.

"I don't remember that."

"Rick did. You don't remember him aiming the cannon at you, spit flying out of his mouth. Everyone was screaming."

"Dammit, Betty, stop it. I hate it when you do that. You know what I mean," says Wanda.

"What do you mean?" asks Betty.

"She's all I've got. Guns can't be her first memories."

Saffire's running around the room mesmerized. She didn't know men could scream as loud as Zach. Hank's scar is giving that funny crooked smile, while D, whose dark skin looks almost as red as Hank's, is trying to unlock his and Hank's legs. D can't, so he presses nails into Hank's Achilles.

"Stop doing that shit," yells Hank.

D throws a hook to the back bottom left rib. Bruce, fed up with Dom and Bode's lackadaisicalness, switches places with Dom, forcing Bode to team with a bruised Coren. Jade and Colt's once playful banter can now be misinterpreted as a severe domestic dispute. Colt, after three knees to the ribs, rears back, snarling to clothesline Jade out of her ponytail.

"Are you ok?" Colt asks, kneeling as she headbutts him.

Colt pins her hands as she kicks at his genitals before slipping from beneath him. Colt's grimacing as hooks and crosses bombard him. He's having no success blocking so decides to use his strength to suplex her and follow with belly flops to take all momentum.

Bruce adds more time and no water break due to the lively atmosphere. An angry Jade rattles Colt with a cross. Before he can regain his bearings, he's caught in a sleeper hold. He lifts himself off the ground to jump onto his back, flattening Jade. Jade, however, is used to him doing things like that and keeps her hold, putting Colt in an even worse position.

Cella's been running and dodging for fifteen minutes. She's always been a good runner, but these last few months have boosted her stamina greatly. It's so good that Rita can't lay a hand on her, but for some reason, the timer hasn't rung, and now Cella's getting tired. Rita's heaving, bearing teeth like some wild beast. She's going to try to kill Cella. It's always been like this.

The ugly ones always have a problem with me. Well, this thick lump of dyke is going to work to get me, dangit.

Five seconds later, Rita's lunging at her. Cella's feet aren't as quick as they need to be, and Rita grabs her. Cella's squeezing her face, but Rita's made of lumpy granite. Rita squeezes tighter. Who puts a woman in a bear hug? Rita yells in triumph, trying to feel for Cella's spine, then yelps and throws Cella to the ground. Cella spits out the taste of sweat, scowling at Rita. She bites Rita again.

"Wait," says Cella, trying to gain her feet.

Rita's got a savage jealous look, and her large manish fist first cocks then fires. Cella's quick enough to duck and turn so only her upper shoulder gets hit. That doesn't stop her from moving ten feet. Cella's up looking to run, but the other women seem to be positioned so that she can't. She turns back to the walrus stalking forward. Rita throws another punch, but Cella ducks and tries to run to the other side, but Rita gets a hold of her hair. Cella's neck is craning back before she knows it, whipping towards the ground. The back of Cella's head smacks hard against the mat, and before she can get her bearings,

Rita has her in a sleeper hold. Cella doesn't try wiggling out of it; she's tapping before those biceps squeeze the oxygen out of her.

Rita pretends to not feel the loud smack against her triceps as Cella's legs kick out. Hank and Rick would be furious if Rita broke Cella's neck, so she doesn't; she just sends a message. She squeezes tighter. Cella's got some hidden strength Rita wasn't expecting. Rita's having trouble holding her still. Cella starts digging her nails into Rita's forearm and then blindly smacks her eye, forcing Rita to let go.

Cella scrambles away and looks back, outraged. She's not so pretty now. Her hair's even more tangled than its natural state. There's a red fist-sized bruise growing on her shoulder and snot coming from her nose from when Rita was choking her. Her eyes are apoplectic and to Rita's surprise, dry.

I thought for sure this prissy bitch would start tearing up about playing too rough.

"Ten more minutes," shouts Bruce.

Rita smiles. Cella glances at the fat-faced idiot, Bruce.

He'll be getting a piece of my mind next time he tries some lame one liner. Elle and Jade too. Both of them probably put Rita up to this.

"It's supposed to be the aggressor—" begins Cella, but Rita's charging.

Cella ducks a right from the enormous woman and begins bouncing from side to side. *I need to pay better attention to these classes because there's no way this butch tree truck has more stamina than me. Rita's too freaking heavy.*

Now some are trying to retire. Most of the guys are enjoying the fighting, but Bode wants no more of Coren. The last roundhouse kick nearly ripped his head off. Coren senses his advantage and throws more kicks. They fall into Dom and Bruce, and it turns ugly. Dede and Elle aren't even trying to take this seriously. Two military women sneak behind the two for belly to back body slams. Dede huffs and squeals as she lands neck first.

Elle grunts deep and cries. Dede and Elle curse and walk to the benches with disheveled heads held high.

D and Hank crouch at opposite ends in a stalemate.

"This round running long?" asks D.

"What's the matter? You tired?" asks Hank.

D charges into Hank's monkey flip. He quickly recovers with a leg sweep adding a straight left, curling Hank's liver. Rick glows at his beating of a fetal-positioned Zach. Rick stops as Zach swings wildly, hitting very near a special area. Rick goes primal and jackknife power bombs Zach into pieces.

D and Hank stop again, collecting themselves. D's ready, but instead of charging, he wobbles to the center dash, waiting for Hank to tow the line. Hank falls motionless from a devastating short right. D's pleased, but Hank's still down. If this old guy croaks, it'll be disastrous for D's plans. He goes to a knee smacking Hank's face. It takes twenty-five seconds, but the senior's eyes are open. D looks around; everyone seems preoccupied, but Rick meets his eye for a moment then turns away.

Most of the civilians have called it quits but can't leave the mat otherwise they'll have a five-minute penalty round against one of the soldiers. Cella can't quit because she's trapped. The military women have formed a semi-circle around Rita and Cella. There's no blood yet, but more bruises are showing on Cella's smooth skin. Rita puffs loudly, trying to land blows, but Cella gets her second wind. She keeps Rita at arm's length with light jabs until Rita is on Cella in a flash with a digging body shot, dropping the woman to her knees. While Cella holds her side, Rita steps back to launch her full weight behind a kick. The thick leg swings through the air with a swoosh and thuds into Cella, knocking her back several feet.

There's a savage pleasure in Rita's eyes as Cella curls into herself, shaking. Thinking it's over, Rita turns her back. She snaps back to Cella after noticing the shock in her friend's eyes. She gears for another boot but mid-liftoff, Cella bites her calf muscle. Rita screams, punching Cella's back. Cella's enraged, but not too enraged to numb Rita's powerful fists. She feels the last one to her core. She lets go but not before uppercutting Rita's perineum. Rita's legs go numb for a moment, dropping her to the mat face first. Cella roars, stalking forward, but feeling's back in Rita's legs, and she's up with bloodshot berserker eyes. Cella's no fool; she runs past a stunned Sabrina and out of the semi-circle with a bestial Rita sprinting after her.

Thirty minutes past the intended stoppage, Jade sits atop Colt with both hands around his neck. He starts tickling her, and she lets go, slaps his chest, then starts kissing him.

"Get back here, you bitch," screams Rita, pulling at strips from the bench.

Cella fits through the opening between benches and hunkers down while Rita rages and spits at her. Betty and several others come over, trying to calm the big woman while Cella crawls to the edge of the benches. She emerges, breathing heavy with a thick sheen of nervous sweat, cobwebs, and bruises, but she's alive and to Rita's aggravation, still very attractive.

"She punched me in the pussy," yells Rita.

"She tried to strangle me," says Cella, twenty feet away.

None of the women can hope to hold Rita, so five of the guys come blocking Rita's path while Cella nods telling them to get Rita under control, which only infuriates Rita more.

"Time's up, goddammit. Get off me," says Zach.

"What the hell took that clock so damn long?" asks D, sitting at the center mat with Hank.

Hank calls a draw after two more flush shots from D. He's an old man, and D is in very good shape for someone who was out there for weeks. It's plain the young man was holding back after that first cross.

"You're not all talk; that's good," says Hank.

Rick laughs at a hurting Zach, accepting water for both. Bruce is happy with the session.

"This is how a real brawl would be except five times as chaotic. Target practice will have to be tomorrow though."

Wanda's rubbing Cella's back while she and Rita scream at each other. Saffire's handing out bottles and ice as usual, thinking of which moves she'll try in private later. Bruce leaves the room to get some healing ointment from the lab while the men group to laugh at each other. The women, on the other hand, are split into the civilian and military camps with a frosty DMZ line one bench wide.

Chapter 13

"**I** didn't appreciate that trick with my leg," says Hank as Betty massages a welt on his chin.

"Survive," says D. "Wasn't that the point of this class?"

"I'd kick your ass if I was younger."

"That's big talk after I had you drooling for half an hour."

"No one's doing any more fighting today," says Betty as Hank opens his mouth.

Colt stumbles towards them, smiling like a boy after his first kiss. Hank laughs, asking if his daughter was too much for him. It's nothing Colt isn't used to by now. Bruce returns with a white tube of ointment. People reach out as it passes around counterclockwise. Using only a small dollop soothes an area the size of a forearm. Most everything on Zach hurts, but he puts some on his knees and back and cries out. He can almost see the ache leave his body.

"Why haven't I heard of this before?" he asks.

"Cella made it," says Bruce.

D turns to her, easy to spot in her yoga pants, glaring at the other bench. *I need to have a serious talk with that woman.* Suddenly, Rick's laughing. He glances at Hank, who's shaking his head. He tells Rick not to bring it up, but Rick pretends he can't hear.

"Seven guys, seven," says Rick. "The meanest, fattest looking slobs I've ever seen. Now in my early days, I attracted a lot of women. It turns out one particular lady had a very mean ex-boyfriend who had trouble accepting that she was gone."

"Says you," says Hank.

"I'm telling the story. I was starting my next tour of duty in three weeks when I saw her. She had on one of those little skirts and a flower ankle tattoo. Man, she was almost as beautiful as Betty." Betty rolls her eyes. "I said, 'I saw you looking at me so I figured I'd come over here help you out.' You know, with the cute ones you've got to show them you're not intimidated by their beauty."

"Get to the fight," says Colt.

"Shut up, young buck," points Rick. "She was hooked before she knew what happened. She tells me she's getting over a bad relationship so nothing serious. Fine; there was only one thing I wanted anyway. I get the number; we go out on a few dates, movies, park, you know. A week before I'm scheduled to leave, I call for another date. She tells me she's back with her piece of shit boyfriend."

"Ok, I'm fine. It wasn't a serious thing for me, but now I need something to do so I call my buddy Hank and tell him I've been dumped, and I need to badmouth women. This is before he met you," Rick says as Betty eyes him. We go to this rundown bar in town. The whole time I feel like someone's following me. Thirty minutes later, a misfit and his band of clowns walk straight to our table asking if I'm Rick. I say, 'Who's asking?' He says, *'The man whose woman I fucked.'*

"I tell him I don't know a Rick, and this asshole punches me in the face. Now when you're punched in the nose, you can't help but tear up. You have to stop for a moment. During that moment, Hank is on his own, but soon after, I pick up the table and smash it over the head of the biggest goon they had. Now it's six on two instead of seven—good odds for any Army man."

"Her boyfriend's got an ego so he wants me to himself. Hank has to deal with the other five. I was sorry about that. The boyfriend runs at me with a knife. I side step it, smack him in the back of the head with a bottle, then break his elbow. The other guys get off Hank to charge at me. By this time, the whole bar's gone crazy. I jump behind the counter to throw glasses while Hank's on the ground holding his ribs. The bartender tries throwing me back over the counter so I slam his head on the beer dispenser, pull out the hose and spray those fat bastards in the face. I'm back over the counter, and Hank's mad now. Knocks out the closest guy to him just because he's there; then we tag team. I take the two to the right; he takes the other three."

"I tell you to this day, I haven't seen something like this. The first guy comes at him, and Hank grabs a full bottle and pushes it through the poor guy's ear. I tell you, I saw whiskey leaking from the guy's mouth. A goon comes at me now. I take a chair and hit a guy fighting behind me, then duck. The guy turns to see my two goons, and all the sudden, it's three on two. I pick up a chair leg and hit my goon right on his kneecap. He falls like the sack of piss he was. The other goon's a pretty good fighter so he's just wiping the floor with my recruits. I move around then jump on his back. He's struggling to get me off when I just go for it. I bite his nipple; took the thing right off. Oh, the other goons see and don't want any part of me after that.

"Hank has one unconscious, one in a leg lock, and another screaming with his arms bent backward. Cops come so we use the crowd to get back to our car. The next day, I see her and tell her I'm too good for her. I should have gotten a girl to kick her ass." Rick sighs.

"Do you remember her name?" asks Zach.

"Kiera Preston."

"You got anything?" Rick asks D.

"Nothing I'm sharing with you," says D taking the ointment.

D checks his body. Having no real bruising, he chooses the now bright red left leg. Hank frowns at it. When did he do that? D straightens his leg, watching the redness fade to match his skin tone in under a minute. D turns the tube over, looking for ingredients, but it's only a clear bottle. He looks back at Cella.

"I love how sexy men are when they get all cavemanish," says Dede as the women nod.

Cella rests her head on Wanda's shoulder, rubbing her chest while Jade tries not to smile. They've agreed Cella gets the courage award for not dying. Dede and Elle take the lowest marks.

"I'm not a fighter, all right," says Elle.

Rita's still smoldering as she walks past, but Cella is matching her glare for glare while Wanda waves Rita on. Cella's not letting it go.

No one tries killing me and thinks it's ok.

"You have a mirror?" Cella asks Wanda.

"You look fine," says Wanda. "Doesn't she look fine?"

Jade coughs loudly then laughs, and several others join in. Cella has murder in her eyes. She'll see how happy Jade is when vagina inflammation pictures are taped to her door. Cella notices D's eyes float to her, and after another quick glance, she nods to herself.

"What else are we doing today?" asks Zach

"Nothing," Hank says before sighing. Betty knows how to use her hands. "Today was supposed to be an off day but you guys threw off our schedule yesterday."

That's when others start to smile. Kellen's looking at Rick. Rick looks at the others. They nod, and he heads for his room, then Room 12, followed by a half-dozen others, including Betty and Hank. Colt shakes his head. *They're supposed to set good examples.* Then he looks for Jade. D and Bruce eye Cella.

"I can't take this anymore," says Dede, marching to Dom.

Dede wants to relax; Dom's grinning widely, nearly hopping as they leave. Zach stares confused and a bit hurt as Coren motions him to Room 12. Colt stands as if psyching himself up, then walks to the ladies.

"Excuse me," he says in a deep, mysterious voice as Jade giggles. "You seem familiar. You see, I once knew a woman who looked just like you. She was as lovely as the sun and sharp as a rose thorn. Sadly, I only saw her once. I believe I've been given a second chance. May we talk my lady?"

Jade's blushing furiously as she gives him her hand. The other ladies are sighing while Cella rolls her eyes. Jade goes into full feminine mode as she and Colt head to their room. Wanda's obfuscating then makes her choice. She's going to Room 12. Saffire's staying with Cella. Cella's yelling no, but the old lady is speed walking away. D and Cella are left alone.

D is up with the easy walk of a predator spotting his prey. Cella smiles at his grace.

D's got an easy confidence about him. I like that in a man.

Suddenly, Bruce is blocking her vision. *Did he really speed walk to reach her first?* How desperate can he be? Bruce is saying something, but Cella's not even trying to pretend to care. Maybe he can take thirty more minutes to come up with a good line.

"Dangit," says Cella as a happy Saffire sits next to her.

"What are we going to learn about?" asks Saffire.

D glances at Bruce, but Cella pats the opening next to her without acknowledging Bruce's presence. D tries not smiling at Bruce's throbbing vein as he sits with Cella, pointedly turned away from Bruce.

"You look relaxed," says Cella.

D eyes her hair puffed out and frayed, thinking about the faces she'll make when he fucks her senseless. Cella starts straightening her hair self-consciously. He holds up the tube.

"You do this for a living?" he asks.

"Not really," Cella shrugs. "Just a hobby."

He raises a brow. "Seriously? That's incredibly unfair. You have enough advantage in life."

Cella laughs. "Yeah, well, life's not fair. Some of us just have to make due." She leans back smugly.

D frowns. "Did you just call me fat?"

"What? No, I—oh, ha, really funny." She pushes him. "Hold on. Were you calling me fat?"

"Of course not. I'm shallow."

"What?" she laughs.

"Yes."

"Ok, mister. You will not sweet talk me. I expect quiet and brooding. This charm fest is not allowed. Do you hear me?"

"Excuse me, young lady." He slides closer. "What are you, nineteen? I don't take orders from anyone. I live by my own rules, and right now, they say, 'See if she's really as perfect as I think.'"

Cella's giggling then clears her throat to say something snappy. She looks at him and keeps looking.

"You got nothing," says D, nodding.

"No, I just. Hold on. I had something. Darn it."

"Darn it?"

"Yes, I said darn it. I say fudge, sugar, and hot tea too. Problem?"

"Are you trying to call me fat again?"

"Ok." She laughs hard and stops as her chest pain flairs. "You didn't win this one. I'm just tired. Gimme that."

She takes the tube. "I'll be back. We're going to have our talk when I return. Saffy."

D noticed the girl sitting with a confused look on her face. She rises, sniffing at D as Cella leads the way out of the gym.

#

"Watch the door," yells Cella, scrubbing her armpits furiously.

The ointment is instantaneous. There's still a little tingling in the bone, but it will fade.

What's important is this hour and a half worth of sweat I built up. My hair is—well D looked like he liked it that way. Men are weird like that.

D's sniffing, then rushes to his room. The stank won't do. *What would General say if D went on a date with all this musk?* His satchel's where he left it, stuffed behind the drawer, blocking the door. The dental tablets double as deodorizers. He puts on a thermal shirt and walks back to the gym. Cella does a double scrub of her vagina.

I'm not planning on giving D any, but still, I have to be clean at all times.

"What are you doing?" asks Saffire.

"I said watch the fudging door."

No one's in the hallway as Cella streaks for her room to a collection of perfumes and a fresh shirt. She tries on five before finding the right one to match sky blue yoga pants and nods at her reflection.

"You changed?" Cella asks, arriving in the gym.

D shrugs. "You have perfume on?"

"No."

Chapter 14

Room 5 opens to a staircase leading down to a white metal door reading Laboratory. Inside, are rectangular desks, beakers, Bunsen burners, microscopes, computers, and two code-locked doors. A large tarp covers the far right corner, gurneys are jumbled with an assortment of medical devices and other various liquids—the main attraction being a life-size model of the human body. It's designed for medical students and biology classes, able to fade between reproductive organs and all other bodily systems. Next to that is the board with drawings of the uglies.

"You have a lot of stuff in here," says D.

"Not by choice," says Cella as Saffire runs to the board.

She points D to his seat then points Cella to hers. Cella is almost indignant but she likes when Saffire shows spirit. Saffire's been helping Cella find the weaknesses of the monsters. The girl goes into rapid fire mode about all the discoveries they want to make if Hank would just let her get out there and find live samples or just intact ones. Cella doesn't even look before pulling out a Tyrannosaurs Rex figurine. Saffire has the dinosaur before D can blink and sits opening the things mouth and slamming it hard while laughing.

"So," Cella begins. "My work's not done yet, but I have a working hypothesis as you can see."

D can't. The board is a mess of scribbles but he nods.

"So," she says. D stares back blankly. "What're your thoughts?"

Cella doesn't seem to have anything. He could just say that flat out, but women don't handle constructive criticism well. The body's all wrong and too small. The drawing has the beast half the size of the van. The brutes are about as big as the van and a little sleeker.

"They're ambush predators," says D. "They can jog long but they sprint when actively hunting."

"How fast are they?"

"Faster than me. Faster than anything I've ever seen. I don't have a speedometer but some looked like they were clocking sixty and seventy miles. With their speed, you wouldn't expect them to be that strong. One can push a thousand-pound rock."

Cella grabs a datapad and stylus pen, taking notes.

"A thousand pounds, you said. Is that typical? Or which type is it? How many types are there? Just the one or are there different stages of physical maturity?"

"Hello," says Saffire jumping between the two. "You're supposed to ask about my pictures." she points to the board.

Cella smiles an unpleasant smile at her pint-sized confidant. "Do you want to show D your abstract thinking skills?" The girl nods.

Cella takes a word puzzle book from a nearby desk and flicks to a page.

"Do all the problems on this page," says Cella, pointing Saffire back to her seat.

Saffire doesn't go back to her seat. The girl moves closer to Cella, eyeing D suspiciously. The girl finishes ninety seconds later, showing D a crossword puzzle and synonym clues.

"She used to need her biology books but not so much now." Cella smiles angrily.

"Can you do that?" Saffire asks D challengingly.

D suddenly thinks of dunking her in cookie dough.

"Did you know whales used to walk?" says Saffire.

"Yes I did. Did you know the earliest known ancestor of the whale is called Pakicetus, from the Pakicetidae family, which means from land to water?"

Saffire blinks. "I knew that."

"Saffy, don't raise your voice; you know better," says Cella.

"Sorry," the girl mumbles then blurts out something else. "Sharks can lose thirty thousand teeth in a lifetime."

"Yeah, that's around nine hundred thirty times more teeth than people have." says D.

Saffire's mouth goes O-shaped as she stares.

"You don't know everything."

D coughs to hide what is certainly not a laugh. Cella's given up trying to force Saffire away. The girl's as stubborn as a mule sometimes but watching D go back and forth with her is very pleasant for some reason.

"I didn't think Carcharodon Carcharias is a favorite of yours," says Cella.

"Scio te non putes multa," says D in perfect Latin.

Cella blinks and Saffire frowns. Was that a curse? The girl loves hearing new ones. Cella for one can't speak Latin and won't even try.

"Where'd that come from?" asks Cella.

"I'm used to dealing with academic types."

Cella's not sure if that was an insult or not but she's taking a second look at D now.

"Saffy, go sit over there and play," says Cella.

"I like it here Cel-"

"I said go sit over there and play," the older woman says firmly.

Saffire sucks her teeth and drags her feet to the far end table with the T-Rex standing on it.

"So what's your story?" asks Cella.

"Which one?" asks D.

"The one that made you learn about sharks."

"I can't just be curious?"

"Considering a brand-new species with supernatural skills has been hunting you for over a year. No. Too much coincidence for general curiosity."

"That's sound reasoning. Did you know they swim?"

"Brogs?"

"Very well. Twelve feet a stroke."

Cella marks that in her datapad quickly.

"You're not a shrink, are you?" asks D.

"Of course not. I'm just curious." Cella winks. "Anything you can tell me about their behavior? Quirks and the like?"

"The one I got my skin from acted pretty strange. I'll admit I try not to be near any of them but this one time I got close to two; they were fighting and hissing the whole time. Not grunting like when they hunt and long thin streams would burst from their back flaps. When they stopped, only one could walk."

"You have skin from one of them. No one told me that. It's not contagious, otherwise you'd show signs. So the disease isn't that contagious. It must just be in the saliva. Can I see it? Please?"

Cella puts on a helpless pleading expression that would make any man do whatever she wanted.

"Do I get something in return?" asks D.

"It depends on what you want." She smirks.

"Good point, I'll have to think on it."

As D passes Saffire, she shouts, "Did you know bowhead whales can live up to two hundred years?"

"Did you also know whales and hippos are genetic sisters?" says D as the girl scrunches her face.

"I don't care about hippos; they're ugly."

"Saffy-" says Cella, then stops.

Elle stands there with a stony expression. D goes into combat mode, sensing the shift in atmosphere. He's glad he's leaving. He gives her a wide birth before opening the door.

"I see how you do it now," says Elle.

"Saffy, put these on," says Cella, tossing the girl oversized headphones.

"This is really unattractive," Cella continues to Elle.

"You backstabbing bitch," says Elle.

"Please don't curse at me," says Cella.

"Fuck you."

"Saffy turn around." Cella takes a step back. "What's your real problem?"

"So are you teaching her how to betray friends too?" Elle points at Saffire. "Did you tell him about how you harvested your last boyfriend?"

Cella's jaw drops. "How can you say that to me?"

"Fuck you."

"This is why you're lonely. You did this with Bruce, Dom-"

"What? What am I doing?" interrupts Elle.

"You're doing it now," shouts Cella.

"Am I?" screams Elle. "Well let me act like you then." Elle sucks in her stomach then does an exaggerated hip sway walking around Cella. "Oh, I'm sorry, I'm lost. Can you help me?" She ends by giggling obnoxiously.

"I don't do that, and you really should take some self-reflection classes. Your feminine energy is at zero right now."

"I should've paid Rita to break your neck."

"It was you." Cella's eyes bulge. "I could've died."

"What a tragedy that would've been. No more simpering to get cheap compliments."

"What'd you want from me, an apology? Fine, I'm sorry you're one of the last women on Earth and it's still cobwebs down there. Happy?"

Cella knows she shouldn't have said that. The words were out before she could think.

"You're a fucking traitor," says Elle then storms out.

Saffire walks to a heaving Cella cautiously. "Why'd Elle call you a traitor?"

#

It's not called snooping, not really. At least not when women do it. D was just waiting for them to finish is all. It's not his fault they're yelling about cobwebs and bitches. Thankfully, there was no one in the halls when he got the skin; only a psychedelic air emanating from Room 12.

"What the hell is that?" says Elle as she exits the lab. "Whatever I don't care. I hope Bruce does shoot you in the head."

Well fuck you, too. thinks D as he enters the lab.

Cella's frowning at the door as he enters. It's a universal female no-sex look. Did that mouse-faced twit just cockblock him?

"What's that?" asks Cella as Saffire runs to the skin.

"It's really soft," says Saffire smiling. "Hey, do you know who Heron Cabal is? My grandma says you remind her of him."

"Who's he to you?" asks D.

"My dad. That's what grandma said. I've never met him but she says he knew everything and acted like it."

D doesn't know what to say to that. Heron Cabel was a military weapons manufacturer. He built the Jupiter fighter jets and is five inches shorter than D. He had five children by three women and was divorced last D heard. What the hell's that got to do with him?

Then Cella pokes him. Well, she pokes the skin and he can feel it.

"Can I have it?" asks Cella fluttering her eyes.

"Absolutely not," says D unblinking.

Cella flinches. She's not used to anyone telling her no.

"A sample?" she asks.

"So long as I pick."

Cella clears space from a desk and lets D lay the skin over the table. Cella wastes no time poking and stretching it with periodic writing on her datapad. It's as if everyone else doesn't exist. D looks at Saffire who shrugs and tries to make her T-Rex eat it.

"Was 'brogs' your idea?" asks D.

"I hate that name," says Cella. "Did you hear the three hypotheses everybody has?" D nods. "The forest made a super predator?" She sucks her teeth at that. "I was hoping you'd have collected teeth too."

"Teeth?"

"Yeah, you said something about a hog tooth. I thought you'd get teeth also."

D stares at her blankly. Cella looks up at him. D isn't one for showing expression but he looks confused. She doesn't know what she's missing.

"You know for samples," she continues. "I want to see if they have the disease in their teeth. Like snakes, they pump their venom through their teeth. I wanted to rule out some things."

"They don't have teeth," says D. "Jagged slabs of bone on each side."

"Really?" she says looking at the board. "So that's why you didn't say anything about the drawings. They're completely off, aren't they?"

"Yes, that one on the end's got eyes. They don't have eyes. They sniff and hear out their prey."

She makes another note. "So ten days?" she adds. "The last case of infection I had was three."

"When was that?"

Cella points to the tarp.

Things start to click in place. The gunshots, ruined dresser. No wait, they couldn't get in. If they did, no one would be here—alive anyway. They were fighting each other. Well he already knew that. Why?

"What happened?" asks D.

"My last boyfriend had a group. One of them got sick and snuck back in through the back way," says Cella.

D gives nothing away, but he almost turns to the doors at the end of the dining hall.

"Bruce shot him. I got samples of the disease, but I've still got no working vaccine yet. No one wants to take my test. It's a virus and you know how unpredictable those things are."

"I thought you made cream," says D.

Cella laughs. "It's a hobby. Biology is my day job. I'm not glad about what happened but I'm glad I came here. This is a level four lab. It's got its own failsafe system separate from the rest of the bunker. Nice right?"

D nods.

That's it? Cella thinks. *No, why is someone who looks like you doing this? You could make a killing as a model, why not that?*

It's not that Cella wants to hear that but she's got an answer prepped and he's supposed to ask. That's how it works.

"Have any ideas about how they breed or how long their lifespan is?" asks D.

Cella blinks as D looks at her, waiting. "Where did I go to school?" she says. "Did my parents go there?" she coaxes.

"What?"

Cella's jaw clenches.

"Owe," says Saffire.

There's a loud clattering as the T-Rex's head falls to the floor. Saffire's hiding her hand as Cella rushes over. Saffire's thumb is bloody.

"I tried to make T-Rex bite it and it bit me," says Saffire.

D lifts the T-Rex head. A film of red covers the front teeth. He looks at Saffire. She looks back over Cella shoulder. Neither blinks.

"D, can we continue this later? I'm not risking an open wound with what I wanna do. Not with Saffy here," says Cella.

"Sure, I'll come back later," he says, leaving the skin.

Chapter 15

An hour passes with Cella testing Saffire and bandaging her hand. She is certain there's no disease because D would be sick by now but she has to be sure. Saffire goes to the kitchen to steal a pear. Cella goes to talk to somebody. If Saffy knows the adults, she'll have thirty minutes to herself. What to do?

"I don't want to hear it," says Elle, tossing the core of an apple at Cella before entering the kitchen.

"You'd rather throw fruit than talk to me?" says Cella, as Elle gives a middle finger before looping around her to enter the hallway.

"Elle, we can't work this out if you don't talk to me," says Cella.

"I don't wanna talk. I'm making silk, you fucking slut."

"Oh really. I'm Dede now."

Jade's pushing Colt off her nipple as the two pass. Colt's got a good grip on both breasts as Jade squirms.

"We're doing caveman, socialite girl again?" says Colt.

"No," she giggles. "Something's happening. Wanda's probably tripping on her high again. Let me go."

"What the hell? We don't have many chances to get this in. You didn't even give me a blowjob yet. You goddam liar."

"What?" exclaims Jade. "You've got me all to yourself tonight. This'll just take a minute. Now get off."

Colt's cursing an endless stream as Jade throws on the nearest shirt. *Acting like he doesn't get enough sex. The nerve* of him.

Elle's saying "fuck" and "shit" and "fucking shit" repeatedly by Room 7 while Cella smolders near the kitchen. Whatever happened, it's Cella's fault. Jade rushes over to Elle with a concerned look.

"You ok?" asks Jade as Elle stomps up the stairs.

"Shut up," says Elle voice croaking.

"Elle, you know I won't judge. What'd she do?"

\#

Once a week, thinks Colt. *I want a blowjob once a week. Is that so unfair? And the complaining? I can't do it without using teeth. They're in my mouth. What a load of shit.*

Cella's biting hard into an orange as the cabinet beneath the sink closes behind her.

"Hey, you and Elle at it again?" asks Colt. Cella nods. "Is it about you not letting her use any of your perfumes?"

Cella laughs. "Do you like desperate women?"

"No."

"Thank you. No one does. You think she'll try to trap you with a baby, right? Not sexy at all."

"Is this about new guy?"

"No. I'm not sixteen. I just know how to be attractive. Is that a fudging war crime?" asks Cella.

Colt has to stop himself from laughing. "You can be a bit of a tease."

"I know. But that's not the same thing."

"It kind of is."

"Whose side are you on?" Cella demands.

Colt blinks. *Never argue with a woman. Ever,* he thinks while rising to leave.

"Wait," says Cella. "I didn't mean to yell. You agree with me, right?"

"That-I-yeah?"

"Agree with what?" asks Jade walking in.

"Desperate isn't attractive," says Cella.

"Beauty's not everything Cella," states Jade.

"I didn't say it was everything," says Cella.

"So why are you trying to bully everyone with it?"

"Because I'm obviously intimidated by everyone else's smarts."

"Don't get sarcastic with me, bitch."

"I'm not. You're just intimidated."

Jade takes a step forward, Cella takes a step back, and Colt gets between the two.

"Didn't your dad say something about no drama?" says Colt.

Jade's fists are balled. Colt's prepping to move and block her punch. It's not the first time he's had to remind her he's six inches taller and ninety pounds heavier. Cella tisks loudly and shakes her head. Jade's eyes go blood red as her ocher skin turns a frightening shade of red. Colt's now trying to get out of the way. He really can't understand female fighting. Jade takes a heavy breath and smiles.

"Come on, Colt. We can talk about that ring you'll get me," says Jade.

Colt's completely dumbfounded. *What the fuck is going on?* Jade takes an iron grip of his hand and pulls him out of the kitchen.

Cella coughs loudly. Colt and Jade turn. Cella crosses her legs and sits prim proper and beautiful on the counter nearest the sink, pursing her lips.

"Bye, Colt," says Cella, eyes fluttering.

Colt stares flummoxed and Jade, if she could, would have fire streaming from her scalp. She's within arm's reach before a strong arm tugs her back by the waist. Cella stiffens when Jade gets close, but she keeps the bright smile on as Jade bears her teeth. She's another one that needs classes.

#

Elle sits in the dining hall as some of the military people head to the war room. She's giving off an antisocial vibe so no one tries to come close. No one even comes to ask. It's like they don't even care. *Assholes.*

"I didn't even say anything, yet," says Bruce.

"What?" Elle snaps. "Go away."

"Come on. Don't be like that. Move over."

Neither says anything for a moment. Bruce just sits while Elle pretends she wasn't crying. Bruce raises an eyebrow and smiles toothily. Elle snorts then tries to cover it.

"There you go," says Bruce. "Feel better?"

"No."

"Well part of feeling better is trying. Try please?"

"No."

"Your face says no, but your body says yes."

Elle laughs. "Don't quote Rick's classic music, please?"

"Only if you tell me what's wrong."

"We're going to die," says Elle. Bruce stops smiling. "You've been outside. I know what you military types say to each other. Fifteen percent if we're lucky. Is it really that bad?"

Dom or Coren, maybe one of them opened their damned mouths. Bruce will have to punch both of them later to send a message.

"It's bad, but one thing I know from all my time soldiering is the biggest threat is always yourself. If you don't think you'll make it, you're halfway dead already." He puts an arm around Elle. "We can't do this if you won't fight. Are you gonna fight or not?"

They look at each other.

"What do you see in her?" asks Elle.

Bruce blinks. He's about to ask who but he knows who she means.

"Fight for me, Elle. All right?" he says before leaving.

Cella hides herself as Bruce passes. She was going to talk to Elle but she'll get D instead and go to the lab. She makes a point to watch for Bruce before walking down the hallway, then psychedelic air is all around her as Betty walks out. Cella refuses to keep a straight face.

"You know where Saffy is? Wanda forgot." says Betty.

That is a really good question. Cella doesn't have a clue. "I have her." Cella coughs, waving smoke from her face.

"Hey, listen. Do you know where my daughter is?" Betty frowns. "She doesn't like you. I'm her mom, so I know you don't believe this, but I like you. And I think you two are trying not to be friendly. I know why, but still. It can't hurt you to call a truce. Give her one of your perfumes. She'll like that."

Hank is there, eyes glazed, tugging Betty back in before Cella can say anything. She'll tell Jade about this later. She knocks and enters Room 7 only to knock into the dresser and fall back out of the room with a yelp. D's at the door frowning down at her mortified expression.

"Can you go back inside please?" says Cella keeping her face turned.

She's on her feet again and brushes off her leggings and shirt. Her sneakers aren't scuffed, and looking around, no one else saw. She takes a breath and knocks again. D opens the door with a very relaxed face. If Cella didn't know better, she'd think he's smiling.

"Hey," she begins. "Let's finish our talk."

Visible red is coming through her sienna skin.

"You sure?" asks D. "After that knockdown you seem a little woozy."

"Shut it, mister," says Cella, a vein popping from her forehead.

"It's nice to know you're human. I thought you glided everywhere. The aura doesn't work on your ass I guess."

"You know what, fine. I didn't come here for this. You can go back to doing whatever it is you were doing."

"Stop. I'm just having a little fun with you. Don't be like that."

"You're supposed to pretend nothing happened."

"Nah, you fell hard. And you yelled like someone looked up your skirt. Terrible, terrible. You gotta learn to keep your composure. I'm disappointed."

"You know you're becoming less attractive by the minute."

D kisses her hand and winks. Cella's shocked by this and smiles broadly. *Where'd that come from?*

"Ok, I forgive you," she says.

"What about the tile you landed on. He's probably offended."

Cella's mouth drops. "Is that how it's gonna be?"

"Yes. And it's completely your fault."

Cella's mouth purses and her foot taps. D eyes her up and down. He doesn't have a smile; he gives her the wolfish glare of a man that knows how to handle a woman. It has Cella squeezing her thighs. D steps closer and she stumbles into the wall. D coughs to hide a snort and Cella stops; she's had enough of this.

She's more frazzled than at any point she can remember. It was that smoke Betty hit her with. Dangit.

D's looking at her as if seeing her for the first time. He takes her hand and walks to the lab.

#

This is a disaster. There's no way Cella's gonna gain the upper hand if this keeps up. She's not going to meet his eye until she gets control of herself.

"You want something to eat?" she asks, walking out before D can answer.

D's quite proud of himself as he stares at her ass with the door closing. She's really cute when she's stumped. It's good she doesn't take herself too seriously. She fell right on her ass. He chuckles thinking about it. He meant to do that to Zach once he got out of Room 12. Stoned people are fantastic to laugh at.

Cella's still ashamed as she reaches the kitchen. Wanda's there smelling like cinnamon and fudge.

"You don't think Saffy went outside, do you?" says Wanda. "I have no idea where that girl went."

Cella grabs a bag of grapes from the fridge and yells, "Look out." Wanda shrieks and grabs a whisk, swatting at the air. Cella loves doing that. Someone's calling her as the hall fills, but she pretends she can't hear and speed walks to the lab.

D's standing, looking at the body model.

"You know our school had one of these," he says. "It broke when the boys kept putting pencils in it when the female parts showed up."

Cella shakes her head. There's no response to that. "You like grapes?" she asks.

"What's in the locker?"

"Which locker?"

"The one you've kept closed since you invited me here. You glanced at it when I brought the skin here, so it tells me you've got important things in there. I hope they're not related to what caused the accident." He nods at the tarp.

D's observant for a man. "Sulfur mustard, otherwise known as mustard gas and an epinephrine cocktail that was being tested the day you came," she says sitting. "You saw the yellow cloud outside, right?"

"Why an adrenaline cocktail?"

"You can't guess? This place is stacked with samples from most of the animal kingdom and insect and microbial world."

"Which means?"

"They can smell us," says Cella as if this is obvious. "It's pitch-black outside, and they don't use flashlights, right? We have to throw them off our scent. So I got to thinking if we could use that against them, we could survive."

"I just use fire," D mumbles more to himself. "You can hold two hundred fifty people here for years; why leave?"

Just then Wanda bursts in. "Ah Ha. You-what the hell? She's not here." Wanda walks back out.

"You wanna see the cocktail?" says Cella, rising.

That was smooth. D likes the way she ignored the question.

"We're using the gas and the cocktail," she says. "Rick says both of them work and to bring both. As if it's easy to make mustard gas."

"Why'd you make it in the first place?"

"I like to mess around. I had nothing better to do."

She hands him a grenade. It's obviously a smoke bomb with the cocktail inside. How they're going to leave is becoming clear. Follow this not that. Maybe these people can make it—some of them anyway.

Cella watches him silently.

"The pheromones cause them to go into hyperactivity," says Cella. "It's a smoke bomb. You-"

She stops at D's blank expression. It feels like annoyance. He must have already worked that out.

"What do you think?" she asks.

"How long have you been testing this?"

"Three weeks."

D nods. So many in this one area. It does work. Just not how they think.

"You should be more careful with this. The uglies learn fast," says D.

"You sound like Wanda now."

"I thought she was in politics?"

"She-what? Who told you that?" Cella asks.

D shrugs. She stares at him, searching his blank expression. "She's about safety too. I think we're way past safe. We need to take risks." says Cella

"You gonna keep eating those grapes or do I get some?"

#

Is five times a charm? No, Zach's not even close, as he hits the bathroom door. People have been taking bets and Colt's up big with 3:1 odds. Zach needs over ten tries. It started with Rick stumbling out of Room 12 in a haze of TGS with a huge smile. The puff, puff pass routine turned into a back and forth with Zach and Rick as others began to leave. Zach's been stressed lately, and Rick thinks he can out smoke anyone. It sort of devolved from there. They stopped when neither could feel their lips. Officially, they ran out of medicine but who knows the truth, really?

Zach's hungry. That he knows. So why won't the goddamn wall move so he can get inside and sleep? Chips—Zach hasn't had greasy chips in so long. *Why am I in the bathroom?* Zach's lost his train of thought. When did he get outside? There it is, Room 7. He needed something in there.

"Ha," shouts Colt. "That's ten. Who wants to go for twenty?"

Zach approaches slowly. This is a battleground. The door's days are numbered. He will win this shoving match. Slowly, slowly Zach pushes the door. It creaks. He stops checking around the edges. Some blocky shape is near the hinges. Zach's got it now. He heaves and pushes through hearing a loud groan and cheer outside. He nods satisfied. Wasn't he hungry?

#

"Noooo," says Cella as D shakes his head. "A thong's nothing like that. Women don't like wedgies. It's sexy."

"I didn't say it wasn't. On a beautiful woman, most anything is sexy but it's still a piece of cloth wedged in your ass. That's an undeniable fact."

"Do I get a piece of the dang skin or not?"

"What type of thongs do you wear? Silk or satin lace? You know a gentleman doesn't take advantage of a poor choice of words."

"Oh, all your years as a man gives you this insight?"

Cella throws a grape at D, and he catches it and pops it into his mouth.

"I hate you," she says. "Don't wink at me."

"You're not playing fair. You won't agree to the terms of our bargain."

"Ask a serious question and I will."

"Why are you leaving?"

Cella blinks, and her mouth tightens. He planned this and she walked right into it. D stares back stone faced as ever.

"Our food's running out. We have to leave or we'll starve," says Cella.

"Why are you-"

"That's one question, mister," she says. "Satisfied?"

D shakes his head but motions to the skin. He gets up to get tools from his bag, but Cella tells him to sit. Does he think she's not strong enough to cut dead skin? Well, she's a self-sufficient woman fully capable of making her own samples.

"Yeah, ok. Relax," says D, waving at her. "Cut the damn skin then."

She's only doing this because D's been winning. Women love to change the subject if it gets them the upper hand. D sits back, watching her profile as she pulls out sharpened micro-scissors with a determined look. A man can never get tired of watching a beautiful woman work. Four minutes and a cramp later, the scissors are dull and the skin is sliced three centimeters deep. Cella's got a stabbing look on her face as she eyes the skin. She's refusing to look at D.

She pulls out a surgical scalpel and punctures more than slices at the skin. Nothing happens, and she mumbles, *Fudging tea*, softly.

"Have you always been a soldier?" she asks suddenly.

D would normally ask where the fuck that came from but he's making progress. Is it worth telling her Marines call themselves Marines? Army calls themselves soldiers.

"Have you always been a scientist?" asks D.

"That's different."

"How? It's a job, isn't it?"

"No. You, you know, have guns and shoot people."

"I protect and prevent. It's just way less comfortable for some people."

"I didn't say I was uncomfortable."

"Neither did I."

"Fine, you don't want to answer the question. That's all you had to say." The scalpel breaks and she yells.

"You ok?" asks D.

"When did you decide to make this your job?" she asks.

"Nine."

"Liar. You were fighting in the third grade?"

"That's not what you asked."

Cella mulls her next question. "Nine? Why, what happened?"

"It's not a big deal. Focus on the skin."

"Forget the skin. What happened?"

"Tell me something and I'll tell you something."

"I'm going to take samples and run tests. Why nine?"

"Why is nine a big deal?"

"Why won't you just answer the question?"

"I don't understand the question."

She sucks her teeth, switching to an even sharper cutting instrument. This is proving as useless as the scissors.

"I read in a psychology journal that people who refuse to answer questions concerning their early life often do so due to trauma and or a great loss," says Cella.

"Did you read that?" asks D nodding sarcastically.

"Why can't you just tell me?"

"Because you're a stranger."

"Punk," says Cella as she upgrades to an electric tool.

"If you want to make a deal, I might remember something."

Cella eyes her tools and skips to her most powerful instrument.

"Are you gonna ask a question about me or the bunker?"

"If it makes you feel better, we can consider this a blind date. I'm so madly in love that I must know more so I decide to play a game. I guess about you and your life and you tell me where I'm wrong. And vice versa."

"What are the rules and what do I get if I win?"

D looks up and down her legs.

"That seems more like a prize for you than me." says Cella

D huffs. "My, aren't we full of ourselves. Ok, you pick your prize."

"I'm not picking until after you. And you didn't explain the rules."

"The rules are be honest with your answers and the questioner has to be reasonable with their questions and statements. For example, 'When did you stop torturing infants?' Answer: 'Right after your mother stopped sodomizing you.' Clear?"

"Prize? And no you don't get to kiss me."

"Has anyone ever told you how humble you are?"

"Prize?" she laughs.

"Teach me how to make your cocktail."

Cella almost coughs up her grapes. This man is not stupid.

"Ok, is this a way to stay close to me?"

"Obviously. Prize?"

"How about I keep that until I know more about you? Start."

"You're rich. Happy kid, good family, seeks Mom's approval but loves Dad more. Dad loves nature, so you love sharks. Mom was a fashionista, so you wear makeup. Your looks and family give you many options, but you choose a challenging one to prove that you are your own woman. But it's still a struggle to be taken seriously because of how you look. However, you've learned the advantages of your physical gifts. Where am I off?"

"Is that a trait they teach soldiers?" she asks and D shrugs. "How do you know if my mom's into fashion. It could be my sister."

"It's not your dad. Women care about fashion much more than men, and you have a mature sultriness about you. A young girl would teach you how to be sexy and slutty. You learn grace like yours from an older woman not a young one."

Cella beams at the matter-of-fact tone. D's got a way of being nice without showing it.

"Careful," she says. "People might think you're brooding face is just a front."

"I could care less what people think. I'm talking to you not them."

D's face relaxes. Cella moves her chair closer.

"What were you before all this?" she asks.

"You're not playing by the rules," he says.

"Yes."

"Yes what?"

"In general, you're right about me and my upbringing."

"But?"

"But I'm not telling you my life story. At least not until I get to know you better."

"Fair enough."

It's Cella's turn now. She can see the appeal in this game. What to ask? She can only stare D in the eye for so long. He has an iron cast to those dark brown eyes that's disturbing.

"You're not a common soldier, are you?" she asks.

"What's common about *marines*? I haven't met many civilians who can do what the average marine can."

"That's not what I meant. I mean you aren't a frontlines soldi-marine. I've been around the guys here long enough to see the hierarchy. The ones who do the planning aren't the ones who take the risk. Hank only gives general information to Colt and Bruce, and they figure it out but with Emmett and Coren things have to be spelled out and there's not much room for initiative. I'm not trying to make them sound dumb, but you get it, right?" D nods.

"So you come here after months outside, about a month after the Three-Mile signal," she continues, "And tooled with two guns and a couple of knives. That's not easy. I only hear about what goes on out there, and I want nothing to do with it. So you are a top-end officer with infiltration skills and an abnormal amount of tenaciousness. What I can't figure out is why you want to go to Three Mile. What's in it for you?"

D nods. "That's pretty good. I didn't think you'd ask those questions."

"Am I right or not?"

"In general, yes, I was a top-ranking officer but that doesn't count for much these days. However, I like to use my hands. Sitting behind a desk typing and running numbers is not interesting. It's fun to learn how people work."

"Really?" she smirks. "Well, I think I am going to have a good prize. But I don't think I have quite enough information yet."

Cella rummages through her tools and finds her most powerful electric tool.

"That's not going to work," says D.

"What do I need?"

"Heat."

Cella digs into one of her many piles of medical equipment to find a blowtorch and a faceguard. A woman wearing and using construction equipment is arousing. She should cut slowly to get proper samples. With a fair amount of effort, she gets twelve pieces. Cella sighs in relief as D feels the cut edges. It's warm like before. He doesn't get it.

"Protein structure," Cella says to her recorder. "This will be a while, which makes it a golden time to keep flirting with me. You haven't even mentioned my eyes yet. Very rude."

"I'll mention whatever I please whenever I please. Got it, woman?" he says, rolling up his right sleeve.

"What happened?" she asks seeing a forearm-length scar.

"Nothing," says D, pushing the sleeve back down.

"Tell you what, how about you think up something personal to ask me, and I answer it and vice versa. Deal?"

"Just one?" asks D.

"Two."

#

Now that's how it's supposed to be, thinks Colt. She didn't use any teeth that time.

What got into Jade is what Colt doesn't get. She flips moods so quickly sometimes.

"Wow," Colt says aloud. "Thanks."

"You're welcome." Jade smiles. "So you wanna join the tournament with me?"

"I hate that game. You know I do. And all that jingoism. I already live that. I don't want it in my entertainment."

"It's a game and you're thirty-six. Cartoons have that big of an effect on you?"

"Rick is a jackass, and I'm not dealing with his big fucking mouth. Sorry, I can't with him. I just can't."

"Killjoy."

"Why do you always try to get me to do shit after I cum?"

"What?" she says blinking, always a sure sign Colt's right.

"You heard me. I know what you're doing."

"I-what? I do something nice for you, and I get interrogated? So kind of you, Colt."

"Don't try to change the subject. Answer the goddam question. What do you want?"

"You know what?" Jade rises. "See if you get anything nice again. Jackass."

Some days, Colt wonders why he shouldn't choke Jade. What are the risks, really? Well, Hank is an issue so Rick would be too.

Just one time, one time. A strong shake, that's all.

#

Cella's back with some chips, fruit, and a loud ruckus that stops as the door closes. Room 12 is clear now, and everyone's hungry. Some are upset that Zach's sleeping and want their money back. D's almost about to leave. How'd Zach get past the extra hinge? D wanted to see him try to force his way in. Rick's medicine must not be that strong.

"Hello," says Cella. "You're not paying attention. I said what's your question?"

D's half-thinking to go upstairs and see how Zach got through the door but stops himself.

"What's your favorite animal?" he says instead.

"That's it? I thought you'd ask if I used to model or something."

"My questions are my questions. Answer it."

How many guys have asked that question? D's not a rookie. You have to ask questions that make them think. Women love to talk about themselves so anything that makes that easier is a plus. And is that lip gloss?

"My dad took us to the water preserve the summer before my freshman year of high school. I got to see the last great white. They named her Victoria."

Cella's trying to keep an analytical presentation but D can see her eyes sparkle. She's back in that moment.

"The keepers are tossing chum in the water. Victoria's killer instinct kicks in. She follows the scent, gradually picking up speed. The enclosure opens into a colossal hunting ground."

"She sways side to side dancing with the stream of entrails. The observation deck moves Cella underwater. The park lets you follow the predator as if swimming beside it. It's amazing, something that has to be lived. Her eyes turn white as she nears. She launches herself from the water clamping her jaws around fake seal meat."

"After I got over the shock, I was hooked," says Cella.

"You got a private show of the last shark on Earth?" asks D as she nods. "I saw a giraffe once." She laughs.

The radiation exam beeps for completion with unexpected results. The modern hazmat suit can withstand close to a thousand rads; this skin is able to withstand 4,128. Cella scrambles to run other tests. She puts three more samples to get an average. Cella's forgotten about D so he rises to leave.

"Where you going?" asks Cella. "You owe me a story. Sit."

D groans before retaking his seat. "How long will these tests take?"

"It depends," she says. "Hog tooth. When I said that you looked at me like I was clueless. Is that a meal or something?"

D snorts. "No. HOG means Hunter of Gunmen. When you train to become a Marine scout sniper, you're labeled a PIG, professionally instructed gunmen. The course is fourteen weeks. Was eight but the Army and Navy increased theirs so we increased ours to maintain shooting superiority. Anyway, upon graduation, you are known as a HOG."

"We are essentially the most feared persons on the battlefield. They can drop bombs, send whole companies, but it won't work; we're too good. We're in the best physical shape, we're masters of evasion and observation, and we're the most accurate shooters. Whatever we see stored in a writing pad or datapad we remember. We know the wind speed, wind direction, what type of vegetation is in an area, the type of people in said area, how far an object is from another object, how far that object is from you, how an object is supposed to naturally move, cars, bikes, topography—everything. It makes us more efficient at eliminating the enemy. The only way to dispose of a sniper is with another sniper. If a sniper kills a counterpart, he or she rewards themselves with a bullet from the barrel of their counterpart. This HOG's bullet was meant for you. Thus, you have won a hog's tooth."

"How many have you won?" asks Cella.

"It doesn't work that way. You only take that first one. If I did take others, I wouldn't be able to carry all of them."

"Humble."

D shrugs.

"How good are you?" asks Cella.

"I'm the best I ever met."

Cella smiles at D's certitude. "If a sniper is the most dangerous person on the battlefield, what's the average number of kills on an average day?"

"Snipers do not work alone," he says. "Every shooter has a spotter. The spotter finds the target. I won't give exact numbers; each day's different. But I can say that it is not uncommon for a sniper to get into the triple digits on certain days. Snipers are a rare breed. Marine scout snipers have the best bullet to kill ratio of any branch with an average of 1.1 shots per kill, that's why we say one shot, one kill. Until we're taken care of, the other side can't do anything. The power can be...intimidating sometimes."

"What's your longest kill shot?" asks Cella.

"Just over two miles," says D without hesitation.

"Is that a record?"

"Someone beat it a year later. It's in the database."

"How'd you get your hog's tooth?"

"I don't talk about work. It gets stressful."

Cella starts batting her hazelnut eyes and D throws a grape at her and sighs.

"You can't ask me about this again. I mean never."

Now Cella's very interested; she agrees.

#

Ten years prior, during the end of the Southern Oceanic War, factions of the old government had trouble accepting defeat. Bombing runs cleared away many of the old rule, stopping all major counter operations. But there were always holdouts. Multiple localities reported a man randomly shooting the citizens. First, their own soldiers attempt to end this disturbance, but after a first squad of ten men were killed and a second squad of fifteen killed and a third squad of fifty of which forty-one died and the rest ran. The new government asked for outside analysis. After D's exploits in counter sniping in Italy and the free Republic of Congo, he volunteered to go help. They made it sound nice, but D was the fifth option. Something about his attitude held up the promotion to major.

D was excited to meet this guy. The file said this sniper was a fifteen-year war vet, 978 confirmed kills, 128 more after the war ended. D learned his tendencies and his weapon of choice, the Rafferty-650, for D the best long-range weapon ever invented. It has a one and a quarter mile sight with night vision and a thermal scope, carries specially made 1,500-grain round with a tungsten penetrator. Only the best soldiers of this country were given this reward. And in every way it's the superior of D's standard military issued m-56.

D's spotter was blown up a few weeks earlier and the Marines were dragging their feet on a replacement. D had his pick, but everyone seemed to think he was full of himself. In any case, D could handle this. On the next 145-degree day, he arrived outside the last known position of the Cleaver, as the locals called him.

On the way to this area, as a welcoming, his driver received a gaping neck wound from a bullet through the windshield. Cleaver did this with the three prior teams also. The car was supposed to be bulletproof for that reason.

It'll be fun to kill this jackass, D thought.

He walked the final three miles to an evacuated township. There were high buildings and built-up waste mounds, a sniper's paradise. D asked himself where Cleaver would be. The sun was high to his right, and the wind was easterly at three to five miles an hour. Cleaver buzzed a shot past D's right ear. D scrambled to get away. General had drilled into D that emotion was the best way to get yourself killed. That didn't stop D from wanting to rip Cleaver's neck out. The shot came from the northwest, the highest building in the area, with a 360-degree view of the battlefield. Moving closer, he saw the second-largest building to the left had a figure in it. D laid flat on the ground, aimed up three mil dots over the crosshairs and two mil dots to the right. His rifle barrel had a left-hand twist to it, and at more or less 1,500 feet you had to listen to physics. His breath calmed and he fired between heartbeats to increase accuracy.

The shot streaked through the humid air, spinning right and hitting the boobytrapped dummy dead center, letting off a huge explosion. It was a stupid shot. D should've taken the time to check the target. It didn't move at all. However, Cleaver showed himself. Seven buildings to the left something shifted. The cloth on the window blew away exposing a person. D aimed again and saw a spark as his shot ricocheted off Cleaver's barrel. Cleaver was down the steps as D sprinted to the building. D's head was back, so he quietly entered the building, steering clear of any boobytraps as Cleaver headed down. At the fifth floor, Cleaver jumped out a window, landing on a garbage pile before sprinting into the shadows. D was close behind but stopped and leaped the other way as Cleaver threw a grenade at him. D leaped into the nearest garbage pile. At the time, he'd never met someone who was better than him; Cleaver might have been that man.

An hour later, D followed the tracks to an alley facing the sun. It was too simple. He thought before ducking Cleaver's first intended kill shot. The two were now even in missed shots. They moved again to see which one would get lucky. Maybe D could set a trap. He made tracks to the corner of a second-level window and put up sticks and a rock, mimicking a barrel and a head while positioning himself in a nearby two-floor complex. D waited but the man did not fire. D didn't expect Cleaver to be so easy to fool, he just wanted to see if something moved out of place.

D saw movement in the neighboring apartment and just stopped himself from blowing apart a feral cat. Another hour passed with the sun forty minutes from setting. He needed to end this, otherwise that Rafferty scope would kill him. D moved away from his trap into the ground-level garage of a nearby building, keeping the sun to his back. Something was wrong. The garbage pile is different. Some of the papers are flying with the wind toward the alley.

Cleaver was too smart to make such a stupid mistake. He probably threw some trash that way then doubled back the opposite direction, looking for anything that would make the best final firing position for his opponent. D marked the territory, so he knew the top of the eight-story building to his right was best, as it covered the entire avenue for thirty blocks. Cleaver didn't seem to think much of D, so he would position himself for the best shot at that position. D just passed that area. D knew where he'd be, inside the twelfth-floor apartment of the building, ten blocks from where Cleaver thought D was.

People thought snipers were stupid enough to have their barrels poking out of a window. Nonsense. There was furniture in there, and this town had a good building code. Each window was three feet six inches from its floor. To hit D's supposed position, Cleaver would have to aim down. So he'd be sitting in the middle of the room, maybe with a table to lean the gun against. The Rafferty isn't a light weapon and he had to maximize accuracy. Each room in those types of apartments in this part of town were about twenty-five square meters. The living room was typically 4.5 square meters. Each block, since the population explosion, was about 440 meters long. D was on the wide end of the street so that times ten is where Cleaver would be. *Hold your breath. Exhale as you shoot.*

His sight was off center. D's shot would be double the recommended range. Well, when he hit it, he would brag about it to his sister. D aimed up. Spindrift would take the bullet right, and gravity would tug it down. The extreme heat would make the bullet move quicker, though. D shot. The bullet entered through the right brow, exiting the base of the skull. A shot like this caused complete skull evacuation. Add to this the fact the bullet hit the fatal T. Cleaver was dead before he heard the shot, a clean kill.

#

"Where's the fatal T?" Cella asks.

"The eyes and down past the nose. You hit anywhere in that location and you're hitting the brain stem. They die before hitting the ground with no reflex action."

"You think of all that, then you shoot?"

"Sure. It's more instinct at this point since I've done it so much."

"What happened after that?"

"I went up to the room and got my hog's tooth."

"Why didn't you take the gun too?"

"I liked my gun. And it's molded for me. The Rafferty was fitted to Cleaver. I'm not gonna use another gun in enemy territory without knowing her first."

"You talk about guns like they're real people."

"Mine was called Tanisha. And I was faithful."

Cella blinks. What the heck is D talking about?

D shakes his head with that relaxed expression of his.

"Well since you lost your tooth, can you get another one?"

"Don't think so. I haven't checked the rule on that."

"How'd he look? The guy you shot?"

"White, black hair, butt nose, clean shaven and dead."

"You feel bad?"

"No. Why the hell should I?"

"It seemed like he was just defending his country."

"The war was over and after that, he killed eighty-three of those countrymen, nineteen of which were civvies and six were under eighteen. That's called murder by every rule of engagement."

D's tone says Cella should probably back off this point. D, for his part, is annoyed she'd ask that. Do civvies think talking will solve every problem? No, they just think its comfortable pretending their ideas work when they don't have a fucking clue what reality is.

"Does it ever get to you?" asks Cella.

"What?" asks D.

"Killing."

Of course she asks that question.

There are military people here. Why would she think that's an appropriate question to ask?

"Why should it?"

D's got a decidedly frosty tone now.

"I've just read that people who have exposure to that amount of violence have a hard time adjusting to civilized society."

Ah, so she understands me. I'm a broken person who needs a hug. And she's not a condescending bitch for quoting some jackass magazine.

"And here I thought no drooling or grunting would help you see the real me."

"Excuse me?" asks Cella, completely blindsided. "You don't know anyone who has committed suicide?"

Fuck you!

"Yeah, hundreds of them. One of my guys went to an aquarium, saw a fish that reminded him of the battle on Lake Constance in Germany. Blew his fucking head off right in front of the fish tank."

"Really?" says Cella, eyes bulging.

D stands, checking his watch as the door opens.

"Yeah, Saffy in here? Wanda can't find her," asks Bruce.

"No. Wanda doesn't want her near dangerous weapons," says Cella.

"Damn right. They'll have inflated views of themselves but go slumming when Sunday brunch gets old," says D, voice getting even more monotone.

"It's Wednesday. And get a mop for all that dripping off your chin."

Cella grabs the blow torch. D eyes her with complete confidence. Bruce steps between both, with D's gun aimed at D's forehead.

Could I take it from him? That doesn't matter, does it? D turns to leave.

"Watch out for the fish tanks, psycho," says Cella, safely behind Bruce.

Chapter 16

Two hours later, people are running back and forth, yelling at each other with fruit and seeds littering the hallway. A depressed Zach comes to the room to tell D it's twenty minutes to dinner. Dede's turned into a bitch, and Elle won't even look at him. *Elle? As if she's got the right to be picky.* D's not listening. He's been drawing a diagram of the bunker, and his things are packed.

"What?" says D.

"Food."

The hall's split into three groups, civvie women, military women, and confused men. Rick comes to D, munching an apple.

"What'd you say to her?" asks Rick.

"Nothing," says D.

"Apologize for your nothing. I've got plans." Rick walks away.

D and Zach stand, looking for friendly eyes. Well, Zach is. D's looking for weapons. Lady sentiment has the men shunning the newcomers as Hank calls for all to take a seat. Betty takes pity on them and motions both to sit with her.

"Don't worry about being attacked," says Betty. "Hank's superstitious about killing before missions. Bad omens and all that. You're fine. It would help if you didn't glare at Colt."

Colt has a familiar bulge in the breast pocket. That's not a wallet.

"So you wanna talk about it?" asks Betty.

"What?" asks D.

Betty's just cost him a staring contest win with Emmett.

"Cella says you called her a self-aggrandizing whore. Well, to be more specific, a prissy, intrusive, know it all."

D can't deny that, and Betty didn't ask a question, so he keeps quiet.

Betty laughs. "Well whatever was said the guys got to be the one who smooths it out. You know why?" She continues without waiting for D to not answer. "Because we ladies have bigger egos than you. It's a fact. When we dig in our heels, no one can change our minds. And I doubt most men care enough to want to be right anyway, so why do men fight? All these years that never made sense to me."

"It's better than choking you?"

"True enough; still it gets the same result. And you don't look like the type who's up for shouting matches anyway. What do you get out of this?"

"Have you ever lost an argument?"

"I'm a woman and a psychiatrist. What do you think?"

D nods.

"Good. Do it tomorrow. The girls need this. Good emotional balance. And it'll be fun to see the guys sweat for a bit," says Betty.

D nods, then stops himself. When did he agree to anything?

"What are we having?" asks Zach.

"I don't care; I'm hungry," says Betty, tapping her fork.

D refuses to look across at Cella, who's doing the same across the table, while Bruce sits near her, gloating. Wanda, with the help of Saffire, carts in the night's meal: leg of lamb, sweet potatoes, red velvet cake, chocolate pudding, and because what would any meal be without it, two bottles of the finest red wine. Rick broke into a wine shop on the way to the bunker. Hank swore Rick took twelve bottles but only five are in the inventory.

"Enjoy," says Wanda as the troop quickly takes shares.

D and Zach are muscled out of the lamb but manage a piece of pudding and red velvet. D switches; he hates pudding. The table's not as lively as yesterday. Jade has a particular glare for D. What for? D has no clue. Don't they hate each other?

Halfway through the meal, Saffire's making the rounds, asking if anyone's unhappy with the dinner. Rick jokes that he's a virile man who needs larger portions. She doesn't have a clue what that means, but her grandma's gonna hear about it. She finds D sitting with Betty and looks for Wanda. She creeps forward; now's her chance. D turns into her juice squirt gun.

A glob of grape and pear pellets slam into D's forearm and face. Betty jumps from her seat to yell Saffire back to her grandmother. Rick lets out a big belly laugh, louder than everyone else. D's furious, but he should've known. That little brat creeping up like no one noticed her. Now his shirt's got a strong sweet scent to it. He needs to get it off before the fruit taste settles. D leaves to a round of cheers and laughs. What does he care? They'll all be dead in two days.

#

It's thirty minutes later when Colt rises, taking Jade's hand. The troop quiets, and Colt clears his throat. "This radiant woman has agreed to become my wife."

"What?" says Hank, as everyone else exhales in shock then quickly rushes to congratulate the couple.

"Why didn't you tell us?" asks Dede, pinching Jade.

"We wanted to tell everyone at the same time," says Jade.

Zach stands with heartfelt commendation while Betty blinks, remaining silent.

"Bruce, you're my best man, right?" asks Colt.

"Are you kidding?" asks Bruce, pulling him in for a hug.

The ladies kidnap Jade as Hank sits, slack jawed. Betty and Hank's eyes meet. Whatever was said, they're in agreement and Betty leaves to celebrate with the ladies. Hank waits a full thirty-five seconds before yanking Colt into a corner. Colt smiles, apologizing for not going old school and asking Hank's permission.

"Shut up, you idiot," says Hank. "What the hell were you thinking?"

"Look, I know you love your baby, but I do too. Don't worry, I'll treat her right," says Colt.

"You're a fucking moron. Did you stop to think about this? What? You thought it'd be romantic to propose to her right before you leave on your tour of duty? That's not original," Hank shouts before controlling himself. "Look here, you little shit, I've seen this story too many times. The night before you leave, you pour your heart and soul out, promising that you'll be back, then she hears that you got blown apart by some six-thousand-pound bomb and she's heartbroken. I am going to tell you one time. I swear on everything that I have ever loved, my parents, my wife, *my child*. If you die, I will beat you back to life and strangle you with your own intestines. Do you understand me?"

"Yes sir," says Colt.

"Good. Congratulations. You're a lucky man," says Hank with a suffocating bear hug.

#

D's on his third round of washing when the bathroom door opens. A small figure and a taller one stand there. D feels for his knife as the smaller one steps forward.

"I'm sorry for throwing fruit at you," says Saffire.

"Yeah, sure," says D, still scrubbing.

The two are still standing there. D turns to them while ringing out his shirt.

"What'd you think of the food?" asks Wanda.

"The cake was great," he says.

"What about the lamb?"

"Rick stole most of it. I didn't get to have any."

"You're not too good at tact, are you? You're supposed to say it was amazing like your friend said."

"Ok, what you said. Ditto."

"That's as good as I'm gonna get, isn't it? Fine, I'll just come out with it. My son-in-law, as miserable and womanizing an ass as he was, knew his shit."

"You're not supposed to curse, Grandma," says Saffire.

"Shut up." Wanda scowls at Saffy before turning back to D. "He knew his stuff. As a military man, he knew all the people of note. Generals and famous soldiers, politicians. He made the—"

"Jupiter fighter fleet. And the Rafferty-650," says D.

"Yes," says Wanda. "He always took the advice of soldiers. 'Real-world application is all that matters,' he used to say. He heard a story about a few snipers that wiped out half a platoon and found out what guns they used. People thought the new design would have been a war winner had the Coalition not found some of those guns and reverse engineered them."

"What's your point?"

"Saffy wait outside," says Wanda.

Saffire, for a change, doesn't argue but still sucks her teeth before closing the bathroom door.

"People think I'm crazy," Wanda begins. "Like I don't know the truth. I know what's out there. You killed one. I saw the skin in Cella's lab. Hank and Jade said you killed one. However true your story is about Zach, the fact is you've been outside for a long time. You know how to survive. Saffy needs to learn that. So how can she learn it?"

"You're excluding you?"

"I'm old. Too old. I'm not gonna fool myself."

"There's other people here. Ask them? They'll help."

"They're not objective. They want to protect her. That's got good and bad attached to it. The important point is she can't be coddled. You don't seem to care about most things. She needs a strong slap of reality, and you don't care enough about her to pull your punch."

"What the hell are you-"

"I'm not going to survive this trip. Most of us won't. Hank's just using a lot of us to maximize the chance of some of us making it. Saffy's going to be a part of that some. You helped Zach and helped Jade. That might have been out of mutual benefit, but the point is that you helped. And for someone who's been out there as long as you have, you looked in better shape than Zach and Hank's team. You've got that luck factor Rick's always talking about. You're a marine. I know the qualities that make a marine. Helping those who can't help themselves is one of those qualities.

Help her."

"A kid's a huge investment. What do I get out of this?"

"What do you want?"

"I take it she means the world to you? There's nothing you wouldn't do to make sure she's ok?" asks D. Wanda nods. He steps closer. "I need access to the armory."

Chapter 17

How is she?" asks Hank.

"I couldn't get her alone. I'll try tomorrow. How are you taking this?" asks Betty.

"I'm fine."

"Did you threaten to beat him with his own severed leg?"

"No."

"Um hum. I remember how you were when she started dating."

"I just didn't want her to go out with the wrong guy."

"More like any guy. My favorite was the one with the dreadlocks. You called him to your office. He walks into blown-up pictures of autopsies on the walls. 'This one was Curry. I didn't like his attitude. The one behind you, Travis, punk little tough guy, thought he knew it all.' Then you pulled out that shotgun Rick let you borrow. I still have space on my wall for more. Do you understand? He was so scared. She came back from the date and wouldn't talk to you for a month. And you said that was a good thing, and that he smelled like he hated showers. 'Next time find somebody with a future.' Then I'd make you apologize and make her accept. Ah, I miss that."

"Me too. So much for no drama."

"Do you have more of an opinion on D and Zach?"

"Zach's harmless but that D, I don't know yet. He's got a good head on him but that kind of worries me. Kid hits like rocks. He got Cella pissed at him, which is hard to do. One thing I can tell is that he's a survivor."

"Now is that a good thing or bad thing?"

"Don't know. He really hits like rocks. We'll test more tomorrow."

#

"What'd you do?" asks Zach.

"The fuck is your problem?" asks D, cleaning his knives.

"You just ran major collateral blockage."

"Oh please, big titties wasn't gonna give you any."

"Not now, thanks," says Zach as the music goes to 1920s English opera.

"I never understand what these people are screaming."

"I can't understand how you got a gorgeous woman to despise you in five seconds."

"Civvies are like that. Damn people are too sensitive."

"You should apologize."

"What the fuck for? I don't even know her."

"You don't have to know someone to be wrong."

"You want big titties bad, don't you?"

"Yes," blurts Zach. "It's Dede by the way. Look man, worse case she says no and in a few days you never see her again but a yes can lead to so much more, for everyone."

D says nothing.

"Don't try to act like you don't care. I saw the way you looked at each other. You were talking with her a while. Who talks that long to someone they're not interested in."

"A couple days and you think you got me figured now?"

"No, I just know mutual attraction when I see it."

"Very persuasive argument," says D, sarcastically. "Now I know why your wife stayed with you after you went broke."

"Let's not bring up my dead wife please."

D nods.

"Oh, that Colt jackass and Jade are getting married," says Zach.

"Maybe she's pregnant. Six months later, a kid 'ill pop out. What a miracle."

Zach chuckles.

"She's got big titties too," says D.

"Yeah, she does. But her ass isn't as big as Cella's, who you should apologize to tomorrow," says Zach.

"You better be better with tech than you are with dumbass suggestions. Go to sleep."

Chapter 18

Hank, Kellen, and Bode storm into D and Zach's room holding a bucket of water, intending to douse the two awake at ten minutes to 5:00 a.m. D, always alert with his knife at the ready, hears Kellen and Bode clumsily slam into the dresser blockade.

"What the hell is going on?" asks Hank. "What the hell is this?" he says, ducking D's throw.

Zach yelps as Hank grunts, ducking late. The knife wasn't even close. Missed by five inches. Zach's backing up to the far wall near the bull's eye.

"Getting comfortable?" says Hank, with an edge.

D shrugs while Zach grips a broken bed frame.

"We're cleaning," says Hank. "Get up."

Hank makes Kellen and Bode clean their mess before heading to the gymnasium, and the rest of the men deconstruct all the equipment and flooring.

Rick's directing some of the men where to begin uprooting the track as Hank, D, and Zach walk in. If the two have any questions about exactly what they will be doing, the answer is yes, the entire room. How long it takes depends on how hard the two are willing to work. Rick gives Zach a hammer and D a pair of construction gloves. Colt leads the combined force of men in, removing the track one lane at time.

Three-quarters of the way finished, the men give themselves a well-earned break. Zach is about ready to fall asleep on the carbon-based floor, so the water's welcome. Not that that anyone's complaining, but what hard work are the women doing? It's a sore subject for Hank as he's not sure how Betty won the negotiation to have the women tear down upholstery after a long speech about everyone needing to help equally. That woman can be so damned annoying sometimes.

No one's laughing in Hank's line of sight, but Rick has his back turned and his shoulders are shaking. Speaking of women, Bode wants details on Dom's day with Dede. Dom sticks out his chest with a big smile. He keeps on about his unequaled manhood as D pulls up his sleeves, half-listening.

"What happened?" asks Kellen. "Cella?"

D rolls back down his sleeves. The men take the cue. A minute passes before Rick asks how D got Cella so riled. Any man over twenty-five has to have noticed the female hive mind routine. Even the ones that don't like each other stick together when they get bored. D claims he didn't do anything he can recall.

"Jade told me you have an inferiority complex," says Colt.

"Your fiancé was talking about me?" asks D, relaxed.

Colt's not smiling and his hammer doesn't look happy either.

Hank taps Colt before anything can happen.

"Tread lightly son," Hank says to D.

Rick still wants to know what D said.

"Mind your business," says D.

"Mind your business? Why'd you tell her that?" asks Rick.

The men start laughing, while D shakes his head.

"You can't curse at her. That's not right," says Hank.

"It usually takes a lot for her to get mad. That's a talent; reminds me of me," says Rick, as Cella walks in.

She's wearing a gold bandana over a bright red sweater and blue baggy jeans. It's a casual look, but on a woman like Cella everything looks good.

"We need someone taller to help Rita," says Cella, smiling.

Bruce is up halfway through the sentence. He wonders why Cella never gives him a chance. She rolls her eyes past D while leading out Bruce. After leaving, the men tell D to apologize for everyone's sake. Some have plans his actions could jeopardize. Rick is planning a rendezvous with Wanda.

"That's not a guarantee," says Hank. "She won't forget that joke about straitjackets."

Rick ignores this. "You don't have to mean it. None of us mean it. We just say sorry so that she shuts the fuck up."

Hank smirks, and Rick smiles at him. It's time for a story. Two young innocent army men and the many women they knew.

"Leave me out of this," says Hank.

"You know, I hate the smart ones," says Rick. "You actually have to be sincere to get them back. I came home on a six-month leave and she was waiting for me. Before I left, I told her 'Baby, I don't know if I'll be back again but if I don't make it, I want you to know that you're the love of my life.' Complete bullshit but I'm literally going to have people shooting at me. So when she sees me—oh man, we went at it for days. So the next week, I'm out partying with Hank. He had just met a certain someone so he had to be home early, wimp. So I stay at the party until I'm too drunk to see, so the bartender takes my keys and calls a cab."

"I tell the cabbie the building address. I can't even figure out how to open my damn door I'm so drunk. So I say, ah fuck it and break the knob. Now I come in and my TV's on. My girl told me that she was going to be out, and that she would be back either in the morning or that night. I go to the shower which is steaming, and figure she wants me to join her. I take off my clothes, open the curtain, and see she's got a new hairdo. I like it; she looks at me like she's surprised. I say '*You gonna let me in or what?*' There was something different about her but I just couldn't tell."

"The next day, I look over and it's her twin sister right next to me. I keep looking around and can't find any of my things. I find out that I'm in the wrong damn apartment. Mine is the fifteenth floor on Thirty-Eighth Street, hers the fourteenth floor on Seventieth Street. I'd gotten so used to spending time there, I gave the wrong address to the cabbie. Turns out the sis had a knack for stealing boyfriends."

"When I get back to my apartment, my woman's telling me never to speak to her again. I say, 'Baby, don't leave me. I could have sworn it was you. Please forgive me.' She's about to leave, and I grab a fork and stab myself. She goes, 'What are you doing?' I do it again, then again, then again. She says she'll stay as long as I don't hurt myself. I say ok before she kicks her sister out. I still have the scar."

"So what happened?" asks Zach.

"I did the same thing a year later and she left. Didn't even threaten me this time. She just packed and left. You can only do things like that once maybe twice before they go. I miss those days." Rick smiles.

"What about Hank and Betty?" asks Dom.

"You don't need to know about that," says Hank.

"I'll tell you," says Rick.

"No you won't," says Hank. "How about we let Colt and Bruce talk about their cheerleader challenge."

"That's a good one," says Rick. "But the new guys want to know about you forgetting Betty's birthday." Hank's eyes flare in shock.

"I was broken up about losing another girlfriend."

"I'll tell it," shouts Hank. "This one over here cheated on another girlfriend and calls me saying he needs emotional support. I tell him I can't today because it's my lady's birthday, and I'm surprising her with a homemade dinner. She cooked for me all the time so I want to show her how much I appreciated her. He starts yelling at me, saying he's going to tell my Betty lies about some stripper ex-girlfriend."

"Lie?" asks Rick.

"Shut up. I say fine, but I can't stay because Betty's waiting. I could tell this was going to be one of those nights. I tell Betty I'm going to be thirty minutes late. I tell Rick two drinks and I'm gone. I didn't have much of my money because Betty's expensive. We have two. Now he wants me to meet ladies with him, something to get his mind off whatever her name was."

"Esmee," says Rick.

"I say no. He starts saying I'm half the man I used to be. Says Betty's turned me into a Eunuch. Being young, I had to prove him wrong. I go for the one with the biggest breasts I'd ever seen."

"Bigger than Dede's?" asks Zach.

"Yes, size M. I couldn't take my eyes off them. She's at least ten years older than me. Calls me over. If any of you tell Betty this, I will fuck you up. She calls me over. She asks if I'm in the army 'cause of my scar. I say yeah. She loves a man in uniform and she wants a 'true gentleman' to buy her a drink. She's got those eyes, you know, so what could I do? I buy the drink, then two, then three. All the sudden, she takes my hand and puts it on her 'area.' I know I should have pulled my hand away, but it felt nice. She wants me to have another drink. I say, 'No, I'm involved. She says, 'But she's not here now.' A valid point, but still I have to leave; it's getting late. One more drink, one. That one turns into two, then three, then four. I start thinking maybe I should take her home because it's late and she seems nice, and as a gentleman, I should at least do that."

"Rick tells me he's leaving with two girls. 'Have fun.' Asshole. She takes off her blouse, for one of those bedazzled bra things. Now I can really see them. She lifts her skirt, takes my hand and stuffs it right on her, area. It was shaved, just beautiful. She takes my finger out and puts it in her mouth. I think I should take her home, for safety reasons. That's when Rick comes back telling me those girls weren't girls."

"That's not true," shouts Rick.

"Ha, then he says, 'Don't you have to be somewhere?' I look at my watch, and I'm four hours late. She called twelve times but I had my phone on silent. I tell Rick he has to get me out of here 'cause I was too drunk to drive. Rick takes me to her house. The lights are on when I knock. Then all the lights turn off. I yell, 'Baby I'm sorry; it was Rick's fault.' Her roommate comes out saying I should be ashamed of myself. 'She's upstairs crying 'cause of you.' I smell like shit, and I can't even stand, and she's blabbering about calling the cops if I don't leave."

"The next day, I go to her work office, and they tell me I'm not allowed in. All the women are staring at me. I felt uncomfortable, so I leave. This damn woman won't talk to me for two weeks. Her roommate says she heard something about me and some old slut. I deny it completely. Finally, I hear there's going to be a USO show. I know she'll be there because I had some MP friends eavesdrop on her. So Rick and I come up with a plan to get her back. Celebs would be there, and they love to look like they love the troops, so on the day of I ask one of the singers to sing his song, 'I still love you' because I know that's Betty's favorite. I give him a picture, and he's supposed to call her to the stage and serenade her before I come out. I wear a shirt Rick made of me that had a big sad face and a caption reading, 'I'm a stupid idiot but this idiot knows when he has a good thing. Please give me another chance.'"

"The crowd stops to know her answer. I get on one knee and say I'm sorry. She kisses me and says, 'You are an idiot and don't ever let me hear about you and another woman ever again.' The crowd goes crazy."

#

"It was so romantic and I never heard about him with another woman again. And he always remembers my birthday. So hear that Cella; he messes up he has to pay for it," says Betty.

"I hear you, Mrs. Auberon," says Cella.

"I have no idea who's telling you these things, but it's a lie, Betty. Gotta give him an A for effort," laughs Elle.

The ladies, done with Room 1, will move to Room 2 as Betty asks Jade to stay for a moment. Betty is silent. Jade taps her feet then sucks her teeth. She hates when her mom does this.

"What, Mom?" asks Jade, walking around her to the exit.

"Hey, get back here," says Betty. "Jade Sayo Auberon turn around." Jade turns. "I know you. Are you sure?"

"What?"

"What."

"Yeah, Mom what?"

"What are you doing, honey? And why?"

Jade rolls her eyes and tries walking around Betty, but Betty puts on her reassuring smile, and Jade knows she's not leaving.

"You know," Betty begins, "You told me once that you'd never get married because you don't want to lose your identity. Whatever that means. Changed your mind?"

"I don't remember saying-"

"You were nineteen, right after coming home from college. You dyed your hair blonde and braided it. You had red contacts too, and painted your knuckles black."

"It was the style, Mom."

"It was stupid is what it was. And you'd gained about fifteen pounds and got dumped by the cute one you brought to Easter dinner. You called me crying about-"

"Yes, Mom. I remember, thank you."

"Are you going to answer my question, or do I have to keep rephrasing till you slip up?"

"Why do you care so much?"

"Why do I care if my daughter gets married?" Betty smiles.

"It'll be a great way to explore the intergenerational family dynamics of a military family. And the inherent differences in generational attitudes during times of great global tumult."

"I thought you never listened to my seminars?"

"I thought you didn't care what I did with my life."

"I lied. Now, are you serious about this or not? Marriage isn't a game, Jade. It's a commitment, not something you do when you're bored. It's serious. Your partner deserves someone who's serious about their end of the bargain. Now stop avoiding my question. I want an answer."

"What the hell is this?"

"Answer."

"What are you doing?"

"Answer."

"I'm not doing this sh-"

"Answer."

"Why not?" Jade shouts. "If we're gonna die in a few days why not be with someone who cares about you. What's the harm?"

"What's the—" Betty sighs before finishing. "Honey, do you think I say things just to hear myself talk? I'm old. I've seen what life can do to people—especially when they make stupid decisions. You have to start thinking long term. You're not getting any younger, but if you do this, you'll be ruining any potential family not just his life because you thought, 'Why not?' I thought I raised you better than that."

"May I go now, doctor?" asks Jade, lips pursed, arms crossed, foot tapping.

If Betty could, she'd choke this girl. She steps aside and Jade speed walks to Room 2.

#

The men finish ahead of schedule, so most go to the bathroom before target practice at three o'clock. Colt, Bruce, Rita, and a few more dress in urban camouflage and check their weapons. Jade's rushing out of Room 2. Colt usually leaves around this time, and sure enough he's holstering his gun. She kisses him, long and deep. Colt backs away, happy and confused before waving to Betty then leading the team away.

#

Rick thinks himself a reasonable man. There's not even fruit here, but perhaps he was mistaken, like the time he showed Saffy how the juicer worked. Wanda's the cook. It's past noon and there's no food. What's wrong with this picture?

"I don't know, you ass. Have you tried drinking what you dumped in the toilet?" asks Wanda.

"What's your fucking job here?" shouts Rick. "Seriously, what do you do?"

"I don't sit around, waiting for some over-the-hill retard to learn how to make his own damn food," she yells back.

"Over the hill?" Rick asks. "Who's the one that wanted Cella to make hair dye. I don't know why, you smashed into the wall decades ago lady."

Wanda tries to smash her hand on the kitchen counter, but it's attached to a string that links to another on the ceiling, letting out a stream of fruit and vegetables from the hollowed-out orange, sailing right into Rick's face. It's similar to tricks done with a yoyo. "What the fuck? What the fuck?" yells Rick.

Wanda laughs and laughs. She tries to leave the kitchen, but Rick's not done. This is assault.

Where is the goddamn food this old bitch is supposed to make?

It's a full-throated shouting match as the two reach the hallway. Zach loves seeing old people fight. Maybe because they know they're about to die, but old folks don't hold back. Zach asks if D's going to watch. D's not much for drama, so the answer's no.

D looks at the ceiling, dripping produce. How'd she get up there? She rushes out of the top cabinet, jumps off the fridge, lands on the counter, does a good combat roll and runs, but D kicks the nearest chair, tripping Saffire. She slides into the cabinet door with a soft puff.

"Owe," she says. "That hurt."

"Get over here," says D in a commander's tone.

Saffire's suddenly not hurt and moving over as told. Another one of those many tricks he never thanked General for.

"How much fruit did you use?" asks D, looking at the ceiling.

"Two baskets," she says. "Oranges and grapes have the most juice, so I used those. I like those."

"More apples and pears would've helped keep the stream straighter for longer. Try freezing the juice next time. And mashing them into balls works well too," he says, picking out all the seeds.

"What are you doing?"

"Not cleaning the kitchen after someone ruined it."

Saffire blinks at him. She didn't think about that.

"But maybe I could help if you told me something I wanted to know."

"Rick likes to steal gun oil from the lab. I don't know why but he keeps talking about his right hand being too strong. What's he talking about?"

D almost laughs, almost.

"Dede and Cella had an argument about using handcuffs and Cella didn't want it back because she said Dede's nasty. Oh, one time, Creighton told Bruce that he'd fuck him with a tire iron if he didn't leave Cella alone."

D's hand is waving Saffire to silence. "Who's Creighton?" he asks after mastering himself.

"He came with Harbour. I liked him. He used his nine fingers and one eye to help me count tens for homework. He was funny."

"It was only him and Harbour?"

"No, it was like fifty of them. Then there was that big fight with Hank about leaving. Grandma made me hide in the closet for most of it. They made Harbour leave. She thinks I don't know but I pay attention."

"How long ago was this?"

She shrugs. "Two months."

"What are you two talking about?" asks Betty. Then she sees the ceiling. "Saffy, you little—"

"He did it not me," says Saffire, running.

Betty tries to grab her collar, but she's old now and that little brat is quick.

"She's lucky we didn't clean the kitchen yet," says Betty.

D's silent on that account.

Cella, Dede, and Elle now walk in. "I'm like, I try to be nice and you're going to talk to me like that," says Cella.

The women stop. Dede and Elle take Cella's lead in not acknowledging D as Betty walks over to D. Cella rolls her eyes and the three women leave.

"Why does everyone care about this so much?" asks D.

"Feminine mystique," says Betty, smiling.

D shakes his head. He should've known; a woman never gives a straight answer about other women. He's about to leave when Betty points him back to his seat.

"You're supposed to try harder to get an answer," she says.

D blinks at her.

"You're not much for continuing conversation. I'm learning that. Normalcy. That's what they want. We've been going full tilt for two months. A new guy comes. He's flirting with one of the pretty girls. For a moment, we don't have to be soldiers. We can act like high schoolers. Normalcy."

That kind of makes sense. Marines find all types of ways to let off steam. D used to pull pranks on NCOs after he got his commission.

"May I ask how the fight started?" asks Betty.

"Didn't Cella tell you?"

"There's her version. With your version, I'll get a good sense of what really happened."

Betty chuckles at D's expression or lack thereof. He's not much for showing emotion, but something bleeds through if you watch long enough.

"You don't care about this, do you?" she says. "Did the guys tell you to do this, so they can get some sex later? Taking one for the team?"

"She's civvie," says D. "One of those compassionate ones who thinks they know how the world works because they gave a homeless guy a dollar. Those people are the worst."

"A lot of that happened earlier. What exactly did she not understand?"

"That understanding your responsibility to others isn't the same thing as brainwashing."

Betty nods knowingly, something D has seen too many times from people in her profession.

"So, when did the insults begin?"

"What?"

"She said something about you hating animals except giraffes. I see bite marks. Is this related to some traumatic experience early in life?"

"What the fuck are you talking about?"

"Have you always wanted to be a marine?"

"What's that have to do with anything?"

"Why don't you want to answer my question?"

"I don't understand your question."

Betty gives a professional smile, fake as any D's ever seen.

"Have you always taken care of yourself?"

"Why don't you get to your real question?"

"I can't know what that is until you answer."

"I think we both know that's bullshit."

"Ok, why don't you tell me what my real question is."

"I'm not falling for that trick. You ask your damn question."

"Will you answer if I do?"

"You won't know until you ask, will you?"

"Will you tell me about your family?"

D frowns, an actual frown not a stone expression you have to guess at.

"I asked you about your mother a day ago and you blew me off. Every time someone asks for something, you want something in return. Trusting people don't generally do that. I just now asked about your childhood and you're refusing to go near it. Will you tell me about your family, or how about your full name?" asks Betty.

"What are you trying to say?" asks D.

"I don't know. What am I trying to say?"

"I don't know. That's why I asked you."

This professional smile is a lot less authentic.

"You've had a lot of these sessions?" asks Betty.

D considers that for a moment. "Yes," he says.

"She thinks your cute. Cella doesn't go for ugly men. Just go talk to her. She's not that upset, and in my experience, women are a lot less upset when good-looking men are around. Tell her something about yourself. Or trade a story. She'll get over it."

Chapter 19

Rick and Wanda are still roaring at each other an hour later, with the others jeering and cheering. D's walking towards the lab quietly as he can, but this bunker's a small place. A couple sneak near as D enters the outer door. D takes a deep breath before knocking. Cella opens the door, holding a beaker of acid. Her smile turns to a frown as she sees D. She has on her lab coat and protective goggles, not her best look.

D's about to say something, but he's forgotten. Women do that to men. It's damned annoying. Cella smirks. She loves getting these reactions from men. D's eyes flick to the acid. He tries miming with his hand, then looks at the acid again. Cella sucks her teeth and places the beaker on a nearby table.

"Is there something you'd like to say?" asks Cella.

"May I come in?" asks D.

"No," snaps Cella.

"I was enjoying our conversation—I don't want—I think you're a very interesting person."

"That was horrible."

"May I come in?"

"No, you may not," Cella says, smiling as he sighs.

D's right sleeve rolls up to run his finger down the scar.

"I got this from a seven-year-old."

The door opens wide. She offers a seat next to her current workstation. For the twentieth time, Cella's testing the protein structure of the skin. It's incredible.

"How thick was the skin when you cut it?" she asks.

"Four inches," says D, seeing she took another three samples from his skin.

"It decayed to six centimeters. How long ago was that?"

"It didn't decay. I cured it over three days. The skin's naturally oily after the first two layers, and when you cut out the layer of fat at the bottom, you can squeeze the oils from that onto the top layer to keep it from mottling."

"This wasn't your first taxidermy, was it?"

"There's plenty of dead ones out there. I haven't seen them resort to cannibalism, but they don't play nice with each other."

"Yes, about that. Are you familiar with animal mating rituals?"

"I don't want to be familiar with animal mating rituals."

She gives him a tolerant look. "Some of them can be pretty violent. Were you able to tell if this was a male or female?"

"No I couldn't."

He spent all that time making a jacket out of the thing, and he couldn't be bothered to look between its legs. Men.

"A southern elephant seal bites its prospective mate. A lot of times, it crushes the female's head in its jaws while copulating. Male porcupines will pee on a female to see if she's interested. If she runs away in disgust, the answers no, but if she rolls onto her back, it's on. Every winter, female quolls, rodent-like animals, go into heat at the same time. All the males go crazy and try sleeping with as many as they can. The mating can go on for a full twenty-four hours, with a lot of scratching, biting, and screeching. A lot of times, the female is bitten to death, and afterward, the male eats her, not in the fun way, and rushes to find another mate. The males exert so much energy that many times they work themselves to death after a few weeks."

"I knew a guy like that. His hands were always clammy."

"Were the brogs making the crackling sound?" asks Cella, smiling, moving them back on topic.

"They always crackle, except when they're unsure about something. At least that's what I make of it."

Cella pulls out her recorder. "When possible, see if brogs have developed a rudimentary language. Something more like how the great apes communicate with each other. Brain casing as well. Is the Brog's capacity for learning as you suspect?"

"You stayed up the whole night looking at this?"

"Of course I—you're not off the hook. I want to know what happened. I know you only said a seven-year-old gave you that scar so you could get in."

"I wasn't lying."

"A seven-year-old did all that to you?" she asks, pursing her lips. D nods. "You know, if you're not going to tell the truth, get out."

"He had help."

"Um hum."

"You want to hear it or not?"

She takes off her protective gloves, goggles, and lab coat before pointing him to the table with liquid nitrogen and frozen skin samples. D looks at her. She shrugs.

"There's a lot of material here, so I use it. Story."

D has to go back to military school. "Professor Baughman had a class dealing with the human psyche. 'As humans, we believe that due to our abundant technology, we are no longer products of nature. This false sense of immunity can be easily ruptured by the taking any of four elements that make a society possible: water, agriculture, structure, and enforcement. Nothing is without water, so it is first. Agriculture stems from water, obviously. Structure or rules make sure the use of resources is wise, and enforcement is so people will abide by said rules, creating a balanced system for all.' If you take away one of these pillars, which segment of the population do you suppose adapts quickest?"

D looks at Cella, waiting for an answer.

"The old are too old, so they probably die the quickest, children are too young, so adults," says Cella.

"Wrong. Its children," says D.

"No its not."

"Yes, it is. Let's hear the professor." Begins D citing an old lecture again.

"'In crisis situations, children below the age of sixteen are the most unhinged element. They do not yet have the mental maturity to conform their frontal lobe to societal norms, so as a result, they simply never receive expected social behaviors. This is the main reason for parentage or guardianship.'"

"Did you know that children below ten are the group most likely to bully one another?" asks D.

"That's not true," says Cella.

"Yes, it is. 'Now for the sake of argument, let us assume we are children. We're alone. It's nighttime, so we are very scared. Even now, humans are afraid of the dark. That's the main reason for night lights, young ones.' Have you been outside since getting here?" asks D.

"Once, a few weeks after we got here. A lot of us kept complaining about being stuck inside all the time, so Hank and Rick made us put hazmat suits on and escorted us topside. The suits were so uncomfortable. It was pitch black. We turned on the little lights on our suits and still couldn't see anything. I wanted to get back inside so fast," says Cella.

"So you understand. Let's look at the kid from another perspective. You're crossing some urban area; Youngstown, Ohio, for instance. There's looting, stabbing, and shooting. You're passing one area to find the same in the next, except this new area is different. Being a trained military officer gives you insight on how to assess threat levels. You expect the normal yelps and whimpers, elderly acting as boundary designations, but it's quiet. Others see you, the stranger, invading their territory. There's clearly something wrong, but you haven't eaten in six days. You walk straight; you know this place. You stop at a cracked rusted gate capped with the words 'Youngstown's Home for Disadvantaged and Troubled Youth.' The gate's almost ready to crumble it's so corroded. There's a film of trash layering the foreground to the main entrance. The stench of spoiled meat makes your eyes water."

"You didn't have a suit?" asks Cella.

"It got ripped up in a fight, but I had my meds, so I'd be ok for a little bit. You look for anything you may find useful. Your nose takes you to the kitchen, where the smell's strongest, excluding the putrefying meat leaking from the stove, and the all-purpose flour spread all over the place. Suddenly, nine heaving juveniles block the kitchen entrance. However, that's interesting. A large cast iron pan's at your feet."

"A bullet grazes past your shoulder. You fall behind the center counter as the bambinos shoot. You take a small aluminum bowl. It has a crack through the middle. With a tug and some stretching, an aluminum knife breaks the tallest boy's nose before ricocheting to burst another kid's eye. The children aren't used to people fighting back. As kids do, they yell and shoot more."

"You have a second cast iron pot. When the shooting stops, you aim for the knee of one boy and see the knee fold back on itself. Everyone hates hearing kids cry, but you have so much cookware here, what're you supposed to do? A cooking pot breaks an arm, a steak knife slices an ear. A forty-gallon gumbo pot bashes two guttersnipes at the same time, and the kids run. Now's your chance; you get the hell out of there."

"Before you can reach those double doors, a young girl sideswipes you into the living room. How the hell did an eighty pound girl get the drop on you? Now her damned urchin pals are crowding in around you with rotting teeth, ready to bite."

"The first boy you saw is there, digging inch-long fingernails into your back until you fling him clear across the room, overturning a couch. Another has a point-blank shot and presses the trigger. He has no bullets. You don't mean to, but attempted murder annoys you. You shatter the boy's face with a punch and take the gun. Now you've got a skillet and a 9mm; see how these little bastards try you now. The eldest is sixteen, looks strong for his age. It's easy to see why he's the leader. He wraps his arms around you as that eighty-pound little shit tears into your right forearm. You raise your skillet hand and swing down. You can feel the skull collapse as she falls limp."

"Now this boy's a bit stronger than you expected, but he doesn't know how to hold a man so you break free and break his finger and elbow and dislocate his shoulder. The kids didn't expect this. The alpha's down. You take the moment to bash the closest kid in the head then make a straight line to the exit. You stumble as a kid spears the back of your leg. The little boys had steak knives in hand, looking to slice your face off, but it digs into your forearm. You can feel it hit the bone and scrape down before popping free at the elbow."

"Block the pain, turn the kids neck L shaped, and run. Another kid's coming. Use him as a battering ram and get to the door. You don't remember throwing the kid away, but you're on the street running as fast as possible to the next area. Some of the kids chase you but have to turn back to their territory."

"You look around, and you're in the same place you started, hungry but you've got a firearm and a skillet; you'll find food. Anyway, I'd like sunlight once in a while. Balance is good, every once in a while right?" says D.

"Cella rushes to a desk to find her ointment. 'This clears blemishes too. It won't completely clear the scar 'cause it's too old but it'll make it look better."

She pushes up D's sleeve without asking, seeing more scars.

"How long was this before the brogs?"

"Can we not use the term *brogs?*" says D.

"What'd you call them?"

"Fernando called them unnaturals, abnormals. I use whatever looks disgusting. I've settled on uglies."

"Ok, ugly dogs?"

"They don't look like dogs."

"How'd you find food?"

"Some local gangs started a big riot a couple of days later. Someone tried to leak out supplies. Before she got too far away, I took it from her."

"Did you—" Cella forms a gun with her hands.

"I didn't need to. She valued her life more than cans of fruit.

Can this cream heal everything?"

"Not bones."

She asks for the left arm and sees more gunshot and slash wounds, though no regrown skin. There's the beginning of a sweeping slash that curls around the armpit down the shirt. She stares at him incredulously.

"A guy took a sword, tried to chop my arm off. It didn't hit the vein, so it could have been worse." She continues staring.

"It's rough out there," says D.

"You've been dealing with stuff like this for eighteen months?"

"Most of this is from before, but yeah. It pays to be careful. Not everyone's as nice as I am."

The test Cella has been running beeps its completion. As with the eight times before, the DNA results are unknown. It's a mammal, but with trace sequences mapping exactly with chimpanzees, but similar skin cells, matching octopi-camouflaged genes. Seventy other species are here, both from sea and land, but that's normal. Thirty-three percent of human DNA is identical to dandelions, and this Brog has squirrel influence and two percent alligator. This suggests multi-generational adaptation of a wild species that has, in her opinion, very recently created a mongrel or abnormal branch of its family, give or take seventy years.

How did people not catch these guys before?

D's been watching Cella talking to herself for ten minutes. She's completely forgotten he's there. She'll try to isolate the important genes, such as the one that makes the protein that produces this skin. It has to have been adapted from some animal of an extreme environment. She'll check desert and cold weather animal groups, find which looks most similar, and cross reference them to find the Brog progenitor. She cuts one piece into about thirty using a Bunsen burner and a white-hot scalpel.

"Oh what bacteria and parasites like these animals?" she says aloud, smiling. "There was contamination, but that can be ruled out after the tests. First, we must deconstruct the body of this new mammalian species. Where are the inner organs located and how large is the brain?"

She blinks, turning back to D smiling sheepishly. "I kind of get involved when I'm working."

"Did you just call me a contamination?" asks D.

"No I—that's not what I meant. If the sample's not completely clean, it's not clean. I don't mean it-you're doing that on purpose. Stop smiling."

"I don't smile."

"Did you know they were mammals?"

"I know they're mean. And are hosts of a new damn virus."

"Do you think it's in the saliva or a gland in the mouth?"

"What's a big, beautiful brain like yours here for, if not to teach me these things?"

That gets the expected smile and as a bonus she bites her bottom lips in that way women do when they're trying to seduce men. This is going great.

"Tell me something about you," says D.

"What do you want to know?"

"Where are you from?"

"Missouri, Jackson County."

"Of course."

Cella purses her lips at him. "I have an older sister and brother, Valerie and Tabari. That makes me the baby of the family. If I dated someone, Tabari would always try to beat them up. My father was a doctor and my mother a chemist. I love high heels and chocolate."

"That was horrible."

"Shut up," Cella says, smiling. "Where were you born?"

"Cleveland, I think."

"You think?"

D's face turns impassive; why did he say that?

"Looks like you're busy," he says, rising and letting out his shirt to reveal a wall of surgical scars and severe slashing wounds. "I'll go."

"Wait, where are you going? Stop."

"Look, we'll talk later. I'd appreciate it if you left that last part out of any conversation with your friends."

She nods as he opens the door for a nosey dozen. She says the room is soundproof but there are ways around that. He steps over the spying bunch before running into Zach and Kellen about to play Deathstrike.

#

The women take chairs near Cella. The pool's gotten a bit bigger. Dede moves close, smiling.

"Tell me everything," says Dede.

"First he knocked on the door thinking I was just going to let him in," says Cella, smiling. "I said, 'Who do you think I am?'"

Chapter 20

An hour passes as the Deathstrike screen suddenly blinks off, with D leading Zach seventy-eight to seventy-six rounds. They step away looking at each other. D tries shaking the machine back to life. Zach thinks the problem's in the circuitry. Zach slides the machine forward to pop out the back panel. As best he can tell, the motherboard's worked itself to exhaustion. The part housing the graphics card is melted and the input chips are burned out. The motherboard needs to be replaced. They slide back the machine while looking over their shoulder at a sleeping Kellen. They don't look at each other as they leave.

Emergency lights flash. D pads for his knives while motioning Zach to Room 7. They sit with innocent expressions as voices fill the hallway. D puts fake concern on his face, seeing people rushing to the dining hall. Bruce and Colt sit wet and winded. D grimaces at Rita. She looks like a sweating craggy stone. Ugly women always make D upset for some reason.

"Damn brogs came right at us," says Bruce, unzipping his suit while Colt shakes bone chips from his torn sleeve. "They were throwing body parts," Bruce continues. "They weren't doing that two months ago."

Jade's helping take Colt's jacket off, seeing no cuts when Hank and Rick run in from the left door of the hall.

"Water's everywhere," says Colt as D and Zach step in.

The others are asking if D or Zach knew about this. Both deny it. Hank calls the troop into the left door. The room works as a panic room. Two-foot-thick wall lined with black reinforced Kevlar, and is more than half the size of the dining hall. There are four cushioned couches at every corner. A circular table forty feet in diameter displayed the presidential seal. Rick tells everyone to sit while Colt taps the clearing to bring up a holographic projection of the state underground system.

Cella sneaks up to D as Zach motions both to sit next with him. Colt and Bruce work on the table screen as the other seats fill. The projection expands to a yellow highlighted section of tunnels and pipes leading to Three-Mile Island. Red represents water. By quick estimation, Colt believes more than forty percent of the route will be flooded by this time two days from now. Collective groans come predictably.

"Hey, that's what it is. Don't blame me," says Colt.

"All right, that's enough," says Hank. "It looks like we're going to be leaving a little sooner than expected but we're prepared for this," he says, moving the map to a half-built recycling plant to the west of their escape route.

Some weeks past a transmission was heard coming from Three-Mile Island. A plan was made. In principle, it's simple misdirection. For the past few weeks, the troop has been testing the effectiveness of the pheromone packs developed by Cella. This combined with the mustard gas caused the desired effect of herding the brogs away from the preferred escape routes. This rising water is ruining that, so the contingencies look more necessary.

As it stands, the charge of leading a decoy team to the recycling plant is with Bruce. The majority of the pheromones for use as breadcrumbs for the brogs will be with his team. The tunnels and pipes provide a number of paths to take that reach the plant. Once his team attracts an overwhelming majority of seven-thousand plus brogs in the area to the plant, he's to incinerate the plant. Cella made the pheromone increase in potency as the temperature rises. Of course, after a certain temperature, the gas is destroyed entirely, but it should last long enough to do the job. When this works, the main body of survivors will have sufficient time and space to reach a military shuttle bay, where the Susquehanna splits the land. Jade, at this time, will use her tech savviness to open the bay. The hope is that the shuttle isn't destroyed. Then, they're home free.

Colt's now going to add his variation. He believes less Brog flexibility is essential. It's not feasible to expect them to comply blindly with troop demands so the troop needs to force their hand. Certain entry points to the troop escape routes need to be closed, specifically the largest convergence points. Yes, the brogs are sensitive to sound, but as previous tests say, smell is the dominating hunting sense, and they are ambush predators. His plan will mean taking some of the substantial bombs meant for Bruce's team with his advanced scout.

Normally, you'd want as many routes to your goal as possible, but the brogs own the tunnels, and the water makes surviving even more of a problem. If anyone wants to live, getting to the shuttle bay is the best option. The escape route now looks like a snake. D's concerned about what happens if some of the passage ways are collapsed, and they need to double back. He'll wait for the civilians to leave before he asks. Civvies are really emotional about things like this.

D sees where this hologram map aligns with his map. It's a solid plan. The civvies forced this option; if they weren't here, Hank might risk more imagination. It's a solid plan given the personnel.

"The estimated time for completion is between eight and fourteen hours," says Colt.

D may have been wrong about Colt's intellect. But a plan's all well and good. Let's see how he executes.

"Are there any questions?" asks Hank.

"Are we going to be taking any breaks?" asks Wanda.

"Don't count on it," says Rick. "But this map shows promising rest spots. We'll decide based on ground conditions."

"How does the decoy team plan to escape after they lure the ugly bastards to the plant?" asks D.

"Please don't curse near Saffy," says Wanda.

D nods then looks at Bruce. Bruce goes full diplomat. There's an unfinished tunnel under the plant that can be used, but D reads through that. He nods, growing a new respect for Bruce. Any blast that attracts as many brogs will kill anyone in the area. Hank gives a grand speech about bravery, but D's not listening. He should've brought his datapad. The people are rising as D comes back to himself. Cella's waiting for him to join but he has more questions.

Zach's the last to leave, following an annoyed-looking Cella. D waits three minutes, making sure no one suddenly returns because they forgot something.

"Did someone talk you out of a better plan?" asks D. "Or are you starting to care too much?"

"Neither one of those is a good reason," says Hank.

"But no one could make you feel better. I guess when you're old, who gives a shit? You'll do what you want."

"You're real invested now, aren't you?" says Colt. "How about you give a helpful suggestion?"

"I don't think I can give one you haven't considered but I'll try. Instead of one ball with a decoy team you have many. Keep the ones over forty in the most dispensable group and make sure two groups with the most able-bodied get the majority of the weapons. Leave the pheromones and a respectable amount of ammo with other teams but ensure that the ones best able to make the trip have the best chance to survive the tunnels. It's harsh but the uglies don't play nice."

"We do care," says Rick. "But some of us older guys are also the ones best able to lead when things get hairy. And when we tried to divide people up into groups, some of us older ones notice the age breakdown, and Betty, Hank, and myself with the younger group. Almost had another war."

"Why didn't you just set up the teams the day of and move out before anyone could ask questions?"

"Hindsight is always twenty-twenty," says Hank. "This is what it is now, and I don't want to give myself up for the greater good, so I'm on the winning side, dammit."

"Which group did you put the little girl in?" asks D.

"That was a hell of a shot you made topside a couple days ago," says Hank. "No lights, a target leaping twenty feet up, and you hit it dead center. I wonder if it's luck or talent."

"That's natural," says D.

Hank wonders just what he means by that. The cocky son of a bitch. "Target practice is two hours before dinner," says Hank.

D has to admit that was a smooth dismissal. After he leaves, Rick tells Colt and Bruce to go.

"I don't trust him," says Rick.

"What's that got to do with anything?"

"Are you crazy? What if he-"

"What if he, what? Sells us out to the brogs? What's he gonna do? Our interests align. We can trust him wanting to live. How's he getting a better chance without us?"

Chapter 21

D rushes back to his room to compare the new information with what is on his datapad with Zach hurrying behind.

"What happened?" asks Zach.

"What are you talking about?" asks D.

"You stayed after to talk. What happened?"

"They don't know me. They're not gonna tell me their plans. But half a day in those tunnels is tough even before uglies. I need to adjust my own plans. You're helping."

"Am I helping them or us?"

"We're helping everyone in the long run."

Zach frowns. "You know I talked with the lieutenant once about why she's helping us. You'd probably be better off with just trained soldiers, I said. She said that there's no military without people that need its protection and that her oaths demand her to take them seriously."

Zach and D's eyes meet.

"Zach, I thought with you being out there as long as you were would beat some sense into you. I guess not. So, let me be plain. If you don't act like an optimistic buffoon, I won't treat you like one."

Jade knocks and enters, as D side steps behind the door, keeping Zach in sight.

Jade sees a red-faced Zach, but where is...

Oh. D's six-inch height advantage is even more imposing in this dark room.

She doesn't yell for Colt, as she was close to doing. "We have to talk," she says.

Zach's glaring at D's back as he follows Jade. Colt's holding court in the dining hall with his own datapad with Bruce pointing. In the lab, Jade takes writing material while asking D to sit.

"Did you do these new drawings?" she asks. "Cella sucks at drawing."

D nods. "What else do you know about them."

"For the purposes of our coming field trip. There's not much to know. Hit the soft spot."

"What about after?"

"After?"

"You think the old people are gonna drag us down. I asked my dad about that. I think he was offended."

"There is a reason old people die quicker in these situations. Nature's practical like that."

"How many brogs have you killed?"

"I don't remember. I'm usually running from them."

"You skinned one. Don't play coy with me. My entire family's here. I plan to make sure they're in Three Mile too. You can understand that, can't you?"

"Have you ever been in the midts of an uglies ambush? I'm sure your fiancé's told you about it, but have you been in one?"

Jade shakes her head. She blinks in the middle of that last sentence. D notes that.

"The fastest person in the world can go twenty to twenty-five miles an hour for a few seconds. These bastards can clock eighty miles in the open field and can keep it up for four minutes. The small ones are a different kind of headache."

"Have you seen them throw bodies before? That sounds ruthless, like they enjoy it. Any theories on why? If they're as smart as Cella thinks, that sounds like psychological warfare."

"You should talk to Cella more about animal behavior. They're not so different from people. The body part thing they've been doing for over a year. I'm guessing here, but I know what I know. Humans, especially early, had a lot of guns. They could hit from a distance. Uglies have to get close to hurt. Less sunlight means less energy, so to compensate for this, they use tools that make hunting less energy intensive. They throw rocks or body parts to catch their prey. I guess they figure an uneaten leg that gets you a whole body is worth losing in the grand scheme with game so plentiful."

"Are you saying there are a lot of people in this area?"

"No. I haven't seen many. I think there have to be other places, but competition's too fierce, so the younger generation branches out, looking for new fertile hunting grounds. If they don't find it soon, they'll get desperate. They'll kill others for scraps, then cannibalism, then starvation, which is why I don't get why you people would leave now. You can just wait a few months and walk there easy."

"They're desperate, you say." She avoids the question. "How about we set up a war game. I'll be the troop and you'll be brogs trying to catch people who are packing enough weapons to be a small army."

"Do I get to keep my numbers advantage?"

"Yes," she says, rising to link two tables together. "Usually, predators attack easy targets. Why do these things search for the real threat first?"

"They haven't met a prey item that's made them respect it yet. Certainly not in this section."

D helps Jade push the nearest table that last few feet before she starts flicking something beneath the table. D had no idea there was anything there. He's getting sloppy. Jade stops at a battle map that looks like an underground pipe system. She'll be microscopes, and D will be bunsen burners. D supposes real game pieces would be too much to ask for.

"Dad taught me how to work this when we got here."

"You have too many microscopes. If we're gonna do this then let's do it right."

She had fourteen microscopes; now it's three, and he went from twenty-five bunsen burners to thirty-five.

"Hey," says Jade.

"Pay attention, rookie. You're about to save your family."

Jade's watching him move the pieces and getting angrier by the second.

"I mean everyone here is like family. Not just the ones I like."

"Ok," he says, flatly.

"What would you be if you weren't a marine?"

"What?"

Jade nods to herself.

"Why didn't you join the war?" he asks.

"I couldn't pass the pullup test," she mumbles.

"You couldn't do-"

"No, I couldn't do three fucking pullups. It's apparently quite hard."

"If you don't take your training seriously."

"Kiss my ass."

"So plan B was computers. Somewhere far from the frontlines.

I'm sure your parents were happy you made the sensible choice."

"What about your parents? Which one thought giving you a letter was a good idea? It was probably your dad. Dad's always give terrible names."

"So Jade was Hank's idea."

"Fuck you." she smiles.

D sniffs before raising his sleeve. Jade's eyes go straight to his forearm. *What is it with women and scars?*

"What happened?" asks Jade.

D pulls down his sleeve.

"Who did that to you?" she repeats.

"Cella didn't tell you?"

"What would she tell me?"

"That I do a man's work, and it's no place for a delicate little flower like you."

"A deli-whatever." She resets the pieces and tries her hand at anticipating Brog movement as D covers a yawn.

"Do you have trouble sleeping?" she asks.

"What?"

"It's dark outside. It's always dark outside. Mom says that can drive people crazy. Or at least exacerbate previous mental conditions."

"Why don't you ask your fiancé? He was out there a long time too."

"I want to build a consensus."

"Or you're being nosey."

Jade's tracking the path almost exactly, but D's sliding nine bunsen burners up the halfway mark of the path. Jade's forgotten to close the last convergence point. Uglies, being the curious things they are, circle around the other end to see if food will be there just as the primary group moves this way pushed by freezing water.

"Is wanting to get to know someone being nosey?"

"It is if you haven't said two words to them since almost getting splattered topside. Makes a person think you're ungrateful."

Jade stops. *That's a fair point.*

"Thanks," she says as D's jaw tightens.

"Why do my sleeping habits matter to you?" asks D.

"We're going to be outside for a while."

"Not long enough for any of what you're talking about to matter."

"Why can't you answer the question?"

"Does this mean you won the bet?" asks D.

Jade's eyes flash for a moment. "What?" She's about to deny it, but D's eyes are—what's the word? Unyielding. She looks down at the battle map. The brogs have them pinned in from three sides. Half of the main group branched off to pick up people fleeing the pincer maneuver.

"Animals don't pull moves like this," says Jade.

"The uglies want food. Most went up to block off the route, some doubled back to herd their prey into a nice big eating pocket. The rest have to settle for whatever's left at the east end. Think like your enemy."

"You seem to understand their relationship dynamics. Why didn't you speak up at the meeting, or is this why you stayed after?"

"Wolves, lions, wild dogs, most predators that hunt in packs imitate these moves. You should learn more about animals. Their behavior will be less surprising that way."

She pauses for a moment. She wants to play again. She's lost ninety-five percent of the troop five straight times trying to do the same war-room plan with slight variations.

"You're cheating," says Jade.

"Boo hoo," says D. "Reset."

Cella walks in as Jade thinks her first move.

"What's going on?" asks Cella.

"Your friend's proving the definition of insanity," says D.

"Shut up. If the point is they adapt, why do you keep doing the same thing?"

"I'm reacting to you. It's not my fault you keep locking yourself into the same positions."

"A gentleman lets the woman win," she snaps.

"A winner fucks the cheerleader."

Jade throws the bunsen burner at him and leaves. Cella's not one for pettiness, but seeing Jade flustered is fun to watch. Her talking to D like they're buddies in her lab isn't ok though. Not that she's jealous or anything, but why is Jade down here talking to him?

What are you doing? Cella thinks. What was that crap about cheerleaders? What were they doing?

"You ok?" asks D.

"What were you talking about?" she asks.

"Tactics."

"What kind of tactics?"

"What?"

"What kind of tactics, dangit."

"Does it matter? The same principal applies to every situation.

Flexibility's the key to success."

Cella has no idea what that means. "Why can't you just answer the question?"

"What about that question did I not answer?"

"Why is everyone patting Zach on the back for fixing the stupid fighting game?"

D's about to curse but stops himself. Women always do this. Whenever they're losing an argument, they change subjects to throw you off. He's not playing that game.

"Are you gonna teach me how to make the cocktail now?"

Cella's eyes bulge. She'd punch him if she knew he'd let her. Or-or ride him like a horse, dangit he's sexy.

"You're really annoying," she says.

"It's part of my manly manliness."

#

Bruce squints at the target. Two shots center mass. "I'm in shape. I have big hands. Is it the cheeks? It's the cheeks, isn't it?" he asks Colt.

"It's not your cheeks," says Colt.

"Does she think I'm intimidated by an intelligent woman?"

"You've been reading Betty's self-help books?"

Bruce sits with a sigh. There must be a reason for his lack of success. D's a psycho. He must have drugged her.

"Show some more of your personality," says Colt.

"You said she liked fit guys."

"Most women do, but when you look like her, you get to be a bit more choosy. It's just how the game is. Look, there's other women here. Just choose one of them. Valenda's not ugly and neither is Sabrina. Elle liked you, didn't she?"

Bruce is doing that droopy bulldog face again. Bruce has always been stubborn about women. Colt was honest with him before when he told him Cella just doesn't like him, but Bruce stopped talking to him for three days. It was early in their stay in the bunker. Colt decided that was the wrong way to go. If Bruce wants to keep making a fool of himself, then Colt has to let him. He'll come to his senses after.

"How'd you get Jade again?" asks Bruce.

"Jade wanted me to come get her. Look, if she likes you, she won't put you through all these hoops."

Of course, there was the laxatives he put in Domelvo's coffee. She was playing both of them off each other, and Colt would be damned if he lost. Dom hated him after that, but he got over it, didn't he?

Bruce won't ask what Colt's smiling about. He's thinking of Cella's lips. The fucking apocalypse happens, and he meets the most beautiful woman in the world after that. That's luck, but it hasn't been working since.

He never had this problem with girls in high school. Colt did most of the talking, and Bruce was able to get his fair share that way. He tries rehearsing his lines but forgets them when she bats her eyes. Does she do that on purpose? It seems like she does.

"Earth to Bruce," says Colt. "Did you hear me? I said find another woman. When you show that she's not the only game in town, she'll get jealous and want to notice you more. That works most times."

"That doesn't make any sense."

"Women never make sense. But this works."

#

The crowd cheers as Zach connects the new motherboard.

"Don't let this happen again," says Betty.

"Yeah, Kellen," says Rick.

"Fuck you, I didn't do it," says Kellen.

Zach meets Dede's eyes across the room. Men who know how to use their hands are very cute. Zach learned that from his father working on cars as a boy. Dede mouths the word later and winks. Zach loves a lady that knows how to seduce. Zach makes his way over. Dede goes extra feminine, sticking out her chest.

"What's a sweet young lady like you doing in a rough place like this?" he asks in a husky voice.

Dede shakes her head, letting her blonde locks flow glamorously. "Looking for a strong man who knows how to handle a woman. You see that anywhere?" she asks in a terrible southern accent.

Zach almost groans. What is it with people fucking up his father's goddamn accent? Zach worked hard to lose it, but he still knows how to pull it out when necessary. He'd do it now if her breasts weren't so damn big.

"You good at Deathstrike?" asks Zach.

"Zach," says Betty. "Can you help me with something else?"

Cockblocking old lady. Betty mentions it won't take long, but its already taken too damn long.

"I'll be back soon, pretty lady," says Zach in a perfect Austin, Texas, accent. Dad would die of shock. He didn't like Zach changing himself to fit in with those uppity tech virgins. He needs to find a way to find what happened to his parents. He knows they're dead, but knowing for sure would be nice. Maybe D can help.

Chapter 22

"**R**eady, fire," says the general as a white flash of metal incinerates a line of two thousand.

"Again." Iron whistles through the skyline. "Take cover," he says as the brimstone shells fill the sky. These new Coalition tanks are more accurate than before. "Get ready," says the Commander, and those are his last words.

D shouldn't be here. He passed the accuracy tests. There's no good fucking reason he should be anywhere near this frontline. Why did that damn pilot get himself shot down while carrying D and his spotter? Not even close to their drop off, D takes the lead to find friendlies and finds a platoon just as it's about to charge headlong into the Coalition lines. D tries worming his way to the back to find a more useful spot, but then a six-thousand-pound bomb drops on the command tents, so he is in the safest place to be. His spotter's having trouble hiding her emotions, but they're all right. Then, the next bomb drops. D's eyes are open with bombs screaming and men stabbing and shooting each other. The boy's there. Maybe two years younger than D. He's looking for a target and runs straight at D. D's blood is pumping now. He's seen that look before. This boy's a killer. He's killed too early in life; he's a psychopath. D's not scared of those types of kids anymore; he's bigger now and trained. D screams a primal scream.

He throws himself off the chair.

What? Oh, Cella left for ingredients.

D fell asleep when she left. Cella's at the door, and that's what woke him up. She saw that. Great, now she'll ask awkward questions, and he'll have to make her drop the subject. He wipes sweat from his brow and sees Dede standing behind her.

Oh, this is wonderful.

"I just wanted some lube," says Dede.

Cella winces. Dede smiles at her, takes the lube from the fridge, and goes.

Cella begins "Are you-"

"I'm fine," says D, cutting her off. "You ready to teach me now?"

#

Cella's a bit annoyed that D's picked up the chemical principals so quick. It's like he's done stuff like this before. He's clearly not going to talk to her about his dream and he's acting a bit more stiff than she planned. Cella was hoping for a little flirting and maybe something more. But D's being real closed off right now. He's already made his own three-ounce mix of pheromones and asked perfectly legitimate questions. It's very academic and not the least bit romantic, which is the opposite of what she wanted. Now, it's time to go to target practice.

"What?" he asks.

"Target practice. You're my partner, remember?"

D checks his watch and nods. "Thanks for teaching me this.

Might come in handy later."

"You're welcome," Cella says, disappointedly.

Cella's not one for this quiet stuff. He's clearly bothered by what he dreamed of, so she'll steer to a new subject.

"You a gun expert, or is the sniper rifle all you know how to use?"

D raises a brow in shock and confusion. There's real emotion there. He must really be flustered.

"A good Marine adapts to any situation. I know how to use everything."

"Is that so?" she asks, glancing down.

"Very much so." He winks.

There you go, she thinks.

He'd better start flirting with her. She leads him down a flight of steps to the soundproof room holding a large shooting range. The ceiling's twenty-five feet high. Monitors show proper posture and ideal bullet spacing. A display case shows the latest in military assault weapons and a projection for each weapon showing its intended uses, firing rate, and attachments should one be interested. There are fifteen shooting booths, six feet wide with six-inch partitions. The range looks to be six hundred yards; that's hardly a challenge.

Hank fires the cannon D saw when he first met these people topside. It was impressive before, but in here that cannon's liable to pop ear drums. Maybe that's why everyone has earmuffs on. Hank's trying to hide a big grin with Betty giving off negative body language with no earmuffs on, while Rick laughs behind them. Cella and Dede guide the men to her clique, staying clear of the military women.

"How's your chest feel?" asks Rita.

Cella ignores the roided out grizzly bear while Dede offers Rita a middle finger. An earmuff wearing Saffire stacks all shooting booths with their own sets of goggles. Wanda's been eyeing Colt and Bruce since they arrived. She's looking for a reason to complain, and everyone's determined to not give her one. She's medically exempt by Betty for no damn good reason.

Colt calls everyone to order just after noticing D enter. The troop will be using nonlethal ammo replicates, not deadly but just as accurate and loud, able to cause serious injury or in very rare cases death at one foot or less, however. The calibers go from forty to sixty, as those are the most efficient against brogs.

Everyone's working in duos. The collective score of each team determines the winner. Each booth has its own set of targets and because certain members complained last time, the targets for this first round would hold still. Thirty shots for a thirty-bullet magazine for a round of a hundred seconds. Colt adds that anyone wishing for more time at advanced difficulty is welcome to stay after practice. To add incentive, each booth gets a score from zero to a hundred based on posture and grouping. Two rounds per person, Jade with Colt, Hank and Betty, Rick and Rita, and so on, until reaching the new groups, Dede and Zach and Cella and D.

Cella is eager to show D her shooting. She's not a completely hopeless case anymore after a month training with Creighton. Their first session, Cella dropped the gun in shock and nearly shot herself and Creighton. It led to a great makeup session afterward. D seems entirely too confident in his shooting, so she'll show him.

The round starts and ends with scores posting on the big board at the back wall, overlooking Booth 7 and 8. The troop's making a good effort not to stare, but everyone wants to see what D can do.

The baseline score is fifty-five. With a score of ninety-one Jade beats Hank and Rick. Coming in last with an abysmal score of thirty-one is Cella. She shakes her head while Dede cheers, not being the worst with a forty-six. She turns back to D as Colt chants, "Sayo, Sayo, Sayo." D asks to see Cella's gun while looking at the five-foot wide grouping on the five-foot wide target. She's been trained but not well, not by a true marksman.

"I don't understand. I was at sixty last time," says Cella, as others laugh.

"Do you ever look at the monitor when you finish shooting?"

"It doesn't make any sense. I did it right."

"You're shooting like the guns a bomb. It's just a tool. Aim where you want it to go, and it goes there." He moves close to adjust her stance. "May I?" he asks, putting his hand on her waist. "Straighten your off arm. Keep the shooting elbow in. Don't choke it. Breathe. Everything should be one motion. And shoot with the padding of your finger, not the knuckle or tip. That's usually what pulls the shot wide," D says, as Cella glances to see the others watching.

He steps back as the light flashes green. The leader board shows number one with a score of eighty-nine, Jade. Rick follows with eighty-seven and third with a score of eighty-four is Cella.

"Yes," Cella shouts as Hank's booth follows and rounding out is Dede with forty-four.

D wasn't expecting that at all. *Eighty-four?* Shit.

"Something's not right here," says Rick.

"Damn right. How the hell am I fourth?" asks Hank.

"Don't feel bad; it just wasn't your time," says Cella.

Rick wants a redo, as Cella hugs D with an ear-to-ear smile. D did something. Rick knows it.

"Don't make me come over there, Rick," says Cella.

"Well, the most important thing is I'm still first," shouts Jade, annoyed, as Colt loudly claps. *How the hell did that girly tart get an eighty-four? Bullshit.*

The second team members step to the firing line, Colt, Bruce, Rita, Dom, and all the way at the end, Zach and D. Cella wishes D luck as the round starts. D waits, seeing if his target will do something unexpected. Cella's getting nervous as the others frown. D's just standing there, looking. Jade's got a growing smile. Others are starting to laugh. Oh, this can't happen. Cella's about to step close, but D breathes, then—does nothing again. Another twenty seconds pass, and Jade and her lesbo friends are smiling proudly. D finally picks up the gun and aims. He doesn't shoot the freaking thing for ten seconds. Two shots hit the head. One bullet per eye. Then this infuriating man puts the gun back down. Cella's jaw could break bone for how tight it is. Jade's not smiling now, but everyone's confused.

"Lost your nerve?" asks Rick. D does nothing.

At sixty seconds, D uncoils, taking the gun in his left hand, spinning it like an old cowboy, turns away from the target, closes his eyes, and fires. It's hard to see D's hand move but slightly. D is done five seconds before the round, blowing smoke from the barrel before laying it down again. He pointedly ignores the target while turning to Cella.

"How'd I do?" he asks as the scores tally.

Cella stares at the scoreboard, mouth agape. A gold star's next to the top score. The score is ninety-five, and the booth number is fifteen. Cella jumps for joy as the others curse the results. Colt and his ninety-three seems unimpressive suddenly. Zach high fives D, though he's respectable with a seventy-three. Cella's making sure Jade hears who's got the top spot while Hank and Rick look at D's target, speechless. There's a four-inch spread shaped like a circle with a check mark jutting out.

That's impressive, Hank admits to himself. *He could've sworn this young man was right-handed. And looking away from the target eyes closed with one hand? That's not bad, not bad at all.* D got five points off for improper posture. You win some, you lose some.

"I'm starting the fucking round again," shouts Colt. "Get back to your places."

"Wanna wish me luck?" asks D. Cella plants a big kiss on his cheek.

D doesn't waste time this round. Using proper form with eyes open and his right hand, he fires two shots center mass, then reloads in 1.86 seconds and continues shooting. He finishes seventy seconds before the round ends. Yawning, D shrugs at an exceptionally pleased Cella. D made a swirl pattern three inches wide. When the scores tally, a diamond marks the top score of ninety-nine again from Booth 15.

"Bullshit," says Colt, slamming the empty gun on the ledge.

Jade's consoling him while the others curse loudly.

"He's cheating," says Rita and her eighty-eight.

"What the hell is this?" asks Emmett.

Bruce has a smoldering quiet about him. What did he do some ask. How's he just shooting perfect like that? Doesn't it take time to learn how a gun shoots to use it right?

"We're going with fifty-caliber rifles now," yells Colt.

"It's our turn," says Cella.

"You wait up, dammit," says Colt.

Cella's about to press the point, but D stops her with a hand. D's a rifleman at heart. The round finishes with Booth 15 holding a ninety-six topping the big board. Another new record, supplanting Colt's long standing eighty-seven. Colt's current score of eighty-four just can't compete with the hoots and hollers of Cella. That settles it. Rick was right. Colt stomps his way to D and Cella's booth, Bruce following, demanding to see D's handgun. D shows it from a distance.

"Hand it over," says Bruce.

D's not doing that. They might mess with it somehow, and he's winning, so no sense messing that up. Colt and Bruce move closer as Cella steps in front of D, telling the two to stop. Jade pulls back Bruce and Colt as D's face relaxes.

"Don't worry about them," says Cella.

The next round begins and ends with D's ninety-seven in first. An incensed eighty-six-scoring Colt pushes the booth barrier before walking to the back wall in silence. Cella chuckles while D looks at the monitor. That thing sucks. His form was perfect, and he got a minus three because the head shot didn't match the center-mass shots. Bullshit. Zach with his seventy-six nods to D as their respective ladies replace them.

"You weren't teaching me like that." Zach smiles.

"Fuck you," says D.

Cella's confident; Creighton taught her rifles first. She went on a rant about being able to handle the bigger guns. She couldn't the first time, but she worked out and swallowed her ego, then went for a smaller rifle and learned. There were a lot of things that went into learning. Her parents are dead; it took a while to admit that, but a scientist can't engage in self-disillusion. Her brother was in Toronto when the bombs hit, and he's dead too. She saw her sister's corpse succumbing to radiation and fire at her house and ran out of Elizabeth, New Jersey, as fast as possible.

Cella is gorgeous; she's known that since pre-k. Jade's pretty, but not on Cella's level. It's the difference between a dime and a nine. The former is one notch prettier with nine times the ease. In school, little boys smiled at her, giving her gifts for no reason. All the little girls wanted to punch her. It only got worse in high school when puberty kicked in.

Cella's breasts grew, not as much as she wanted, but they were respectable, her hips developed, her butt got perky, and thanks to her mom's beauty advice, her skin was flawless and on a sunny day, it looked like it glowed. When friends had boyfriends and Cella clearly looked better than them in every single way, well... those relationships didn't survive long. Cella can admit she wasn't a pure-hearted good girl and had a very high degree of conceit, but to be fair, she's never met a man who found her unattractive, and she's always had tenacity. No lasting friends meant working to make sure people saw her as more than super model material. So, she worked and worked and worked at science and math. Yes, she may have played a few geeks into thinking they'd get dates, but she got the concepts down.

She ripped through the science competitions and used flirty eyes and suggestive smiles to get her way, but she got into the science programs, adding another notch to her perfection belt.

Then, the bombs came, and she was humbled. For the first time in her life, her money, looks, and smarts meant nothing. She left her big sister in the street. Luck is why she was alive and being a coward was why she was still alive—never again. She fires. The round ends with the shock of all shocks. Cella with a score of eighty-two, just ahead of Jade's eighty-one is first.

Cella screams her jubilation. Jade's dark brown eyes turn red like flames and a sharp object twinkles in her right hand. She stalks forward, teeth showing. Colt gets over his sullenness and hurries over to his fiancé; that smile is dangerous. Cella's playing it cool, but she notices the knife. A few girls tried to slash her face freshmen year, but Jade's combat trained; that could be an issue.

"Jade," says Colt with a firm grip on her wrist.

"I'm gonna fucking gut you, you bitch," says Jade, hissing the words.

"Well, you sure can't use that gun to do it," says Cella.

"You wanna talk, you slut? You're trying to fuck a new Commando schizoid."

"At least mine wins. Yours has help and he still can't top out," says Cella.

"Top out? Well, we all know you lost your gag reflex a long time ago."

"Maybe if you were that friendly, it wouldn't take thirty-seven years and the apocalypse to get a marriage proposal."

Jade roars as she lounges at Cella. The others come between them as Betty tells Jade to go back to her booth. Cella finds herself behind D shouting for Jade to do as told. Jade's cursing fluently as Colt carries her back to Booth 1.

"Good, come back," says D to Cella, slowly stepping around.

"Right." Cella smiles. "She never beats me in wordplay."

"I think you got her off her game. If you get anything over a sixty-five, we win this round easy."

Cella does some quick math, and yes, D's right. Oh, this will be fun. The next round begins and ends with Jade scoring an eighty-six. Cella posts a seventy-five and smiles a sincere smile at Jade, batting her eyes at Colt out of spite. Then there's the telltale pop. Everyone stops and stares at Cella clutching her arm staring at Jade in absolute shock. Jade shot at her. The bullets are fake, but still.

"Maniac," Cella screams.

"I should've aimed for your nipple, bitch," says Jade with a savage smile.

Despite nonlethal bullets being known for being just that, it doesn't mean they don't hurt—a lot. Cella's not exactly the type of person who takes bullets for breakfast so for her, the shot hurts like hell. It's all she can do to not breakdown, crying from the pain. D's there dispassionate as ever, looking at the arm. A nice plum-sized welt is forming just below the shoulder. He pokes it.

"Hey," says Cella, slapping his hand away.

"Are you kidding?" says D. "That's a love tap. Suck it up, lady. We're doing sixty-cals next."

It's not as if Cella expected a guy like D to be caring and considerate, but he's supposed to say nice things. She stares at him.

"Your first time?" asks D. "You wanted to get to know me? Know this boo-hooing over flesh wounds don't impress me. This is really not that bad. So stop acting like the world needs to stop for your feelings. Block the pain and keep moving."

Cella just stares at him. After she went to defend him. She was shot in the arm, and block the pain is all he's got?

"You're not gonna console me?" says Cella.

For about two milliseconds a look crosses D's face. It's a look she's never seen any man give her. If it's because of her whining or complaining, she's not sure, but it's a look of disgust. D's hefting the sixty-caliber shotgun and waiting for the green light. D ends the next two rounds with a ninety-four and ninety-six, respectively. Cella's still behind him, staring in shock. It's almost as if D's lost complete interest in her.

"Your turn," he says, with eyes as unyielding as stone.

"We're talking after this is over." she whispers.

Cella's two rounds end with an eighty and eighty-one. An average of 87.7 is better than the 82.5 of Colt and Jade. Valenda's standing near a nearly comatose Jade as she sits, dripping incredulity. Stoneface D is gone, and the guy she's been talking to for all of yesterday is back. Cella doesn't understand this man. She grabs D's hand and tugs him back to the lab.

The military people watch them go, then look at each other.

That was—well none of them have ever seen shooting like that. Worse thing is it didn't seem as if D was taking it seriously. During the second round, D's final twelve shots hit dead center with one hand while he was showing Zach with his off hand how to position his body to shoot a shotgun more effectively. That's where the minus six and four came from. It makes Hank wonder what D can do when he's trying to hit something. It's been fiftyeight years since nineteen-year-old Hank stepped into boot camp, and he's never seen shooting like that.

"That," begins Rick, "wasn't bad."

Chapter 23

Cella's rubbing the salve on her arm as D sits, checking his finger for gunpowder residue. After the welt clears, Cella's ready.

"Who did that to you?" she asks, nodding to D's covered arms.

"Are we playing the guessing game again?" he asks.

"Yes."

"Well then. I forfeit. What's my punishment?"

"Getting hit in the jaw if you don't answer my question."

"My life's none of your goddam business, stranger."

"Really, we're back to that? Well, how do you expect anyone to not be a stranger when you don't want them to know you?"

"You don't want to know me; you wanna win a bet."

That stops Cella right in her tracks. She's trying to recover when the door open. It's Colt.

"We need to talk," says Colt.

D nods to Cella, then follows Colt.

"We're not done," she says as the door closes.

"Were you ever in any shooting competitions?" asks Colt as they walk back to the war room.

"Sure," says D.

"Ever lost?"

"No."

Colt nods. That was as expected. "How long have you been shooting?"

"Twenty-one years."

"You always been that accurate?"

"I've always been more accurate than anyone in my age group. I still had to develop my skill, though."

"What else do you know how to shoot?"

"What else you got?"

Colt looks at D. Colt's been a soldier for sixteen years. He knows the real deal when he sees it. Maybe Hank's onto something. He nods to D, then motions him into the war room.

Something's wrong. The big table's not there. The couches are the same. Hank, Rick, and Bruce are trying to hide behind the door. D kicks the door back into Bruce as Colt spears him from behind. D twist loose with a spinning elbow. Bruce slams the door shut as Hank and Rick sprint in to kick D back to the ground.

Colt's trying to hold D's legs while Hank and Rick stomp on him.

When someone's trying to hold your legs, keeping them bent until you can strike is a good option. People always try to pull out the feet to negate any kicking power. If the legs are bent, you can get decent force out of a kick. If the fool's trying to grab you with the hands instead of flopping over the body, keeping organs and head protected, the hand has to move, absorbing the kinetic energy before bringing the leg under control. This means that if the hand is close to the face that energy has the potential to slam back into your opponent's face, which is what Colt finds out when his vision goes dark. D rolls to whoever's kicking to his left. It's Hank. D spins back to Rick first, knocking him over like a pin. D throws a short stinging hook into his calf muscle, causing an instant charley horse.

The silver man yells, as D rolls back to his feet. D wastes no time staring; he charges Hank with Bruce coming in to spear him from the side. D spins off Bruce, ducks Hank's left to deliver a right cross to the ribs. Hank folds like an accordion, but Colt is behind D with a straight right to the kidneys. D grunts as he falls, and Bruce is there to kick him square in the jaw. D's dizzy, but he knows how to take a hit. In three seconds, he'll recover and—a boot slams into D's other ear.

#

D wakes up in a chair, hands bound behind it. D would try to jump and slam the chair at an angle, but seeing as it's metal and his feet are tied to the front legs, that's out. He's caught. No use fighting—yet.

Rick's massaging his leg while glowering at D. The charley horse hurts like hell. Bruce is holding up a broken nose, Colt's got a black eye, and Hank is hoping that this young man didn't break three of his ribs with that body shot. D's happy. At least they know they've been in a fight.

"Do you know who Harbour Dax is?" asks Hank.

"I ain't answering shit, you old bitch," says D. "Fuck you twice."

"Ok, let me make this easier for you. Why do you have Harbour Dax's magazine clip?"

"To fuck your mother up the ass. That bitch likes the kinky shit."

Bruce yanks D's head back, applying a sleeper hold.

"Stop," says Hank. "He can't talk if he's asleep, can he?"

"Is Creighton Frost still with him?" asks Bruce, twisting D's neck.

"Sure. We were gonna gangbang your little sister once we take care of you guys."

Colt punches him just under the sternum.

"Is he leading them now?" asks Colt. "Harbour's dead?"

"Yeah. Sat on a toilet and shat his guts out, literally. Couldn't believe it when I saw it. Flew off the fucking seat like a goddamn missile."

Colt punches him squarely in the jaw.

"I'm not gonna ask you again," says Colt, voice growing calm and menacing. "We're not going to let you sabotage our plans.

Your side lost. Accept it."

"I haven't lost shit. My mission still goes so long as I'm breathing."

"We can help with that," says Rick, limping over, still upset over his leg.

D sighs and looks up because Bruce is still holding his head. Something like sadness passes over his face then resolution takes hold.

"I guess," D begins, "you have to do whatever you have to. I'm ready."

The four men blink. Who the hell is this guy?

"You'd give yourself up for Harbour?" asks Colt. "Well, he's always had good leadership qualities."

"Where is he?" asks Hank. "Is he-no he's waiting at the exit, isn't he? We'll be dead soon as we exit, won't we?"

"I don't know or care who that is, but I hoped he fisted you in the ass when you were three. Fuck all of you," says D.

Bruce gives him a solid punch to the left ear. There's liquid leaking down D's neck, and he's woozy. Punches there do that; it just can't be helped.

"Stop," says Hank. "You don't know who Harbour Dax is?"

"No."

"Well then how many fingers am I holding up?"

Hank is staring D in the eye, puckered scar leering, holding nine fingers.

D raises a brow. *Is there a code on the nine fingers?* "Are you serious? Fat face didn't hit me that hard."

Hank continues staring, giving his best intimidating look. The scar really adds to his fierceness. If one looks closely, they'll see folded skin inside the lips of the scar, stretching like a thin membrane over pink folds of muscle. Anyone who doesn't know Hank would piss themselves at this terrifying glare. But D's met quite a few monsters in his life, human and Brog. He just can't manage the fear Hank wants.

"Ok," says Hank stepping back. "Say I believe you. How'd you get his gun?"

"I don't know who Harbour Dax is, but I passed a dead guy on the way here. Fourteen walking hours to the west-southwest. He had one eye. Urban camouflage gear on. He was at least three weeks dead. I couldn't tell his age, but he looked to be mid-fifties.

I think he shot himself. Is that your bogeyman?"

"Let him go." The others blink. Bruce is about to protest, but Hank is firm. "You heard me."

Bruce unties D's hands, then the legs. He can't bring himself to look at D, as Hank begins talking.

"We were ready to kill you," says Hank.

"I don't doubt it."

"You weren't worried about Zach?"

"Zach's a civvie, and he knows as much about you people as I do. If you were going to kill me, it meant he was already dead. The type of people that would do that can't be negotiated with."

Valenda comes into view, handing Hank a card. It's the answers from Zach's interrogation. He doesn't know who Harbour Dax is and claims he only met D a few days ago. He was on a boat before that and named all seventy-seven people on the boat with him. The names are broken down by gender and categorized as military or civilian. He says his father was a big game hunter. That's where he learned to use a gun.

All he knows about D is that he kept him from getting eaten, he's four inches above the average height, black, fast and shoots real well. Valenda's an experienced interrogator, and Rita, Emmett, and Dom were there. They believe Zach.

"Do you believe him now?" Hank asks Rick.

"Lying at this point kind of defeats the purpose," says Rick. "All right. He's still hiding something, but I think our interests align."

"What are your interests?" asks Hank.

"To get to Three-Mile Island by any means necessary," says D.

Hank looks at Rick, who gives a defeated shake of his head.

"You're with Domelvo's team. Wake up at zero four hundred.

We leave at 0445. And get that ear looked at."

D pops out of the chair with a relaxed expression. "Does this mean I get my guns back?"

"No. Who's gonna hurt you here?" Hank smiles. "Dinner starts in forty-five minutes."

\#

Cella has been thinking up arguments for the past hour.

How'd he find out about the bet, anyway? That's not important. He's cute, and she just wants to talk to him; get to know him. There's no harm there. They're probably going to be dead tomorrow. What's the point in closing yourself off?

The door opens slowly. She takes a breath.

"All right I know-" Cella stops short.

D has bright blue and black bruises on his face, blood leaking down his ear, and a boot print on his *freaking cheek*. Is this an attack? No; a few of the others are standing behind them as a pseudo escort.

"What happened?" she demands, rushing over to D.

Her eyes are full of concern as she drags him to a table to look him over. Zach's face is just as bruised. If one accounts for him not being a trained soldier, his injuries might need more immediate tending. However, Cella doesn't give one bit of a crap about that. D's a sweetheart deep down. She hasn't found out how deep yet, but it's there. *Who had the nerve to hit him?*

"I'm ok," says D, pulling her hands down. "We just need some of that salve."

"No, who did this?"

"You sound concerned. Isn't that sweet."

"Stop with the tough guy thing. You're bleeding. Colt and Bruce did this."

It's a statement not a question. There's a fire in Cella's eyes D is surprised by. Now this is a girl with potential.

"I'll be right back." she says.

D takes a firm grip of Cella's arm. "It's over. No hard feelings. I gave as good as I got. It's over. Just stop."

"Look what they did to you."

"I've been hit a lot worse than this. And Bruce has a broken nose, Colt has an eye as big as an orange, Rick will have a limp for a few hours, and Hank's ribs are pretty tender right now. It's over, don't go making a big deal over nothing."

So Hank and Rick helped, did they? Cella pulls out of his grip. She's still angry, but D doesn't seem to be too bothered by this. He's a strange man. And for some reason, his nonchalance is really turning her on. She will have to talk to Bruce later. This has to stop.

"Why are you still standing?" she asks Zach.

Zach coughs as Cella's pointing at the seat near D with an expression that will not be argued with. He sits gingerly near D who's shamelessly staring at Cella's ass.

"Nice girlfriend you got there," Zach whispers.

"I think so," D whispers back.

#

Cella's mother instincts were on high for an hour, meaning D and Zach are late to dinner by fifteen minutes. She drops a bottle of ointment on Zach's lap before caressing D's face over and over again, asking if anything hurts. D keeps pretending something's hurting, even after the bruises completely fade. Dede comes in once to get a salve for Colt and Bruce, but Cella almost throws a beaker at her before locking the door. She's genuinely concerned about a perforated ear drum, but D's insistent that it's fine. Nonetheless, Cella stays very close, running hands over his face and shoulders and abs.

Zach's about to leave twice before Cella orders him to sit. She isn't letting them jump Zach again either. They can't leave until D gives his word to come back after dinner, so she can make sure there's no lasting damage. The scandalous look she gives D gives Zach an erection. Then, they have to wait for Cella to clean up with lip gloss and some eye shadow. She'd deny it if accused, but smoothing out her yoga pants, letting out her shirt to show off her six-pack, and smiling was outright teasing.

The dining hall is loud as Cella walks in with D and Zach. Even if the interrogations didn't happen, Cella would've stopped traffic, but right now she has a serious expression on her face. It's the type of look that makes all men cautious. Rick was about to smile but thinks better of it. Jade's about ready to shank Cella as she holds Colt's hand. That eye looks as if a swarm of beetles took a shit on it. Bruce had to reset his own nose, but it's still as crooked as the letter K. Hank's having trouble breathing. He's had broken ribs before, so he knows what they feel like, but there's definitely a deep bone bruise. Rick is favoring his right leg. They made sure their best men dealt with D, and all of them have visible injuries while the gauze covering D's ear is the only sign of his injury. The optics are fantastic for him right now. Cella knows why they did it, but since it was proven D's no mole, the whole situation in her eyes was flat-out bullying. She takes a firm grip of D's hand and walks—no sashays—to their seats for dinner. Having the best-looking girl at the party is always a good thing.

There's tension between Cella and Jade, but she slides over the ointment as a gesture of goodwill. Betty and Wanda had to talk Jade out of going down to the lab. Dede was sent instead. Jade's been boiling since the denial, but Cella's offering an olive branch.

If D were to guess, he'd say Cella's doing this now in front of everyone to show that the aggrieved party can be magnanimous after the fact. She looks like the understanding one, while Jade looks angry and unremorseful. Women are great at this game.

D glances at Cella, who shrugs, then purses her lips seductively. D's thinking about how many ways he can twist her.

Is she a loud one? Probably. Of course, all women are loud when you fuck well enough. Cella's going to be really loud tonight. D's whispers something in her ear now that makes her smile. Betty's shaking her head at the two, as Hank returns, felling much better after the ointment does its work.

"Are we ready now?" asks Hank.

Cella giggles at whatever D's whispering, so Hank takes that as a yes. Right on cue, Wanda and Coren cart in the food with Saffire staring jealously at Coren for taking her place. The featured dish of the night is leg of lamb. Dessert will be chocolate mousse cake made by Coren with the guidance of Wanda. Hank asks both to stay while he rises for a toast. There's a glass in front of D, but there's no way in hell he's taking anything from these people. Cella, however, is offering wine from his glass. This isn't the liquid D wants from her and tells her that.

"You are not getting it that easy, mister," says Cella. "I want chocolate before you get any of my sweets."

"Chocolate's damn near impossible to come by right now."

"Which means it's worth getting. Don't you agree?"

"That's feminine mystique I should've expected."

Cella winks. Yes, this is the type of trouble D can handle.

"To loved ones lost and for new ones to be gained, cheers," says Hank.

D lifts his empty glass while Cella fills hers halfway with red wine and starts downing it. She's halfway done before taking a breath. It's impressive, but she's not the biggest woman, and she'll be drunk by the end of the glass if she's not careful. Everyone else is taking food. Dede's next to Zach, asking about his interrogation, and Zach's shrugging it off. He's just happy he went to the bathroom before that war-room meeting; otherwise, it might have been a spectacle. She doesn't need to know that, though.

Cella's blinking now. She may have overdone the glass. She drinks when she's nervous. She'll get some water in her to stop any hangover tomorrow. Across the table, Jade's making it a point to not look at Cella while holding a knife. She and Colt are eating the meat substitute and enjoying it. D and Zach missed out on it yesterday, but tonight's the last night, so the meat takes up half the table. Dede's cut the tailfeather portion for Zach. He's got a look he had leaving the lab to get here. Betty was able the make this stuff taste close enough to the real thing. Zach's taking in all these features to stall eating it. D's watching, waiting. Zach takes a breath and bites. Zach chews and chews.

It took twenty years, but eventually, the formula for making fake meat that didn't taste like grainy shit-stained ass chunks was cracked. It's not quite the real thing, but for today, it is the best meal since Betty's breakfast. D nods he wants part of the leg; it all tastes the same, but still, he wants a leg. The others are smiling and laughing an hour into the meal, but no one's touched Coren's cake, opting for fruit and drinks.

This happens to be when Coren, Wanda, and Saffire come back to finish the meal with everyone. Coren's scowling. These fucking people; they think it's easy making dairy with powdered milk? *Assholes*.

"I helped him," says Wanda. "It tastes good."

Betty sighs and cuts a slice. The verdict? It's actually pretty damn good. Betty gives Hank a stern look to try and he does. He shrugs so that two others take slices, and suddenly half dig in as well. Cella inhales three slices in a blink.

"Chocolate as promised," says D.

Cella's shaking her finger while swallowing. "This isn't yours."

"You never specified that. Can't change terms and conditions after the fact."

"You are a jerk of the highest magnitude."

"True and you have the greatest legs I've ever seen on a woman, so there."

Cella smirks, no reason to argue with that one. She takes a fourth slice. She's thinking about a fifth. D's curious if she can fit that in her small frame. This more than anything has Cella putting back the slice.

"I want to, but I have to watch my figure," says Cella, calmly.

"You could use a few more pounds. Eat the cake," he says as she elbows him, then takes three more slices.

"I really like chocolate," says Cella.

"I see," says D.

"Can you cook?"

"A little bit—eggs, pancakes. It's hard to find a good woman so I do it myself."

"What do you mean it's hard to find?" asks Cella.

"Do you know anyone?" D asks.

"You're not funny."

"Neither is the way you're shoveling the cake."

She pushes D or tries. She nearly slides off her own chair trying to move him. Cella glares at him as he nods imperiously, flexing his biceps. She's definitely kissing him later.

"I'll be right back," says Cella, looking for anyone with uneaten cake.

"You can make eggs?" asks Betty. "I guess that makes sense. You're on your own a lot. Has it always been that way?"

D's about to answer, then eyes Betty. "You're pretty good. Did you work in the private sector or military?"

"Military. It's where Hank and I met."

"Are you part Japanese?"

"Yes, great grandfather on my mother's side," says Betty.

"How long have you been a military psychologist?"

"A very long time. Why do you ask?"

"You remind me of a friend."

"Were they a psychologist?"

"She thought she was. How'd you wind up in the military?"

"Well, I studied in college. I had just received my PHD and was looking for something to get me out of my student debt. It was hard, but then I heard the army was looking for medical and psychiatric specialists. If you were of fighting age and stayed seven years, all of your debts would be forgiven. I didn't have any money and wasn't going back to my parents, so I went to a recruitment office and signed up."

"Best decision she ever made," says Hank.

"Excuse me, I'm telling the story," says Betty, smiling. "The first warriors charged with stopping the Coalition advance are getting too old. The obvious is there, but no politician in their right mind would purposely bring back the draft. People underestimated the threat the Coalition is. Low on resources high on population and weaponry, needing to preserve their lands from nature and civil war. Why wouldn't they attack the countries with ready access to water? It's simple enough to see. It's supposed to burn itself out."

"Just politicians on their last legs, looking to make one last hurrah before their countries crumble. But the big one hit—a 9.6 magnitude earthquake hit California. Then eastern floods. All monies allocated for insuring certain governments around the world don't come. So, allies have to fend for themselves and lose. The Coalition grows to the new power in the world too strong now to be anything but a true enemy."

"New recruitment ideas start until they could get the support for a draft, anyway. Huge advertisement campaigns begin. All types of perks for working professionals and people needing new homes can join in return getting preference for family relocation. The recruiter tells me that I'll have the best conditioning and can see the world. In seven months' time, despite my parents' objections, I join the army, but the experience is different from the hard sell. I'm in fantastic shape, but I hate the food and the constant yelling in my ear."

"Upon graduating basic training, I realize the true scope of my duties as one of a growing number of fighting-age professionals. The new military quota is one psychiatrist per seven hundred soldiers on a base that averages over nineteen hundred. However, I'm the only head doc on her base. I just needed to find the ones that might go on suicide rampages. The other soldiers could handle themselves."

"Other recruitment practices go for even more low-income people. If anyone could use a job and help its them. The marketing's too good. The average people per base jumps to thirty-two hundred."

"I rethink this commitment, but the fine print says leaving early means not only that the debt returns but the money spent training as well as housing and feeding me is due immediately. The total number would be close to two million. I stay and they send me to dozens of active and nonactive war zones with the purpose of keeping soldiers in acceptable mental shape for reentering a war zone or ending their tours. In the outset, the instructions are three interviews with each soldier. Soldiers get a rating from one to six, and all soldiers who score a four are mentally stable."

"I continued for two and a half years. Sure, there was resentment for jumping to lieutenant rank because I had a PhD and other soldiers had to work harder to climb the ranks, but I earn a reputation for having an above average case completion rate. I fly to the most problematic bases, meaning those with the highest rates of suicide. Nigeria, during the first occupation, is where I met Hank and Rick."

"She wanted me as soon as she saw me," says Hank.

"Yeah, right," says Betty.

"The first words from Hank are, 'Would you like to go to dinner sometime?' I say no and hope that's the end of the nagging. The base suffered fourteen suicides the month preceding. For lack of a better term, I consider Hank at the time to be a *conceited jerk*. Rick's no different; the two make my job that much more difficult.

"The first meetings are disturbing. All the men and women give the impression of being quite disturbed. The next week, during my second round of meetings, is when I catch on."

"All the men are giving false statements to have more meetings with me. My counter was threatening dismissal for those who participated in faking severe mental instability. Suddenly, the interviews fall back in line with the average. I am not fooled. Hank and Rick backlog my work because they're six years old. They get what they wanted, which is extra time with me. Hank doesn't try to hide his grin in our next interview. I don't smile. After the next two rounds of interviews, it's two years before we speak again." "The military abruptly sends me to South Korea due to the execution of four base psychiatrists. I am quite well known in and out of military circles at this point. There's a future in the private sector once my obligations are fulfilled. Then, an incident occurs. A soldier goes on a homicidal rampage, killing fifty-nine civilians and thirty-seven military men and women, including the base psychiatrist in South Africa. I am on the next flight, charged with giving the soldiers at this barracks a seven-day four-meeting examination, starting with the new lieutenant, Henry Auberon."

"She tried to pretend she didn't remember me," says Hank.

"I didn't remember you. I was doing more important things. Now hush," says Betty. "The next day, while on his usual morning run, a car bomber drives into the base checkpoint, sending shrapnel flying in every direction, including a piston that rakes across the young lieutenant's face. Hank is distraught that half his face was ripped apart, and he has outbursts at the medical staff."

Betty leaves out the time he almost shot himself and the paranoia that ensued in the ten years following the accident.

"That's when she started to lighten up," says Hank.

"Be quiet," says Betty. "Times are different now with the need to understand what the stresses of battle can do to an incoming and outgoing soldier. The standards and practices for entering the civilian world as recommended by scores of military psychiatrists for the past twenty years is one month of daily psychiatric evaluation and a three-month stay at a readjustment facility. However, in these pioneering days, I went with what felt best. It takes a while to bring back Hank's one-liners. I try almost everything to bring back the old narcissist."

"Except go out with me," says Hank.

"Against my professional judgment, I use my position to clear a special request. Rick is stuck in an intense firefight on the hills of Ireland. He's transferred to South Africa a week later under the guise of special forces training. Hank and Rick passed the exam a year and a half ago. Rick doesn't like being jerked from his responsibilities like this, but I outrank him, so he'll bend over and like it. Rick's lost his attraction to me for this, but Hank's his best friend and not going to war isn't horrible. Rick does help, unfortunately."

"It's amazing that no matter where you are, prostitution is always a big industry. In war time, it's even worse, or in Rick and Hank's case, better. It's strip clubs and late nights galore for two weeks. I am annoyed at the tactics, but I can't be upset about yanking Rick away to help his friend then be upset that he's helping. I could see the help when Hank starts asking for dates again."

"I was just wearing her down," says Hank.

"The final meeting comes and I feel Hank is no longer a threat to himself or anyone else. One minute after this final session, he asks me to come to the traveling circus. I haven't been out in a long time, mostly because of his case, so I figure he owes me a night. I say yes."

"I wore her down," says Hank.

"The circus is, as one should expect, loud, dizzying, and exciting. We are enjoying ourselves. Then, the ringmaster asks if any soldier is brave enough to participate. Hank volunteers us against my obdurate demand. It's actually great. We do the one where you have to swing from one bar to another. He plays the guy who catches me. I almost slip, but he holds on. It is the most fun I have had on a date. When he escorts me back to the base, he asks if I wouldn't mind doing it again. I turn him down."

"Why?" asks Cella. She has three more slices with her as she sits.

"Patient doctor rules. It just felt wrong," says Betty.

"But technically he wasn't your patient anymore," says D.

"That's exactly what I told her," says Hank.

"A week later, with nothing to do, I ask Hank if the offer's still good. Hank takes me to a picnic on a secluded beachfront found on his first day, arriving in the country."

"The occupation ends a month later. The Coalition is calling for a ceasefire to regroup. Hank and I exchange contact information before separating, me to Chicago, Hank to Iowa. Five weeks pass, and Hank's bored and can't keep me off his mind. He makes a decision. He's driving through Illinois on his way to the address I gave him."

"Why'd you wait five weeks?" asks D.

"I was an idiot. Rick stopped by, saw I was depressed, and brow beat me into going to see her," says Hank. "She is on the twentieth floor, Number 2077. I knock to find a very black, very stout older man at the door not pleased to see me. It was her father."

Betty continues the story. "I come to the door, eyes wide, jaw tight. I push Hank deep down the hallway, while my parents leer. Why didn't he call before coming? Hank tells me I was on his mind and he had to see me. He's apologizing for a few minutes, wearing me down, with people in the nearby apartments pretending they're not eavesdropping. I am actually enjoying giving him a hard time; I didn't forget that stunt he pulled the first time we met."

"I wasn't doing anything, and the thought of a man traveling hundreds of miles to see me is great for the ego, but if I could get more from a deal there's no reason I shouldn't try. I would go on a date, but first he has to meet my parents. The big tough Green Beret is rightfully cautious about meeting the parents, but he decides it is worth suffering through."

"My dad doesn't like Hank. He can be a Green Beret all he wants to, but according to him, I was too good for Hank. My mom is just happy her daughters not a lesbian. That means a real chance for grandkids. She knows I like Hank. A mother can tell these things."

Betty doesn't look at Jade when she says this.

"My mom strikes some type of deal with my dad, and after some threats, the usual 'You hurt my daughter, I'll kill you, thing, Hank and I have our first real civilian date. It is some trashy Horror flick with no plot but lots of cheap scares. It forced me to grab Hank a lot for protection, just as he planned. This is a weekly event for six months until Hank's recall."

Betty glosses over the worry of Hank not returning, the secret nature of his missions, the borderline abuse of power to make sure they were housed close by when she was recalled, the first time they had sex.

"Two years later, on a clear August night, Hank finally proposes. A year later, Hank's Iowa farming family meets the inner-city Jenkins clan at a beautiful ceremony. I have the pictures on my datapad. Jade came five years later."

"Wow Hank has a romantic side?" says Cella.

"Hell yeah. They taught us how to treat a lady back in my day. Now it's this 'Let's chat from four thousand miles away' crap. You gotta talk face to face. That's the only way to truly get to know someone."

Colt and Jade roll their eyes, having heard this rant countless times.

"If there's one thing I've learned in all these years, it's that life is about choices. You are what you've done in life."

Betty's showing Cella pictures of the wedding and trying badly to pull Jade over. She needs to quell this problem now.

"Who's doing the dishes?" asks Wanda.

Everyone's looking at Kellen. He was playing Deathstrike longer than anyone; who the hell else could have broken it?

"I didn't break it," shouts Kellen.

The matter's settled. Rick rises deaf to the four-letter storm from Kellen, welcoming all challengers to the best view of his ass.

Rick pulls down his pants and moons everyone. Why? Because everyone should have a nice view of the champion's ass. Deathstrike is something serious, and the champion must maintain order.

"Pull up your goddamn pants, Rick," yells Wanda.

Saffire's mouth drops open, but Wanda gives her the 'be quiet' look. Jade forgot to get a partner. Colt was beaten with a perfect score ten straight times, so he's refusing to go near the game. Dom, Bode, Dede, and a few others are in. Zach's in, but before D can nod, Cella's looking at him.

Shit, thinks D.

As much as Cella loves men, their strength, their protectiveness, their height, and their athleticism, she's annoyed that all of them have an unfailing need to protect their pride.

"You're gonna chicken out of the tournament?" yells Rick.

Cella also knows how to use that pride to her advantage.

Zach's looking at him. D said he'd join Zach. D's done a lot of things in his life, but breaking his word is not one of them. Of course, he wants to fuck the daylight out of Cella and screwing that up could be something he'd never forgive himself for.

"You get a few love taps and you're terrified of me, is it?" says Rick. "Typical weak-ass Marine."

That settles it. D's up. He's not grinding his teeth. D's got too much self-control to slip like that in front of people, but there's an extra vein in his neck now.

"Sorry, Cella, we'll have to reschedule," says D, locking eyes with a smiling Rick.

Cella sucks her teeth. That idiot Rick overdid it. If there's one thing she's learned about these military types, it is the inordinate amount of pride they have to the average population. She wants D back with her in the lab. *How to play this?*

"What are you gonna do after you win?" asks Cella, pulling D's eyes back to her. "There's a lot of night left after the tournament you know."

"You're right. So, you're coming to support then?"

"Well, you kind of left me dangling in the wind. I think I'm owed a gift in return."

"Like what?" asks D.

"A nice long talk would be nice."

Why the hell would he wanna do that? That sounds horrible. Cella almost laughs at the twitch in his chin. He's such a man.

"We could make this easier. You could just answer a few questions."

"About?"

"You, silly."

"How many?"

"Five."

"Two."

"Four."

"Three."

"Three and three, two-part questions."

"Three and two, two-part questions."

"Deal," says Cella, as they shake hands.

Cella's not satisfied. She should've started at ten.

Chapter 24

Most of the troop's gathered in the arcade room for this last bi-monthly Deathstrike tournament, with Hank, as always, retiring early the night before a big mission. Rick is, as always, up enjoying his last night before business. Betty's tournament emcee. The tournament officially begins when all the teams are settled or eight o'clock comes, whichever comes first. Rick's stolen Rita from Dom; the other teams are D and Zach, Dede and Coren, Cealen and Camille, Emmett and Elle, and Mark and Sabrina.

Jade's current mood has everyone steering clear of her. There's no other way to say this, but Bode sucks, so Dom's not asking him. Valenda's available so that's another team. Bode's been hiding from Jade because she can be a bit of an overbearing bitch in these tournaments. Never again, he told himself after the first tournament, but as things are looking, no one else is going to be her partner now either. Why did Cella have to start shit with her today of all days? Jade smiles at him. she's a pretty woman, so that usually helps make any man do what she wants, but it only terrifies Bode. So the last team's called, and the four-time reigning champion Rick can put on his game face.

The teams gather to flip a coin to determine seeding. They face each other with one calling it in the air and repeat until there's a top four, then again for the bottom four. Rick and Rita are number one with Jade and Bode second, while Zach silently agrees with Dom to be third. D's angry until Zach nods at the bottom four seeds. Five is Dede and Coren. Coren's awful, and they'll win by default. Betty's stating the rules. Each round is ninety seconds, each team member must play at least one match per series, a concession to curb the bullying of the last three tournaments.

"Will you hurry up?" asks Rick.

"Shut up, Ricky," says Betty. "First round series are best of five. Seconds and third rounds are best of seven. If a fifth or seventh game is needed, the computer will randomly pick each side's fighter. Oh yeah, the fighter you pick will be yours for the entire tournament, excepting ace matches."

The players will be vying for Saffire's shoddy molding of a man in what must be a martial arts stance. Rick can't wait anymore. A wave of impending doom is coming, aimed at his first victim, Camille. His fighter's a well-rounded top tier Kung Fu master, great for combo linking. Camille's fighter is a mid-tier military girl with a gun, ideal for zoning.

Camille's a very nice woman, so the others don't mean to laugh, but how the hell do you lose in eighteen seconds? Seriously, the damn game's flashing *cataclysm* in neon red after a thirty-nine-hit combo while the gravelly voiced announcer yells, *Perrrrrfect,* with an echo box. Rita's next with her beefy stone monk warrior vs. Cealen's Bruce lee knock off. Rita's win is in a less *spectacular* twenty seconds. The screen says,

Speeeeectacular, in glowing blue. Cealen got chip damage on one hit that was blocked by Rita, so no perfect. Rick's already delirious with joy.

"I've never seen it go blue before. You wanna tell us something about your sex life Cealen?"

"Rick, it's your turn," says Betty, keeping her grin under control.

That last line got to Cealen. Dede wouldn't shut up about how disappointed she was.

"Fuck you, Rick," spits Cealen.

"Oh, all the other girls shut you down, huh? Why don't you try Palmala?" says Rick, moving his right fist up and down.

Cealen kicks the nearby game screaming gutturally and walks away.

"Cealen don't be like that," says Betty, losing her battle with that grin. Camille should take his place, but she's forfeiting. There're jeers, and Valenda throws paper at the quitter, but this is supposed to be fun, and these guys always take this tournament too seriously. The hell with this.

The next series is Jade and Bode vs. Mark and Sabrina. Jade's choosing the game's fastest fighter, a female with a lighting whip and a bionic arm claw. She dismantles Sabrina's wolf with an enormous forty-six-hit combo, ending the match in thirteen seconds, as *Suuuuuperstrong* lights up the screen. She's roaring as the crowd hoots. Sabrina's red, an anger tick is in the corner of her lip. Jade's flexing her bicep before chest bumping Colt.

Bode's next vs. Mark. Jade's still shit talking when the match starts, so she doesn't notice Bode's playing until seventeen seconds later, when he's raising his hands just like his character, a high-tier, self-aware shapeshifting rock.

"Yeah." Jade punches Bode hard on the shoulder. He smirks but that punch hurt.

Sabrina's quiet but Jade keeps clapping, raising her hands, imploring the audience to help Sabrina get one fucking hit this time. Normally, Sabrina wouldn't stand for this, but Jade won their last five fights and tomorrow's important.

Seventeen seconds? Again? Jade's doing a mock shirt stretch like a famous superhero, chin held high as she salutes the crowd. Sabrina couldn't get one damn hit, not one.

"Your fucking character's OP. Play with someone normal," snaps Sabrina.

Jade laughs harder so Sabrina goes apoplectic. Betty's between the two before Sabrina can try a body slam. She always thinks because Jade's twenty pounds lighter that means she can flip her. Wrestling's about leverage, and that's never been Sabrina's strong suit. No one's gonna risk hitting Betty, so Sabrina won't vault off the machine like she was planning, but that doesn't stop an astonishing array of four-letter combinations from hitting Jade. That last one about a black hole between her legs gets under Jade's skin. Cella used that on her once.

"Oh yeah," begins Jade, "well it's too bad they don't make vibrators tough enough for sandpaper."

Sabrina's eyes flash as she lets out an animal roar with spit and curses flying everywhere. Mark's tugging her back while Jade nods behind Betty.

It's the three-six match of D and Zach vs. Dede and Coren.

Zach and D play rock, paper, scissor for first dibs. Zach's facing Dede first.

The first ten seconds are close, with Zach's undertaker cyborg pressing Dede's magic elf stripper into the corner. Then, Zach's hand slips, allowing Dede to unleash a thirty-two-hit *uuuuuultracrazy* combo, ending the match. The crowd cheers. Dede's one of them, not Zach. Meanwhile D's cursing Zach's phony excuse of sweaty palms. Zach's standing up to D. D's not in his body. His goddamn hand slipped.

"Bullshit, you fucking turncoat," says D. "You did that on purpose."

Betty has to yell into the mic to get D's attention; it's his turn. Cella's smiling at D.

What is it with military men?

D's ignoring Coren's hand. These assholes ambushed him earlier and Coren's cooking sucks; fuck him and his friends.

Coren's tight-jawed now. The hell is D's problem?

It takes twenty-five seconds, but the result is a dismantling. *Perrrrrfect*, echoes across the screen again, as D's high-tier well rounded Muay Thai shaman master calls up the spirits of victory. Coren's cursing under his breath as D turns away. The fucker didn't look at him once, then kicked his ass. *What the fuck?*

Zach's about to step to the machine, but D turns back. He's not letting sweaty palms lose another match.

"It's my turn dammit," says Zach.

"Fuck you. Go get a towel, bastard," says D.

Some are laughing as Betty eagerly announces the change. "It's the battle of the D's. I was hoping I'd get the chance to say that," says Betty.

"That was awful," says Rick.

"Shut up."

"You'll take it easy on me?" says Dede softly to D.

D sniffs and the round starts. An early barrage by Dede has D backing. Her elf stripper has a high breast strike that's hard to block with its plus frames. D goes low. His shaman has weak low attacks, but he can link into a strong mid-combo and knock her into the corner. The high attacks won't work. D's blocking her mid-level attacks and parrying into high-low combos. That elfling's never had a good defense even after all these years. D ends with a tribal superflame up kick to knock her out of the screen.

"Fuck you," growls Dede.

D nods to her and walks away magnanimous.

"Better than expected?" asks Zach angrily.

"It's your turn, clammy," says D.

Zach lets off a devastating fifty-six-hit combo to end the series. "Sorry," he says to Coren.

"Kiss my ass," says Coren, smoldering. No one's ever done that to him before.

D's shaking his head as Zach comes over. Where'd that sudden talent outburst come from? Cella's off to the side, laughing at the two.

Meanwhile, Betty's begging someone to make a good series. Next series is Dom and Valenda vs. Emmett and Elle. It's clear how this will turn out. Emmett and Elle aren't patient players, and Dom loves to counter. But Emmett looks serious, so maybe that counts for something. Dom's Kung Fu werewolf annihilates Emmett's military sergeant. Emmett's sergeant is great at range but when the werewolf gets close, the sergeant has terrible defense. Valenda lets off two thirty-one-hit combos, shattering Elle's leopard cyborg with *Incrrrrredible* flashing on the screen. Elle's face gets extra mousey when she's angry, and right now she looks like an enormous squirrel.

"You sure that kick button's working?" asks Emmett

"The goddamn machine's fine. It's your turn," says Dom.

"Then why is everyone losing on this side then?"

"Because everyone on the other side's better. It's your fucking turn. Now get up here."

"There's some goddamn tomfoolery going on here?"

"Tom-what?" says Valenda. "Who uses words like that?"

"I wanna switch controls," says Emmett.

"Bullshit. Stop stalling," says Valenda.

"I knew it," says Emmett.

Dom throws his towel at Emmett. Emmett throws a middle finger back then starts screaming, "I want to switch."

Dom was going to switch but now Emmett's being a little bitch, so no. It's nearing the point that a real fight will happen, so Betty steps in. She points out that Dede won with those controls, giving Dom a point, but then asks him to switch. The classic "give a little get a little" ploy. Dom shrugs. The match starts and Emmett loses.

Ultrasick is pulsing on the screen after a fifty-two-hit combo.

Emmett's forehead is scrunching, cheeks contorting, eyes reddening. He got one fucking hit.

"The fucking machine's broken," he yells.

"Emmett, get away from the game," says Betty.

He got one fucking hit? Bullshit. Something's wrong. Why can't so-called friends understand this? He's past the point of caring about the collective groans. His cheeks are a respectable red while he rages. Elle's tapping his shoulder. Colt, Rick, and Dom are about to carry him out of the room, so best he leave with dignity. Emmett's still yelling, but getting closer to the door.

"I hope every one of your future kids suffer sudden and painful infant deaths by leprosy. You fucking cheaters."

D's no expert, but leprosy can't do that, can it?

"Only with this," says Cella. "It's just a game."

"Leprosy?" asks D.

"What?"

Kellen rushes in. Cella fills him in as Rick enters the hallway to return with a shirt with his likeness between two women licking him from head to toe.

"All right I'm ready," says Rick as Betty yells him back into the hallway before Saffire can take a closer look. The back shows a thought in bold writing:

Superiority is a fact of life. Evolution states that some are better than others. One can be athletic, another can have a high IQ, yet another can be confident. But few such as I possess all these attributes. If you are upset by my statement, it is clear you do not have any of these qualities.

"What's the problem?" asks Rick.

"Take it off" says Betty.

"Have you ever thought about us?" asks Rick.

Betty blinks, completely thrown. "No."

"No?"

Betty's getting off this topic asap. She's calling Wanda. Now with double the talking power, both women deflate Rick into taking off the shirt. Rick's not taking this lying down, so as the old hags walk back into the arcade pleased with themselves, he walks to his room, then enters the arcade with no shirt.

"Dammit Rick," says Betty.

"Not your husband lady," he says. "I did what you wanted."

He stands imperious as the crowd takes in the full glory of the oiled gray chest hairs.

"You flabby abed bastard," says Jade.

"Careful," warns Rick. "I remember when you were too young for teeth."

Dom's not ok with this. Didn't they make rules for this? Rick's body hair, at the right angle, hits the light giving him the illusion of a glowing aura. Dom's confused now. What the hell is going on? Betty's tight-jawed while Wanda stares at Rick with bulging eyes. There's no rule against going shirtless; she should've expected Rick would pull something like this. Dom and Valenda are staring at Betty, but she can only shrug. Dom mumbles something in isiZulu while refusing to look at Rick, who's sticking out his chest like the *after* picture of a bodybuilder.

This match is fast and furious with Dom taking an early life lead before Rick recovers with two eleven-hit combos, kicking Dom to the corner. Dom's adjusting using low counters on Rick's Kung Fu master. It doesn't work so well as on Emmett. Rick's character has plus frames on low attacks but it gives Dom space. It goes back and forth with bluffs and energy beams. Each blow gives Rick or Dom the life lead.

The round expires with both seeming to have the same amount of life, but Dom's werewolf turns human and howls in victory. The crowd roars as Rick temporarily loses sanity. Rick's cursing and spitting. D's never heard anyone go that long without breathing between words. It's quite impressive.

"That machine's fucking broken," yells Rick, as Jade claps purposefully in view.

"Clap all you want, you little shit. I remember when you were fat."

Rita raises her hands after an epic battle with Valenda no one was watching because of the twitch in Rick's chin. Somehow, it's jumped from the eye, forehead, then upper lip and pulses in all places every five words. D will have to find out what a *fuckshgutfitdamn* is. Probably some old people slang. He'll ignore the shiny object Jade has in her hand. That fat thing must really bother her.

Rick high fives Rita so hard his palm's imprinted on her hand. Dom's laughing hard as they reach the machine. He's speaking that Zulu shit again trying to confuse Rick. Well, fuck him.

Silence. That's the word to describe Rick's combo. "Godly" pulses in bright gold as Dom blinks at the fifty-four-hit combo. Dom can't understand.

"It's my silky smooth wrinkles, kid," says Rick smiling. "I overawed you and now the world's back in order."

Dom calls him something in Zulu.

"Your mom's from Nevada. You better curse me out in American, Dom."

"It's called English you ass," screams Dom.

With Dom cursing Rick, no one sees Cella keeping back D as Kellen accuses Zach and him of breaking the machine. Zach doesn't see why Kellen won't let this go. It's over now.

"We were thirsty," says D. "You didn't see us on the way to the kitchen?"

"What type of fucking answer is that?" yells Kellen.

Dom is refusing to play until Rick puts a shirt on while Saffire moves closer.

"Why is Rick's stomach showing a sad face?" the girl whispers.

Betty lets out a big belly laugh while Rick threatens to kick Saffire. Again, no one watches as Rita pats a frustrated Valenda after a fifty-hit combo sendoff. Rick gives Rita a shirtless bear hug as Rita reminds Valenda that emotion is the enemy in battle. Rick wants the machine to move so Dom can feel the heat of Rick's pulsating aura. Twenty-two seconds of three *massssssive* combos proves Rick right.

"Yeahhhhhhh," says Rick. "Four-one, bitch. How's it feel? I beat you like your daddy didn't." He high fives Rita. "You knew you were going to lose; don't try to make it suspenseful."

"He's cheating," says Saffire.

Rick turns, asking if Saffire wants to go a round.

"Rick, get away from the machine. Next series," says Betty.

"Just admit it," says Kellen.

"You need an enema, you jackass," says D. "Happy."

Kellen's lip starts quivering. Cella's laughing, and Zach's staring at Kellen with a smile. He has a few seconds for a comeback or D's won.

"I-you," Kellen begins.

"One slot is filled," says Betty. "Who is next, the newcomers or Princess Jade and her loyal confidant, Bode? I can't believe you made me say that."

"I love you, mommy," says Jade.

Jade and Bode discuss matchups while Rick flexes. They both think Zach's better so Bode's facing D. D's nodding in the corner while Kellen's forehead bulges with a vein, as if in great thought. Cella's almost about to fall down she's laughing so hard, and Zach's giving D a thumbs up.

"How'd you fix the motherboard so quickly?" Kellen asks.

This is a stupid question D won't answer, so Kellen better back off. Cella's laughing hysterically at Zach's shocked expression.

"Will you two hurry up?" asks Jade.

D pays no attention to Bode's outstretched hand as the match begins. Four *riiiiighteous* seventeen-hit combos later, D's back by Cella and Zach.

"How was that?" D asks.

Cella gives him a shrug. "You need to win the tournament if you wanna impress me."

"Really?" asks D.

"We high-class girls have standards," says Cella, holding her chin high.

D flicks it; she squeaks then pushes him.

"You have nice eyes," says Jade to Zach who blinks, then realizes she's in the middle of a *megaaaaaabusive* sixty-six-hit combo that is breaking his fighter apart. Another perfect for Jade.

As Jade laughs, Zach walks back to Cella asking D to calm down. She's a buffer between Zach and an ass whipping. D hasn't blinked since Jade's combo started. Cella's intrigued. Her mom told her once stripping naked will cure most men's everything.

The thought of trying that now makes her laugh.

D's moving around her suddenly.

"You gonna show him how it's done?" asks Cella.

D blinks, a good sign. "What?"

"I like winners. Remember that."

D nods after shaking his head. Cella learned when she was twelve how much a word and wink could affect a man's pride and focus. After she won that beauty pageant, she had a whole textbook of ways to make men notice her. D's more aloof than most men, but he's still a man.

D gives fourteen consecutive five-hit combos to Bode to take back to an ill-tempered Jade who has no justifiable words for Bode. Kellen, after seeing D's triumph, moves closer to the machine to give off stronger bad juju vibes.

"One fucking hit, you pussy. Don't you have any pride? No wonder Dede wouldn't give you a blowjob. Do you have a hormone imbalance? Do you need my vibrator to make the transformation complete?"

Jade keeps going, adding other insults which have Bode thinking back to when he said yes. Never again, never again.

Dede joins Cella in her wall between D and Zach. The two are refusing to look at each other.

"Are dim wits and sabotage mutually exclusive?" asks D aloud.

Zach's been quiet for over a minute. That last line about being a cuck stuffed underachiever wasn't called for. Zach slams his hand onto his thigh.

"You think you can do better?" Zach shouts." "Fine, let's switch."

D eyes Zach, nodding. It looks like respect on his face but Zach's still seething. Cella's not understanding this at all but the back and forth is fun.

Bode and Zach head to Deathstrike red-faced and determined. They shake hands and face off. It's brilliant. Zach almost has it when he launches a thirty-hit combo, but Bode yells for no reason and breaks Zach's concentration. Bode counters with a twenty-five-hit combo then Zach gets cheap. He starts zoning, throwing projectiles from a full screen away.

"Pussy," says Bode.

"Winning," says Zach.

Bode starts grunting, trying to get close, then Zach hits him with a seven-hit combo and is about to back track to zoning again but Bode anticipates this and sprints forward with a nine-hit combo, ending the match.

D is now an unnatural shade of brown verging into red, which is something to see on his dark skin. Dede and Cella are staying between him and a returning Zach. Damaged vocal cords, combined with the v-shaped vein in his forehead give D a truly demonic presence.

"I did the best I could," says Zach.

"Fuck you," says D, trying to move around Cella. If she doesn't stop, he'll pick her little ass up and move her.

Betty, closely observing, is now calling out the change.

"Can D make up for his partners ineptness?" says Betty, as Zach throws up his hands. "Sorry, facts are facts."

"Ineptness?" whispers Rick. "You better leave your college speech in your textbook."

Betty swings a slap at Rick that misses. Her heart wasn't in that one.

D wants to hurry up; there are two games to play. Betty hears him mumbling to himself. He does that a lot.

"Did you hear, ladies and gentleman? The new guy guarantees a victory." She raises her hand dramatically.

"Boo," says Rick. Betty gives him her middle finger then hears a gasp from Saffire.

Rick smiles and Betty growls. This is his damn fault.

Jade steps to the machine looking D up and down. "I didn't notice how tall you were before. Is it proportionate?"

"You do anal?" asks D.

"Excuse me?" says Jade, blinking in shock as D lands ten six-hit combos.

"Shit." She tries regrouping before D lands a twenty-seven-hit combo, stopped only by the games rendering engine.

"Fuck," shouts Jade as a calm D stands, waiting for Game 7.

Perrrrrfect blinks across the screen. Jade hasn't been held hitless since she was six when Rick regularly beat her silly. D's a lot better than she thought. The cheating bastard.

"Owe," says Jade, holding her hand.

D frowns at her gripping her pinky.

"Is your thumb ok?" asks Colt coming over.

Jade promptly grips her thumb. She needs a five-minute break. "The pain, oh the pain."

"Are you kidding?" asks D.

Jade's holding her ring finger now pleading with Betty.

"Mom, I think I might die," yells Jade, grabbing her index finger.

Betty has a decision to make. Can one truly know another's pain tolerance? Does she want her daughter to get crushed by this new guy? No and no.

"Five-minute break," rules Betty.

"Bullshit," says D.

"Stop cursing, young man," she says while Colt rubs Jade's other hand.

D shakes his head, returning to Cella.

"No one's perfect. This has gotten out of hand," says Dede.

D's pretending he can't hear while focusing on the bowl of fruit Cella's holding. She moves it away. D stretches out further, and she slaps his hand away.

"Fruit's across the hall," says Cella.

"Really?" says D, raising a brow.

Cella bats her eyes, moving closer.

"Please talk to Zach. He's really depressed right now."

D pops a grape into his mouth and nods. Cella looks down to see her vine of grapes missing. She throws a peach at him, and he catches it without looking then bites it. The jerk.

Jade's finished the longest five-minute break of all time. There's no sign of hand trouble, but Jade looks concerned. She's been trying to figure out how D countered her speed rush. The shaman has weak mid-attacks. Everyone knows that. That's why he's never picked at top-ranked fighting tournaments.

What she doesn't know is D won with this character weekly during his high school's private semi-illegal tournaments. Everyone respected D's shaman and now Jade's getting the same lesson.

He cheated, she thinks. There's no way he's better. It's the only explanation. Period.

"Feel better?" asks D.

Jade smiles, shaking her wrist. "It's tough, but I'll push through."

D grunts.

"Careful you almost smiled." says Jade.

"Trying this now. Well, the last one didn't work too well, did it?"

Jade narrows her eyes at him. That was a good line. As both icons jump across the game's thirty-nine characters, Jade bites her lip, thinking of a comeback. D tells her it's too late for a comeback. She calls him an ass, and he winks at her. He winked that's—

"Well, I didn't know robots could do that," says Jade.

"Funny," says D going grim-faced, but it doesn't seem as genuine for some reason.

D's icon lands on the least intimidating looking character in the game, "Moi Culte Merde" or simply Manôn, a French stereotype complete with a beret and striped shirt but dismal in all fight categories except maximum magic rating. He's a boss and hidden character. Which means the computer cheats all the time with that character and most humans can't play with him effectively. Jade's icon lands on her own fighter making D groan in outrage as Jade fist pumps. Colt's on her right whooping extra hard. He didn't much like the whispering these two were doing while the screen was up.

D hasn't played this character in years. It's a hard character to master, and you can lose quickly if you're not careful. However, D's always careful.

The fighting stage is a white forest D vaguely remembers. A scrambled clock shows without the announcer signaling to start. D starts doing combination experimentation while Jade frowns before realizing she can move. She goes for an all-out vicious twenty-hit combo, taking half of Manôn's life meter and unscrambling the clock with brown streaks running from where Manôn was first hit. Manôn's special moves unlock. D starts making brown bubbles. Jade comes again with a fourteen-hit combo, halving Manôn's life meter again but streaks now track onto Jade's fighter as the forest grays. After Jade's third attack, the damage to Manôn is nothing; now D throws brown ball projectiles and squats, causing tremors. Jade's fighter is pale and slowing, while the forest is turning into a toxic sludge. Manôn's faster now, moving through the muck easily.

Jade's losing life with each second. Manôn squats again, holding his stomach and vomits, trapping Jade for a moment. D's not happy. He should've used the big one. That always ends the game with this character. It's been years since he's played, so it takes time to remember the button sequence. Up, down, low punch, low punch, block, up, up, left, block, down. That sounds right.

Jade frees herself, desperately searching for a win by unleashing her most powerful combo as D pulls out a huge brown bubble. Just before releasing the bubble, Jade connects, causing the bubble to envelop Manôn, suffocating him instead.

Jade wins. That quickly, it's over.

D blinks at the screen. It's as close to slack-jawed as anyone will ever see on his face. No one understands what has happened but Jade's puffing out her chest, hands raised.

"Yeahhhh," she yells as the troop catches on seeing the victory stance of her character. D looks like a walking catatonic heading into an unlit kitchen.

He's cursing about forgetting that counter. Jade's back in the arcade, smiling as if she's a fucking right. D's in an unlit kitchen, mumbling about luck.

"You all right?" asks Zach.

"Of course I am," says D, without looking at him. "You know that character beat me twenty-eight consecutive times on suicidal mode?"

Zach hasn't said anything but D keeps going as if he asked. "My military instructors thought Deathstrike was a good teaching tool for tactics. It was a new-age learning tool. That's what General called it, anyway. The staff stopped playing us kids after we got too good."

D sees Zach's expression and realizes he's talking to himself again. D will need to resolve this habit he's fallen into. Later though; he's still on a mission.

"The maker of the game was a French Coalition defector," D explains. "Brute force only serves to bolster an idea; evasion does the same. Only at your weakest can you realize your strength and win."

Zach has a blank stare.

"You can't attack an idea head on because Coalition ideas are magic, can't stand scrutiny, which is why even the weakest can beat them. Did you notice? You can only counter Manôn right when he attacks. If you don't, you allow credibility to nonsense. I got two days off my suspension for figuring it out."

Zach still looks confused.

"You ok?" asks Cella, leaning against the doorframe.

She didn't know that last bit. Who knew games had propaganda elements to them?

"I want a rematch," says D.

"I know," says Cella. "Come see who wins."

"I don't care."

"You can't spend all your time on something then not care who wins. It's not normal."

"Fuck normal."

"Please?" asks Cella, pouting those luscious lips.

D's no match for those, and the dimples kind of double team him.

"I still don't care who wins."

As they return to the arcade, they find Kellen clapping something about justice. He's apparently been doing this since D lost. Rick's got a punch out stance ready, and Jade's whispering about how she's going to kick his dick any second now.

"Kellen," blurts Betty, pointing him away from the game before continuing. "Which of the two remaining teams will win this beautiful trophy?" She points to it after shoeing Saffire away from the peeling leg muscle paint.

Saffire wanted to try molding but maybe drawing it would have been better. Betty said it looked very nice. But she might have been lying.

"Saffire, I said get away," says Betty.

"But the head's all wobbly."

"The head's fine. Get away."

Saffire shambles over to her seat.

"May the best team win," says Betty with fake host smile plastered to her face.

Jade is keeping away while mouthing, "You can do it," to Bode until Rita lands a fifty-six-hit combo to go up one to zero.

"You can't do shit," says Jade.

Bode's looking down while Rick laughs, high-fiving Rita. They flex while the crowd boos.

Rick goes stone faced, giving Jade the thousand-yard stare. She's trying her best to keep a straight face while Colt starts puffing out his chest, telling Rick to mind his manners. Rick's giving him obscene gestures while shouting what a real man is.

"Hold me back. Hold me back," shouts Colt, while Rick slaps his chest.

She fails. Jade's howling with laughter as Rick curls some of his gray chest hairs. In high school, Jade was the starting shooting guard for the Monmouth High Bruisers, averaging 18.8 per game against the hated rival Mercer High Wolverines. It was for the state championship and the whole family came to support. Jade's counterpart was a six foot four inch beast of a woman with five D1 scholarship offers. Jade was not. In girls' basketball, someone as big as the beast plays center or power forward. Why the shit was she playing shooting guard? That was just bullshit. At halftime, the Bruisers were down 47-19. Coach was not happy with Jade.

"You gave up thirty-one points in one half, girl? Get a damn grip. How'd you let her take you to the hole five straight times? You gotta foul. Let her know you're there."

Jade already had three fouls. Two more and she'd be disqualified. Things were looking bad. Her family was there. Hank thought a girl that big should be on the front lines. Betty wanted to kick the other girl's ass. No one left her daughter scoreless. Rick was the only one willing to do what was necessary.

There were tables with cardboard signs reading what you could buy for a dollar from the students behind the desks. While Hank and Betty were undecided on sour candy or chocolate bars, Rick went to his car. Hank gave him a questioning look, but Rick just shook his head. When halftime was over, Rick didn't sit with Hank and Betty. He sat next to the family of that gargantuan woman. Hank had a feeling what was going to happen and was about to stop it, but for a change, Betty was hoping Rick would do something outrageous.

The beast drove right past Jade again, looking to score, but Jade all but clotheslined her. She looked like she was about to cry. Maybe Green Beret training helped, but Rick always was able to come through in the clutch. Timing was everything. The beast took her time going to the line. She smiled at her mom and dad. Just as she was about to shoot, Rick held his stomach, smiling and turning ever so slightly, and aims his mouth for the mom's ear and vomits.

This wasn't some trivial vomit. Rick made sure he ate something spicy before drinking the ipecac. The mom shrieked in outrage and disgust. The dad had no idea what was going on. He guessed quickly and yanked the mom away with pure disgust on his face. The dad wanted to punch Rick and was damn close until Rick vomited again, right into his mouth. To this day, Rick's never heard a man yell, curse, cry, gag, yelp, and twitch all at once. It was most satisfying.

Security came just as disgusted demanding Rick left. The parents were shrieking, gagging, and spitting out Rick's vomit all the way out of the building. Well, the beast saw all this and was completely distracted. Rick heard after that the beast seemed disengaged for the rest of the game. It was a huge comeback. The Bruisers ended the game on a 26-3 run, winning 75-73. Jade hit the go-ahead free throws. She ended with twenty points and dominated that second half.

Jade left the building holding her tournament MVP trophy. She saw the beast crying with her irate parents outside while Rick was shouting back at them. Two officers shoved him into the cop car. Rick's connections and the fact that not being able to aim bodily fluid away from someone is not a crime, meant Rick got out in a day with no charges. Sure, the parents threatened action, but after a quick overview of Rick's background, they thought better of it. The next day, Jade gave Rick the biggest kiss on the cheek. Not everyone has people willing to help them like that.

"You're adopted," Rick says,

Jade breaks a smile at the limitless tactics of this man she has known forever.

"I'm giving you one last chance to forfeit," says Rick.

Rick starts with a salvo of energy beams that Jade dodges. The two are now trading taunts while trading combos until Rick finds Jade pouncing on another of his bluff charges, and with an *ultracombo*, she knocks Rick into and out of all four walls of the fighting stage, tying the series at one. The crowd cheers while Rick's bottom lip quivers violently. These people are pathetic. That last move was clearly a fluke.

"A fluke," Rick says aloud, adding curses for some of the louder people. "You little brat," he says to Jade. "I don't give a shit about you, this game, or anyone associated with you."

Rita's nodding while pulling Rick away.

"You want some too?" says Rick to Saffire, who's screaming with her hands in the air.

Betty stands between the two before shouting at Bode and Rita to come forward.

Bode jumps on Rita with four massive combos in twenty-nine seconds, giving his team a two-one lead.

"Now, I know you're cheating," says Rick.

Jade shouts at him to stop whining as D steps out.

"Where are you going?" asks Cella in the hall.

"Bathroom, Ms. Nosey," says D. "Do I need your permission?"

"Yes."

D sucks his teeth and keeps walking.

"Hurry up." she says.

D waves at her without turning back.

#

"But this shit's gonna stop now, big mouth," says Rick as Jade scowls.

The match begins and ends quickly. Rick is genuinely surprised. This is a rare event, in fact one might say unheard of, Jade executes a forty-nine-hit supreme combo, finishing a perfect match where he gets not one hit. Down three-one. Highly irregular.

"Yeahhhhhh," says Jade, flexing her biceps.

Rick is in a frightening state of perplexity. Betty pauses to see if he's in full control of himself while Saffire jumps and cheers behind her. Jade's warning Bode not to mess this up for her before walking over for a kiss from Colt. As Jade cuddles up for more kisses, the crowd hushes. She snaps her head back to see Rita in the midst of a seventy-four-hit supernatural combo. Just like that, it's three-two in just thirteen seconds. Saffire is yelling for someone to do something. Rita is cheating too.

Rita was saving that combo. This character can't link like that. Jade has to admit that was impressive, and worst of all, it has Rick rising up, filled with old man aura. Bode's sheer incompetence is going to get him shot one of these days.

"All you need is one more win," says Rick, pulsating with his trademark silver-haired confidence.

With anyone else in this position, Betty would have some lame emcee catch phrase to get a contrived reaction from the crowd. However, she, like everyone else, senses the change in momentum, and this is her daughter, so there's no need to add to it. Jade gets a squeeze from Colt before heading to the game.

"Don't drag your feet, girl. Get up here," says Rick.

Jade's biding her time, but Rick is raising his hands, welcoming the boos. He swells up again as Jade reaches the game then glares down his nose at her. She would laugh if she weren't so upset with Bode. She refuses to look at Rick's chest hair as the match starts.

Rick comes quick with energy beams and follows with combos. Jade blocks and dodges for the first ten seconds. This damn character is relentless. She could never figure out how Rick links combos this way. She can't get a flow going. She's not a defensive fighter; she likes to do what Rick's doing to her right now, and it's fucking annoying.

She tries to force the issue, but it doesn't work. Rick hits her with a twenty-hit combo before she backs away. It's another five seconds before Jade tries again, and again is hit with a twenty-hit combo.

"Shit," she says.

She tries to sidestep Rick's next attack, but he's ready and give's her another twenty-hit combo. Jade curses again and tries some low attacks and takes the last twenty-hit combo, ending the match. The series is tied at three.

"All you need is one more," shouts Rick, beating his chest. He scowls at the crowd, giving his ugliest war face.

"We're taking a ten-minute break," says a disgruntled Betty, with Saffire shouting that Rick is cheating.

Rick's doing body building poses while Rita claps.

"Make it fifteen. It won't matter. You all know who's winning." says Rick.

D's back in the arcade with chalky knuckles. Cella frowns at him.

"How flexible are you?" asks D.

"Why?" asks Cella.

D gives her a salacious look that has her smiling and moving closer.

"Your hand ok?" she asks, gliding a finger over his chest.

"Just getting all my tools ready for later. You like variety?"

Cella has a big grin at that. "Look here, mister. You might be the type who gets your way, but you're going to work to satisfy me."

"I've heard that before. It's usually the other way around after an hour."

"Is that so?"

"Yes," he says, refusing to look away.

Cella loves a man with confidence. She has to admit, military men have a bluntness and controlled violence most regular guys are missing. It's a maturity in their skills and willingness to be aggressive if necessary. It's erotic. She likes it.

"We'll see," she says, pressed against him.

Outside, Jade's furious. That felt like when Rick beat her senseless as a kid. She couldn't do anything against that goddamn Kung Fu asshole. Colt gives her a peck on the cheek as she frowns.

"I don't know how he did that," she says. "I only got four fucking hits. Bullshit."

"You lost because you lost patience," says Colt. "He pressed you, and you played into his hands. It's like I told you about your shooting. Same principle applies."

She glares at him. She didn't want good advice; she wanted to hear Rick's a cheating jackass.

"Don't look at me like that," says Colt.

"Like what?"

"Like being a good drone is all I should think of."

Jade blinks at that.

"I didn't say that. I wasn't even thinking-"

Rick walks into the hall then backs into the arcade as he sees the two about to argue.

"What is it, Rick?" asks Colt, not turning around.

"It can wait," says Rick.

"No, it can't. I'm leaving," says Colt, brushing away Jade's hand as he walks to their room.

Jade's blinking at Colt. It's a full minute before Rick speaks.

"I want to up the stakes," he says. "You have to wear one of my shirts if I win. It's a new one. You'll like it."

"What do I get if I win?"

"You won't but if the impossible happens, I'll admit you're not adopted," says Rick.

"You're such a dick," says Jade as Rick warns her to watch her tone, and Jade has it. "Yeah, if I win, you have to wear a dildo on your forehead."

Rick blinks. "What the-what?" Rick's brow is wrinkled hard. How'd he get into this? "There's no reason for this disgusting proposition. Does your mother know you have these types of toys?"

"Leave mom out of this," says Jade.

"Colt not fulfilling his obligations?"

"He's doing plenty, you jackass. Deal or no?"

"I'm gonna tell your daddy."

Jade rolls her eyes.

"So, do you want a small or medium?" They shake hands.

Saffire's close to the trophy again.

"Do you really think it's nice?" she asks Betty again.

"You keep asking, expecting a different answer. I said what I said," says Betty.

"You said I shouldn't lie."

"You shouldn't."

"So why are you?"

Betty blinks at her. "You wanna go to bed early? Keep at it, little girl."

Saffire huffs but backs down.

"Mom, make him put it back on," says Jade.

"Not hurting anyone," says Rick, poking a disgusted Jade.

Betty's hiding her grin. Rick's oiled his chest again.

"Hurry up and get to the screen," she says. Jade's slapping away another poke as the icons jump. Once the icons stop, both Rick and Jade frown. The icons have stopped on each other's main characters. What are the odds?

Betty steals another famous line and yells for everyone to rumble. Both are trading basic four-hit combos because they don't know each other's character combos. Suddenly, Jade takes the momentum with three four-hit combos. Rick, feeling the shift, breaks off to buy time and experiment with combos. He may have something, but Jade's on him now but makes disjointed moves, forgetting this isn't her fighter.

Rick comes with more three-hit combos before inexplicably yelling, causing Jade to flinch. A few seconds pass, and Rick slaps his side of the controls, causing another flinch by Jade. Then Rick smiles. He's played this game for years with every fighter. He remembers one of her combos. He waits and she comes. It'll hurt to do this to his Kung Fu but not that much. He unleashes a twenty-seven-hit combo, taking the match and series.

"Yeahhhhhhh," Rick yells as Rita comes to start a synchronized handshake formed for the eventuality of their win. Now is a song to commemorate this glorious victory.

I am the only man, you dogs. And I will defeat thee, oh yessss. I am the only man. I am the only man. Kiss my ass because you lost. I am the only man. You are a loser. You lost, I won, you lost, I won, you losssst, I wonnnnnn. Thank you, thank you," he sings to boos.

"What the hell are you singing?" asks Valenda.

"It's inspired by old rock, losers."

"Ok, Rick," shouts a dejected Betty.

Jade's frowning in the corner while Bode stands at the machine repeating, "We were just up three-one." He's not too happy with Jade's behavior during the tournament so hasn't come within ten feet of her since she lost Game 6.

Jade was expecting him to give her a pat on the back, but he's all but ignoring her now. What's his problem?

For Bode's part, it's nice to see she blew this lead, not him. He knew he shouldn't have teamed with her.

Kellen's still saying to anyone in hearing distance that D and Zach broke the machine.

"I don't give a shit, Kellen. Shut up," says Dom.

Betty is in a hurry to finish this trophy ceremony while Saffire is bitterly upset at what rules make it ok to scream people into mistakes. This is cheating. Rick and Rita are smiling in their extended route to Betty. She's scowling while congratulating both, but Rick doesn't think it's genuine.

"I'd like to speak," says Rick, taking the mic from Betty. "Yes, our complete and utter domination of the field was expected, but it is not complete. To my lovely goddaughter Jade, for not knowing to always concentrate no matter the disturbance, I must say thank you and collect my debt." Rita hands him a folded gray shirt while Jade is ungraciously walking to him. "I got a medium just to be safe," he whispers.

Jade smiles a predatory smile while taking the shirt. She unfolds the shirt to see Rick's likeness bracketed by two women with huge breasts and big asses, polishing Rick's nether regions.

"You are a disgusting old man," says Jade with an edge of laughter while Betty shields Saffire from a closer view.

Betty's trying to get herself angry enough to not laugh but this is ridiculous. How many times has Rick done something like this?

Colt's back in the arcade. He can't find his shirt. He can't sleep without his shirt, and Jade loves moving his things around so now he can't sleep. He sees the shirt and smiles at the picture. Jade turns it around at Rita's suggestion.

"Perfection is discipline in the face of obscurity, where fear and doubt meet their true master. I am perfection; I conquer all."

"It's going to look great on you," says Rita.

Jade puts on the shirt, making Rick beam before pulling her into a big bear hug. Jade's laughing as Rick holds her up for Rita to take pictures. Jade pushes off her godfather, refusing to smile now. Betty's concluding the night as Jade finally notices Colt leaning at the door. Colt motions her over.

"It looks good on you," he says.

"Haha."

Saffire's able to see the shirt. What are those cartoons doing?

And what the heck does that thing on the back mean?

"All right to bed," says Betty.

"Why?" asks Saffire.

"Little girl, we're not doing this."

"I wanna help clean up."

"No you don't. Go to bed."

Chapter 25

The troops are planning to enjoy the rest of the night. At least half are planning on sex. The other half wants sleep so they can have more energy for tomorrow. Zach's smiling stupidly while following Dede to her room. Elle has a vice grip on Emmett's arm. She locks the door before Cella has a chance to get there. Too many times Cella would be the one to lock out Elle when Creighton wanted some comforting. Betty's going to wake up Hank while Rick's doing his best silver-haired devil routine on Wanda.

"I can't. Who's watching Saffire?" asks Wanda. He banged on her door, waking Wanda up to see an angry Saffire.

"I've got earmuffs, blindfolds, and p.m. cough syrup," says Rick. "She'll never know."

"Gimme some more poetry," Wanda says smiling.

"Your eyes speared my lust for other women."

Wanda laughs as Rick escorts her to his room.

Cella wasn't planning on this, but there's nothing for it. D's coming to the lab; its soundproof, and D's room looks like a warzone. Computers log off while D makes himself comfortable on the stretcher. The irony's not lost on either of them.

"That thing of yours play music?" asks Cella.

D has a sixties love music playlist ready; women seem to respond well to that music. Sure enough, Cella's humming to the songs while sensually walking to the freezer. She pulls out some lube she made, tossing it to D.

"What?" she asks, seeing D's look.

D just shakes his head as she teases him by slowing pulling off her shirt then pants, showing more of her magnificent hourglass shape.

"All right, Marine," D mumbles to himself. "Don't get too excited. See your goal and break through it."

"What?" asks Cella, showing off her lacey bra and panties.

She wraps her hair into a bun before stretching. D didn't know when he took his sweater off, but he is now showing broad, scarred, muscled shoulders. Cella nods in approval. She doesn't run as much as she does to sleep with a jiggly slob. Cella's not sure when, but one second D's on the gurney admiring her body and the next they're kissing.

D's good, excellent, extraordinary. How many women has he kissed to be this good? Any other questions fade as her legs weaken. He's damn good at kissing. The door clanks open.

"Get out," Cella snaps, pulling D closer for more.

Jade's smiling. All she wanted was that lube. There were like five bottles in there last she checked but this is interesting. She could ruin this for Cella, but no. Cella might walk into her room and stand in front of Colt naked. She swore she'd do that if Jade told Creighton that Cella thought her first love was better in bed.

Best not to risk it.

"I just want the lube," says Jade, raising her hands, palms open.

Cella nods her to the freezer, her cold eyes tracking Jade, who is taking her time. Jade thinks, That D is built and those scars— well it's fun to fantasize. Jade wanted that fruit flavored one but Cella has that, so she'll settle for arctic breeze.

"Thanks," says Jade with a big obnoxious smile.

Cella looks at the door then back to Jade.

"Sorry about that," says Cella as the door closes.

"You taste like peaches," says D.

"Peaches? You sure? Check again."

D's checking—first her neck, making her giggle, then her ear and collarbone. Cella's surrendering. She was a little worried D was all looks but no. He knows what he's doing, and she's about to explode any minute. He's working on her nipples now. It's been months since she's let a man touch her. Too long. She's not sure when he got his hand down there to start rubbing her other lips, but in a flash she's having spasms.

"Stop, stop, stop," says Cella, panting.

"That was quick," says D. "You a one-minute girl?"

"Shut up," she says, half-laughing.

"Want me to do it again?"

Cella spreads her legs and D goes to work.

Most people think sex is some mystical fantasy that should be treated like second-century Bronze Age artifacts. Ridiculous. His early life on the street showed him how people treated sex. General talked about how to see sex responsibly. Being an intel expert showed D the power of information. In sex, mechanics is crucial, and D knows proper motion. When he thrusts left or right it causes friction. Women love friction, but the trick is to go at a rhythm. Like all art, this takes time to learn, but after forty tries, even a fool should get the gist of it. However, D is a man who likes to perfect every new skill he learns. So when he thrusts to the left and Cella yells, "Oh god," he keeps doing it. Every woman's different, so one spot might not work as well as another. This is why he takes his time to find out where he should thrust for maximum impact. Cella's got one shallow spot and another deeper inside.

"Ahhhaauughhh." screams Cella, digging her nails into D's chest.

D likes that sound. It's not hard to find out if a woman likes it. She's gushing all over him. D barely needs the lube. Her legs are twitching, she's sweating, and her eyes are dilating. Women are good actors, but certain bodily movements can't be faked.

"Oh god. Oh, oh, what, oh, dammit. Oh god."

Most men get too excited when they're doing this to a woman. They want to go faster, but you have to be consistent. Train your most valued partner to behave himself and maintain the rhythm. Most sex only last between three to seven minutes. Fifteen minutes of sustained pounding will blow away most women, especially since most people aren't that good in bed. D likes to go for between twenty and forty minutes. If he's with a true sex goddess, then he'll need to stretch for two to three hours, but those women are rare.

Cella's average in D's experience. Most pretty women don't get the shit fucked out of them, so when they meet a man who knows what he's doing, he turns into a valued asset. But there's a danger. The woman might get attached. For that reason, D's not going to try to find all Cella's spots and fuck her to oblivion. He's made that mistake before. He's just going to fuck her real good so she's happy before they leave tomorrow. It's the responsible thing to do, and Cella's too damn pretty for any less. Women love to talk, so he wants a good review when she tells the other women.

"You—oh, uh, uh, uh. Keep going. Keep going. Yes, I love it. Do it, do it," she screams.

Cella doesn't have many thoughts at the moment; unless you want to count "whoa" and "ahhrrah" as coherent thoughts. She was hoping but really wasn't expecting this. Faolan was the only man who could make her drool during an orgasm. D's relentless.

This is a great day. She's floating.

"Crap," she says, landing on her shoulder.

D fucked her off the gurney. She loves men.

He's pulling her back onto the gurney as the door opens.

"What?" says Cella, eyes flashing. She snatches D's sweater to cover herself.

Dede is holding out Zach's arm, showing a softball-sized bruise.

"It's nothing," says D. "Put some ice on it and get out."

Zach's groaning. He thinks the arm's broken. Neither D nor Cella could give a shit.

"Get out," says Cella.

D's looking for his pants. If he doesn't throw Zach out quickly, it could ruin the mood for Cella. Women always need certain conditions to keep going. They're weird like that.

"Cella, I'm really sorry about this, but I think I broke it. He can't leave tomorrow with a broken arm," says Dede.

Zach yelps as a shirtless D drags him to the door. Zach noticed but didn't quite realize how strong D is. He's never been thrown up steps before, let alone with one hand. It's emasculating, and he landed on the hurt arm.

D's eyeing Dede now, asking Cella with a glance if he can toss her intrusive ass out too.

"Cella, come on, it'll take you five minutes to fix then you can go back to doing whatever you were doing."

"D," says Cella.

Dede's yelling, slapping D's back as he tosses her atop Zach and closes the door. Cella's pushing the nearest table across the door after locking it. D yanks her to him and throws her back on the gurney.

"Bite my neck again," she says.

#

Cella has an all too familiar afterglow to go with a silly grin. It was only supposed to be twenty minutes, but D felt another forty minutes was needed to make her forget what that jackass Zach tried to pull. He thinks it worked. He also ate her out to make sure she forgot everything else.

"So, you do have to watch out for the quiet types," she says, half-laughing.

Her hair's a mess, she's drenched in sweat, and she's still creaming between her legs, but dammit she looks gorgeous. Her flat stomach and toned legs are heaving and twitching; her nipples are still erect. All good signs.

"You ok, or you want another round?" says D.

"You're not tired?"

D's slightly winded, but Cella's average, so it didn't take much energy to give her an orgasm.

"Jarheads are built to last. No one told you?"

She giggles. "I'm done. Thanks. I really needed that."

"No problem."

He pecks her on the cheek, and she holds the back of his head then starts kissing him again.

"You staying here, right? There's nothing upstairs," she says, eyeing him with those brown hazelnut eyes.

"I thought you were done."

"Well, I might change my mind later. And maybe I like to cuddle a bit. It's our last night here after all."

D stops himself from groaning. He doesn't get the whole cuddling thing; it just doesn't make sense.

"Let me clean up then."

"Put this back first." She hands him the lube. "Combination's A489G3."
There's no way D's letting this stay here. He pockets the other three lubes and some other things.
"You like handcuffs?" he asks.
"Hurry up and come back." she laughs.

Chapter 26

D hates cuddling, but he has to admit Cella's a gamer. After he came back, she was ready for another thirty minutes. He didn't think she could ride like that, but maybe she just needed to warm up. A lot of people are like that. The good thing is, she's finally asleep. He had to find another one of her spots and grind away for five straight minutes before she passed out. He probably shouldn't have done that, but he's a competitor at heart, and she has pretty good riding skills. He was winning this fight, and that's that.

He's careful as he maneuvers his body from under hers. She drools a lot. He wouldn't have expected that. If she survives tomorrow, he'll need the recipe for that lube. That stuff is excellent.

"Shit," he says once in the hall. He's stumbled over a bat in the pitch-black hall.

Well, it looks like Zach and Dede found a way. D knew Zach was faking. There's loud slamming on Door 9. A woman's voice is screaming, "I love you Colt," and a man's voice is saying, "Fucking take it." There are women and men in Doors 8, 11, and 5, cursing about who's momma or daddy and how long they can go.

All the things in D's bag are still in the right places. He's got enough to leave tomorrow but he'd like some more tourniquets. That's why he's heading to the gym. There was leftover rubber workout bands there. Two of those could work.

Six of the gym's overhead lights make a straight line above the boxing ring. There's a man punching a heavy bag at the end of the hall. Ambient light shows half his face. It's a fat face. No reason to deal with this now. Who's going to object wanting rubber if he goes later when everyone's awake? He'll go back to Cella, wake her up, and fuck her some more.

"Where you going?" asks Bruce. "I could use a partner," he says, fading and reappearing as he steps toward the ring with two pairs of gloves.

"Bye," says D, turning to leave.

"Scared?"

"No, my legs are a bit weak is all."

D turns, catching the twitch in Bruce's face just in time.

"I was checking the count in the armory. It's off. Is that where you went after you lost in the tournament?"

"She's really athletic. I went to do some stretching."

"Fuck you."

"That's just about what she did."

Bruce is visibly calming himself. He really wonders why Cella's not interested.

"I know you," says Bruce.

D stares, waiting. He's damn sure he's never seen Bruce's face before.

"My boss wanted to hire you. I was one of the people in charge of dossier compilation. I know what type of person you are.

"You're a merc?" says D.

"Was. That type of thing doesn't matter anymore."

"Corliss Bedingfield of Red Wall, Inc.? No, he goes almost exclusively for retired Navy Seals. Boris McMichael's of Tsunami Borders. No, he was Marine and Navy Seals only. You and Colt are Army. Sampson Coaldagger of the Thunder Clap Crop. That was like three years ago."

"I know your body count. Most confirmed kills on a battlefield. 1k men are dangerous. They don't act like regular people."

"I'm getting a morality lesson from a merc? Only thing that makes you different from a whore is whores get you off when they're fucking you."

"You were pretty famous in our circles. Guys like you always leave early. Spend more time with the family once you finally pop. I read about you almost ripping off your CO's head then slaughtering town villagers.

"You don't know a fucking thing. The entire reason I punched him was to—" D stops himself. He doesn't have to defend his actions to anyone. "If you know I am who I say why'd you let Hank attack me?"

"Because you deserved it. I know better than anyone here how hard it is out there. You walk in looking like you barely walked a mile. There's no way you can be as stable as you're pretending to be. You're dangerous and we'd do better without you."

"How many times did you say that speech before you actually believed it?"

"I'm willing to show you out now, right now with as many guns and ammo as you can carry. The route we showed was for a large group to travel. There're smaller ones that lead to real nice secluded zones. No brogs, other people. You can lose us there and just go on your way. Leave us alone or I'll be forced to do what Hank won't. He thinks your interests align. He doesn't know people like you only have one interest. What's best for you and worse for everyone else. Just leave us."

"There is no *us* with you fat face, and there was never a chance for one either. You need to accept that and move on."

Bruce throws something shiny at D. It's hard to see as it fades in the light, but D catches it and charges Bruce. Bruce tries side stepping, but D's prepared and presses the attack. Bruce pulls another knife from his back, slashing wildly to keep D back. Bruce falls from the force of his wild swing, as D, face like an irate animal, bears down.

Bruce tries another wild swing to give himself time to roll back to his feet but D judges the arc of the swing and grips the hand as it passes D's face. Body mechanics won't allow Bruce to stop his swing midway, so his arm's trapped across his own body. D's grip is so strong Bruce's pinky literally pops off. D registers Bruce's artificial finger rolling out of the light before setting up the kill shot. D stabs with no hesitation. The blade punctures the mat where Bruce's eye was just a millisecond before. D pulls the knife out and plunges down, but Bruce's other arm catches D's forearm, so now D's slowly but inevitably moving his arm down. Then, he really sees Bruce.

Bruce is terrified. He's got a vein popping out of his neck, trying to stop D. D's made too many men look like that.

What are you doing? D says to himself.

An iron grip has D's hand, and it's prying loose the knife. D lets go and is slammed to the ground face first, right arm twisted behind him. Bruce stomps on the left one, and D feels the base knuckles on his index and middle finger dislocate. He just fixed those three weeks ago, and they pop out again.

Bruce feels the dislocation too so grinds his boots into the hand. D doesn't react outwardly. He tries to ignore pain. Bruce lifts his legs and stomps down one more time, breaking D's ring finger. There's an audible crunch for that, so Bruce is satisfied.

"Told you," says Bruce.

"I know," says Hank.

Chapter 27

Of course he was baiting you. You idiot, D tells himself. *How many times did General tell you to control your reactions, watch that temper?* This is just like when he broke that kid's face in eighth grade and General made D fight him to make a point.

"Just because someone's trying to hit you doesn't mean you need to kill them." General said. "You can break an arm. Force a submission, or, and here's my favorite, you cannot get into the fight in the first place." General gave D boxing gloves. Then started the bell. He knocked D senseless with a jab right cross combo thirty seconds into the round then made him get up to finish the round. General knocked him down four more times that round. D had blood pouring from his nose and two swollen eyes. "Becoming a man means knowing when to fight and when a fight's just not worth it, son. Now try again."

D smiles at the memory. *Is that old man still alive?*

"I don't know why you're smiling. We're fucked because of you," says Zach ten feet away, handcuffed to the other post of the boxing ring nearest the wall. "I was fucking her good. You know how long it's been since I've seen a woman squirt? She was letting the water out. Then Bruce comes in and pulls me right off. I'm fucking naked and he just yanks me off. No fucking decency because you've confessed to—"

"I heard you the first twenty times, Zach. You can shut up now."

"Why would you try to kill him now, now of all the times."

"I told you. I lost my head."

"You were supposed to be losing it inside Cella."

"She was asleep."

"So you try to murder someone?"

"I didn't—oh fuck it."

"Are they going to interrogate us again?"

"No, if they think we were lying to them the first time then nothing we say now will convince them. They'll make a decision then we'll find out what they'll do to us."

D can feel Zach's scowl. He's had that damn scowl on since Bruce handcuffed him to the post. The fat face idiot smiling like a triumphant ass. Cella was still asleep when he went to check on her. He looked like he wanted to stab D in the chest. Cella only had D's sweater layered over her when D left. He hopes Bruce smelled the sex in the air when he walked in, the desperate piece of shit.

"You're fucking kidding," says Colt, looking at D then Bruce.

"He tried to kill you but you beat him."

Colt pats Bruce on the back then walks to D, lights flickering on as he approaches. He punches D right on the bridge of the nose. D's head bangs against the post, making his ears ring as his eyes blur.

"That's for my eye, you fucking punk," says Colt.

#

"He comes to the war room and says, "Look, General, I can prove it," says Hank to Betty and Rick, also eating at the breakfast table. "The count's off. Someone took two guns and three 9millimeter magazines last night. It was him. If we don't deal with him now, this will mean disaster when we leave tomorrow."

"Do the count yourself. If I'm right, he might come to the gym or kitchen later to see if there's something else he could steal. Just watch him." Hank shakes his head. "Me, I'm thinking the way Cella was looking at him tonight there's no way in hell she's letting him out of her sight. But sure enough three hours later, D's creeping out the lab. He goes to his room first then heads for the gym. I stay back, checking if he took anything. I find two 9-mm pistols in the drawer and three magazines stuffed inside the bull eyes he carved into the wall a few nights back. That's it. He's a thief and probably just as dangerous as Bruce says. I creep down to the gym and see him trying his best to dig out Bruce's skull."

"So do we kill him?" asks Rick. "We probably should."

#

"All I know is he's grinding away and Bruce comes in and yanks him off me. I'm like, What the fuck? Get out. And he's all like, 'This is for your protection. Stay inside. We have to check for Harbour's people.' I'm about ready to jump on him and kick his ass and drag Zach back into bed, but then I see your dad there, and he says, 'Get back in your room.' So I get back in the room. And lock the door," says Dede, eating her bacon strip.

"But I thought they decided he wasn't with Dax's group," says Jade holding a cup of orange juice, half of it spilled over the dining hall table.

"Bruce said he was stealing supplies to bring out to them. Now, they're going to decide to execute both or leave them here to starve," says Rita.

"No, Rick will want some answers first," says Dom.

"You really think they'll believe anything those two say after they were so convincing the first time?" asks Bode.

"No, Rick and Hank are deciding between execution and exile or in this case leaving them here. He won't risk Dax's people jeopardizing our plans."

Cella comes up the steps, humming in satisfaction. There's a glow about her, the women and a few of the savvier men notice. She waves at everyone then sits down with a broad grin.

"Hank is keeping me out the kitchen. They're having a meeting." Cella smiles while helping herself to bacon. "So did everyone else have a good night?"

The others look at her. Dede doesn't want to bring down her mood, especially after almost ruining it, but Jade has a predatory grin on her face.

"There's been a development," says Jade, leaning in.

#

"Look at the route that's flooded. It almost covers our route exactly. He knew. And now he's here to drive us right into Dax's arms," says Bruce.

"Then, it's simple," says Rick. "We execute him. We can't risk him figuring a way out then telling Dax's people where we are. After all, this time they'd rip us limb from limb and smile while doing it."

"Are you sure this is him?" Colt asks Bruce again.

"I spent two months of my life and a whole lot of favors making an accurate dossier for Mr. Coledagger. I know him. It's Dice."

The men shift uncomfortably around the table.

"Honey, why don't I know him?" asks Betty.

"I'm sure I mentioned him a couple of times. Has the kill records for every theater of war he's fought in. Second longest kill shot in history. Best shot anyone's seen in the armed forces."

"You never gave a name."

"Dice isn't a name more than a statement. A coalition enemy hears that, they shit their pants."

"Well from what you've told me and what I've observed in this young man, something seems off. If he's the man you say he is and he was clever enough to last eighteen months out there with brogs crawling around, why wouldn't he have been smarter at stealing guns?"

"I don't know why. Story is he cracked two years ago, tried to kill his CO then mowed down a village of seven hundred in the Amazon by himself."

"He's too dangerous," says Rick. "I say kill him."

"Wait, the man you're talking about teamed up with Harbour Dax?" says Betty. "Harbour was a fine person and like it or not, he knew how to get people to follow him. But he's not in my husband's league on the leadership front, and D chose to follow him? He barely tolerates you, honey," says Betty.

"If Harbour poisoned him against me that could explain it. Three days just isn't long enough to change someone's mind," says Hank.

"You were convinced he didn't know who Dax was."

"He wouldn't be who he is if he wasn't a good liar."

"Kill him," says Bruce.

"That's three," says Colt, raising his hand.

"We're military, Colt. We protect democracy. We don't practice it," says Hank waving Colt's hand down before rising. "Let's look at this from his perspective. If I ran into Dax's people, just been forced out of the only safe places for hundreds of miles, what would I think? Dax tells me a mad man forced us out, killed thirty of us, used chlorine gas. Stole all the women and left us to die in exile. What would I think?"

"That's not what happened," says Rick. "I told Cella to make chlorine gas to minimize casualties."

"And how would I know that unless I was there to see it?"

Hank looks at Betty. She's shaking her head.

"You were wrong before, wife," says Hank. "You said let them leave. How can they survive out there? No meat, no fruit, no air, no sunlight. If starvation doesn't kill them, then they'll go insane from the lack of sun. They're still our people. There's been enough blood. Please don't do this. You remember that, Betty?"

"How is any of that D's fault? If—"

Hank raises a hand and Betty stops. The others have never seen Betty show deference like that to Hank.

"I've made my decision," says Hank.

#

D's trying to feel at his left arm while Zach keeps cursing.

"Eighteen months," Zach mumbles. "I survive eighteen months and I'm going to die at the corner of a boxing ring tied to a fucking ring post. This is bullshit. Bullshit."

The door opens and Hank stands there flanked by Betty, Rick, Colt, and Bruce, all with severe expressions. The rest of the troop file in after them.

D has a mental sigh. Well, he tried his best. Maybe someone else can get to Three Mile.

"Major, otherwise known as Dice." Begins Hank. "Decorated war vet, owner of two medals of honor, five purple hearts, nineteen battlefield commendations, given such names as Wolf of Buckingham, Dragon of the Devil's horn, Black Tiger of Versailles, and one of, if not the, best riflemen in the history of our republic. We thank you for your service. However, it has come to our attention that you are a known party member of a traitorous group of rebels led by the exiled Harbour Dax. The evidence shows that you willingly infiltrated and sought to sabotage and kill members of this community and ruin our journey to Three-Mile Island. For this, there must be a price. This decision for that price was mine and mine alone. As leader of this troop, any ramifications of that choice rest with me."

"Following the orders of a man known to us all as Harbour Dax, you are guilty of sabotage and attempted murder. However, because you were following orders you believed came from an aggrieved party doing your best to help, and because all of your known records not including that for which you have not been convicted of show a dedicated officer with a more or less clean track record, I sentence you to imprisonment beginning now and not lasting more than your natural life."

"I can't kill a man that thought he was doing right but your reasons for following bad orders do not excuse those bad orders and for that, short of execution, this is the fairest judgment in my book. Do either of you have anything to say?"

"Fuck you," says D.

Colt rushes over to punch his head into the post again. The ringing in D's right ear is louder this time.

"Colt stop it," says Hank.

They look to Zach. He shakes his head.

"We're done," says Hank.

"All right, people, let's go get ready," says Rick, motioning people up the stairs.

Cella's standing with Dede and Elle, a look of blank shock frozen to her face since she walked in. The look turns to betrayal as she meets D's eyes. D keeps his stony expression. He's nothing to feel bad for, except failing his mission. Cella moves to Rick, asking for a private word with D. He nods, and she marches forward, righteous anger all but pulsating from her.

"So you're a high-class con artist," she says, leering down at him, standing between his sprawled-out legs. "But before you put your master plan to work, you decided to have a good time with me, huh?"

D would laugh if he wasn't so depressed right now.

"Answer me." She steps closer. "Or, is it that you're not man enough to tell the truth to my face?"

D remains silent.

"You owe me three questions. Are you a man of your word or not?"

"Ask your damn questions."

"Don't curse at me. Is it true what Bruce said? That you've killed over a thousand people in battle?"

"Yes."

"How many? And that's the second part of the question."

"Three thousand two hundred forty-three. That includes the fourteen I had to kill after the bombs hit."

Cella's mouth hangs open. She let a man who's killed three thousand people inside her last night. He's a monster, like Bruce said. He's not quiet—he's empty. He's not ashamed of what he's done.

"You were going to kill me last night, weren't you?" she asks.

D snorts. "I was doing that for two hours. Over and over and over again."

She smacks him across the face, hard. The sound echoes in the gym. She kicks his balls and slaps him again then rushes from the room with Dede and Elle.

#

She is such an idiot. Her mother taught her better. Get to know a man before you decide to sleep with him. You idiot. Cella chides herself. *You belong to one of the richest families in the country. Why would you even look at that type of low life?*

It's 4:02 a.m. Cella's going to take another shower. She needs to wash the scent of him off her.

#

"Three thousand two hundred and forty-three?" asks Zach.

"You're a morality cop too?" says D. "You can save it. People like me make it so you can go on a dumbass boat trip and pretend you're too important to care about life. If it weren't for somebody like me, someone a lot meaner would steal that boat and break every bone in your body while another fucks your wife in front of you just to show you they can. I keep them away so you can pretend they don't exist. So save your fucking opinions."

"I wasn't going to say anything," says Zach.

"Good."

#

Colt's holding up the updated map while Jade uploads the new routes into everyone's datapad. Colt thought Jade would be upset about what happened last night, but when Jade heard the details she had that sinister smile on her face. He's never going to figure out women. The only good thing about this is they can put the better plan in place sooner. It'll save more people.

Sometimes it's good being petty. Small victories can make all the difference to how a day goes. Jade's going to declare herself champion of choice in men. And she had great sex last night, so this day couldn't have started out better.

That self-absorbed, conceited bitch. It's about time she got that ego deflated. Bitch.

Cella knows there are more important things to be concerned with. However, she's human and had spectacular sex last night so finding out that the guy she slept with is a psychopath is hard to get over—and that pack of jealous harpies and second-rate queen Jade... Whatever. Cella made sixty gallons of mustard gas. If anyone gets hurt, Cella's going to be the one fixing them.

How could he leave right after screwing her brains out? Faolin never did that after sex. Even Creighton had a good sleep after they had sex. D just left for a deathmatch. Seriously, how's a girl supposed to feel about that? Was she not good enough? She thought D seemed interested but with an international murderer who knows and why is she still thinking about this? She waited five months before having sex with anyone, and she'll do the same after this. Maybe a year after a screw up this big.

The others are snickering loudly and glancing at Cella. Well, Jade's own dad said that Cella's probably going to be the best help against the brogs.

They'll be hoping I can fix any injuries they get, so there.

#

Bruce was about to go to Cella, explain why he did what he did. She looked even prettier today with her hair tied into two thick braids going down either side of her head and no makeup. There was a passion mark on her neck. He ignored that, like he ignored the frayed hair and D's shirt over her naked body last night. He just wants to say her safety is all he cares for. Women like men who are willing to protect them.

"Wrong," says Rick. "Women like men they're attracted to, to protect them and only when they like it. They're real complicated that way, and what I said makes no logical sense. That's women. They're all emotions, and right now you're the guy who ruined her night. She won't thank you. Don't."

One of these days, Bruce is going to get that woman. He is always up for a good chase. She will be his. He'll figure it out.

#

Betty prides herself on not being a complainer. She worked hard over these eighteen months to be a moderating force for everyone. Yes, the Dax incident was a colossal failure on her part, but that notwithstanding, she's done a great job with these people. Only four of them committed suicide and that was in the first week of them being here. No one else gave up after she got to know them. Dede even got her sex coping mechanism under control. She was hoping Jade and Cella could work out their differences but that ship's sailed. Maybe whatever's in Three Mile will make for a better social situation. Doubtful, but she's old dammit; she's allowed to be unrealistic.

She glances down through the floor to the gym. Leaving both of them there to starve sounds cruel, but her family comes first.

If D's resourceful, maybe he'll be able to kill himself before he starves. D seems just stubborn enough to bang his head open. Zach doesn't seem to have that type of constitution but a desperate person can always surprise you.

#

Hank's reviewing the map routes. Knowing Harbour as he does, Hank highlights ideal ambush points. He's told Betty to stay as close to Cella or Jade as possible. When they split, there won't be time to get in the proper groups. Damn that woman if she gets distracted by someone getting hurt. He's not losing her or Jade.

#

After checking all the likely places D would have hidden something, Rick, Dom, Bode, and Cealen head to the shooting range to drag up the rest of the equipment. The count's back to its proper number. That arrogant Marine. Did he really think they wouldn't count how many guns they had. How'd he get into the armory in the first place? There's an alarm on it. They pack the excess parts also. Dice isn't going anywhere, but best to be safe. And who knows, maybe they'll have to replace gun parts on the way to Three Mile.

"What are you doing?" asks Bode.

"Just checking," says Dom, zipping up the vest of D's suit. "He won't need it, and this is some quality material. Why can't I wear it?"

"That's top-grade omni-weather military tech. Only spec-ops get that gear, and it takes them six weeks to learn how to use everything in it properly. That's version 8.36. The newest gear as of eighteen months ago."

"Oh I'm definitely wearing it then."

"Dom, I want you to think. We're heading into infested enemy territory. You've trained with the standard infantry cold gear for months now. You think you'll be able to learn how to use new equipment that you just put on today as effectively as the gear you already know and trust?"

Dom's still wearing the vest, trying to think up a counterargument.

"Bode," snaps Rick. "What is the rule on equipment?"

"You must know and trust your equipment as you do your body. Your equipment is what protects you in the field of battle. If you cannot trust your equipment, you are good as dead," says Bode.

"Dom, do you trust that equipment?" asks Rick.

Dom shakes his head.

"Then put it back in the box." After Dom throws the vest in the box, Rick smiles. "Tell you what, if we make it, I'll show you how to use it properly. Ok, men, lift on three."

#

Saffire was hoping to see D in action. That shooting was so cool. He had his eyes closed.

How'd he do that? But he left? He left early? Snuck out when she was sleeping? Why would he do that? That's stupid—all the people are here. Wouldn't leaving with the other people be better because more people can protect each other?

It wasn't nice to leave like that. She wanted to see how he moved. Was it like in those ninja movies? She wanted to see who was better at scouting, him or Bruce and Colt.

Now how's she supposed to become a super-agent spy killing master swordsmen if she doesn't see all the best people show their stuff? Like Master Onwuemelie of the Augment clan says in her favorite show, "Embrace death and you will know life. There is no end only the cycle." She had her notebook ready and everything. And why is Cella so upset? Saffire lost another potential teacher. Well, everyone says Colt and Bruce know what they're doing, so she'll settle for them. But she doesn't have to like it.

#

Hank calls everyone to him after Rick distributes the weapons. Rick's standing there proudly holding that monstrosity Mr. Buckshot. An old guy like him shouldn't be able to walk around with a thing that big. Colt's got his trusty forty-caliber rifle with laser sight and jam proof bullet chamber. Bruce has his dynamite and fifty-caliber rifle with a silencer built in. Dom's got his forty-caliber heatsink laser sight. He bet Colt for that one last week and won it.

These people have really grown up. That split with Dax hurt, but it forged a tougher unit. Not so naïve about the new world. A unit that's actually worth a damn in a fight.

It's 4:28 a.m.

"No speech," says Hank. "You know I'm not good at that. I just want to say that I wouldn't want to do this with anyone else. You are family. That's not something easy for me to say, but I love all of you. Now, let's go for a walk."

The door's open, and Hank leads the troop into the blackness.

His heart is pounding five times for every one step he takes.

Chapter 28

Colt's lights take in the damp, rusted, cobwebbed tunnel secreting some unknown liquid as Dom shuts the bunker

entrance. He presses two fingers to the door in thanks.

"Don't get sentimental, Dom," says Rick.

"Never that, sir. I'm ready to do my job, sir," says Dom.

"Our job is to protect Corporal. Let's go do that."

Colt's at the first network of passages, all trickling water. Bruce's team would have left at this point, but instead they stay waiting for Harbour's people to attack. Nothing happens. They wait for five minutes, aiming at shadows, then move on.

Everyone's tense, so no one notices how the civilians are grouped. Cella does though. They're set up much like they were when they first set up this plan. Bruce is always five to twenty feet from Cella at all times, and she's right in the middle of the young people. All the civvies under thirty are here along with Betty as Hank walks alongside them. Jade's up front with Colt and Kellen. Colt tried moving Saffire closer to Cella, but she wanted to stay with her grandmother, so those two are up with the other six people between thirty and thirty-five. It works to hide what Hank's doing though.

Colt leads them right into a corridor of five tunnels. Colt takes the right-most tunnel. Long, slick, and winding declines are threatening to twist and break joints, but Colt and Jade are jogging ahead as Dom lets off the first explosives. It was a risk leading Harbour's people to them but stopping brogs from circling them was a bigger threat.

Bruce is helping Cella down a slide. He's gentle as always. Too gentle. Cella should have done something about him months ago. He's nice, but she's not interested and never has been. She knows she can be prissy, but she's nowhere near as bad as she used to be. The world ending has humbled her.

It means she won't use a man's affections to play off another and get everything she can from both then dump both. She can be honest even if it's against her selfish interests. In a way, the world blowing up was the best thing for her. When they get to Three Mile, she'll do it; make it clear how she feels. It's cruel to give him hope. When they get to Three Mile, she'll do it.

"Stay close," whispers Colt. "We're going into a waterlogged section. It's supposed to be waist deep at this point. It was knee high last time we scouted."

The others go quiet. It's an ideal ambush location—fifty yards long, with jagged pieces of pipe pointing at them from all angles. Most haven't been outside since the bombs came. They haven't seen what happened. The blackness is also unnerving. Some bounce against the walls and slip in the water, splashing and causing a ruckus. Cealen nearly falls over one of the civvies while ice thickens on the sides. There's no proper footing in this place, but before they know it, they're past the watery tunnel and at another convergence point. This time, Colt takes the second tunnel from the left without skipping a beat.

After heading down for some time, many ears pop. They're deep into the earth now. This next convergence point is buckling.

They don't hear the metal groaning, but it feels like it will fall, so they walk slowly instead of the half-trot Colt's been using. Betty's gripping Hank's arm tightly. Cella's holding Dede's arm. Bruce tried taking Cella's arm, but she made her decision. He's helping Elle instead.

They're past this tunnel, and Colt leads them to the next. There's water here, and it's deeper. Colt didn't expect the water here to rise so high. In the light, the pool looks as welcoming as boiling oil. There's a crack somewhere. The water's rippling and freezing. Well, there's nothing to it.

"Careful, everyone," says Colt, taking Jade by the hand and heading in.

#

D's rubbing his arm again while Zach tugs at his restraints. D's impressed; Zach's been at it for thirty minutes. There's blood around his wrists. It was a good thing D saved this one. He needs someone with spine to get out of here.

"Uhhh," Zach wails. "My fucking arm's killing me."

D's sitting calmly, watching the clock.

"This is your fault," yells Zach. "Aren't you gonna do anything?"

"I'm giving them a head start," says D. "Don't worry. I'll get us out of this."

"You have a way out? What are you waiting on?"

"I just said. Relax. In fifteen minutes, I'll be sure they're not coming back, then do what I have to."

"Are you gonna dislocate your thumb and pull your hands free like in the movies?"

"That's fucking stupid. And my hands are too big for the cuffs. It won't work."

"How do you know that?"

"You think I've just been sitting here for four hours with hopes and wishes. I know how to get out, but it won't work if we get stuffed back in cuffs because they're still close and don't want to take chances."

"I saw you fight Hank. You can't take some little guard?"

"Look, Zach. I fucked up. I'm going to get us out, but first I need to be sure they left. I'll get us out alright. I don't break my word."

D looks Zach in the eye, and Zach searches those eyes. There's something unyielding in them. Zach didn't quite notice before, but with proper lighting, he sees. D helped Zach when he didn't know or owe him anything. That's one point in D's favor. Those others named D some kind of war hero—*a war hero that went crazy.*

He wouldn't be the first. Those news outlets against the war have plenty of stories of soldiers suffering battle fatigue. But Zach was with him; it was only for a day, but he didn't look crazy. He did everything he could to get them to this bunker. He killed a lot of people, but Zach grew up under a man that loved the military, dad was army but still. Dad never quite forgave Zach for being a tech geek rather than having a real job like a soldier. Zach doesn't give a shit why he killed all those coalition people and doesn't care. The coalition had it coming. What he knows is D saved his life, twice.

He owes him that much trust. He nods and they wait.

"Alright." D mutters to himself, moving for the first time in four hours.

"What are you doing?" asks Zach.

"Shut up."

D tries biting at his left arm again then nods. He starts rocking back and forth as if psyching himself up for something. Zach leans forward. The cuffs dig into his wrists as the links press into the steel ring post. D presses his left palm into the ground. The other arm's pulled behind the post at an odd angle but his eyes look forward, seeing nothing. D groans now, face feral with concentration. Veins pop from his neck and forehead. D grunts louder than roars and the elbow cracks loudly, folding back on itself like dried wood.

"Aaarg," D yells, heaving down and sweating.

D bites his arm, feeling the bicep, then finds his mark. He bites deep. D rears his head back, ripping a black metal object from his arm, blood spurting.

D's cursing now, really cursing. Some of it sounds Spanish; some of it's French and Haitian Creole. There's some Latin and Portuguese in there too. D is visibly calming himself. When he stops shaking, he spits the keys over his right shoulder onto his hand. He angles the metal piece in into the keyhole. The cuffs click open. D falls over cradling his ruined left arm.

It takes a minute, but D stops shuttering and lifts himself up. His eyes are focused again. He rises, ignoring the pain, then turns to Zach. Zach has a horrified expression on his face. D has his own blood dripping off his chin and a ferocious look in his eye. *So this is Dice? He's intimidating.*

D presses the top of the metal stick and pulls it from the keyhole. With another press, lines jut out from the stick and Zach's cuffs pop loose. He'd say something about the blood from D's arm dripping onto his pants but thinks better of it.

"Alright," says D, voice ragged.

"Are we gonna try to catch up?"

"No. I'm hoping they clear the way for us."

"We're not going to try to help them?"

D has a confused look on his face. "Why would we?"

"Well, they're civilians like me. I thought you wouldn't care what they did. People like you protect."

"I have a mission, Zach. That mission's more important than these people."

"What does that mean? There's women and children in that troop. Are you really just gonna leave them?"

"I have to clean up. See if you can get into the war room. There might still be something useful in there."

"What is this place?"

"It's the Pennsylvania governor's secret nuke shelter. She never quite made it here, though. A pity."

"D, tell me straight. You know better than me how brutal it is out there. I'm getting the sense that you are one of the few people in the world to trust in this situation. They have a seven-year-old girl in the troop. Are you really going to leave those people to fend for themselves?"

"I've got my priorities."

"Just answer the fucking question."

"Have you ever seen someone die of hunger? I have. Hell, I almost starved to death three times before General found me. First you see the weight loss, the gaunt face, sunken cheeks. Then comes dizziness. It gets real bad when they start fainting.

"There's a smell, you know. Flies start crowding around, waiting. Your body starts eating itself to fuel its primary functions. Maybe your teeth will fall out. You start walking like a zombie, back bent, hovering around stores and restaurants, waiting for garbage disposal day. You might have a seizure or three. Maybe you start thinking about where else you can get food.

"Late night in the quiet alleys, you'll look for someone and maybe eat them. Or, you'll try to eat part of your own body to keep the edge off. Your organs break down. You won't care—you'll be too hungry and tired to care about that. Then, complete system failure occurs. There's no last push or yell, you just wither away. Then, the flies eat. Your body's resilient so it could take up to three months before you die."

"It's one of the worst ways to die I know of, and I've seen plenty of death. They weren't doing us a favor by leaving us here to starve, Zach. We don't owe them anything. Fuck them."

#

The path is branching into six more one hour later. If Colt didn't have his map, he'd be hopelessly lost. As such, the paths are stable. He was expecting a collapse soon, but there hasn't been any cave-ins yet. Colt was certain that shockwave from a few days ago was a collapse but maybe he was wrong. He's starting to think Dax's group might not be here.

An army doesn't wait to attack like in those war movies. If you're going to attack an enemy, it's best done quickly at the point of maximum impact. If Colt were trying to attack the troop, he'd have attacked right when the bunker door closed. It would have taken too long to reopen while twenty men fire down from the tunnels. Everyone of them would have been slaughtered. That's why he had Bruce set up explosives on their last scout. Now they're deep into the route and still nothing.

If this keeps up, they can make it to Three Mile quickly. Colt's hope was twenty, but if he can push the pace, he just might be able to get everyone there in under eighteen hours. Those old guys will slow them down, but his priority is everyone who can still have children. It doesn't matter how he gets them there, just get as many of the people who can make babies to the shuttle as possible. Those were direct orders. He unconsciously looks back at Wanda.

"What's wrong?" asks Wanda.

"In half a mile, we're going to run into a frozen lake," says Colt. "This ain't an ice rink. There'll be jagged rocks and steel poking through. There're pockets of water too. Be careful."

Jade stiffens as they move closer. She asks about the places he scouted a month ago. She always wanted to know about the most dangerous places. Hank refused to let Jade check those passes until Colt told him what would be needed in a worst-case scenario. This was a path Colt said he'd avoid if he could. There're many compromising positions on this route. That's not including the brogs. He might get a severe talking to when she finds out the rest of the route he's taking. Colt's not going to make an ambush easy.

Jade doesn't say anything for the next five minutes, but has not been more than three feet from Colt and even grabbed his hand once. She doesn't usually do that in public.

"We're here," says Colt. "Remember to follow the scouts."

The troop splits into four groups. It takes longer now than in practice, but it takes less than ten minutes. Colt owes Bruce a round of drinks now. Jade wanted to stay near Colt, but she's leading ten people by the submerged earth mover. Colt's standing where the ice is thickest. One thing annoying about no light is that you really can't see anything. When Colt and Bruce first found this place, the opening was twenty feet wide.

Then Colt fell flat on his ass, and the ground cracked. Bruce was about to laugh, then the ground sucked him in. The water froze almost as soon as he sank past the surface. Bruce caught the lip of the submerged floor and smashed his rifle through the surface. They silently agreed after Bruce dragged him from the water to never let anyone know about this and that it was Colt's fault.

"Colt, my route's changed," says Rita.

There's a new whole mound of snow and ice swirling in the blackness covering a dead body that fell through the collapsed roof over a year ago. Rita's glad the snow covered that face, even if she'll never admit it. The blue skin, bloated and deformed, bothered her.

"My route's changed too," says Bruce, frowning.

There was an upturned patch of tunnel locked in place by a mound of ice five feet wide and seven feet tall. Now, there's only a frozen six-foot-wide crater with jagged pieces of ice sticking out at odd angles.

"It looks like there was a snowstorm last night," says Colt. "We all know how bad those can get. Be more careful. Let's move."

Cella and Dede thought the partner system was insulting, but Elle's almost slipped three times. She's annoying Bruce even if he won't say it. His left hand fidgets whenever he's mad at women. He never yells at them. This doesn't stop Dede from telling Elle to get her fucking shit together. The others in line are nodding. It's no fun to have to overcompensate for someone that can't remember to keep her fucking feet on the ice and glide slowly to minimize slipping risk and ice cracking from too much pressure at one point.

The suit lights of the troop make the water look like white ripples on ebony. Bruce did most of the route-making for this part and even he didn't measure to the sides. So, the tunnel could be 120 feet wide, as the troop is spaced out, or it could be two miles wide. Bruce didn't check that far, nor did he want to. The job was to find the quickest safest route for forty-four people. So as far as the lights can reach is how wide he's making the route, roughly two hundred feet.

Betty loves her husband, but sometimes Hank can be excessive. He didn't have to bully Dom out of his anchor role.

"I'm old, son," says Hank. "I'll be the one to warn you to get the hell away. Now move in front of Betty."

Dom was in front of Betty in a flash, grumbling but doing as he was told. She'll talk to him later, explain that actually he's more important than Hank. People his age are why they're moving, so it's actually Hank being overall mission commander. Caring for his men more than their feelings. That's flimsy but Dom was only made a corporal by Hank in the bunker. It'll probably work.

She smiles to herself then looks back at Hank. She'd never say nuclear winter was a good thing, but retirement did not suit Hank at all. It's good to see the man she fell in love with fifty-two years ago. She'd never change him.

"What the hell is that?" asks Betty, having the good sense to whisper.

Hank swings his light left, trying to spot what Betty saw.

"It walked like a cat," she says quietly.

Hank is trying to extend his light. If he were brave enough, he'd tell Betty she's seeing shadows, but she had that glaucoma scare a few years ago so Hank hasn't made vision jokes since. Hank is about to pull free of Betty and go over to make sure, but Betty's got quite the grip. Rita's tugging them forward, and the others are looking back at Hank. He can't see their faces with the helmets being tinted, but he'd guess they're glaring. He lets Betty drag him forward. He makes one last survey with his rifles light and stops. He saw something.

"Shit," says Betty, slipping.

Hank slips over her, and the two pull down Dom. Then, the entire line falls.

"What the fuck is going on?" snaps Rita with a feral face.

Technically Betty fell, not Hank, but as the leader he'll take blame later.

#

Zach knows he was helping, but it still feels wrong snapping someone's arm back in place. D came back from the bathroom, asking Zach to move his arm back in place so he could clean himself off properly. Zach didn't realize just how badly D mangled his own arm. There was another series of pops and clicks. D stopped Zach when the arm was in more or less the proper position. He'll need major surgery on that arm or more likely an amputation since there aren't any surgeons anymore.

Now D's just flexing his fingers. The pinky and ring finger aren't moving. D's trying to pretend it doesn't hurt, but Zach can see the sweat form every time he tries moving the arm. Zach's no good with field medicine, but D showed him how to fix his own arm and wrap it properly.

Zach, for his part, is looking through the government files. There was some weak passcode on the war-room computer:

Oldm@nsyndrome. D said Jade was good with computers so Zach guessed Jade was having fun with Hank. The files are fascinating. There are nine of these bunkers located around the state. Only five were finished, and this one was top priority. There is a status log for the activity done in the bunker too. Something to gauge CO_2 levels and optimum food requisitioning for a maximum of 350 people. That part is damaged. It keeps reading Repair of Nutrient Assessor needed. Catastrophic damage for nutrient tanks 2-11.

There are other things about state evacuation plans. There's a curious bit about which party members will be allowed in the bunker should shelter be needed and a personal note for the governor's boy toy to be found. Wasn't that lady sixty when she took the oath of office. *Scandalous.* What's important to this mission took some digging to find, but the layout of the state underground system opens up completely with preferred escape routes and a path to Three-Mile Island for some reason. There's not supposed to be anything on that island, not for a hundred years. Yet, there's a big classified sign on the computer file. Zach has to know. Government files are a hacker's wet dream.

It takes five minutes to hack this so-called top military-grade encryption. He smiles to himself. This is quite clever. There's nothing in the file. Only the governor can access these files and only after coming here to verify that they are authorized. Then, they are linked to a site where they further authenticate their clarifications and then download the information. All of that is easy for Zach to bypass, or at least it would be if he had internet access. Those paranoid government hacks. If the governor did get here, she'd have been locked out of vital information for her own state. All the money these people get paid, and hardline access to priority intel was never a concern? The idiots. He's cursing when D walks in, raising his eyebrow.

"They wipe the mainframe?" asks D.

"Oh, please," says Zach. "You can't wipe anything off a mainframe. The only way to clear history from a computer properly is to destroy the hard drive. No, the problem is all the red tape people have to go through to get information."

"I've known that since I started my way here. Can you download what you do have?"

"The network is the same thing we copied a few days ago."

"They stole our bags."

"I thought special forces are trained to remember everything."

"No, we're trained to learn everything pertinent to an operation. Unfortunately, the underground network of an entire state is something beyond my ability."

D slides two blank datapads over to Zach.

"So Dice is a call sign?" says Zach. "And your real name's Dorian?"

"It certainly is a name. Hellenic, did you know that?"

"What?"

"Zeus, Poseidon, Hercules, the titans. Greek. As Greek as I am."

Zach blinks at him then frowns, looking past the computer screen then back up at D.

"What?"

"No."

Zach looks as if he's about to have a stroke. "No what?"

"It's not my goddam name."

"Why didn't you just say that?"

"There's an art to getting information. You don't ham fist people into giving you what you want. You need to guide them. Say I need to know where you grew up, but I don't know you. How would I guide you to the proper state of mind? Well, first you start with a nonthreatening smile."

"You smile?"

D gives a comforting smirk, not quite a smile. It looks so genuine, Zach's stunned stupid. It's gone in a flash.

"Maintain eye contact," says D moving closer, holding out his hand to shake. "Firm grip. Keep that winning smile. Ask him, 'Do you know the best place for drinks? I'm new here."

He nods to Zach.

"Oh, um, it's down the street about three blocks from here.

Make a left at the stop sign and keep going straight."

"Thanks. What's the name?"

"Oh, it's called the Sandpit."

"Yeah, what's the best time to go? I like the ladies. I wanna get off to a good start here, you know."

"I get that. You should go on the weekends after nine. That's when the best ones show up."

"Is it? All types of women or twenty-somethings. I like variety."

"Perfectly understandable. But, yeah, it's mostly eighteen to twenty-five on that night."

"Regulars or tourists? Those all-girls weekends can make for great memories," says D, giving a bigger grin.

"That's why I said the weekend. Bright-eyed girls in the big city for the first time. It's a goldmine."

"Yeah, where from?"

"All over, you see pretty; it don't matter where it's from."

"True, but I was looking for a southern girl. Had a friend of mine said they were the best. I think he's full of shit but had me thinking."

"Southern girls are like any other woman. I think it's the accent city guys like but once you get past that, they're like any other woman."

"You sound experienced."

"I grew up in the south."

"No kidding. I can't hear the accent."

"Haslet, Texas. Just up the road from Fort Worth."

"So do the women there have big breasts or not?"

Zach chuckles. "Some do, some don't. It depends how much money their husband or boyfriend has."

"Ah, well thanks again. Sandpit, you said. Make a left stop at the sign and keep going straight?"

"That's it."

D nods and returns to that stony expression.

"That's good. Why didn't you try that with them?"

"I'm cranky when I don't get sleep. And they had a gun pointed at me after I helped them out. And soldiers and marines don't get along. Not to mention that no one lives this long being a happy faced fool. Everyone would've pegged me as a psycho that second."

"So that conversation was for a civilian who doesn't know any better?"

"You're getting it," says D as the download starts.

"So why'd you steal the nine millimeters then?"

"We're trained to prepare for the worst but hope for the best. What's the worst-case scenario when we get outside?"

"The fucking brogs."

"And what caliber gun brings down a brog?"

"Thirty and above."

"So why the fuck would I steal three 9 milli's?"

"You didn't? He framed you?"

"I should've known that fat-faced fuck would be upset I fucked the girl he wanted. I bet he thinks she'll see him as a real hero. Idiot. How long will this download take?"

"Six minutes."

"Let's gear up.

"Didn't they take everything?"

"No, they took as much as they could carry."

They walk down to Room 7 and open the door. Usually, D would be careful about moving furniture because loose parts might splinter and catch him, but he and Zach both have bad arms at the moment, so he just kicks the door. The thing falls apart with a racket. Bruce and Hank stripped all of D's weapons when they handcuffed him to the ring post, but D doesn't need his knife for this. He kicks in the lower left-hand side where the hinges are. He tugs a bit, and the door pops free. Inside are two .45 caliber bullet chambers, trigger boxes, hammer spring magazine chambers, and two fifteen-round magazines.

"You did steal something."

"It's not theirs to own first of all, so no I didn't."

"They didn't find it in the door?"

"Who the hell ever checks the door? It's the thinnest part of the room. And why would they check this door? The lock's broken. The door's got bullet holes in it. There's no way we could hide anything in here."

"When did you do this?"

"Two nights ago. You were sleeping. Dom was doing the rounds that night. I moved the drawer in front to block the light from my datapad from showing shadows under the bottom of the door. I just had to time his patrol. It wasn't hard."

D tugs and pulls the gun parts from the door with adhesive, dragging pieces of the door out with the plastic covering. D rips it open with his teeth and takes out a retractable knife. Where did that come from?

"They had account of the guns, so I took parts. Most people don't count how many spare parts they have," says D. "It'll be cold as shit in those tunnels, so we need protection. The urban winter gear they have is good, but I like added protection. So, we'll take extra arm and leg padding. We'll give them an extra hour. I wanna make sure they're far ahead so we don't have to deal with the uglies."

D ignores the twitch in Zach's face as they head to the armory.

"They told us they locked it dow—" Zach stops mid-word.

D types in c89geg5, and the door slides open.

"How'd—"

"Zach, do you ever get tired of asking stupid questions?"

D strides through the emptied armory picking through the leftovers. The troop left a few duffel bags and all the nonlethal bullets. There's over a hundred cold weather suits and the same number of heat resistant suits. Everything's the same: white, gray, and black camouflage color.

"Find something in your size. Remember to put the padding on first." D stops, thinking he should be clearer. Zach's no idiot, but he's not familiar with military equipment either.

"Your size should be whatever fits loose enough to fit the padding underneath. I'll show you how to reduce noise on it."

Zach nods. He had no idea. Zach has never been scrawny, but he never really saw how much weight he lost. He had to walk down the row of suits until he was near the extra small section. These suits are enormous. That's the problem, not him. D's almost grinning thirty feet away as he tries to fit his injured arm into the jacket. Zach should've known. This is the women's section. He throws the suit down and gets a large. D snorts but Zach ignores it. Sometimes, you just have to be the bigger man.

D's really trying not to yelp, but his arm really hurts. This should be an easy job. Just put the padding on the elbow and into the sleeve. The problem is the pads are tight. They're supposed to be, but it doesn't stop D from cursing them for being tight and his arm for shooting lightning strikes of pain through his neck whenever he tries bending it. If he still had his bag, those pills might come in handy. This is when he remembers his dislocated and broken fingers. He forgot the pain when he freed himself, but now that he looks at them, the throbbing from his fingers returns. Well, he's not having that. He moves his arm again and forgets all about his fingers.

"This won't do," D mutters to himself, snapping both back in place and straightening the broken one. "I'm going to get ice."

D comes back, seeing Zach flexing the suit. It fits him perfectly. He actually listened to what D said.

"Tie straps around the upper thigh and upper arm," says D, dropping a bowl of ice and duck-tape on the gun counter top.

"No plastic," says D. "In a place this fucking big, not one stich of plastic wrap."

"You need oil to make plastic."

"That doesn't mean you throw out the stuff you already made."

D frowns at the ice, then his arm.

"If you need—" Zach begins.

"I'm fine," says D.

D gets that focused look in his eye again and dunks his arm into the bowl. There's some twitching but to his credit, D doesn't remove his arm.

It takes fifteen minutes, but the arm's numb with cold now. He can still feel the twinges of pain, but it's at a level he can ignore, so D wraps strips of tape around a fist-sized piece of ice and rolls it around the arm. There's a nice sheet of ice cube pressing into the deformed bones. He'll feel that later. He wraps a second layer around the tape now to keep the first layer intact and a third to reinforce the second layer of adhesive. When he's done, it looks like AstroTurf mated with his arm, but it's functional.

D finds the largest size to fit his makeshift cast in and dresses himself. The large bulge is odd. It makes D look like he's suffering from elephantiasis. The top half not matching D's black armor pants just screams of crimes against fashion. Zach laughs, and D gives him a middle finger.

D decides to cut the suit open at that part. D cuts just to the edge of his duct tape cast then duct tapes the edges, making an imperfect seal. There are little droplets of water seeping through the tape already, but those tunnels are cold. He could just leave this part exposed and let any water that forms refreeze and make a more stable cast. He'll see if it works. They pack duffle bags with gun parts and after turning on the only working nutrient tank, all the food is ready in an hour.

D looks like he stuffed ten meals in his mouth at once, but he needs the calories. He didn't sleep last night and the arm is going to zap more energy from him during this trip. Zach was surprised the nutrient tank worked as long as it did. It has seven bullet holes in it and the other ten have hundreds. D waits for seven o'clock before moving out. They have thirty bullets between them, and with D's leg and arm as they are, Zach probably has the best chance of getting there alive. D won't say that, of course, but he does give him the other gun.

"Try not to shoot unless absolutely necessary," says D at the door.

Then, D writes down several numbers on a paper and explains part of his mission to Zach. Zach's eyes widen, but he expected something like this. The doors open, and D and Zach head into the tunnels.

#

"Get him out," yells Jade.

"I'm working on it," snaps Rita, hooking an arm around a thick piece of wall while Hank splashes in the water.

Rita pulled six from the water thanks to the buddy system, but part of an ice block sandwiched Sabrina's hand against a jagged metal protrusion under the water, and her grip loosened. She slipped under with Dom, Betty, and Hank behind her. Sabrina now pops to the surface, breathing heavy. It's a good thing Rita's abnormally strong for a woman. Sabrina's suit is ripped open at the side. She has a second layer of padding on, but even with that, the freezing water is sending needle-like pricks of pain through her as it leaks down her leg.

Rita's back in the water, looking for the others. Her beam of light can't see much past fifteen feet. It's as if she's dropped into a plane of liquid blackness; then, three lights flick on and off below her. If she could see, Rita would know that Hank, Dom, and Betty are clinging to a slab of tunnel floor held in place between two columns of ice. Ice is above, carving down like a sword through this unfortunate pass. The other ice block made in the subsequent months after winter, grew as the sun faded. Now the ice blocks meet where hank holds betty.

As Rita swims what she doesn't know is that these columns are only two of a network of ice columns that collectively hold back sixty thousand pounds of dirt and debris in its current position. It's waiting for a chance to shift again. The weakest point just so happens to be between Jade and Bruce on the other side of the tunnel. No one has moved since Rita's group fell. Ice is nothing to toy with.

Hank, Betty and Dom are lucky they didn't fall to the bottom of this death trap. Rita sees this place has changed since they last scouted. She figured this place was forty maybe fifty feet deep. But it looks like big plans were meant for this location because huge swathes of earth are missing. What could you possibly build that would need this much room underground?

In any case, Hank offers up Betty first. She's not a civilian technically, and young people are the priority for this mission, but Rita can't argue right now; cold is creeping into her fingers. Rita punches through the thin ice and guides Betty to where Sabrina sits shivering as she tries keeping her suit closed.

Rita's back under the water using the pillar to pull herself to the two men. This will be tougher. Both are at least three times heavier than Betty, and they're carrying a disproportionate amount of food. Everyone carries some food, but the military people decided they'd carry the majority of the weight just in case things got difficult. It means that Dom and Hank each have thirty pounds more equipment than Betty. Rita wastes no time. Her knife is out cutting through the straps on each man's bag. Neither man could cut through their own straps because they were sinking and instead of trying to cut, they chose to find a place to hold on to and hope help came.

Rita takes Dom first as he mentioned he was not a good swimmer, and Hank swims up behind them, tugging at the ice column to guide their way.

"I had to ditch some of the food," says Rita to Colt.

"Shit happens," says Colt. "Get your squad together. We're moving soon as you're ready."

Rita's clapping her hands, motioning everyone back to their feet. Sabrina's still shivering, and two civvies move closer. Rita's gut tightens. There was a reason she left Sabrina by herself. The floor's unstable and now the others are moving over. Three bodies cluster around one location.

The ice cracks. Like an earthquake, the tunnel shakes and dips.

A large fissure opens between Jade and Bruce.

"Glide," says Colt, keeping his team locked in the buddy system.

Colt's route has the thinnest ice, which is why he took it and most of the strongest swimmers on his squad. However, ice is ice, so his carefully prepped route is ruined. They just need to move 150 yards, and they're safe. He glances back, seeing his anchor, Valenda, moving her gun side to side.

"Hurry up, Colt. I could've sworn I saw something in the water," says Valenda. Her face is obscured by the helmet and the bright light shining back toward Colt.

Colt glides quicker. He clips a jagged piece of ice but doesn't fall. Jade's gliding her team, looking past Colt to Rita's squad. She hasn't paid much attention to her anchor, Rick, since she saw her parents drop out of sight.

"Jade," yells Rick. "Stay focused. We've already done this twelve times, right? This is easy."

Jade breathes deep and comes back to herself. "We might run into Colt's squad while we're moving. Do not let go of your buddy. Now move faster."

There's a persistent grinding echoing and reverberating through the tunnel. Colt's team is in a synchronized groove, swaying with him around mounds of frozen rocks and metal. He was lucky to have Saffire up front. She holds onto his free hand while Wanda grips the other. The little girl hasn't slipped once.

She's got potential.

\#

Bruce has a tougher job. His newly made island is tilting left faster than the larger block the other three teams are gliding on.

Water's already bubbling close to him, so Bruce makes a decision.

"Everyone, glide toward the side of the tunnel," he says.

Bruce takes Cella's hand and tugs the squad up the ice. Someone slips on the ice, but Bruce's squad has more men than the others. Everyone knew he'd insist on having Cella near him, so he had to take a larger portion of women civvies with him. It's balanced by having more strength on his squad. The compositions are no accident. Having some of each in every squad ensures a healthy mix of people. It also means Bruce can make his plan work.

"Everyone, we're gonna jump on three," says Bruce. "Three."

They jump, and as they do, the edge of the ice juts up. Then, as they come down, the side closest to Jade rises from the depths in a wave of freezing water splashing into her team. Bruce's island rides the wave into the other ice column with a loud thud. It worked.

"Glide," yells Bruce.

He keeps the squad to the edge, the combined body weight keeping the island from tilting as much as it wants. He periodically checks the noticeably sinking ice pillar. The rumbling sound grows as it sinks. Kellen, Bruce's anchor, fires a shot into the water. It's a useless move, as water slows the bullets. Bruce would curse him for wasting bullets, but as he looks back, he see's something reflected in the ambient light. A too familiar creature's shifting, flailing an arm as if looking for a way to escape.

\#

That wave did nothing to help Jade's balance. Being open to the topside elements makes the comfortable fifteen-degree tunnel dip to negative thirty. The wave crest turns to ice and snow before showering Jade's squad in white. Her toe clips a new ridge of ice, but somehow, she maintains balance and glides forward.

Bruce's stunt has complicated Colt's route even more so. He was already on the thinnest part of the ice, but after Bruce's island collided with the pillar, cracks sprang up around him. They sealed quickly, but he can't trust his feet there. In that moment, Colt changes tactics. Wanda might kill him for this, but he's going to use Saffire. He was keeping her at his side, forcing her to stay at his pace; now, he whips her out in front. She's about fifty pounds, so she'll warn him of new ice traps, and he's more than capable of pulling her to him if she falls into one.

"What are you doing?" yells Saffire, as she rockets from one side of Colt to the other.

"Relax, Saffy," says Colt. "You're helping. Try not to shift around so much. I don't want you to slip."

The end of the tunnel is only twenty yards away, but Saffire's fallen into an ice trap. Colt almost falls forward, the shift of Saffire's body tugging him forward. He yanks and Saffire's little body kicks as a new layer of ice forms immediately. Colt's last swing dragged Saffire over five feet of unstable ice. Keeping momentum, Colt tugs Wanda and the rest left before swinging Saffire out front again. Everything is stable until the edge breaks and forms a gap between Colt and the solid dirt. He throws Saffire across the gap without a thought then yells for everyone to be ready for a jump.

"Break into two-man teams," says Colt. "Ladies, hold on to the guy next to you."

He leaps, using the momentum of his glide to carry himself over the now two-foot-wide gap. Wanda's holding on for dear life. He's at the edge, but Wanda stumbles over shards of ice forming as quickly as water is exposed to the surface. She falls into the water, but they're close enough that Colt has her on land before she sinks. Bode's next with his woman and throws her across first then, like Colt, uses momentum to jump to safety. It works this way until the end with Valenda. She's flying over the four-foot-wide gap before her partner lands beside her. Valenda's a bit ashamed she didn't have the strength to toss him instead he tossed her then jumped so it all worked out.

Colt directs everyone deeper into the tunnel to make room for the next squad, which will probably be Jade's. She's only thirty feet away and was watching Colt's squad. This is why Cealen's in front. He launches her over the five-foot crack. She had no idea he could throw like that. Cealen's leaping just as she pushes to her feet. He lands with a splash, flecks of ice kicking up around him. He misjudged the gap; it's six feet wide now. As he stretches a hand for Colt to pull him up, he's yanked off his feet. Colt's no weakling and Cealen's not so weak that he's manhandled like this. It's clear what happened a second later. Cella is screaming as she arcs into Cealen's back while his feet still can't manage to grip the black ice atop the firm land.

"Hurry up," yells Bruce.

His island is cracking apart as the pillar falls, hitting it on its way beneath the surface. Dede's next, but as she lands, a primal grunt from Rita has her partner sailing and almost squashing Dede. Colt doesn't have time to slow the three teams down. The ice is breaking up around them, but he knows what just took Cealen. Instead of doing something stupid and fruitless like trying to stop the squad from jumping over, his squad aims at the water just in case something pops out.

Elle's in Colt's arms before she hits the ground. Bruce should've jumped after Cella, but he's trying to get all the women on his team off first. The chivalrous idiot. That's not the plan.

"I'm not priority. Go," yells Rick.

The three men ahead of him grumble, but then, one after the other jump the seven-foot-gap as Bruce jumps with the last of his squad. Rita's leaping with only Hank and Dom left from her squad. Colt's got a rotating shift of people pulling others from the water but something odd happens. Rick sees two of the men sink. Most drowning victims just sink with no gasps, not like in the movies. It seems like that, but Colt's yelling for everyone to pull harder and four more soldiers charge forward, aiming guns at the water.

Colt hasn't even looked at Rick yet, but it's clear that he thinks brogs are in the water. Rick takes a deep breath. He's done dumber things. His old legs turn, pushing him up over the eight-foot gap. He falls five feet short, and as he does, someone else sinks. Ice is crumbling loudly, but Rick doesn't dare turn back to see Bruce's island disappear or Rita's patch of land crack into random large ice chunks. He pushes forward, slapping the ice down as he dog paddles forward.

This can make someone more attractive to a predator as Rick knows well. He loves his classic horror movies, but he also lives in the real world. And in the real world, predators go for the easiest prey because the object is to eat and finding easy food saves energy for the most important thing creatures do; produce offspring. There are twelve people in the water now, so Rick has an eight percent chance of being eaten; damn good odds for any Green Beret. As soon as the thought comes, Rick feels ashamed of himself. He grabs the nearest man and tugs him along.

The ice is shifting. It's an odd sensation. It's as if half of his body is being engulfed. A loud crashing scream of ice and metal causes everyone to lift atop the wave as the last foot of the pillar sinks. This is when the rumbling pattern changes to a more frantic howl. It's so loud no one hears the two people closest to the pillar being sucked down in its wake.

One of them is Rick. The ice black water looks beautiful as he floats down into the darkness. The pillar's shattering against the ridge of land Hank held onto back when Rita found him. That falls into other slabs of ice and rock with the sound pulsing through the water at five times that of air.

Rick's suit is not quite built for a sound attack like this. He sees a brog silhouette trapped against ice; they fall into the depths with humans falling with them. Then, the currents have him. The multi-ton slabs form many rip tides, snatching Rick. Sounds bombard him. Only good luck twists and pushes Rick toward the rest of the troop.

No one sees Rick floating at the surface. Hank and Dom are sending waves of scorching air at the surface so everyone still in the water can swim without pushing away the ice constantly forming on the surface. The flames allow everyone to see the bubbles of air and mini whirlpools forming and disappearing as the ice beneath Hank and Dom bucks. Rick checks himself, noticing his shotgun is gone. Dom is using it.

When did that happen?

Rick's still missing many things. He's not noticing the random silence while the cannons are firing, the world tilting as he stands still. That ringing sound. All he knows is he shouldn't fall asleep. Something tells him that would be bad.

Hank and Dom heave the weapons at Colt then jump. Colt aims the cannon now. Colt's always thought the cannon is too impractical, but Hank makes it work. He sends sheets of superheated air in a semi-circle. Steam clouds form, turning to snow in seconds. It's an eerie sight, as if the world is undecided on what temperature it will be from moment to moment. Rick just keeps swimming, ignoring all the movement in the water. Colt nearly fires at Rick when he reaches out a hand for Hank and Dom.

"Where the hell did you come from?" yells Colt.

Three people tug hank and Dom onto solid land.

"Give me my shotgun back," says Rick.

"Spot me," says Colt.

Emmett is still in the water. Colt ignores Jade's yelling and dives in. He never takes his eyes off Emmett. Rick's aim is a bit off. His hands are cold, and he's too close to Colt. Proper cannon firing when looking to create a passage is to aim at least ten feet from any allies that maybe near the firing solution. Rick's line of fire is two feet from Colt. Colt reaches Emmett as another sheet of fire illuminates more of the water. Colt's not distracted by his fear, but the tension is growing. He saw brogs in the water but nothing's grabbing him as he tugs Emmett to the edge. Before he's aware of it, Colt and Emmett are on land.

Hank's bending over Emmett about to open his helmet when Cella stops him. The open air would cause more harm. She presses one of her medical tools against her chest, the warmest part on her body at the moment, the other into Emmett's suit. Everyone is wearing winter gear. Soldiers always prepare for the worst. Rick made sure Cella knew how to access these suits with her equipment. A scanner goes in through a folded flap at the back of the suit.

After twenty-five seconds, Cella sees that Emmett has a mild concussion and whiplash due to heavy sonic waves and the furious rip tides. Cella checks Rick next his hearing integrity in his right and left ears are down twenty-two and fourteen percent, respectively. Rick never listened much anyway, so not a big loss. The bigger issue is the bruising on his brain. Rick still isn't registering Bruce holding him upright. Cella will fix that before moving on the others. She gives him slightly more of her adrenaline cocktail before increasing his perception and focus by seven percent.

It's a delicate procedure even now, but she doesn't want Rick having a stroke mid-fight. Her simulations show a 93% chance of success. The cocktail Rick had her work on will get its first real test now. Rick stands unaided feeling the drugs do their work. He nods to Cella with more meaning the others don't see.

"He's fine," says Cella. "Who's next?"

"No time," says Colt.

He's been looking at the edge for over a minute. Nothing has popped out yet. Yet.

If you see one you should think thirty.

"How many did we lose?" asks Colt, shaking bits of ice off himself.

The troop does a quick count. They've known each other for over a year. It takes under a minute. Nine people.

"This is on me," says Colt. "Bruce."

"Already on it," says Bruce, setting up explosives with proximity fuses.

"We're still on schedule," says Colt. "Let's move."

#

D and Zach are making good progress. D's arm is frozen now. Exposing it to the tunnel was a good move. Icicles are dangling from the thing. D's trying to hide his limp, and these past fifteen minutes, Zach's been the one slowing to let D recover. D would argue about this, but there's a throbbing in his elbow, sending a pulse of pain with each heartbeat. It's enough to make D think about taking those pain killers. Without the vest, he can't regulate where the fabric should tighten. So now it's just very comfortable warm pants instead of something more useful. All of this has D wanting to change routes and find the troop. Zach would notice if D changed routes, so D's not giving that prick the satisfaction.

They reach a depression about fifteen feet deep that takes up the entire width of the tunnel. It should curve up to the other half of the tunnel in half a mile, but D's not sure about going down a known failed structure. The other paths on their datapads seem worse though, so he slides down. This underpass has old footsteps, likely the troop's scouting missions. It's unsteady rock and pieces of rust based on

Colt's notations. The problem is D has to keep placing the datapad to his body because the cold is zapping power from the thing. His other datapad had better insulation. If he does meet the troop, he'll need that back too.

The fucking thieves.

It takes an hour, but finally D tells Zach to stop. He almost blacked out with that last pulse. They climbed a half-broken ladder past a partially caved-in tunnel that was groaning as soon as they stepped inside. D had to run, and the real pain hit with sparks of agony popping in his eyes with each step.

The spike of pain is constant. He's sweating inside his helmet, but the light is turned off, and he's turned away, so Zach can't shine his goddam light in his face. Cella took all the pain meds from the lab, and the troop stole his bag. This can't continue. D's going to have to suck it up and deal with the pain or find the troop and get his things back. His arm hurts. And dammit, he's not dying here.

"Alright," says D. "Slow the pace a bit. We're changing routes. There's some flat surfaces if we go left and take Route 3 from the right at this convergence point in two miles."

Zach looks at the route in question on his own. As best he can tell, instead of the relatively straight route the troop proposed days ago, it's a route that looks like a question mark with an L at the top, tilted thirty degrees to the right. When they waited for that hour, D showed Zach the intended route and where he would lead the troop if he were scouting. The route they're on has points that come close to the troop's route but they left late to avoid meeting the troop. The problem is that Zach and D are making better time; about an hour if Zach's reading of the map is right.

Zach's not going to say this aloud, but he can see D's hand shaking and knows why D's in this state in the first place. Zach's pieced together the broad strokes of D's mission and knows something of the man. Four times now, D's gone out of his way to protect Zach, and in his compromised state, D's battlefield effectiveness is less than a hundred percent. Is D trying to ensure Zach gets to Three Mile? That's how D could rationalize going near the troop after swearing he didn't care about civilians. Well, it's a good thing because Zach isn't going to fool himself. He needs D's help if he's going to survive.

"This might take five to seven hours," says D. "But, then we'll be back on course unless something happens."

"You wanna eat first?" asks Zach.

"I'll eat on the road. Let's move."

#

Rick's still blinking as Colt pushes the pace up front. The civvies have been trading Saffire since this walk turned into a light jog, then slow run. Bode is moving stride for stride with Emmett, and they haven't had to slow once. The others seem impressed. Cella is better than they hoped. Aside from that, everyone knows Colt thinks the brogs are chasing them. Instead of panicking, people are focusing and following Colt without question.

Rick's still feeling well but would've like to be told Cella would use that experimental shit on him. He did say he'd volunteer for whatever experiment she was planning after he asked her to make the gas. She was really upset about doing that and how well it worked. She shouldn't be, that Creighton was an asshole and probably dead. She needs to move on and not use him as a guinea pig without his permission.

It's unsettling; he can see Betty and Hank keeping pace but slowing. None of them are twenty-five anymore, are they? Wanda is in the worst shape. She didn't want to follow the training regimen Colt and Hank set up: eleven miles every other day with four hours of core strengthening each day between.

#

"I'm too old for that," said Wanda when Betty tried persuading her to join for set ups.

"Saffy's going to need her grandma when we leave," says Betty.

"Back the fuck off. I said no. Leave me alone."

Wanda ran to cry in her room after that.

Rick was listening outside his room. Betty found a compromise a week later.

#

"Wanda's slowing us down," whispers Bruce.

"I know," Colt whispers back. "Nothing we can do right now."

Colt keeps his eyes forward, but Rick catches his body shifting slightly to Wanda off to his left. Jade's jaw stiffens as she jogs next to Wanda. She's at the pace Colt's going at despite trying five times to up the pace. Even Saffire ran two miles twice a week. Being so small, they couldn't risk stunting or injuring the little girl by expecting her to run like adults. The little girl's almost about to collapse too. That's why she's in Bode's arms, head on his shoulder, drooling.

Everyone else is keeping pace, though. Then, the tunnel collapses.

#

"He's not dead. There's a pulse," says a female voice.

"Then wake him up. We have to run," says a male voice.

"He's got a concussion; he might have serious brain-"

"I don't give a shit, Cella. Wake him up."

Suddenly, energy's pulsing through Rick's veins as Cella tells three men to lift him up.

"Did you use that damn cocktail on me again?" asks Rick, standing on wobbly legs.

"No," says Cella. "Just regular adrenaline. I didn't want to risk giving you a stroke. You'll be a bit on edge for the next two hours give or take. Probably longer based on your metabolism and age."

"Cella, get inside the circle," yells Colt.

He just told her to try to wake Rick up; now he's yelling at her to get in the circle. Colt gets mean when he's nervous. Cella's back in the middle of a line of soldiers. This is one of those unfortunate things that made Cella more unlikable. Since she has the best practical support skillset, she was made a priority. She taught the others some basic field medicine, but she is still best skilled at healing, so she gets the most protection.

Valenda took a swing at her during the first run through. Cella didn't have to call Valenda a serial killer's rape child, but Valenda didn't have to make that wisecrack about Cella going asexual after launching chlorine gas at her boyfriend. Now Valenda's shoving Cella next to Saffire and crowding the others around the two. The soldier in her comes out now as she jogs next to Bode with dust swirling in the rifle lights. Cella knew—no, she had an idea—things were dangerous out here. She tried forgetting what was outside after she left her sister, but now there's no pretending. That pipe almost killed them. Partial collapses suck. Cella's beginning to lose control of herself.

#

It's an hour later before D calls for another stop.

"I'm hungry," says D all but falling onto a flat rock wedged against the tunnel side.

"You got any more of those calorie bars?" asks Zach.

"No, they were in my bag, remember?"

This walking is tough. Even with the extra calories they stuffed themselves with, Zach just doesn't have the muscle mass or stamina to do this type of traveling. He's not complaining. D's working with one arm and hasn't said anything yet. They both punch their suit induction ports into their pouches and squeeze the flavor into their mouths.

"Since when did people start calling metal straws induction ports?" asks Zach.

"If you call it something fancy you can charge more for it," says D.

Zach didn't realize he asked that aloud. They should only stop for five minutes then keep walking, but D wants to wait longer.

"We're gonna be out here all day. I don't want to overtake the troop," says D.

That's what D says, yes. However, Zach can see the shaking hand again. D's staring down at the hand with that familiar intensity. After a few moments, the hand finally stops shaking. D flexes his fingers twice, then stands and walks. He doesn't give Zach a courtesy glance as he taps the tunnel sides.

They keep walking. It's not as bad as the first days with D. Maybe Zach's body needed that recovery time, but he's not quite as tired as that first day. D's pace, however, is noticeably slower, and Zach can see his limp is worse.

"D, my arm's throbbing. Can we stop again?" asks Zach.

Zach's arm feels fine, but D's so stubborn, he'd never admit to his discomfort. Zach knows D's his best chance of making it out of here, so he'll pretend his arm hurts to give D extra rest. They're about to open another food pouch, when the shockwave comes. D actually falls to the floor as the tunnel rumbles. D doesn't even bother helping Zach to his feet.

"That was an explosion, not a cave-in," says D.

"How can you tell down here? The sound's bouncing everywhere."

"I've set off explosions in tunnels before. And started cave-ins on purpose. Trust me, I know the difference."

"Can you tell where it came from?"

"No. but I have a guess about who set it off."

D gives Zach a significant look.

"This doesn't change anything. We're keeping to the current route, but we'll detour at the next convergence point and double back away from the troop." says D. "We're not close now, but a blast like that means the uglies, wherever they are, are coming to check on that blast or set it off. Enough of them will hear the troop. A group of that size, with that many civvies, won't move silently."

They continue their way, then the crackling comes. D and Zach both shiver at the sound.

"It's a horde," says D before pulling out one of the grenades he made in the armory. "We'll find a tunnel that looks like it's about to quit then let this off. We don't have to bother keeping our voices down. The louder we are, the more it'll confuse them at this distance."

D doesn't say that it's a cheap plan that only works for a few minutes, but if they're as clustered as he thinks, then being so excited will slow them down in these tighter tunnels. Yelling will make them more excited at the chance of getting prey. It's a desperate and stupid idea, but it will buy even more time. D and Zach have a burst of energy as they reach the convergence point. "Shit," says D.

The horde is already here. D doesn't think as he releases the grenade.

#

"Keep going, people; we're almost at the convergence point," yells Colt.

Everyone heard the crackling. It's a large horde somewhere behind them. Bruce falls behind everyone, looking for a particularly unstable part of the tunnel to release his explosives.

Colt pulls Jade behind him. The damn woman tried to take the lead. What the hell is wrong with her? There's a huge horde behind them and probably a few spaced out in front. Brogs will set up preemptive ambush sites in a proven kill area. Colt lost seven people that way a year ago; he's not losing his fiancé. Just as he's about to call to the troop that they've reached the sixth route convergence point, five brogs sprint from the tunnel directly ahead, closing in on the troop.

"Stop," yells Colt. "Soldiers up front."

The soldiers take more time to get to Colt than it took in practice runs. Too much time. Only Colt's five-men squad is in position.

"Fire," he yells, as the brogs come within two hundred yards. The tunnel is wider at his end. The tunnels always widen at the convergence points but brogs are thick, bulky creatures, so they can only fit in two shoulder to shoulder. It'll buy the troop precious seconds, Bruce will need to blow the tunnel. It may kill some of the troop, or most, but the mission is to get people to Three Mile. An exact number was never specified.

Colt's team opens fire and a wave of sound pulses through the tunnel, knocking everyone to the ground.

The troop is up quickly. The helmets are made to absorb shockwave pulses at this scale, and that felt like a crowd-dispersal bomb, not meant to be lethal but it hurts. The helmets protect against these types of weapons well. Against a thing like brogs, its effect is multiplied. The creatures aren't dead, but they're unconscious, which is as good as dead.

The soldiers rush into position and fire on Colt's mark. They unload half a magazine each into the five beasts. One was carrying a dozen of those damn pygmies. The shockwave had the biggest effect on the small things. Colt puts one shot into each, then steps over the things and jogs to the troop behind.

Bruce rushes back up to Colt. Jade is back close to the main body. She's not so willing to be in front now, so there's enough room they can speak in private.

"We don't have those types of bombs," says Bruce. "I can make some out of parts, yeah, but the armory never had enough for me to make a shockwave bomb."

This is a statement by Bruce, not a question.

"I know," says Colt.

"Say it then."

"There's another group of soldiers in the tunnels."

#

D wants his other vest back, but this one has earned a commendation, as the force he felt from the shockwave was minor. Zach's breathing a bit too heavy for D's liking.

"Slow down, or you'll make yourself pass out," D yells behind him at a comfortable slow run.

"How many more explosives do you have?" asks Zach.

"Only two and that was the last disperse round. I'll use one of them, and if we're fucked, I'll blow us up so they don't get the satisfaction of eating us alive."

"I didn't need to know that."

"Did I hurt your feelings, princess? Is the stress too much for you?"

"Ok, ok. No need to be an ass."

"I'm changing routes. We're going to curve back toward the original route, then cut east. The map shows some real tight tunnels on the route. It'll keep the uglies in single file, that way they can't swarm us like they'd like."

"How long will it take us to get there?"

"You got a better idea?"

Zach doesn't.

"Why didn't we shoot those uglies back there?" Zach asks instead.

"There over a hundred and fifty back there and we have thirty bullets. On top of that, they can track gun smoke. It would've been a waste of ammunition and would give them something else to use to track us down when they wake up."

"How long will that be?"

"They hear better than anything I know of, so a weapon like that, even when it's nonlethal to us, will have a big impact on them. I'll give them an hour and a half before they wake up, maybe two if we're lucky."

His adrenaline's pumping now. It wasn't when he heard the first crackle, but when he let off the bomb, D thought they were dead. He was fairly certain it would work as planned, but those parts weren't of the highest quality. Dying because of a malfunctioning grenade would be so embarrassing. But it did work, and he can't feel his broken arm—a win-win if there ever was one. Now all he has to worry about is a possible fifteen hundred more uglies who are up and angry.

One problem at a time, D tells himself. "We're going into a decline now. The notes said water, so watch your footing."

Zach doesn't feel the shift down, and if his ears popped, he can't remember. All he knows is they're past the two hours D guessed, and there's a crackling. It's like how it was topside— nothing but blackness chocked with an overwhelming urge to crawl inside yourself and pretend you've already died. Zach didn't know he felt this way when he first saw the brogs. Maybe he just refused to think about it. He can't do that now. Those fucking things are crackling again, and all he can see is Pat exploding and Lilly's broken body tossed like a piece of garbage.

"Zach," yells D. "Stay focused. You're lockin' up on me."

D shakes Zach. He's seen this before. The fear just breaks someone, and then D has to dig a knife in their brain to keep their screaming from killing everyone else. Or, in some rare cases, D would leave a person where they are because they've shut down completely, but the chase is on and their bodies could feed an ugly and hopefully buy time for him to get away. D hasn't had to do that in over a year. Anyone that weak should've died off by now.

D's wrestling with that decision right now. If Zach's too weak to continue, then D will have to do what he has to do. He punches Zach in the stomach. Mucus flies from Zach's nose, splattering against his face plate as Zach drops to his knees.

"Get it together, or I'm leaving you here," says D. "Make your choice."

Zach nods and D lifts him up, handing back Zach's gun before running. D has to cut back three times, making nine detours because the explosion earlier forced a cascade of tunnel failures. It means D's having to think on the fly which routes are best. Of course, he can't know that without checking these tunnels first. Conversely, all this doubling back and taking random paths makes it so the uglies can't find the two either. Confusion always hurts a larger force more than a smaller one.

D's updating his datapad continuously as they run. For the past three hours since the first explosion, the viable path has changed from a loop that cuts through the middle path to a semicircle that bends straight halfway, like an upside-down question mark. D's moving closer to the path he guessed the troop would take. The crackling isn't distant, but not close either. There should be a construction site for a classified something up soon. The notation says it should be deep but frozen with ice mounds of radioactive dust and puddles of ice.

What's not in the notations is that the constructions site is only a foundation, so it's exposed to the elements. They've been running downhill for at least an hour, and they're still going to be topside. D would laugh at the irony if his heart wasn't trying to burst from his chest. He hasn't looked back at Zach since Zach's little moment, but he does now and the civvie is keeping up well.

"You need to stay close on this next pass," says D. "The grounds going to be bumpy as shit. The last time they checked this location was two weeks ago. That's two weeks of ice and snow to build up on uneven ground. Do not pick your feet up. Slide as much as possible and step where I step. My boots have better grip then yours, so I'll help you out if you're stuck."

In fifteen minutes, they reach the construction site. D sees something is wrong. Where his lights can reach, he sees large snow mounds and a solid layer of ice. It looks like it snowed recently. There are dips in the snow. So either the wind made some incredible funnel vortices in twenty-five specific spots or the ice is thin and the weight of several snowstorms over the weeks has buckled the surface. There had to be some hellacious and long snowstorms to break through ice in temperatures this low.

D groans to himself. He's not sure if it would be better to have water or not. Water falling through the ice could mean that the entire underwater foundation is weak, and parts of it could fall and crush D then freeze over him. If the ice is completely frozen, then is means air pockets near the surface broke open, and irregular tubes of ice are waiting to swallow the fool dumb enough to fall in. The solid parts of the ice are easy to walk on if someone knows where to step.

D has no possible way of knowing without stepping onto the ice. Also D's only working with one arm. The real problem D's having is with the notations. It says that this site is about fifty feet deep. A service ladder should be right at the edge. D can feel the tips of the ladder. His ice arm cast has expanded, blocking the wind from poking through his airtight duct tape. This is where the problem lies.

Either Colt made up this part about the level of ice or fifty feet of water filled this construction site since it was last checked. For that matter, D can't see how far to the west or east this site goes, as pitch black as the sky is. The map shows state plans for the underground network as it was eighteen months ago, but for at least a mile and a half there is effectively a hole in the map. After a year and a half exposed to the elements, some of the buildings could crumble, pipes could burst, and the sewage pipes leading to the river could have filled in this area for a solid five miles. The map shows the geography dips in this area for about that distance. All this goes through D's head in the ten seconds it takes to make the decision and come up with contingencies.

"Remember to stay close," says D, stepping onto the ice.

Zach's having stomach cramps as they step onto the ice as cautiously as they can. The wind's trying its best to knock them off balance. There's an unnatural ebb and flow to the wind. At times, it howls its fury unmerciful and all powerful, then it's as if the force forgets its nature and stops. If Zach could see in the distance, he would see the remnants of buildings that lost their fight to the wind with stubborn pieces keeping the wind from a clear path across the construction site.

So far so good for D. Zach actually grabbed his back once when they almost fell into an ice trap. D had to rip the hand away. If they fall together, they're both dead. Zach should know that much. After he gets over his annoyance of the civvie, D's battlefield senses are back at high alert. He can't wait for the sun to come back; not having it has really ruined D's sleep cycle. He puts up a hand to signal Zach to stop. D feels something. With the wind howling like it is, he can't hear, but he knows danger well; danger he can run from or fight.

Something's happening off to his left. It's clear as the wind blows west to east that the ten-story building on his map crumbled some time ago. His light's not strong enough to see what's coming from that direction but something is. This is when the ice shifts beneath him. D signals Zach with a hand swooping across his body to glide. As they glide, a full crack forms in front of them, water seeping in and freezing almost as soon as the ice opens. They glide quicker. Then D sees it. A massive ugly thing shambling its way toward them.

It's within fifty yards, and D can see frost and ice on its skin. One of the back legs looks like it's bent at an odd angle. Did the thing break free of a trap? Maybe it went into hibernation and woke up when it sensed food? D doesn't think uglies hibernate, but they've surprised him before. He still doesn't know enough about these animals. D hasn't seen an ugly voluntarily jump into waters this cold unless they were hunting food. Well, it looks like D and Zach are the food. He's not wasting time shooting. In this wind, with this little area knowledge, it's better to avoid a fight.

This is when more of the ice breaks and more uglies show themselves as silhouettes sprinting toward D and Zach. Each of them have either missing or bent limbs. D can tell by their gates that there has been a severe accident, causing many of these fucking things to die or be injured. It won't stop them from chasing him though, so what to do?

D glides left with a brief glance to see Zach right behind him. *Good man.* More water is flowing in and freezing beneath them, and it's working to keep the ice mostly stable for as long as the two men need. As soon as both men step off, ice crumbles or it doesn't. Ice is an annoying bitch sometimes. Being in this blackness means having no sense of how far he is from the edge. D's running out of options. The claws on the uglies' feet help them maintain balance on slick surfaces. They will catch up if he can't do something.

As more silhouettes come, D's breathing increases. He's going to lock up like Zach almost did. Then he remembers he's Dice, the most feared man on any battlefield. He is not going to die in an open void of blackness. People are depending on him. Suddenly, his brain works again. The nearest snow mound is to the left, closer to the advancing uglies. He glides diagonally toward it with Zach close behind. For once, Zach doesn't ask questions.

D reaches the mound and stops holding his arm out so that Zach can't come too close. He doesn't want too much weight at one spot yet. When most of the uglies are close enough to see features, D glides away as fast as he can; Zach is close behind. They don't hear the ice crack; the wind is too loud for that. They feel the ice move in great shuttering fits. D glances behind, seeing nothing.

The snow mound is gone along with most of the uglies. One of those things is more than twice as heavy as D and Zach put together. All of them converging at one point—what did they think would happen?

D pushes hard east, keeping a rhythm like speed skaters back when international relations were good enough to have Olympic games. He runs too far away from Zach, so he slows down. D can see twelve more shapes moving toward him. D has to be a bit more careful here. He can see fifteen uglies, and they're are about sixty yards away. He's heading into a section full of mounds scattered randomly. This means quite a few air pockets and unstable ice that he will try to glide through.

Despite his better judgment, D keeps Zach closer. This means D can keep Zach from getting lost as he navigates the air pockets, but it also means more weight localized to one point. It's a risk no matter what he does, so D glides through the snow mounds. To D's great pleasure, ice cracks minutes after he enters the section. If D could get a clear look at the uglies behind him, he would see the uglies slowing as they approach the snow mounds. Many of their friends died when they chased that other pack of two-legged prey; now this smaller pack is proving very clever. They have to be careful if they want something for them and their offspring to eat. If not, then the other horde in the tunnels will get food for their young and starve this horde out.

D and Zach are making great progress. Their route is heading toward the shore but in a large zig-zag route. In a way, this is good, as it gives D more information about this ice field. It makes it easier to set a trap for these animals. Some are still chasing directly for D and Zach, but he's lost track of three. Finally, his light reaches the edge of the site and a beautiful tunnel blocked by three uglies. The ones chasing D and Zach haven't fallen into the mounds; they broke the air pockets and looped around to stable ice and repeated the process to seal off D and Zach's escape route as the ones in front close in.

Those clever ugly fuckers, thinks D. Then, without warning, he shoots the nearest ugly in the soft spot.

The huge beast convulses and drops to the ice, as the others charge. D can't retreat, so he and Zach glide forward at the remaining two uglies blocking the tunnel. At ten yards, both jump, looking to smash down onto D and Zach. D was waiting for them to expose their stomachs again. He shoots twice: one for each ugly, and they both twist in the air as if some great force is tearing them inside out. They land with two huge thuds that break the ice around them. D can't wait; he yanks Zach by the hand and runs along the backs of the beast into the tunnel as twenty uglies crackle and chase them.

#

Bode's now pacing the troop as Colt falls back to assess his map. He's certain there was a big snowstorm yesterday and it blocked off four potential routes. This is why Bode's up front checking this latest tunnel, so Colt can remap his datapad and hopefully not lead the troop into a horde of brogs.

"Turn right at the next convergence point and then take the first tunnel to your left," Colt yells to Bode.

Bode raises a hand to show he heard as Kellen steps forward as a spotter. During the past ninety minutes, two brog-scouting groups found the troop and tried charging into it to wreak havoc. Hank's cannon killed the first group, but seven more brog scouting teams followed. Now fourteen troop members are dead. They've switched to two-man scout teams to protect the troop; it's working.

"Stop," says Kellen, pulling back Bode as four sniffers charge out of the second to left tunnel.

He cracks his fifty-caliber rifle, almost falling back from the recoil. The sniffer stumbles to the side as the bullet slams into its shoulder. The thing shakes itself then charges again, burgundy blood spilling as it runs directly for the gun barrel. Kellen's inexperienced with fighting brogs; this is why he doesn't pay attention to the other three looping around the first to flank him. No one really conveyed how agile these things are or how hard it is to have a clear look. They say aim for the soft spot, but how can you do that when they're running on all fours?

The one to Kellen's left reaches him first and leaps as two loud bangs fill the tunnel. Kellen's flat on his back with the open vertical mouth of an eight-hundred-pound freak fogging his face plate as something pops in his shoulder. This is when a blinding light fills his eyes. This is how he dies, eaten by the ugliest animal in history? Suddenly, strong hands are tugging him from beneath while others lift the burning beast up. Bruce is hovering over him, while Hank stands close by, checking the fuel gauge on his cannon.

"Sorry," says Bruce. "It was either shoot the one to the left or the two coming from the right."

"Thanks," says Kellen, gasping.

"He's fine," yells Colt. "Now, everyone, keep moving. First tunnel to the left."

Colt's back in front now. Jade wanted to track with him, but he's in soldier mode now, and he told her no. Emmett's with him while Dom keeps three steps behind. At the back of the troop, Bruce is setting another proximity charge at the tunnel entrance while Rick spots him. Bruce is only placing two this time. That last explosion was too strong.

Colt's checking his datapad and scowling as they run. They're an hour behind schedule, and the tunnels ahead are more fragile than the ones closer to the bunker. It's probably because the pipes are closer to the river. In any case, Colt's making a new route as he runs. The original route was a big snake that cut through the path, the one Colt presented at the last war-room meeting. He wanted to split the troop and confuse the brogs. Whoever's left would meet up at the shuttle location. He can't see a way to make that work right now.

The routes he wanted are shut off right now, and he's had to double back twice to get around dead ends. Colt's leading them more on a straight line parallel to the main path. This is not good. There are too many people to navigate this without losing more as the brogs close in.

"Shit," says Colt, almost falling.

Everyone's heard it. Crackling, a lot of crackling, and it's close. This tunnel is wide enough to fit three men side by side. It'll work as a choke point, but there's at least a thousand brogs in the area. They might have the firepower to take out half, but the others would be smart enough to change tactics. Then, the troop would be in real trouble. The brogs know this area better than the troop. He's moving them toward a place he did not want to go, but this entire route is something he wanted to avoid, so why not go further?

"Push forward," yells Colt. "Soldiers up front. We may have to make room."

Seven? Yes, seven brogs stand waiting for them. There's no hesitation. The bullet storm's as loud as the wind topside. The tungsten penetrators slap at muscle and nerve bundles nearly sawing the creatures in half. It feels like minutes, but two hundred bullets tear apart the brogs in under fifteen seconds. Colt motions everyone forward, then hears more crackling. Not like what he heard moments ago, this is like when the beasts first showed up on everyone's radar. It's an entire horde. They're coming from all angles except the one directly ahead. These damn things smoked out the troop using the seven brogs to trap them in a pincer move.

Where the fuck did they learn that?

It doesn't matter. Colt runs forward as the horde closes in behind them, crackling so loud Colt can almost see the sound vibrating off the tunnel walls. It's enough to make someone lock up and crumple to the ground. Colt's going to pretend he can't hear it. His lights reflect off a shiny surface a hundred yards ahead. With all the new water he should have expected this location's water level would rise. This is when the roof of the tunnel buckles. Colt runs faster; maybe if he can get to the water first, he can— shit, he needs the tunnel to not collapse.

Dust flitters down, more so near the water. It seems to be localized in that point. As he moves closer, he sees the left and right tunnels blocked by some cave-in that happened months ago. The depression is now filled with ice and water. At ten yards, the roof above the water falls, crashing through the thin layer of ice as two men yell, falling. Brogs fall in after them, but with their agility, the brogs manage to grip part of the rock and swing to dry land. Colt's squad doesn't wait; bullets punch through the two brogs, several hitting the soft spot.

The two men flail; both have on urban combat suits, but one has a gravelly voice and some big bulge around his elbow. The gravelly guy yanks the other guy down below the water. Colt doesn't stop to ask who they are; he just follows, diving in. They swim twenty yards down before looping up and diagonally.

"Come on," says gravelly, dragging the other to the lip of the metal platform.

The two climb the submerged ladder 40 rungs tall. Last Colt saw, the ladder had twenty rungs above the water line, now it's only four. The man with the bulging elbow does an odd hop leap with his right arm and leg to reach the ledge. The other man throws himself against the thick composite metal door. He tries leaning on it and slapping it, but that's a bombproof bunker door. Neither man notices the dead man in the corner wearing the same urban camouflage. The other troop members bob up to the surface, looking around the 160-yard-wide circular room. There's a current coming from the right where a visible crooked gash puckers out, letting water gush in.

Colt helps Bode up the ladder before moving to the edge of the platform near the gash. He looks back at the ladder seeing only 3 rungs above the water line. Two things are clear. This room will be submerged soon and someone, recently blew a hole in that wall. It's twenty feet to the bunker door. It's clear now that this guy can't use his left arm but it doesn't stop him or the other one from yanking at the door as the troop members join in looking for henges to pop off.

"Hey, friend," says Colt to elbow bulge. "Save your energy. We can't get through that door."

The guy ignores him, so Colt grabs his shoulder. The guy works with the motion to twist himself into a liver shot dropping Colt to his knees. The guy kicks him twice, hard enough to force Colt back five feet. The rest of the troop is out of the water, and Jade is on the platform, yelling. Colt can't hear what she's saying because of the pain in his stomach.

"Stop hitting him," yells Jade. "And put your fucking hands in the air."

The guy pulls out a tiny grenade and arms it. It's a dead switch. If his grip loosens, then everyone is blowing up with him. Jade blinks at the thing in shock. She doesn't know what to do. Hank helps Betty onto the platform, then identifies the situation in two seconds and steps in front of Jade. "Who are you?" asks Hank.

#

"Zach, you still back there?" asks D, running.

"I'm here," says Zach.

"There's supposed to be a hidden construction room in a half mile. If this path isn't blocked off, we'll be right on top of it."

"What do we do then?"

"We'll blow it. Then, as the uglies get close, we'll double back through one of the tunnels. There's a lot of them focused here, so if we play this right, we can block off access to the rest of the tunnel for most of them. We'll still have uglies to worry about, but it'll be fewer, and they'll spread out to try and catch us. Hopefully, the energy it takes to eat us will be too much."

"You mean like the troop?"

"Yes."

Twenty minutes later, an ugly pops out forty yards behind them and starts crackling. Others crackle in return, seconds later. The tunnel makes it so hard to pinpoint where the sound is coming from. There's hissing and grunting after that, and most of the crackling fades. There's an ear-splitting fire fight happening somewhere. D can't tell, but most of the uglies are probably over there. D doesn't stop as the tunnel turns into a ramp leading to a path above. The ground is rugged.

Crackling tells D at least two uglies are behind them. In under a minute, D finds a dead end and below that a crusted manhole. D stomps on the manhole and the surrounding rock. This ground is already weak so D stomps down hard, once, twice, then tells Zach to jump with him, and together they crash through the floor and keep going into ice water with the uglies hurling themselves after both.

#

"Who are you?" asks Hank.

"Fuck you," says D.

That voice sounds familiar. Hank has no idea what to make of that arm. It can't be Dice. How could he get out of those handcuffs? The post was a steel welded to the floor. Hank refuses to believe he got himself out. It doesn't matter how much his friend stands like Zach.

"Help me up," says Bruce.

Hank does a quick glance back to see Rick pull Bruce from the water. Bruce is the last one up, then he presses a button and the water lifts high in the air before splashing down over everyone.

"What the hell did you do?" asks Rick.

"I set a charge at the base of the tunnel. The brogs should be blocked off now," says Bruce, shaking mud from his suit.

That was a damn good idea, so Hank has nothing to say on it. He looks back at the two men. It's tense in a way that means a fight might break out. There's a man standing with a grenade over his head. Behind him is another guy, and in the corner is a slumped figure. That one looks dead. What the hell happened?

"You're wearing our suits," says Hank. "Are you with Dax?"

"I don't know who the fuck that is, and I don't care," says D.

Everyone hears the voice. It's Dice. How did he get out?

Rick steps closer. It's clear to him that Hank is in shock. They need to take control of this situation.

"Look out," says Dom.

Bruce ducks and Dom's shotgun sprays the brog with thirty-gauge pellets, many hit the soft spot.

Bruce has no idea what happened. He blew the hole. Dirt and rock should've filled the path. What Bruce can't know is that though he set the explosion, luck both good and bad can play into any decision.

When he blew the charges, rock and mud fell but only a weak under layer. A thick section fell into the deepest point but didn't bring the rest of the tunnel down with it. Instead, water displaced and filled the space above so a flattened curve leads to this pocket. The rest of the rock just didn't fall. Bad luck.

Hank eyes D, certain it's him behind that helmet. But they can't do anything about that now.

"Form ranks," says Hank. "Shotguns up front. Rifles behind that. Civvies on the wall." Hank turns away from D. In his long years of life, he's learned simple motivations are usually the correct ones. Right now, what would be the incentive for anyone to not help?

"Are you gonna help?" asks Hank.

"I need a rifle for that," says D.

Hank pulls his secondary weapon from his bag. It's a sixty-caliber rifle, single shot with a wicked recoil. D hates these guns. They're too strong for their function. He takes it anyway and checks the chamber after ripping off the protective wrapping.

"You sure you can shoot that with one arm?" asks Hank.

"Of course I can," says D.

D moves closer to the wall and off to the side. This is when he notices the dead man in the corner. The blood is a sticky brownish color that's stained his entire front and the back wall with bits of shriveled gray chunks. Whoever this was, his death is hard to tell with as cold as it is. He has a gun in his left hand and a bullet wound through the bottom of his mouth and out the top of his head.

"Get on the wall with the civvies, Zach," says D, maneuvering himself into a comfortable position to the far right five feet in front of the dead man, flat on his stomach, barrel tilted up fifteen degrees on two stand legs, and sixty armor-piercing bullets.

Zach would protest, but he's here to hack things, not shoot things. He slides left seeing Wanda. The woman looks like she just recovered from a stroke. Saffire doesn't look much better, clutched to Dede. A lot of others are missing. Zach counts twenty-five people. Seven soldiers are missing.

"Live fire exercise. Testing," says D, and before the others can turn, the thunderous crack of the rifle sounds.

"What the fuck is that idiot doing?" yells Rick, holding the sides of his helmet.

Ambient light from the others is enough to make out details on the far wall. There's a dark blotch about thirty inches above the water. From fifty yards away, it looks the size of a quarter. D hits the top left corner of it. Now, he'll try to hit the same exact spot.

"Live fire exercise. Second test," says D and shoots again.

This second shot pulls to the right by 3.5 centimeters.

Unacceptable.

"You done?" demands Hank.

A brog leaps from the far left, and the combined shooting of Bruce, Rita, and Valenda pulverize its soft spot and the brog splashes back down into the water with a wave that wets everyone on the far left. Just before the water can settle, another brog leaps to face Colt, Bode, Jade, and Kellen in the center. It flops back into the water dead as the first. The next leaps to the right, and D sends a bullet straight through its soft spot before Hank, Dom, and Sabrina can fire.

"Nice shot," says Hank as three more jump from the water.

Everyone aims in that direction, and the sight is spectacular. A beaded stream of white-hot steel peppers the blistered skin of the beasts as they fall back into the water with the fog of gun smoke filling the chamber. Another three emerge from the far right. Hank's team fires soon as the water ripples. Hank's cannon melts the top half of the closest brog, and bullets just about explode the other two. Pieces of their limbs float atop water before other arms pull them beneath the surface.

Nothing happens for over a minute. During this time, people fidget, check their guns, and aim at the emergence points. D glances at the door for the sixth time. Those clever ugly shits are deciding something. He doesn't want to be here when they act. They're too smart for normal animals. Another minute passes. Some start groaning. Others are breathing heavy. Bruce is sweating much harder than he should for someone standing still.

The water is still rippling west to east due to the gash in the chamber, but some subtle waves are coming from the gap at the far wall. D's thinking about what they could be doing. Uglies aren't human, and in some ways, they're much more practical than people. When one dies, it's either nothing or useful, maybe food if they're desperate enough. If D were one of them, attacking this superior position, what would he do? It'd have to be simple but effective, something that helps the rest of the horde as a whole.

"Hank," says D. "How about firing that cannon at the water."

"Why?"

"We need to flush them out before they're ready to attack again."

Hank has no time to contemplate D's words. The brogs are out of the water. It's the brogs they just killed. The bullet-riddled beasts are moving forward like zombified abominations. Everyone fires on Hank's command, tearing out chunks of flesh, but they keep moving. At the edge of the platform, severed arms jump from the water, slapping troop members; others shoot the limbs from the air. Then, with an ominous wrenching sound, the dead beasts are on the platform with living brogs behind them, pushing forward. D crawls forward, moving his gun left forty degrees, and fires. The ugly and the dead ugly drop as D hits the living ones soft spot. With a four-degree angle at the middle, D wasn't sure he could make a shot like that with this gun, but he has to admit, stopping power does have its merits.

Five more brogs climb the platform using the dead brogs as battering rams to plow to the civvies along the wall. Bruce's side collapses as Valenda loses it.

"They come back to life?" screams Valenda, pumping round after sixty-caliber round into the dead beast while the thing beneath pushes forward.

Other brogs climb up now and bum rush the left side. Kellen is first to try to help push back the brogs but before he can aim for the soft spot, the beast dislocates his hip without much effort. Kellen screams a scream he didn't know was in him as the beasts crushes three civvies against the back wall. A brog in the water clinging to the side lets out mist from its back flap, and all the brogs swim for the left side.

Bruce has no choice; his line is broken so he arms a grenade and tosses it where the platform meets the wall. The explosion bounces soundwaves back and forth off the walls six times before the fire reaches the troop, blowing them off their feet and breaking the left side of the platform off into the water. Someone falls. It's a small frame. The light shows her clearly. The terrified face of Elle falls under the water.

Hank stands front and center, letting his cannon burn everything coming from the water. The steam mixes with gun smoke to coat the entire chamber in a light orange fog of war. D only fires twelve times but has twelve kills. With all the shooting and screaming, the troop can't hear him, so D shoves Dom out of the way and smacks Hank on the shoulder. Hank almost turns to burn D alive but stops.

"Hit that thing by the opening in the wall," says D. "We need to buy some time."

Hank doesn't notice the one by the wall until D points to it. Then, the stream of heat sweeps across the water and melts the sniffer pumping mist from its back. At the same time, Mr. Buckshot blasts three brogs away from the civvies. Sixty calibers pump into the sides of the brogs, holding off the beasts in front of them. They're mostly dead now, but three brogs that came after are still on the platform slashing at Colt, Jade, and Rita while they protect Cella, Wanda, Saffire, Dede, and Betty. No one can fight a brog in close quarters. Rick's about to shoot out the platform beneath them, but that husky voice is telling him to hold still. A bullet wizzes past his head, crumpling a brog tearing at Emmett. The other two shift and charge at Rick. With one tug, his arm snaps as he's pulled down into the vertical mouth of the beast. The other is about to chew through Rick's other arm when another shot makes it flop to the floor, shaking the platform even more.

The brog about to eat Rick drops him as another shot nearly hits the soft spot. The thing crackles and stomps on Rick's arm, shuddering as it steps towards D. D tries running around the thing, but it can hear and move quicker and better than D and pounces on him. D's ice cast doesn't quite break as it digs into the platform, but it is fracturing. The vertical mouth opens as a bullet flies through it.

Zach keeps firing, breaking off bits of teeth from the beast. The beast pushes off D to charge at Zach when Colt hits it from the left. The thing shifts with supernatural agility to pounce on Colt.

Jade, Rita, and Sabrina blast the back half of the brog off with forty bullets. D's back up yanking Saffire, Wanda, and the others to the far right as another seven climb up onto the platform that's tilting into the water. Only one rung of the ladder is visible now.

One handed, D fires and kills the closest brog with a center mass shot. Another charges, and the platform dips as the weight of seven brogs nearly drags the rest of the platform into the water. The others charge D now and the troop fires. The remaining uglies rush at the troop while one continues its charge for D and bull rushes him into the wall.

The strength of this thing is astonishing. D can feel his insides about to squeeze into a pulp, then another shot nearly takes off D's leg as it hits the brog's side. The brog pulls back, about to crush D into a fine powder when another shot hits the brog's right side tooth slab. It turns. Before D can think, he grabs at the soft spot. Without a knife, he can't kill it, but grabbing such a sensitive area gets the brog's attention. Before it rams D a final time, a bullet goes through its soft spot somehow missing D's hand.

D looks back at Zach, but Zach is looking at Saffire. The little girl's holding the smoking gun of the dead man in the corner. The next batch of brogs are climbing the platform now, but D can't help. The fucking beast's nine hundred pounds are draped over him. Zach is trying to pull, but he has no chance to move something this heavy.

"Help me," says Zach to everyone who can hear.

Rita, Rick, and Hank are over yanking at the dead brog while Colt, Bruce, Dom, Jade, Sabrina, Valenda, and Bode fire at the newest brogs. D kicks the dead beast off the rest of the way, grabs his rifle, and shoots past Hank's cannon to kill a brog that's about to grab Colt. Then, the door opens.

#

Cella's closest to the door, and she all but shoves the figure down to rush in. Hank lets out another stream of super-heated air, letting it work as a buffer between the brogs and everyone else. It's a bottleneck as people try pushing through, so Rick kicks Bode in the back, making him fall onto everyone else who, like dominoes, fall into the door. Wanda's almost catatonic with fear so hasn't moved an inch. D, with his one working arm, picks up the woman and throws her through the door, then picks up an equally shocked Saffire and dips in. Hank slowly backs into the doorway while sweeping the air over the platform until both feet are inside, as D slams the door shut.

#

There are actually two figures, but no one could see the other when the door opened. The first has a man's voice; he's tall, about six feet, wearing dark blue and black camouflage. The other is about 5'9", wearing traditional green camouflage. The first is cursing as he rises, helmet tinted to cover his features. He turns to the door then back at the troop. He sighs as if resigned.

"Follow me," he says.

He leads them down a six-flight staircase as Bruce falls back to throw mustard gas down the hall leading to the door. The figure enters another hall and walks down the pitch-black thirty-yard path using his and everyone else's ambient light to turn left at a fork and enter the second door of only two in the hall on the right. The room is large, and chairs are scattered around rectangular tables. A large industrial CO_2 converter buzzes in the corner as the first figure turns on a soft white light.

"Hey, I'm private Garnet Harris," says the tall figure.

He's no older than twenty but looks as if he's seen some things. Most of the troop isn't listening. Cella's telling them to put Kellen on a table, so she can look at his hip. Valenda's foot is leaking blood after that brog stepped on it. Rick's trying to hide his arm, and Jade's checking Colt's ribs. That thing made a slash at him. Emmett is looking for Elle. He's almost about to go back to the platform to find her until Bruce stops him.

D's trying to peel Saffire off but the little girl's got a good grip. She keeps staring over D's shoulder, thinking the monsters are coming. Betty comes close to Wanda, but Wanda shoves her away, screaming, then moves in a corner away from everyone. Betty can't do anything about her now, so she looks for Saffire. Betty didn't see if she came with them. In the moment, Betty forgot. She's ashamed she did, but she did. She finds the girl in the arms of some strange man.

The girl finally loosens her grip as she sees Betty. Betty sees the face of the strange man.

"You?" yells Betty.

Everyone stops and turns. Betty drops Saffire. Garnet is about to yell again as Colt, Bruce, and the others see the face in the tinted helmet.

"What the fuck is this?" says Colt, aiming his gun, followed by Bruce, Rita, and everyone else with a gun.

Most don't understand what's going on, but they can't be too careful. D pulls out his grenade again, arming it.

"How'd you get out?" yells Colt.

"I'm me. That's how," says D.

"Hey," yells Garnet, then there's a shot.

Bruce shoots at D, then everyone else shoots at D. Garnet crumples to the floor. D sees Wanda in one corner so tosses the grenade at the opposite corner away from everyone and lets off a blast that knocks everyone to the ground. D dives behind a table, flipping on its edge before shooting at the troop in return. He doesn't aim to kill. Three shots knock Colt, Bruce, and Rita's guns from their hands, then an electric pulse shoots through the room, numbing everyone.

D blinks awake with a stash of guns piled in front of him. The table is right side up again, but he's still on the floor. He blinks again; something must be making him hallucinate.

"Tag?" he says to the woman hovering over him.

"Hey D. Miss me?" she asks with a huge smile.

D lifts himself from the floor, peering at her in utter confusion.

"I'm me, D. You're not dreaming. I'm alive, and so are you. The family's back together. All we need is General, and it'll be just like high school."

D hugs her tightly, and she hugs him back just as tightly. Zach stands over both of them just as shocked as the rest of the room. Maybe they have different moms or dads. No, people like D are born in a vat at some government lab. They don't have families, right? In any case these two don't look anything alike. Lieutenant Jamie Varnum has a brother?

"I thought you were dead," Jamie whispers.

"You know how stubborn I am. The nuke got tired of me. Kicked me out of my own death. Can you believe that shit?"

"With you? Yes."

D's smirking. It's not quite a smile, but it's as close as anyone thought possible with D.

"So my brother saved your ass, huh?" says Jamie, turning to Zach. "No wonder you survived."

"Jamie was the lieutenant, you meant?" asks D. "I'd have been nicer to you if you told me that."

"Somehow I doubt that," says Zach.

"True enough." D nods fairly.

"Who the hell are you people?" asks Hank, standing across the room with the others.

"Like I said the first time you asked," begins Jamie, "he's my brother you're shooting at. And the one you just killed is the young man that saved my life when I got to this stupid fucking state. You're not my favorite people right now and you're not moving until I know what is going on. And I trust Zach and D's word better than any of yours." she ends with cold fury in her voice.

"What'd you use to shock everyone?" asks D.

"His friends have some cool toys." She nods at Garnet's body lying at the edge of the room, arms folded. "You have to admit Coalition dissident suppressor tools are damn effective."

D can't argue against that.

186

"Now, I need you to talk. Did they try to torture you?" she asks, clenching her fists.

"It's done now; it doesn't matter. I need to get to Three Mile. Will you come with me?"

"Wait—what, hold on. You're going to Three Mile too. Did everyone hear that fucking message?"

"Sounds like it," says D, lifting himself off the ground.

Jamie tries helping him, but he gives her a look and she backs off. He's stubborn as ever.

"What happened to your voice?" asks Jaime.

"Look at you with all the questions," says D, showing her his neck scar. "It's rough out there."

Jamie will have to ask about that later when they have more privacy.

"Who are these people?" She motions to the troop.

"We met them on our way to Three Mile. We don't have any agreements. They're just assholes."

"So should I give them their guns back?" she nods to the pile behind them.

"No. Those two next to the tall old guy are trigger happy. And everyone's a bit too keyed up right now. We'll decide after everyone takes a breath."

"All right, then," she says, turning to face the troop. "This is a proximity charge. I hope you know what those are, but for those who don't, it means if you come within five feet of these guns, then everything explodes. I'm going to put it on this table, so everyone has a good look and no one forgets the boundary. Now with that out of the way, you, the prissy one, can go over there by broken hips and try to fix him. You can have three assistants' help but no more. The rest of you will spread out. The ones who are injured will sit on a table and wait for the prissy bitch to come to you. Now, to ensure none of you try something stupid, the pintsized shooter will sit by me."

Betty and the others are about to rush Jamie, but she shoots a bullet an inch past Betty's ear, one past Hank's ear, another between Rick's legs and then swivels the gun left to shoot one into the table, holding Kellen and letting bits of faux wood kick up an inch from his head and fall back onto his face.

"Wow," yells Jamie, eyes blazing. "I can't believe my aim's this bad. Let's hope I don't have to shoot again. Something might happen."

Jamie motions for Saffire. Saffire pulls back, trying to hide behind Betty. Betty meets Jamie's eyes and sees no yielding. She lifts the girl up and walks with her. Jamie disarms the proximity fuse just before Betty enters then turns it back on. Hank's jaw is so tight, his teeth are about to break.

"I wouldn't test my sister, Hank," says D.

As their eyes meet, Hank sees the monster in D. He has no doubt D would kill his wife if Hank tried something. D knows Hank thinks he might. Reputations matter. Hank sits directly across from Jamie. Jamie sits Betty and Saffire between her and D with the pile of guns behind Jamie against the wall.

"What's wrong with the other old lady?" asks Jamie to Betty.

She's staring at Wanda in the corner. The woman hasn't moved since she walked over there. The shock bomb did nothing to her, and when Jamie tried to drag the woman over to the other unconscious troop members, she lashed out. Jamie decided to just leave her there.

"She's in shock," says Betty.

"So, what are you gonna do with her?"

Betty blinks in shock at the implication, then turns to D.

"You're the psychologist," says D. "No one's more qualified to answer that question."

Betty glances between both Jamie and D and sees the similarity now. Betty's seen many people in her profession. She knows truly dangerous people when she sees them, but neither has even looked at Saffire. And D is the one who was holding onto the girl as they came down here. They won't hurt the girl, but she can't be sure of that.

"Are you going to kill me because I killed your friend?" asks Saffire to Jamie.

Jamie turns to her, raising an eyebrow. "Sweetie, if anything happens to you, it'll be because of your people."

Saffire frowns at that. Jamie didn't answer the question.

"Why'd you leave?" asks Saffire to D.

"Is that the story?" asks D, glancing at Betty. "Well, I'm here now."

D didn't answer the question either. He must be mad at her too. She didn't mean to shoot that guy but it went off. When D pushed everyone into the corner, the gun was there, and she knew how to use it, so she picked it up and shot. She missed the first two times, but then she hit that last time and the monster fell. She did the right thing. But in here, everyone started screaming, and the gun just went off. She didn't mean to do it. Tears leak from her eyes, and she starts shaking.

"What's wrong?" whispers Betty, putting an arm around the girl.

Saffire hides her face behind her hands. D slides his chair away and back, giving the two space, but keeping the guns in view.

Jamie had the same idea, except she moves closer to the gun pile.

"What happened to my team?" asks D. "Where's Andre? Is Captain Jackass dead?"

"Tiller and Andre are dead, yes," says Jaime.

"Let me guess, he came up with a stupid idea and you tried to fix it before he ruined everything, but this time you couldn't fix it."

"D, he's dead. Let it go."

"That piece of shit cost me my promotion."

"No, you're punching him cost you your promotion."

"War crimes are not valid orders. You fucking know that."

"Dice, please. I know, but you could've done more to help that relationship too."

"There was nothing to help. He was an idiot with no standards and power. Bad combination."

It's been too long. She loves her brother dearly, and they've just found out the other is alive. She's not arguing this point, especially since it's clear they're not talking about the same thing.

"So Zach, what'd you make of my annoying and cocky brother?" asks Jamie, purposefully ignoring D's stare.

Zach blinks at the question. He was hoping to see more of how these two act around each other.

"I think he's a hell of a lot crazier than you. He needs to work on his self-preservation skills a lot more," says Zach.

"He's got you there," says Jamie. D grunts and moves over to the weapons pile. His duffle bag is at the bottom. He pulls out his vest and seven knives. Everything else is in there too, except the pain killers.

"D. D," yells Jamie. D turns back, frowning. "You let him believe you still have the longest confirmed kill shot in history?" D rolls his eyes before unrolling the brog skin.

"I beat his old record by .3 miles," says Jamie, smugly.

"That's only cause I catch them before they get too far," says D.

"He's still upset about that. You can tell."

"So his call sign is Dice," says Zach. "You're Tag, right?"

Jamie nods. Zach was a nosey ass on the boat, and the soldiers weren't any better. He overheard the soldiers talking and picked up things.

"So you two were on a team?"

"The best raiders team in the world," says D, stripping off his jacket.

The ice cast is melting fast, helped by the ugly almost cracking it on the platform.

"I'd love to know more about young Dice," says Zach. "He's not the loquacious type."

"Loquacious?" says D. "Look out now, Jamie. Our little techie is going to intimidate us with his fancy college speak."

"I know. Next thing you know, he'll be calling us insensate or doltish," says Jaime.

"Nah, Zach plays it safe. He'll want us to know he respects us in his way. It'll be bellicose or pugnacious."

"I see it now," says Zach, pointing at both.

Jamie smiles, and D points a gun over Zach's head.

"Get back in your fucking spot," says D in that stone husky voice.

Colt moves back to his place, hands up. Zach catches Jamie holstering her gun and D kneeling again, checking his vest a moment later.

"What'd you wanna know?" asks Jaime to Zach.

"What was life like with him?" asks Zach, motioning at D.

"First, you tell me what you've been doing since I let you out of my sight, and I'll share a very embarrassing story about D."

"I've got dirt on you too, Jaime," says D. "You talk, I talk. How about we use a mutual story?"

Jaime scowls at D, but he has a serious look so she nods grudgingly.

"Talk," Jaime says to Zach.

Zach tells her everything while D slices the rest of his jacket off. The ice cast is ruined. Most of it is a puddle at his knees. D pulls on the vest and presses into his palm, sealing the helmet around his head. The systems come back on, and D scrolls to the bright Red Cross. It does diagnostics check then brings up an image of D's arm. The helmet reads multiple fractures and shows best recommendations.

Major reconstructive surgery: Recommended ASAP.

Chance of returning full arm use: Eight percent.

Biomechanical joint replacement: Recommended.

The vest compresses around D's arm, making a cast.

"D, dammit," says Jamie. "I'm about to tell him about our race."

"You can't just start there; you have to build it up. He needs proper context to understand."

"That'll take forever."

"We need time to recover."

Betty pretends to be uninterested, but Jamie spotted her subtle shift in body posture.

"What's your name?" asks Jamie.

"Betty Auberon," says Betty, extending a hand.

Jamie slides back, holding on to her gun holster.

"Nice try," says Jamie. "So, you're a psych doc. Should I call you Dr. Auberon?"

"Betty's fine."

"And I'm assuming he's your husband?" Jamie points her chin at Hank.

"Coronel Henry Auberon," shouts Hank.

Jamie points to Rick.

"Lieutenant Coronel Richard Cabido," says Rick.

D names the others around the room before stopping at the last one, Cella.

"She stole my pain killers," says D.

"You let someone take something from you?" Jamie stares at him curiously, then back at Ms. Prissy. There's something about how Ms. Prissy looks anywhere other than D's direction. "You fucked her, didn't you?"

"Shut up," says D.

"Watch it. I outrank you now. Second lieutenant." Jamie smiles at D's scowl before turning to Zach.

"So believe it or not, there was a time when we were innocent children trying to find our identities." D throws a piece of his ruined jacket at her.

"Hey."

"Talk about that later," says D. "How'd you make it? I saw a full-on ambush topside."

"I thought I told you. Garnet saved me." Jamie glares at the little girl. "Pulled me into a manhole right as the building was collapsing. He's with a crew of sailors. We all went scouting for stable routes and were supposed to meet back here a few hours ago to map out the best way to get to Three Mile. Then, those ugly bastards attacked my squad. We barely made it to this rendezvous. We've been waiting for the others to return. They should've been back two hours ago. Garnet came up to check if you were them, then you killed him."

"It was an accident," says Betty.

"I'm sure he feels a lot better now," yells Jamie. "Who gives a kid a gun anyway?"

D looks at Jamie, asking her to relax with his eyes. They'll need these people later. He's developing a logical reason to help. That can't work if Jamie makes them too pissed off. The nonverbal conversation happens within five seconds.

"How many are in your crew?" asks D.

"Fifteen. We lost Jacob on our way back."

"Was he the guy outside?"

"What guy?"

D describes the visible features on the man outside.

"No, he must have died a while ago. The cold kept him in decent condition. I haven't seen anyone else wearing your camouflage gear."

D nods; that was a long shot anyway. "What routes did they take?"

"Why?" she can sense where D's going but wants him to say it.

"Jamie. These people started out as forty-four this morning. They'll need help. I'm sure if we can find your crew, maybe they could work together to make it to Three Mile. Of course, seeing as they've already killed one person, this might be tough, but I'm willing to call it an accident. They know you. You can smooth things over so that all the humans can get along to achieve a common goal. Everyone wins."

D stares at Hank. The contemplation's practically written on the old man's bulging forehead veins. They could rush the two after they get their guns back, but Jaime will insist on keeping Saffire near her, and D might still have another bomb on him.

Where the hell did he get the first two anyway, and how the fuck did he make a dead-man switch? D smirks at Hank reading his mind.

It would be risky, and D's reputation alone would make it a hell of a fight. Add civilians and some injured soldiers that could be used as hostages, and it's in Hank's best interest to play along for now. He nods at D.

"I'll need to hear that aloud, Hank," says D. "And I'll need your assurance that your troop won't do anything to try to harm me because it might harm the kid or your wife."

"I give my word that the troop will not do anything to harm you or Jaime until after we reach Three Mile."

D points to Zach.

"The same goes for Zach," snaps Hank.

D looks at Jaime, and she nods.

"Great, would you like to let them move around now? As a sign of good faith?"

"Fine, you can move so long as you do it away from the second table closest to us. And the girl stays here."

"That sounds plenty fair, Hank. Jaime's making a real effort to be friendly even after you killed a member of her team, after he pulled your asses out of a fire. It would really show the character of a Green Beret if you tried harming his teammate after those facts."

"I said we wouldn't try anything," yells Hank. "I'm a man of my word. No one's going to do anything or I'll shoot them myself." Hank stares at Bruce and Colt for a long moment before they nod. Hank looks at D. D looks at Jaime. She nods, then D nods. Hank rises slowly and moves to Valenda. Everyone else does the same after nothing happens.

#

Cella's taken control of the room as far as injuries go. Jamie was about to protest, but she saw the loophole in her instructions. She said Cella could have no more than three assistants, but she didn't say it needed to be the same three and every table. That clever, prissy bitch. It's a great way to send messages. As for Cella, the rules for care are clear. Leg injuries are top priority. Those get an A marked on their foreheads. Everything else gets a B except scratches or tears. Those are an X. One of the soldiers will deal with those.

"They didn't look like dogs, Colt," says Coren at a table with Colt and Bruce.

"I heard you the first time. Shut up," says Colt.

"We got lucky," says Rick, standing by Hank at a table right next to Colt and Bruce and Coren. He's refusing to let anyone near his self-slung elbow. "We won't win another fight like that." He adjusts the arm for aim. "I'm a B. Leave me alone," he shouts at Dede.

"Can your new eye see colors now?" asks D, motioning to Jamie's cybernetic right eye white on a blue steel pupil which doesn't match the dark brown natural eye.

"Yeah. It took the brain time to adjust. Of course, now everything's shades of gray so I don't think I really need color," says Jamie. "Did you get a new left ear yet?"

"No, Captain Jackass put me in the back of the line after I put him to sleep."

Jamie shakes her head. "You got a lot thinner."

"I'm on that new doomsday diet; it works."

Jamie snorts then eyes Sabrina coming within three feet of the redline.

"This pocket isn't on the maps," says Sabrina.

"I know. My crew found it. There's lots of places like that all over the States from what I understand. You just have to look harder."

Hank needs to update his datapad but Jamie's not moving from behind that line. When they're in the tunnels, he might have to start the second phase of the plan. These pockets might help a lot more people get to Three Mile. At this rate, there won't be anyone left. Hank thought they had enough firepower, but now he sees more experienced soldiers would have helped in the tunnels. He'll have to play along until he meets these others. Being able to survive out here for weeks is impressive. They could help each other. He needs to make sure no one does anything to D. This could make getting to that other unit and Three Mile nearly impossible.

"I hate it too," says Rick, reading Hank's face as if seeing his thoughts. "We've worked with people we don't like before. We'll do it now."

Colt's twitching with fury. How did D escape? He'll beat it out of him when he gets the chance. Colt's not going to take this lying down. And using a kid? This guy has one arm and somehow managed to come out ahead against twenty-five people. What the fuck is going on?

"Colt, pay attention," says Hank. "She's been looking at you for longer than a moment. See if you can get that datapad from her when we're back in the tunnels. These little pockets could be damn useful."

Jamie's a bit too bulky for Colt, but there are uglier women in the world, and it'll be dark. He'll see what he can do. Jade's a foot away and keeps quiet. If Colt weren't so mad about D getting the drop on them, he'd see her hands balled in fists while looking between Colt and Jamie.

"What's the name of the cute one with the green eyes again?" asks Jamie.

"Colt," says D, adjusting his sleeve cast. With some of the bones displaced, the cast pinches at some angles.

"Are him and that other one serious?"

"From what I've gathered she's the type to agree to marry, then divorce him a year later, talking about irreconcilable differences. Does that help?"

Jamie nods. After the mission, if he's still alive, she'll have to glam herself up a bit. Guys like him don't date average-looking women.

This is when Jamie sees Betty eyeing her critically. Family, yes, Jade looks like her. She glances down at Saffire. The girl's still crying. What the hell's she crying for?

"Why does that prissy one keep not looking at you?" asks Jamie.

"I was honest for once." says D.

"Why?"

D gives her his middle finger before readjusting his cast again. Zach is nodding at Jamie. He's got a big mouth. She'll get the real story from him. As of right now, she doesn't like Cella at all.

With everyone cataloged, Cella turns to Kellen. His joint is sticking out at an odd angle so Cella's going to be blunt.

"I have pain killers to help with the pain, but I need to realign the hip before I can give them to you. And these painkillers can cause addiction quickly," she says.

"I don't care. Give them to me," says Kellen.

Soldiers are stubborn so Cella doesn't bother telling him no. She looks at Jamie, controlling her features so as not to glare. Jamie nods and Cella calls over three guys to hold Kellen's limbs down. She gives him a towel to bite into. She lifts his leg to a ninety-degree angle. Kellen's screaming, and the guys press down harder.

"Kellen, you're tougher than this," says Hank, holding the right arm. "You just fought a ten-foot freak, but you can't do this?"

"Coronel, this is immoral," says Kellen with tears forming in his eyes.

"Kellen, I'm going to count to three, then you're going to stop being a pussy and let Cella fix you."

"Can you not go slow?" Kellen asks Cella.

"Sorry. You don't want me to mess up, do you?" asks Cella.

The leg is lifting again bringing a roof-shattering scream from Kellen. Cella pushes forward, tightening her grip. With another scream, the hip pops into place.

"I think I got it," says Cella.

"You think? Get off me," yells Kellen, feeling better but still angry and panting. "Don't ever fucking touch me again."

The troop is laughing while Kellen glares at Cella, feeling exhausted. Jamie sees D's attraction now.

"He's done," Jamie whispers to D, who nods in agreement.

Chapter 29

So he didn't mention anything about a family?" Dede asks Cella. "I probably wouldn't either if they looked like a transvestite."

Cella starts chuckling while standing in front of a laughing Sabrina checking for any frostbite.

"She's kind of bulky," Cella agrees.

"How do you think he got out?" asks Dede.

"A key obviously. He probably took it off Bruce when they we're fighting. Or, he got it the first day here. Or he made one based on the locks he saw around the bunker. Or, he already had one on him that the guys didn't find."

Dede frowns at Cella.

"Well, it wasn't magic," says Cella, defensively.

"You don't think he tried to rip his arm off to get free?" asks Sabrina.

"He didn't deny his past."

"Go find out," says Dede while Sabrina nods. "You already slept with him, so this is nothing."

Cella's jaw tightens at that.

"Dede," begins Sabrina. "you've got a real strange knack for being a cunt. You know that?"

"What's in it for me?" asks Cella.

#

"Let's get back on track here," says Rick. "Obviously, they're a lot smarter than we thought."

"They jumped into our line of fire three times. That doesn't sound smart to me," says Colt.

"No, they probed for weaknesses," says Rick. "Did anyone see our old friend in the corner? The brogs did that and that means they knew the area, just didn't count on all our firepower."

"They used their own as shields. Was that spur of the moment?" says Hank, walking back to them. "Damn, things are full of surprises aren't they?"

"We need to find these other segments," says Colt, updating his datapad. "Something about these dimensions on the map always felt off. We've got one point of reference. If we can find Jaime's friends, they might be able to give us two points. I can probably map out where the others along our route are from there. Not all, but enough to protect more of us."

"Did I hear you just agree to work with D?" asks Hank.

"For right now, it serves our purposes better than not."

That's as good of an agreement as Hank's going to get. Young men like Colt don't like being hamstrung like this, but if he feels it helps people he cares for more than it hurts, he'll suffer through it. The same might work for Bruce, but Hank will have to make sure. He's not risking Betty's safety for those hot heads.

"What's our time and distance?" asks Hank.

"Nine and a half hours and fourteen miles," says Bruce immediately.

"I thought you said we were ahead of schedule?" Hank turns to Colt.

"That was the estimate before the flooding was known," says Colt. "The new one I gave you adds six hours to our time with ideal conditions. Which these aren't."

There's no inflection in Colt's voice but the defensiveness is there.

"Ten to one says that asshole knew about the flooding," says Bruce, scowling at D.

"Whether he did or didn't doesn't matter," says Hank. "We're heading into unknown territory now. It'll be just as foreign to him as to us."

"We don't know that," says Bruce.

"What we know is that we don't know the battlefield. What we know is that even with a head start and more firepower Dice somehow managed to get ahead of us. Right now, we know that he and his sister have friends. Can we know how close they are to us? If we attacked him, could he lead us into a horde of brogs? Or, if he escaped, could he trap us in some ambush where his friends are waiting? What if Dax's crew are with them? There's no women in that group. What do you think they'd do to our women if they could get us out of the way?"

Hank doesn't say it. He'll let Bruce reach his own conclusion.

"What would he do if we broke our word? Could I trust you to not find out?"

"We'll wait," says Bruce.

"I'm not sure I understood that," says Hank.

"I won't fucking touch him or the other two unless you say otherwise."

Hank nods. Being the husband of a psychiatrist means you pick up a few things over the decades.

Jade glances over at D and the walking she-bolder sitting next to him. She had her doubts about Bruce's story, but holding her mom and Saffire hostage isn't the act of a good person. There's no way they can trust them. She doesn't care what dad says; they need to do something about them once they have the chance.

"Mind telling me what happened to your arm?" asks Betty.

"Yes," says D.

Betty gives a professional smile and leans in. "You mind if I deduce then?"

D shoots into the ceiling, sending everyone into alertness. Several grab for weapons they don't have, and others pull out sharp objects. D and Jamie mark them, then nod to each other.

"Thanks," D says to Betty.

Betty gives a genuinely shocked expression. This is why D said thanks.

#

Cella's okaying Emmett's left leg bone bruise as he shifts uncomfortably, keeping his arm from spiking with pain. He's looked up at the exit five times in as many minutes. She'll have to note this to Hank; Emmett's distracted right now.

"Want a pain killer?" asks Dede.

Cella takes the cartridge from Dede. It was a full bottle of twenty-five pills when Hank gave it to her. She's at eleven now; that means only the worst cases will get more. Everyone else will have to deal with the pain.

Valenda's doing a bad job of hiding how much her crushed foot hurts. As if the twitching wasn't a dead giveaway, she's curled in on herself, giving off a completely defensive posture. Her face is drained of blood. She'll get one pain killer, for all the good it'll do.

Rick's being stupid about his arm. Everyone else is as healthy as they're going to be at this point. Wanda's an issue they need to deal with now. She doesn't have to be a psychiatrist to know that one is about to pop. Cella herself was about to break. That crackle—well, she's not too interested in studying these animals anymore. They're so powerful, and large, and terrifying, and, and—

"Cella, dammit. What's wrong?" asks Dede.

Cella blinks at Dede while Dede rubs her shoulder. She was shaking. And judging by the drops on her hand and heat in her eyes, she was crying. Dede wipes Cella's forehead.

"I need to check you for scratches," says Dede firmly.

"What?" says Cella. "I'm fine."

"Is your mouth dry?"

Cella's getting upset. The brogs didn't even get close to her. But over Dede's shoulder, Hank and Colt are moving closer while Rick stands between Bruce and everyone else. Sabrina is behind her, while Jade is about to flank her. Cella can see she doesn't have a choice.

Sabrina's not too subtly hovering a hand over a hidden blade on her belt line while Jade covers her face with her undershirt. Everyone else takes off their jackets in the forty-degree room so Cella can strip with some privacy as Dede checks her body for wounds. Cella's got some bruises but no broken skin.

"She's clean," says Dede while sliding a sheathed knife in her panty line.

Hank doesn't glance at Cella but the glint of steel is obvious. The steel disappears behind his hamstring as Sabrina shifts behind her.

"That's enough of that," yells Jamie.

Why did she bet D on this? Of course, he'd know what they'd do. Now she has to stick with the old lady while D gets to carry the much lighter girl. Bullshit. There's a loud thumping crash coming from above, and Jamie orders everyone up.

#

"How fast can you run?" D asks, staring down at Saffire as Jamie tosses everyone back their things.

Saffire blinks at him. D snaps his fingers in her face and her tongue comes back. She moves closer to Betty before speaking.

"Aren't you mad at me?" she asks.

"Mistakes happen," says D. "Now, you can wallow in self-pity or do better. What are you gonna do?"

Saffire nods.

"I don't speak nodding."

"I'll do better."

"How fast can you run?"

"Um, I don't think I can run as fast as you."

"That's all right. You'll have to stay close then. And do what I say. Understand?"

Saffire nods then before D can correct her again. "Yes, sir."

"We'll see."

Saffire has a firm grip of D's hand as Jamie instructs everyone to move away from the far end exit. She's standing just behind Betty with her gun out, not pointing at Betty. Everyone does as she says and with a hand at Betty's back pushes her toward the exit as a growing racket forms above them. That mustard gas Bruce threw earlier has the uglies confused for the moment. Jaime nods at Wanda still catatonic in the corner then jogs away with D. Bode lifts her in a fireman's carry before following the others.

D's impressed that the girl's keeping to his steady pace just ahead of Betty and Jamie. It was smart to keep Betty near so the girl doesn't get difficult. Betty had an idea D was clever, but this personable streak was unanticipated. More than his shooting prowess, this has Betty concerned. The young man knew exactly what to say to the distraught girl and put her at ease. Betty's honest enough with herself to see that she's keeping detached from the situation because she's afraid. She's seen killers, and Jaime and D have both shown that side of themselves, but logic says they won't do anything unless Hank does first. She knows her husband; he won't do anything, and everyone's waiting on his signal, so for the moment she's as safe as she can be.

Jaime's trying to keep more than an arm's length away from the rest of the troop. Zach is just behind them but already struggling to keep pace. Something Betty's just noticing is Jaime favoring her ribs. *What happened there?*

D's looking back and forth at his datapad as he runs into a T shaped fork in the road.

"Go left," says Jaime.

The darkness makes it easy to miss D plowing face first into the wall. Jamie didn't notice, so D will be keeping that to himself.

"Why don't you have markings on the walls?" asks D.

"There are, but I lost my black light getting back here. I remember the way. Just follow my directions."

She's tugging Betty along while Zach huffs and puffs behind them. Jamie's really hoping these ribs don't make her fall before they reach the main tunnels. D'll never let her hear the end of it. D slows as they enter more corridors. Jamie calls out the way, left then right, around the corner, and so forth until they reach a dead end and its idle five-rung ladder. She says five, three, one, four as she falls more than leans against the wall. D's smiling in his helmet while Jamie gives his tinted face the finger.

The others reach them and start grumbling.

"You have no idea where to go, do you?" says Jade.

"Shut up you combat blow-up doll," pants Jamie.

D, like every man, knows better than to enter a woman's argument, so he feigns deafness while repeating the sequence.

There's no number pad; you have to tap the rungs, which is what he did twice, but nothing's happened. He looks back at Jamie.

"Try leaning on it," she says.

D hops on to the bottom rung with both feet, then hops down and onto the hops onto the third, ending the sequence by hanging off the fourth rung. There's a click but nothing after. He looks back at Jaime. Jamie's frowning. Maybe something on the other side is keeping the door loaded down.

The troop starts cursing under their breaths. D keeps Saffire from wandering off. Then, he comes up with something. He hops on the bottom rung as before, then sits Saffire on the third.

"Zach, come here," says D. "Hang off the top rung."

It's an odd thing to look at as D is keeping Saffire in place while holding onto the side bars. Zach hangs, then D steps onto the fourth rung and the wall slides half open.

There's a rumble, then rock falls in. It's as black on the other side of the tunnel, but as Jaime peers over his shoulder with her light, they see scorch marks on the rock. Some of the tunnel has collapsed. There was a recent fire fight. The cold has kept D from seeing any temperature differences.

"Everyone, the uglies are probably close by. Be ready," says D.

"On my pace."

D's lifts Saffire and starts a steady trot. In seconds, it's a slow run; in minutes he's running flat out.

"Slow down, slow down." pants Jamie.

She feels like she's about to have a heart attack. D shakes his head at her. She gives him her middle finger. No one else notices. The troop members are all suffering. Sabrina's toes are shouting at her and Kellen can feel his hip pain through his entire body. Rick's elbow has him sweating buckets, but they're making time. The route's taking them through a choke point about two feet wide. Saffire has no trouble getting through, but D and the others need a bit more time.

Everyone's out but longer than D would like. Wanda, especially with her ranting and punching, really clogs things up. D's tempted to leave or shoot them. Bruce is the last out so D's back to the running pace, switching his vision from sound waves to infrared periodically while going left, right, left again, then right, reaching another convergence point branching left, right, and straight forward. D just goes right as the shuttle is northeast of their general location.

The datapad by says they're nearing the tip of the question mark about to loop back around to enter the last leg of the journey. If they hurry, he can make it to the shuttle in eight hours, maybe five if they get rid of the dead weight. D's thinking of Wanda, but keeps his eyes forward, holding tightly to Saffire. The ground is getting soft like dirt. It's concerning, but D can't feel wind.

"D, slow down," says Jaime, slowing as her light shines on white feces and bone fragments.

D stops near a rib cage he sees through a coagulated mess. He spots a tattooed dog tag of a navy officer. Beyond that is shrapnel, shell casings, and limbs, one of which is still gripping a live grenade. The pin is still in it, but D nudges the severed arm just to be sure. Nothing happens, so D picks up the arm. The hand has a death grip on the grenade, and though stiff with cold, D can see this incident happened recently.

The pipe seems to have taken the brunt of many explosions and may fail soon, so the troop is thinking they should find another way, but D is calling everyone forward until there's a crackle. For a change, the tunnel gives a straight line view, but D's lights can only reach about a hundred a fifty feet, and it's three miles to the bend. Saffire runs to Betty, and D lets her. There's no point in playing that card anymore. D's helmet goes infrared, but he changes the color output to a green. He likes switching colors from time to time.

"D, where's the next segment?" asks Jamie.

"Four miles ahead and around the bend," says D.

"We should talk about—" Hank begins, as D yanks Saffire to him and starts sprinting.

He's setting a very fast pace. Saffire's being difficult, kicking her legs to try and get back to Betty, but D has a strong grip. He's not waiting to see how close the troop is; the footsteps and squeaking tell him the troop is about fifteen steps behind him. They weren't this fast before. He should've started at this pace. Lazy bastards.

About a minute into the run, a few people fall, and someone's telling D to slow down. Not going to happen. The moment he stops, the troop will ambush him. He doesn't trust Hank. He's getting to the next segment whether the troop is with him or not.

This is when the ground starts rumbling.

There's a loud crash and boom that makes D stop. The crash was behind them and to the west. D switches to soundwaves and sees ripples coming from behind the troop. There's more waves coming from the ceiling. The waves are multiplying, and the sides are about to buckle. D tells everyone to move forward and runs, switching back the infrared. Saffire's still kicking, trying to get back Betty. He might have to put this girl in a sleeper hold if she doesn't stop being annoying. The telltale groaning starts. Seconds later, there's another crash of rock and steel. D doesn't stop. People are calling to see if everyone is ok while others are chasing D; Hank's leading the way.

The ground bucks beneath them, opening fissures and cutting paths branching into, once closed tunnels. Now Saffire stops squirming, holding on tight to D as he maintains his balance over corrugated steel and gravel. Parts of the path ahead yawn open, letting to ice and snow. D keeps moving; they're almost there. The rumbling stops.

As they approach the bend, D looks back. Hank and Rick are sixty feet away, trailed by twenty-five suit lights. D's surprised Wanda's still alive. That nut case is slowing everyone down. The collapse means they can't go back, so D drops Saffire and trots forward. He sighs. He should've known.

According to his map, the next segment is three hundred yards ahead. All they have to do is walk through a horde of uglies hissing and grunting in confusion. D looks for Jamie to his right.

"A bet?" asks Jaime.

"First to twenty-five must be acknowledged as the best the other has ever seen," says D.

"Deal," says Jaime, aiming her barrel.

Rick's back with Dom and everyone else holding fifty and sixty caliber guns. Hank slides Betty and Saffire into the middle with the rest of the civvies. Colt and Jade are in front, right next to D. The uglies start crackling and turning toward the troop. D fires, dropping the closest one about a hundred yards away. The rest of the horde, in one fluid motion, turns and sprints, tracking the gun smoke and the rest of the troop fire.

The sound of two thousand bullets exploding in unison is deafening. In this confined space, echoes prevent anyone from communicating or thinking. D can feel the soundwaves pounding against his suit. The muzzle flashes are so consistent that for five hundred yards there is full illumination. There's a savage glee bubbling up from D as twelve 1,500-grain rounds saw through a sniffer. A brute all but falls apart from another barrage. Streaks of iron slam into the horde, creating a gurgling, repeating boom.

It can't have been more than a minute, but there are rows upon rows of dead beasts forcing the other uglies to fall back and reassess.

"Forward," yells Hank.

The troop steps forward slowly, practiced, alternating between calibers as D, Jaime, Colt, and Jade stab and poke the eviscerated bodies looking for surprises.

"Six," yells Jaime before pressing gently into a pool of steaming blood. Most of her pant leg is already stiff with frozen blood.

Is it too late to switch pants with someone in the back?

"Twelve," yells D before pulling up an arm and using it to poke into the layer of dead uglies.

Like Jaime, D takes pride in every shot. They'll let the others unload clips into the horde. They'll look for the sneaky ones using the excitement to get behind the troop and cause havoc. D has to admit the rate of fire is consistent. Hank trained these people well.

"Fifteen," yells Jaime, aiming at the ceiling.

Jamie's starting to enjoy herself. She can't see the bloodthirst in her own eyes, but it's clear to her brother. D freezes, crouching low beside her, gripping a smoldering arm dripping with gore as Jaime bares her teeth poised to kill something else. D's only seen that once, a long time ago when Jaime felt powerless. She made D promise never to talk about that. D hates seeing that look. It's a look that makes him want to kill everything in sight. He drops the arm and focuses.

The uglies on the frontline are cannon fodder with this much ammo being pumped into them. D's looking for the clever ones behind them, letting out plumes from their backs. He fires and fires and fires. There's loud crackling as the sniffers fall. They must aim at a softball-sized target from eighty yards away while the hulking beasts shift and contort in on themselves in grotesque ways as the bullets fly. It'd be unnerving and as difficult a shot as anyone can make, but D's damn good at what he does. That's when he sees it—an opening on the left side of the tunnel with several uglies disappearing into it.

"All right, you win. Showoff," says Jaime.

D gives her a glance, but he's thinking up options. Where are those uglies going? The collapse opened up holes in the tunnel.

He saw them.

"Shit," he says.

"What?" asks Jaime.

"Keep these two from getting killed." D points to Colt and Jade. "I'm going to the back."

He waits for the left side of the troop to stop and reload before making his way through them. Hank grabs his arm.

"What's wrong?" asks Hank.

"We're about to get hit from both sides," says D, pointing down the black tunnel.

D trots to the end line. Dom's reloading on one knee as D taps him.

"I need you to take down the ceiling," says D.

Dom blinks and looks back to Rick, then Hank. Hank nods. Dom's confused but aims up and shoots as the first ugly trots forward. Dom curses and fires at the thing.

"Aim at the ceiling, you idiot," yells D.

Twenty more brogs sprint into the light. Rick fires Mr. Buckshot, and a sheet of pellets slam into the horde. No one can hear the animals grunting in pain, but Rick's team is no longer shooting at the horde blocking the segment. They've stopped guessing how the brogs got behind them. This is foolish. They need to take down the tunnel or more of these ugly bastards are going to loop behind them splitting fire.

It's bad form and flat-out stupid to do what D's about to do, but it'll probably work, so he'll ask for forgiveness later. D tosses the grenade then lifts Rick's weapon up to the ceiling. Cracks form in the ceiling. The tunnel groans, and the sides buckle. Rick yanks his weapon away, ready to punch D, but D's already backing into the troop as rocks and steel tumble over everyone with an ear shattering rumble.

D keeps glancing up as he retreats, but the collapse stops.

Sometimes, it's better to be lucky than good.

"Dad, get back up here," yells Jade.

The front team is stuck. With this much fire power, the brogs should retreat but they're fighting with everything they have to stop the troop from going through them. And there're so many. Did they just stumble onto the main hive of these things? Some of the brogs are running into the tunnel forming the holes in the left side and letting off plumes.

"Kill the sniffers," says D.

The bodies of other brogs are forming a mound that both sides will have to get over to reach their goal. Now Hank fires his cannon. He's careful to aim just above the eight-foot mound, so that he doesn't bring this part of the tunnel down on their heads or block them off from the segment.

"Grenades," says Hank to Bruce.

Just as Bruce is about to throw his grenade, the mound bulges at the center. A stream of brogs sprint for the troop. The troop fires, turning brogs to pink mist as fast as they appear. Colt fires again just as a huge, clawed arm comes down on him. Colt slams into D so fast it seems as if he was teleported to the ground. There's a brog hand indentation in his helmet.

Jade yells, seeing him flop to the ground. Twenty bullets fill the offending brog's side, punching into the nerve cluster.

"Just do it," yells someone.

The brogs are easily through the frontline, slashing at everything as a yellow fog forms. The brogs grunt heavily. The brogs pushing in from the mound retreat from the growing cloud. D's trying to get free of Colt. Somehow his gun strap's tangled with Colt's. He'd let go of the weapon to properly untangle it, but there's a sniffer shuddering ten feet away. No way is D letting go.

"Stop moving," says Jade.

Jamie's shooting into the back of a brute when she sees Jade's knife aiming at D. She sprints to gut punch Jade, making her drop the knife onto the brog-littered floor. Jamie aims her gun.

"Don't. She was helping," yells D.

Jaime frowns, looking at D, and pulls her own knife to cut him free. Hank's ordering the troop back, away from the cloud as D turns, seeing a brute swing wildly, breaking the top seven vertebras of Coren's back. Kellen is hit next, sternum destroyed as he folds in on himself. Luckily the cloud seeps into the brogs nostrils. The thing shudders and grunts letting out strangled sounds it suffocates on its own fluids before falling dead.

"Good thinking, Cella," says Hank.

Cella looks shellshocked, nodding at the words.

"This cloud won't last long," says Hank. "Get in your positions. We'll make 'em pay for every inch." He looks at Rick. "Get an ammo count."

Rick tells everyone to count their remaining clips. It doesn't take long. They have about a third of the ammo left and a few grenades. No one says it, but they have a contingency. Hank moves closer to Betty, keeping his grenade in easy reach.

"Same formations as before," says Hank.

The fog is fading. The brogs trying to break through the cloud are frothing on the ground as the mustard gas does its work.

The cloud fades enough to show brogs gearing for a sprint. This is when pygmies leap over their bigger brethren and the cloud to land in the middle of the troop. There are screams and gun butts swatting at pygmies, and some people, after seeing these things clearly for the first time, break. Dede just about screams her lungs out as she pulls her hand back from a mouth with rigid spines coming out of it. As Dede pulls back, the suction pulls the glove off. Another pygmy's mouths latches onto the other glove. Sabrina panics as four pygmies pile atop her, looking for an opening. Her gun goes off. She's not certain if she pulled the trigger but the bullet leaves the chamber and rips through Cealen's chest.

Rick can't use his weapon around the troop; he'll trust that the others can take care of themselves, so he aims Mr. Buckshot at creatures in the thicker part the fog, blowing two into gray mist. The last of the mustard gas fades as thirty brogs surge forward, crackling at a deafening pitch. Hank's getting control of the situation. There're only five pygmies left, yanking at helmets and squeaking—or is it crackling? Maybe their size affects the type of sound they make. He'll ask Cella later. That's when his shoulder dislocates. Hank crashes into Sabrina as her foot shatters. He rolls into Valenda, who gives no resistance as the air leaves her body. He stops with one last rotation into Wanda. The screaming woman's been yanking at two pygmies trying to pull off her helmet. All that stops when the crown of Hank's helmet breaks through her faceplate, knocking her unconscious. The pygmies squeak and the remaining three pile into Wanda's helmet.

A brute is swatting at everything using Dede's frost-bitten arm, while two sniffers are dragging the rest of her body toward the mound. Dom sees this, and switches to firing grenades. The blast tears chunks from the animal, making it drop the body. Twenty more brogs aim for Dom, and he fires again aiming high and blowing off part of the tunnel taking down all the brogs but killing ten of the troop members and sending a spike of rebar through his thigh.

"Dammit, Dom. Don't do that again," says Rick, pulling his leg free from under a rock. "Dom, answer me."

Jamie and Jade have their backs to the wall to limit pygmy maneuverability while twelve have D off his feet, biting at his suit and looking for openings. Jamie's trying to pick off what she can, but the tunnel's turned into a nightclub with random spurts of fire and flash. Colt's still knocked out, and Kellen is stuck beneath him and a dead Coren. Kellen screams as he tries pushing them both off his broken hip. This is when someone yells, "Kill everything."

Rick pulls out his grenades as with Jade and Bruce and everyone else still standing. They lob them at the mound. As Rita is about to throw hers, a pygmy catapults off a brute and into the back of her knee. The grenade sails wide, into the civilians with a burst of fire. Cella's blown off her feet, feeling the whoosh of air, as her helmet nearly melts from the heat. Her bag flies open, and half of the mustard gas canisters go off. Many troop suits are compromised so the fog seeps in, blisters break out, causing more yelling and screaming.

Zach hasn't fired a shot. He's frozen. That last blast from Dom was close, so close Zach was nearly cut in half by a foot-long slab of debris. He wasn't cut in half, but it tore a huge gash into the suit along the belly and the cold gripped him immediately. The sweat from all that running has turned into ill-formed icicles. He had enough presence of mind to close the opening in his suit, but he's shaking as he instinctively curls in on himself.

Zach's father would be so proud of him. He'll go down as the only person in history to freeze to death in a gun fight.

Pathetic.

At least freezing is pleasant in the end. Several people on the ship froze to death, and it was always quiet. Rick lets off another blast near Zach. It helps a little; it makes him think he can see help in the distance.

D's raging, trying to get these ugly little bastards off. Every time he slices one, another has its spines on another part of him. D calls them spines because Fernando called them spines, but to him they've always worked more like tentacles, and they're slimy. Why is he trying to categorize the teeth of these little shits? It's because he's stuck. D's been in plenty of stalemate situations, and they get boring after a time. The suit won't let the pygmies in, and he can't get the pygmies off, so he's stuck without—bullets slam into him. He tenses instinctively, flinching as blood splatters across his faceplate and bullets strike his limbs.

When the bullets stop, Jade's on the floor again with Jaime climbing over her to reach D.

"You ok?" asks Jaime, wiping away the blood.

"Yeah. It's a good suit," says D.

"I told you it would work," says Jade, pushing herself up.

This Jaime bitch punches really hard.

As D's about to rise, a brute's fist squeezes around his vest, claws digging into the armor. A second fist is around his hips, pushing in the opposite direction. The thing is trying to snap him in two. There's a slight pain then nothing. D loses all feeling below his belly button. Then, the ugly falls. It has a hole where it's soft spot should be. Feeling flows back to his legs. He's about to thank Jaime as explosions burst from everywhere fast and furious. Uglies are hissing and sniffers are letting out plumes while retreating to the left side opening behind the mound. Six people are ushering the troop forward while shooting grenade launchers. Jamie's screaming for D to follow. D sees Dom sitting against the wall, wanting water while feeling at his gnawed legs. When did that happen?

"D come on," yells Jaime.

"I'm coming. Go."

D reaches Dom.

"Take your helmet off," says D.

As soon as Dom's helmet comes off, a bullet goes through his brain. Coren's body is being shoved off a bloody Kellen. Kellen's suit is torn. Blood is already freezing, but there's no way he's not infected. D puts a bullet through his eye. Dede's body is mutilated along with most of the other civvies. He doesn't see Cella though. Someone is writhing with a face so mangled D can't tell if it's a man or woman. That gray hair gives him a clue. He puts a bullet through its head all the same.

No one else seems alive, so D's about to catch up when little hands poke out from under three bodies. Saffire's freeing herself. D hesitates; there's blood all over the girl's suit. If she's exposed, killing her now would be best. Later no one would be willing to kill the girl. The troop is getting further and further away. Children are a liability; this girl won't help the situation. The practical thing would be to leave her. In a few seconds, circumstances will make his decision for him, so D makes his choice now. D runs. He passes Hank, Betty, Jamie, Colt, Zach, Cella, Emmett, Bode, Rita, and Bruce. Just as he's reaching the six people, the ground disappears. Others are falling after him. As the last person drops, the segment entrance closes, with uglies crackling above and D clutching Saffire.

Chapter 30

The remaining people in the troop are cursing, scrambling for something to shoot, as a blinding light shuts everyone up. The light doesn't fade. A man, it's definitely a man, 6'5, broad shoulders, and a familiar deep baritone voice is telling everyone to calm down. As their eyes adjust, the troop notices the man's holding a pure white orb over his head.

"You need to put your guns down," says the man. "That's not a request. You put them down, or I will make you. I won't repeat myself."

Jaime's the first to drop her rifle. Hank does the same, then everyone else. Another light from another man appears as the first fades. The first man rubs his hand and speaks again.

"First thing's first. Each of you need to check yourselves for suit integrity. You're covered in night tracker gore and probably some of your own people. The white stuff mixed in there is night tracker shit. I definitely don't want any of that on my people so if you want to come any closer, you'll make sure that you're all clean. Otherwise, we'll just shoot everyone and hope you were all infected to clear our consciences. Is that clear?"

"Who are you?" asks Hank.

"I'm your fucking lord and savior. Zeus almighty. Odin or maybe you'd like Tlaloc, god of thunder, rain, and earthquakes. Whatever you call me, know that I am blessed with a singular ability to kill people who ask stupid fucking questions. Now do what you're told."

Hank's seething but steps back slowly with his palms open, showing no hidden weapons.

"You guys stink," says another man. "The fuck. Commander, it's Jaime."

The commander steps forward, lifting Jaime's helmet. A piece of tendon comes off, and he takes out a powder that crystalizes the gore immediately for an easy clean.

"I thought you bit it with Corly. We found his body near the rendezvous point. Is Harris with you?"

Jaime bows her head. "No, Commander. He's dead. I found these people around the same time. I told them about you."

"Good things, I hope. What'd you do with Harris's body?"

"I folded his arms. Left him looking peaceful. I have his dog tags too."

Commander watches carefully as Jaime slowly takes the dog tag from her pocket to show Commander.

"Put it on the ground," says Commander.

He sprinkles more of his powder on the tag and scans it with a three-inch large black metal object then puts it in his own pocket. "Keep checking yourselves," says Commander.

It's not long before everyone is checked. Everyone is fine, except Emmett and Zach. Emmett and Zach's suits have large gashes, but they don't see any break in the skin. Commander orders both quarantined anyway. Just to be safe. Rick is about to protest, but a gun is at his head before he can get the words out.

They enter a room a quarter full of all types of munitions.

"Don't get any ideas," says Commander.

After the other soldiers rig their lights up to a turbine, there's enough light to illuminate the room, soft white paint over concrete. Commander does a quick survey of the room and lingers on D. He hasn't taken off his helmet yet, and that suit is top military hardware. He needs to speak with this one.

"I'm Commander Cassian Maize of the Navy Seals," says Commander. "These are my people, Captain Teague; Sergeant Majors Andrews, Carlton, Hidalgo, and Saccarria; and Private Terry. Who are you?"

Hank introduces everyone in the troop. "D and Zach aren't with us, and you already know Jaime. So that's that."

The Seals were paying close attention to D as soon as they got a look at his suit. Now, they step closer. One of the men, Andrews, who seems to be in his mid-thirties with receding black hair, gray eyes, and pock-marked skin, scowls at D.

"Too scared to take your helmet off?" asks Andrews.

"No, I just can't," says D, motioning to the deep gouges in his vest.

"Aren't those suits self-healing?" asks Maize.

"Yes," says D.

With his helmet fully tinted, Maize can't see his eyes, but somehow, he knows D's looking at him. A feral grin forms on Maize's face.

"I can tell I'm gonna like you," says Maize.

"We don't take kindly to sassing the Commander," says Carlton. "You better show some proper respect, or I'll crack that suit open, and fuck you in the ass."

"Whatever gets you off, Sergeant." says D.

Andrews doesn't telegraph the leg sweep. Carlton doesn't telegraph the armlock that will transition to a sleeper hold. D just understands what they're likely to do based on positioning and how to counter.

Andrews will go low first, aiming for the outside leg to take away D's foundation. A half-second later, Carlton shoves then grabs the flailing arm using his body weight to press D into a joint lock that will end with an arm around the neck to keep pressure on two places.

This is what would happen if D didn't step into Carlton before he was ready, out of range of Andrews' sweep, then turn Carlton into Andrews. D has a hand lock on Carlton while moving him in front of Andrews. To anyone watching at full speed, it looks like Andrews squatted and D side stepped Carlton, but the ones who know what they're looking at are impressed. This doesn't stop all the Navy Seals from pointing guns at D.

D raises his hands in surrender. Carlton wraps him in an armbar as Andrews kicks his helmet. It doesn't hurt, but as Maize steps closer, he sees the tightness around D's left arm.

"Something happen?" asks Maize.

D doesn't answer, so Andrews kicks the arm. D flinches as white-hot pain shoots through his body. Maize has no facial reaction, but he does see Jaime aim her gun at Andrews.

"He your friend, Lieutenant?" asks Maize. "His height and build match the brother you told us about."

"Yes," says Jaime.

"You'd better tell your brother to mind his manners. I'm not gonna take much more of his shit," says Maize, staring at D.

D stares back, anger rising with the pulse of pain that's returned to his arm. Carlton moves his arm lock to the left arm, and the pain radiates, but D keeps staring. What people don't understand about pain is that it's only a warning about what might be wrong. With enough time, you can ignore that warning. Training can shorten the time it takes to ignore that warning, and breaking arm locks is an old trick General taught D years ago. And General didn't do weak holds; he held him as a man would hold a dangerous suspect because only when you're desperate does the training count.

"He'll understand, sir," says Jaime. "Can you please stop? He's a better marksman than me."

The Seals blink at Jaime. They saw what she could do when they challenged her to a competition two days ago, after all her bragging. She beat all of them easily.

"Please, Commander," says Jaime.

Maize looks back at D on his knees, breathing as the pain in his arm fades to a distant echo.

"Family's important. You should show more consideration for yours," says Maize, giving Carlton a dismissive wave.

Carlton lets D go.

Jaime's by D's side before he tries anything.

"Andrews, he's your responsibility now," says Maize without looking at D. "Make sure he doesn't try anything else." To the rest of the troop he asks, "What brings you to Pennsylvania?" He looks at Hank when he says this, motioning him to a table, one of nine in the room.

"We heard a transmission," says Hank.

"So you're not from Pennsylvania?"

"I didn't say that."

"Well then, why don't we be clearer with each other. Seeing as my people helped you out of a cluster fuck for no other reason than good karma, I'd say a little insight is the least you could provide. Wouldn't you like that in my position?"

"Fair enough."

Hank tells a shortened version of how he and the troop made it to the bunker. He skips the fight with Dax. Maize doesn't need to know about that. Maize listens carefully and asks Hank to rewind to their decision to leave. Something doesn't make sense.

"My team's from a bomb shelter. Fifty-one people there, and they need us to come back with supplies. We have a reason to be out here, but it sounds to me like you had it good. The only shelter around here that can house the people you're talking about is the governor's shelter. And if I'm not mistaken, that shelter's around here."

Maize pulls out a datapad pointing to the exact coordinates. "What happened, Hank?" asks Maize. "It feels like you're leaving something out."

Hank tells Maize about Dax, and the Seals perk up. They heard about a Dax from Creighton. Most of the troop stiffen but Cella has the strongest reaction. Maize notices but keeps focus on Hank.

"Are they still alive?" asks Hank.

"When we met them, there were maybe ten left. Dax didn't like you. When one of his people tried running back to you, he shot out one of his eyes and ripped off his finger. If you wanna know where they went, they said they were heading south. They heard rumors about a big colony south of the Mason-Dixon line. If they made it, I don't know, but they were going that way."

Hank nods. "We're going to Three-Mile Island. If you can help us get there, than that's good. If you can't, that's unfortunate, but we're going to Three-Mile Island. We've sacrificed too much to not go there. Now is any of this conversation going to get me to Three Mile, or are we just going to keep talking. If so, you should know, I'm too old to want to talk to you. I don't give a shit about you or your damn people. My only priority is the people who put their trust in me. So can we help each other, or are you planning on killing us?"

"I like straight talk. In my position, it's hard to find people who can be honest with you. The truth is, I don't know if we can help each other. We seem to share a goal, but for operations like this, there must be trust. Your friend over there—"

"He's not with us," Hank interrupts.

"Ok. That's a good start. How much more ammo do you have for those cannons?"

"About fifteen canisters worth."

"And my men swear they saw some yellow gas that kept the night trackers back."

"Mustard gas. We've got a few gallons collectively."

"Ok, I think we can be friends."

"He's awake," yells Jade.

Colt's just opened his eyes.

#

"You sure he's not infected?" asks Andrews.

"It's been ninety minutes," says Cella. "He hasn't tried scratching himself or going for water. There're no breaks in the skin, and his suit only had a dent in the helmet. What more do you want?"

"I'd like a bit more respect in your fucking tone, girl."

"I'm not your girl."

"You won't be anything if I break your fucking neck. Don't test me. You're not tough."

Cella's heart beats faster as he steps closer. Rick steps to Cella's side, and Andrews looks at Rick smiling. Private Terry moves around Rick. Jaime, Zach and D are sitting against the wall about two dozen feet away. Emmett is in another corner, ringing his hands.

"Andrews," says Maize. "Be nice. Keep him here next to that one." He points at D. "If he turns, I want D killed first."

Jaime is sitting slightly ahead of D, as if to protect him. D hates when she gets like this.

Rick walks over.

"That's a weird one," says Rick about Andrews. "It's like he's looking for a fight."

D nods. His helmet is fading to a lighter tint. The claw marks are getting smaller also.

"You seem to have that effect on everyone you meet," says Rick.

"Thanks," says D.

Jaime slaps his leg lightly.

"Didn't you owe Zach a story?" asks Rick.

Zach's still recovering from the cold but he looks up from his table. He's still in quarantine there are no scratches. As Rick goes to pull him over, Teague coughs loudly, letting Rick know that he's watching.

"Come on. You're fine," says Rick. "Just shake it out."

"Zach, did you want to know how D and I grew up?" asks Jaime.

"Sure," says Zach.

"What should we tell him?"

"Your call," says D as his suit sparks and the helmet retracts. "All right, finally."

The Seals look back at him, ready to shoot in an instant. D pokes at the shrinking claw marks, pretending he didn't notice.

"I know. I'll tell them about how you tripped me in our race," says Jaime.

"You fell."

"After you tripped me."

Zach doesn't understand. After what just happened, these two marines, in fact most of the military people, are acting like nothing happened. Betty told him that soldiers have to compartmentalize while on a mission. Otherwise, worse can happen. And when you've been doing it as long as they have, you learn any quiet time is a good time to reset and detox mentally. That's what's happening here.

"I was a good kid," begins Jaime. "I want that made clear. D was always a son of a bitch, but I was a good kid."

D sucks his teeth at that.

"How long have you two known each other?" asks Zach.

"Since tenth grade?" says D.

"Ninth," says Jamie.

"I thought you two were related?" says Rick.

"Do you wanna hear the story or not?" asks Jaime.

Jaime was transferred to the prestigious Denver Youth Military Academy halfway through freshmen year. Her father was a Marine gunnery sergeant who'd finished his tour and was asked to go recruiting. If he enrolled his daughter on campus, then they'd get fifty percent off rent so it was a no brainer. And it was the only way to make sure Jaime was being taken care of while he worked.

"They don't care about all that," says D. "You were scrawny and had a big head and that ridiculous blonde tassel jacket with the bright pink sneakers. Remember?"

"Shut up," says Jaime, her face turning red. "That jacket was the style in Tennessee for everyone under twenty-five. The shoes were the best Dad could afford, and they were durable. So kiss my ass."

D chuckles.

"D was a vile, childish—"

"Hey, don't besmirch my good name," says D.

"*Besmirch*? Fuck you."

"She came at the wrong time. It was the start of tolerance week. We had some kids of coalition defectors complaining about not making friends. General thought an anti-bullying campaign at the school would get more attention and funding to the school, and the administrators voted with him. He didn't always have the best judgment about these things."

"There was bullying in military school?" asks Zach.

"Kids are kids wherever they are," says Rick.

D continues the story. "The war meant children shuttling into and out of the academies every year, but of course, this was during the ceasefire, so it was a rare time when all the enrolled kids would be in the same place for an entire school year. The Denver Academy's reputation for producing the most commissioned officers made it a magnet for career soldiers, and conscripted soldiers got a thirty-five percent discount on rent. Jamie came the week before Thanksgiving. During this time, to coincide with the festivities, they practiced what one of the administrators coined the Week of Tolerance. I thought it was a bit too spot on, but I was thirteen."

"The press heard that the nation's toughest were practicing a week of tolerance, and they asked to bring cameras to document the occasion. General agreed. He also agreed to let a panel of speakers come give lectures regarding tolerance, including a transgender woman. General was a fair man—hard, unyielding sometimes, extreme in his discipline—but fair. He cared for everyone; otherwise, he wouldn't have been an educator. Still, he was conservative, and all this emphasis on fairness made him feel soft, something he wasn't accustomed to. He just wanted the week to be over."

Jaime was enrolled and had her first class on the day the transgender woman was to speak. The children assumed she must have arrived that week because she was part of the Tolerance Week. Jokes started pouring in, comparing Jamie to the presenter. This speaker started her presentation with a documentary on the history of the LGBT movement that transitioned to the first homosexuals elected to office, early drag queens, and the new-age torch holders, complete with strobe lights and sound effects. The only clear outcome was a history of verbal ammunition against the new girl, Jamie.

"This extravaganza had people talking." D continues. "There were supposed to be more speakers but mothers demanded a stop to the week *for fear of child bewilderment*. I swear that was the headline. As for Jaime, for two months, children would rhyme Jamie's name with elements of the documentary, mostly from female classmates. Jamie liked to talk to people but she didn't like these kids. They were all bastards. She did what her father did when the stress was too much. She worked out every day after class. She started out small, since she was so skinny. People noticed the subtle change in her appearance. The kids started coming up with better nicknames for Jaime. The most popular ones were 'Jamie the Juggernaut,' which came with the singsong, 'the juggernaut ma'am is stronger than three men,' that naturally led to the corresponding nickname 'Madam Six Balls.'"

D's face is as relaxed as is possible without smiling. The pure imagination is admirable.

"I hate kids," says Jamie, still sore about the taunts.

"Drag queen's offspring," says D raising a finger. "That was a good one."

Jaime's still a bit sensitive about that name.

"I'll admit you had some inches on the other girls, but it wasn't ridiculous," says D.

"Fuck you," says Jamie, scowling, but D winks at her, and she laughs.

"The names continued past winter and into the spring term when the school held their annual skills competitions. The contests included shooting accuracy, teamwork, endurance runs, agility, speed, and swimming. Winners were separated by grades and gender for all events, excluding the mandatory teamwork event, which was a month after end-of-year exams."

"Everyone knew me as General's son. I lived in General's house, so most times I didn't participate because if I won, most kids would think General cheated. General was sensitive about this, so as a compromise I got to do just about whatever I wanted—within reason. This year, I used the tolerance mishap to enter the competitions. Everyone knew I'd win the competitions, and this school was supposed to be about doing your best. How could the other kids do that if they never faced the best? I also started playing pranks on all the kids, increasing in danger. General couldn't prove how I did half the things I did, but I made my point."

"As for the rest of the kids, like Jaime, there would be six weeks to prepare for their chosen events. Jamie's professors, because she was so skinny, steered her toward endurance running. Most children didn't like the endurance competition so this is also why she chose distance running. Jaime went for the one-mile run. She did all her training at night, away from everyone."

"A week before the competition, the records of each event were posted along with times and minimum requirements. The endurance record was the longest held record. I received a special plaque for breaking the six-year-old all-ages shooting accuracy record and won all other events by double the second place finisher, including the—"

"So you two didn't talk the whole year?" Zach interrupts.

"What for?" asks D.

"He never talks to strangers, and I couldn't stand any of them, so there was no reason to talk," says Jamie.

Colt is up now, trying to stand, but Jade's pushing him back down. He slaps her hand away.

"I'm fine. Let me breathe," says Colt, stumbling but not falling, as his knees wobble.

Three Seals turn from ogling Cella to eye Colt. Colt sees D sitting next to Jaime and walks over. "You should've left a day early."

"Tell me about it," says D.

"What was your time in the mile run?" asks Rick.

"Three minutes and twenty-six seconds," says D. "The next closest was thirty-eight seconds slower."

"Whatever," says Jamie. "My time was better."

D continues the story. "The girls stepped to the line at two o'clock. The gun sounded, and that was it. Jaime finished a full fifty-three seconds ahead of the competition. Jaime was as happy as anyone had ever seen her. Her time was three minutes and twenty-four seconds. There was a 14-mile wind at her back so it shouldn't have been a record. The supervising instructor was in shock."

"You were jealous."

"The supervisor got a hold of himself and ordered one of the corporals to retrieve the plaque they'd given me. But I wasn't giving back my plaque. The corporal wasn't going to argue with me; he tried to rip the plaque from my hand, but I kicked him in the shin and ran off with the plaque."

"In the meantime Jamie's standing waiting for her special accommodation while her competitors stand off to one side, scowling at her and whispering. Jaime was shocked when General himself returned to hand her a scuffed plaque while I stood off fifty feet away, eyeing her with murder in my eyes. General was clearly upset with me, but he hid it well and congratulated Jaime for her stunning run. She beamed while the other students planned. No one was stupid enough to call Jaime names now, but later they asked questions."

"The next day, all of her competitors claimed she cheated. The ringleader, a girl by the name of Krystal Wellins, even got her dad to make an official complaint. The word *mountebanking* was used. Who uses *mountebanking*, seriously? Well General couldn't ignore all these complaints, so he authorized an investigation. For the time being, the school accepted me as the true record holder. That's when Jamie snitched to her father."

"I'd had enough," says Jaime.

"Jamie's father marched to the General's office the next day, demanding an explanation. It just so happens, I walked in at this point."

"Jaime jumped up, pointing at me and her father stood up, trying to intimidate me. I've never been one to back down from a threat. Jaime was furious, so she took a swing at me. She telegraphed it, so I countered with an arm grab into a hip check." "She screamed like I stabbed her or something. I didn't think I flipped her that well. But she was so skinny it was nothing to slam her. Her dad roared at me. I thought he was going to snap my neck."

"General got in the way," says Jamie. "He wasn't gonna let anyone hurt D."

Both have a laugh at that, a real genuine laugh. It's odd to see on D, but pleasant to think he does things like that.

"General told my dad to be patient and the investigation would show the truth of things," says Jaime.

"Jamie was cleared of all cheating charges. However, a replay of the race, clearly showed Jaime step onto the line before the first four hundred meters were cleared. That's a disqualification, but the incident would have been too much of a problem so General compromised. She would have to race again. Since the only person in line for this record was D, he would have to race also. The winner would own the school record clearly with no ambiguity."

"Bullshit," says Jamie.

"You know I slowed down the last fifty meters. I was dustin' your time."

"Bullshit." Jaime points at D menacingly. "General saw an opportunity. D's always been a solitary person. Even with his likability at an all-time high, D couldn't stand any of the kids in the school. I was different. I was a bit of an outcast, and General knew enough about my father's financial situation to see that I'd be staying at the school for the entire four years of high school. I could be the one emotional link D had beside himself to guide him into stable adulthood."

D picks up the story. "General encouraged me to get a read on Jaime. He couched it as learning who his opponent was in order to achieve victory. I knew General was lying, but I did it anyway. The night before the big race, I found Jamie in the hallway heading back from dinner. I asked Jamie if she cheated. She said that she didn't—with some real conviction. I believed her, so I proposed a plan; to let her win. It would shut everyone up and she'd get everyone's respect for beating the best in the school. Jaime was insulted. She found the nearest mop handle and tried her best Hank Arron swing."

"Before the race, we refused to look at each other. General ordered us to set. As the gun sounded, I asked if Jaime had fun with my property. The taunt had Jaime stumbling off the block."

"But I started to slow, and she sprinted, closing the gap. I go into a full sprint but Jaime's momentum has her pushing ahead. Right before the finish line, Jaime tried to cut me off. I let her pass, which surprises her, who stumbles, catching my foot. She face plants into the turf. I crossed the line at three minutes and thirty-five seconds as the winner."

"You tripped me," says Jamie.

"You fell," says D. "I dodged a swing from Jamie's dad. General and the instructors had to hold back the man. Jamie was absolutely furious."

"The next day, I went to the main office with plaque in hand. I said I didn't want the plaque any more after hearing what Jaime went through."

"Trying to sound all noble, you piece of shit, he cracked the frame behind it." says Jamie. She picks up the story from there. "Our rivalry continued for months. I still wanted to leave but my dad and General thought this could be a character-building experience. Later, my dad was suddenly called to an emergency black ops mission in Coalition territory in an effort to maintain the peace until the country was ready to restart the war. After weeks of my dad being gone, General called me into his office one day. He informed me of the untimely death of my father. I was distraught."

"I was hardly the only child orphaned by the war, so a streamlined process was in place. For academy students, if there was no living relative, the school would have guardianship over the child, with periodic visits by a childcare professional. Dad had no known teammates and his mission technically didn't even exist, so I was left at the Denver academy. General had a good record with kids, D being his best example."

"D and I continued to be short with each other, especially me, because I was still trying to get over losing my dad. D and I both had to work in the kitchen, according to General. One time, D left a rubber mouse on one of chef's knives that almost got him stabbed. I couldn't help but laugh at that. D kept pranking the staff.

There was one incident when a rat was stuck in a rice bag. The chef screamed like a damn Oprah singer. D and I killed the rat by bashing the bag with rollers. After we threw the bag out, we laughed so hard. Chef tried threatening D to keep quiet. D wasn't scared. I respected him after that. Eventually, I joined in on pranking. We weren't friends but it was fun.

D somehow bought movie squibs packed with red colored water. Since he and I prepared the plates, it was nothing to drop the squibs in and watch people bite into lasagna and spit out gobs of red fluid."

"You forgot when he fumigated the cafeteria for three days."

"Oh yeah, you planted fake roach eggs in his apron." They laugh at that memory. "We just needed to understand one another."

"That's it?" asks Zach.

"You only asked for one story," says D.

Emmett screams as if being scalded by lava while tearing at his side. He charges forward. The closest person is Cella. His strength is exceptional; Cella feels as if her heads about to pop off. Rick tries prying

Emmett's fingers off, then a bullet pulps Emmett's brain. It's a special made hollow point for killing humans without spreading gore everywhere.

"You're welcome," says Maize, holstering his gun.

"Sir, we should leave now," says Teague.

"Give them a minute."

The troop gathers around Cella, asking if she is ok, while D pokes Emmett. There's a small scratch on his side about three centimeters wide, easy to miss.

"You didn't check as well as you should have," D says to Cella.

She can't argue the point; at the time, Bode's injury appeared to be more severe. Cella's heart rate is rapid but falling. The scratch was so small it didn't even break the skin. She should recheck Zach.

She rises but Maize locks her in place with his eyes. The other Seals have their guns aimed and the woman, Saccarria, is standing before her with gloves on. Cella doesn't fight it. Saccarria has calloused fingers and a face hard as stone with small nicks on her cheeks that make her look like walking exposed rock.

It fits that a normal woman wouldn't be a Seal, but Saccarria is singularly ugly and musclebound even more than that walking she-obelisk Jaime. Saccarria is quick and dexterous as she checks Cella's neck. The only ones that don't seem tense are D and Jamie.

"I could've sworn she'd enjoy this?" Jaime whispers. "I guess she isn't a lesbian."

D coughs over a laugh, and Cella tenses, refusing to look at them.

"She's fine," says Saccarria, in a deep voice.

It fits, thinks Cella. She could have a career in cement breaking.

The mood lightens palpably as Saccarria heads back to her position near Hidalgo. Hank whispers something to Maize, and Maize lifts an eyebrow.

"You were serious about that?" asks Maize.

"It works better now that they're on our trail," says Hank.

Maize can't deny that. "I take it you'd like some of my people with you?"

"What I want is to maximize the odds of my people reaching Three Mile. That will be much easier for both of us if we work together."

"Why don't you just send more of your people. My team is smaller. We'll get there quicker."

"You won't if we cause a fuss."

"Is that a threat?" asks Maize sternly.

"It's reality, Commander," says Hank, without blinking.

"You first."

"Colt, activate the second part of the plan."

Colt nods to Bruce then Rita. He keeps looking. A lot more people are dead then he hoped would be at this point. Who can he trust at this point to create a successful diversion? He looks at D, who's poking his suit again for some reason. No way.

"Me," says Colt.

Maize looks around at his team and Terry the Kid steps forward.

"No," says Maize. "Do you know what your mother would do to me if I let you do this?"

"Why am I here then, sir?"

"Because there was going to be another riot if something didn't change. She had to send you, or she'd be dangling from a rope. You proved her impartiality and sincere wish for the safety of the people. That doesn't mean you play hero. If we all die, your objective is to go home, not finish the mission as you were told on numerous occasions." Maize is shouting by the end.

"So you're a coward who's scared of doing his job even after you take your oaths. This is why you weren't on the first team. Those men had integrity."

Maize punches Terry. Terry can't remember seeing Maize get up from his seat, but he's blinking watery eyes up at a furious commander.

"My answer was no kid. I need a volunteer."

Hidalgo and Saccarria look at each other.

"I'll go sir." says Saccarria.

"Colt, here's your fourth. She's determined and fit. Bring her back." says Maize, refusing to look at Terry.

Maize calls his team in, but is loud enough for everyone to hear.

"Coronel Auberon has been so gracious as to let us have some of these pheromone packs, and in return, we're giving his team some reload. Now, the plan was to go back and get Jaime and Harris, then scout ahead again, but that's dust now. We're going to protect these civilians and get to the shuttle. Saccarria's going with a decoy team to clear the way and get her ass back to us before we can activate this shuttle. Should the worst happen, we get Teague to the shuttle and anyone else who'd like to not die. Understood?"

The Seals say, "Yes, sir," in unison.

"Good, pack up. We're leaving."

Chapter 31

"**W**anna make another bet?" asks Jamie. "Over or under fifty uglies within a half mile of the shuttle."

D's mumbling to himself about riots as he stares in Jamie's direction. This mumbling is new. D's often aloof when preparing for combat. It's his way of maintaining a healthy mind for the mission. This new thing is concerning as it doesn't have much of a point to it. She didn't talk to him much after the shit show in the Amazon and she paid no attention to the rumors about him going off the deep end. Should she have?

"Are you still having trouble sleeping?" whispers Jaime.

D blinks at her as if just noticing her. "What?"

"Did you sleep?"

"Sure."

"And the night before?"

"What the fuck does this have to do with anything?"

"Answer my question."

Zach comes over, and D hands him another clip, pointedly turning away from Jaime.

"You notice anything about Teague?" D asks Zach. "His jacket has a few more pockets than the rest. You see it?"

Zach nods.

"He's got tech and a few tools to open cases like motherboards. Watch."

Teague is careful about it, and if Zach wasn't looking he'd miss the glint of copper and silicone off his hand as the officer double checks his equipment.

"You heard Terry talking about what Teague does right. Well, that makes you backup," says D. "You look at him as your reference point. Wherever he is you go the opposite direction. The two of you must never be in the same location because if both of you die then the missions over. Got it?"

"All right. What about you?"

"I'm going to try and stay halfway between you two. That way if and when shit hits the fan, I've got a decent shot of keeping one of you breathing. Now repeat my instructions back to me."

"Stay on the opposite end of Teague at all times and whenever possible, get to the shuttle."

D nods.

Colt takes a moment for himself before wrapping his arms around Jade. Betty gives him a good luck peck on the cheek after the two are finished. Rita hums bible verses while hopping on either foot. Saccarria has a look in her eye like she's reconsidering joining this decoy team. Bruce is throwing up in a corner. Maize frowns at him, but no one's coming back here.

"You've been fucking my brother." says Jaime. It was a statement not a question.

Cella blinks at her and tries turning away. Jamie moves in front of her and Cella sees just how formidable Jaime looks.

"You're not barren, are you? I want nieces and nephews to play with." adds Jamie.

Cella's eyes flair and Jaime smiles. Cella visibly calms herself. "What is it?" she asks.

"So you're not an idiot. That's good." Jamie nods to herself almost disappointed. "I have to make sure he's making a good choice, you understand?"

"A good choice? There's nothing going on."

"That might play on guys, but women see differently. You look like you got the shit fucked out of you yesterday. And you're making a point to not stare at D. I know what's up, Ms. Prissy. I'm watching."

Jaime turns away pleased with herself, and Cella stands mouth open and utterly speechless.

Saffire slips away from Betty to find D. D stares at her then looks for Betty. This is her problem.

"My grandma died," says Saffire.

"Sucks, doesn't it?" says D.

"How do I get stronger?"

"Why are you asking me?"

"Because you're not scared."

Before D can answer, Betty starts yelling out for Saffire, who scurries back.

"You're a liar," says Cella, appearing before D.

"Is this supposed to be your pep talk?" asks D.

"Oh get over yourself. You slept—who are you?"

"Is this your next question?"

"No, it's not you, insufferable lunatic," she says, raising her voice. "If I had to guess, you tried to rip your arm off to get free. Zach's been glancing at it the whole time we've been here and that walking she-man says you're a better shot than her. Something's not adding up here, D. Where are you from? Are you seriously the best Marines have nowadays?"

"And what the hell would you know about the Marines? You're a pampered rich kid whose parents got her out of doing any military service."

"You don't know a thing about my parents, and at least I have a birth certificate," says Cella walking away.

Andrews looks between both. "You two got a thing?"

D sucks his teeth before walking away.

Colt's arguing with Maize about explosives.

"Those are the only things powerful enough," says Colt.

"I don't give a fuck what's powerful enough. These are ours not yours," says Maize.

"One of your people is on our team. We need failsafe's."

"A few days ago, there was a large explosion. There's only a few things that would do that. Tell me you didn't let off one of these things."

Maize blinks. "You felt that? We got ambushed. Sergeant Elvin let off the bomb to help us escape. What's that got to do with you?"

"We walked through a swamped trail that I know personally was clear days before. A large part of the route I had planned was cut off because of a collapse."

"Bullshit. There was a big snowstorm. That could've caused any number of problems. You're not guilt tripping me into anything."

"Are you kidding? What do you want for them?"

"A little respect would be nice. And more liters of that gas."

Colt's jaw tightens as he looks to Hank. Hank nods, pulling out a bottle.

"Commander," begins Colt. "Sir, I respect what you do for yours and humbly ask that you allow me the chance to have the ability to do for mine as well."

Maize nods. He didn't think the pretty boy had it in him. He hands over five sonic bombs. He knows how deadly those weapons are and takes a step back. The bombs are circular objects with horizontal grooves running down the entire 4.5-inch diameter with a screaming mouth on the top and a button inside the mouth that blinks red when armed. A clockwise twist to the center grove sets the timer and with another press, the bombs detonation sequence locks in. To disarm the bomb, twist the center groove counterclockwise three times, then hold the top button.

"Last resort, you hear me?" says Maize.

Colt just smiles, caressing the bombs. He hands one to Bruce, Rita, and Saccarria. Now they're ironing out the details of this final stretch.

"You don't have any footnotes past the next two miles," says Teague.

"That's because I didn't take this route past two miles. It's a death trap. I wasn't confident I could get through let alone get a group through," says Colt.

The other seals suck their teeth. The other tunnels are cut off from them for at least six miles.

"Ok, then, we're going to take a horseshoe route that forks left and right in six miles," says Teague. "Your team can break off at that point and we'll time your departure. It's a set time limit. You don't return within that time, we're leaving."

"Time to go," says Colt.

Chapter 32

The troop and Maize's team are at the main pipeline entrance, a sewage line that leads straight to Philadelphia. Each team sequences their times before Bruce, Colt and Saccarria check their ammo. Teague taps blocks on the dead-end wall and suddenly they're into the main tunnels.

Teague's out in front with Hidalgo as bodyguard while he reads Colt's tunnel map. Everyone is in a gentle trot. D is about forty steps between Teague and Zach and is constantly analyzing the area by tapping his helmet.

This is when everyone stops. That sounded like a crackle but D's sure it wasn't. His suit's still recovering but it saw the sound waves from an object falling 150 feet ahead before the view faded. In these close confines with people nervous, it wouldn't be hard for shooting to start. Teague tells them to keep moving. This is when the ground shifts. Now those cackles sound like a cascade of pebbles. Teague goes into a fast jog, forcing everyone to keep pace. On cue, a section of the tunnel buckles and pops, sending rusted iron chips flying.

Teague is sprinting now, yelling for everyone to move. Everyone's already running, as the tunnel crumbles around them. It feels like an hour, but it only takes them two minutes to reach the fork, and in that time, many things happen.

Teague is all but thrown ahead by Hidalgo. Saccarria slips on shifting rock falling behind the others. Hidalgo tips forward on the same ground. Colt, who was inching his way left, falls into a hole made by the tremors as Bruce nearby, grabs him and pulls him up. D, who was closest to Zach, moves forward, looking to help, as a thick piece of stone falls, forcing him left.

Jamie is in back and nearly impales herself as rocks buck Zach clear off his feet, sending his legs smashing into Jaime, who falls back near a spike of rusted iron as rock engulfs and bends the spike just as Jaime falls onto the harmless flat side. The rest of the troop is suddenly on a slab of rock, pushing up toward the crumbling ceiling. As the tunnel finally falls, a wave of rippling rock rolls out, and everyone is checking themselves. A wall of rock with a foot of space near the top cuts the left of the fork off from the troop. Several people are missing.

"Terry," yells Maize. There's no answer.

"He's back here," says Colt.

Terry was panicked during the collapse and ran. He didn't know where he was going. When the ground shifted, he fell forward into the left side of the tunnel. The ground was stable, so he waited there until it stopped. He told himself he wouldn't let fear drive his decisions again after the ambush at the state border. He said it again after the ambush several days ago. He tells himself that now as Colt flicks his head light on and off as he moves closer.

This is when a shadow moves behind Colt. Terry's eyes go wide, and he fires, hitting the target center mass.

"Hey," yells D.

Colt flips around, gun primed and eyes wide as D, takes the gun from Colt with a step and a hip toss. Still moving, D is on Terry before Terry can do anything. He takes his gun and punches the soft spot in his armor under the ribcage of his suit doubling Terry over in pain.

"You done?" asks D, annoyance clear in his voice.

Colt is up, rage rushing into his cheeks, but D has both guns and managed to dismantle Colt's rifle, while Terry is groaning on the floor. The battle is already lost, but Colt's still angry. He needs to assess the situation before D kills him. If D wanted to shoot them both, he would. He hasn't, so everyone should calm down.

"I'm done," says Colt palms open.

D nods and turns to Terry. "Check your target, kid," he says, barely containing his anger at being shot, then flicks on Terry's helmet lights and slaps the crown of his helmet.

Footsteps race down the path now and Bruce and Rita appear, guns out. They see Terry's light shine on D's suit, and Colt behind him kneeling unarmed. Colt puts up a hand making Rita put the gun down, but Bruce isn't so ready to lower his.

"So, we're it, then?" says Rita.

"Looks like it," says Colt. "I'm not risking moving that pile. It'll have to be us."

Terry doesn't show how shocked he is to see Bruce and Rita coming the other way. It's clear he missed two people running by him while he was running. That is unacceptable.

"Is Saccarria with you?" asks Colt into the opening of the fork.

"Yeah I got tripped up during the collapse." says Saccarria.

"You're alive, good. We're leaving now," says Colt "Let's sequence our times now."

"All right," says Maize and Hank. They look at each other, then sequence their times without acknowledging each other.

"Wait," says D. "Jaime, Zach, are you ok?"

"We're fine. Hurry up and get back." says Jaime.

This is when Colt remembers to ask about Jade. He just assumed since she was near Hank, she'd be fine, but he should have asked. The two share assurances that sound heartfelt, but D doesn't really buy Jade's emotions. This isn't his business though. The decoy team is off.

"I had a bet before your fight with Bruce, you know," says Colt quietly as they walk slowly with Terry, Bruce, and Rita ten feet ahead. "I bet that you would skip out on us when you had the chance."

"What were the odds?" says D.

"Three to one."

"You should've started at five."

"I did. Bruce can be a cheap son of a bitch."

D nods.

"I think I'm gonna lose," says Colt.

"How's that?"

"Jaime's clearly important to you. So it doesn't take a genius to see that you'll make sure she's ok. You don't strike me as the type to skip out on someone you care for."

D says nothing so Colt stops and faces D.

"Can I trust you to see this mission through?"

"If doing this mission gets me to Three Mile then I will see this mission through. If along the way I see it better for me to leave, then I'll tell you before I leave."

That's as good as Colt expected.

They should be running, but the last collapse has everyone being cautious until they're far enough away from the collapse site. It takes several minutes, but eventually Bruce calls back for everyone to double time.

"Colt, what do you want to do here?" asks Bruce, holding out a bottle of pheromones.

"Wait half an hour more," says Colt. "I want to be far enough away that the brogs won't smell the troop when we start."

No one's sure if it's the adrenaline or not, but thirty minutes passes quickly, and Bruce squirts a full quarter of his first bottle over the area. The map shows this route to be a five-mile-long zigzag that leads to a looping three-mile eastern curve that winds its way back northwest. This is what the five-year-old map showed. No one from Colt's scout party took this full route. It was just too dangerous.

"Two minutes per spray," says Colt. "Give your spray a five count. Then we'll alternate. Remember, we want most of the pheromone to ignite when we hit our target. If we can't, then we need to be close enough."

Colt is repeating this for Terry and D. Thirty-six minutes pass when Terry is spraying his bottle again, just as that crackle hits his ear. He squeezes the bottle tight, letting out half of its fluid.

"Control your pouring, private," says D.

Terry straightens sheepishly.

"No sprinting," says Colt, in forced level voice. "This is the point. Bruce, lead the way."

Fear is a curious thing. Most militaries train to suppress fear, as with most emotions, it's more than likely to cause mistakes. Terry's been afraid of many things. He was afraid when his father died. He was afraid when his mother stopped talking for a year after. She was almost stripped of her commission before she went on that extended vacation. Even after that, she was never the same. Terry couldn't understand why she was the way she was. She never told Terry how proud she was of him. Now, he understands.

"Terry," yells Colt. "It's Rita's turn, not yours."

"Sorry," says Terry.

"I don't give a shit about sorry. Just pay attention."

#

Teague's leading the way. Everyone heard that crackle so no one questioned it. Jade's been stride for stride with him since Saccarria got pulled out of that ditch. Her ankle's broken. If she survives, that joint will need to be replaced. For now, two powerful pain killers have her eyes bulging.

"You make a habit of fighting lost causes?" asks Teague.

"This is why I like army guys," says Jade. "They're just so much smarter."

Teague snorts and leaps ahead with a quick burst. Jade slips, trying to catch up.

"Shit, wait up," says Jade.

Jamie's huffing at the back, holding her side, with Cella and Rick two steps from her. She's too ashamed to look at either. Her ribs are howling, while Ms. Prissy and the old guy hold back to stay with her. Even Zach is doing better than her. She's so glad D isn't here to see this.

"Thirty-four minutes since they left. So we're just under four minutes," says Rick.

Four minutes? Jamie thinks it has been forty minutes. She can't keep this up.

"Hey, Ms. Pris—um Cella?" says Jaime. "You have more of those pills?"

#

D is last to top this collapsed portion of the path. His head crests the pitch-black landscape, but he feels the gust of wind shove his head forward. A storm's coming again; he can feel it in his elbow. This is very inconvenient.

"It's your turn, D," says Colt.

"A storm's coming from the east," says D, releasing a pheromone pack at the opening. "It might be better to start lighting fires a couple miles before the plant if we want maximum effect."

Colt was thinking much the same thing when he passed through. He's worried they may have to start firing the pheromone now and hope they attract enough brogs to achieve mission success.

"We'll give it another hour," says Colt. "If it gets worse, we'll split up. Can I trust you to not skip out on me if I order that?"

"As it stands now, I have to see this through with you. The routes have probably changed, and this plan is the best way to get me to Three Mile. I'll follow that order," says D.

Colt frowns at that answer. It sounds good, but he wanted someone he could trust on this mission. He doesn't believe D, but he'll have to trust that answer.

#

"Eight minutes," says Jade.

The troop slows, finding their path partially blocked. Water's trickling through the cracks, forming a layer of black ice that's impossible to see in this blackness. Teague's the first through and promptly does a near full split on the ice.

"Shit," yells Teague.

"You ok?" laughs Jade.

"I'm fine, hurry up," says Teague angrily.

Hank's the last to push through and finds the water trickling in from five points. The water is forming into a funnel of ice. With the temperature as it is, it's more likely that walking through here caused the water to find new cracks. Another collapse is coming.

Eight minutes and thirty seconds.

#

There's an echoing crack that sounds through the tunnel. Bruce stops, turning to Rita. They both turn back to Colt. He was prepared for this. There's no time for an uncomfortable silence.

"As soon as we have a chance, we're splitting up. We're twelve minutes from the end of this zigzag zone, then there'll be a fork about 250 yards after that. Bruce goes with Rita to the left, and D, Terry, and I take the right."

There's a quick nod of the head as everyone continues moving now in a tight circle. There's a soft hissing that sounds far off, but they keep moving and reach the end of the zigzag to find a stable path about 250 yards long. No one's conscious of how much time it takes, but they cross the 250 yards in record time. The cursing comes when they see six paths, not two as the map showed. This is a recent addition that map makers hadn't added to Colt's map.

"Change of plans," says Colt. "Everyone pick a path and hope it meets at the plant. If you find you've hit a dead-end, double back. If you are trapped by brogs, release everything and take as many of those fuckers with you. Whoever reaches the plant first will wire explosives. Wait at least four minutes for everyone else to show. If no one comes in that time, assume everyone is dead and blow the plant. Are my instructions clear? Good luck everyone."

Terry was really hoping to have two people with him when the split happened. He can hear crackling and hissing. He's breathing so hard he's about to pass out. Checking his map for the fourteenth time, he tries to find any landmark to tell him he's going the right way. He passed two paths that lead left and one going right but he feels going straight is the best option.

Colt is cursing his map every second. Why wasn't this new construction put on the map? This is bullshit. He just about throws the empty pheromone bottle while cursing at his map again.

D is hiking over gravel to find dozens of uglies speeding across his path. This is concerning since he's also just found out there's other paths connecting to his own, which probably means there's paths connecting to the others as well. They've walked into a maze, and it's packed with uglies. Perfect. He doesn't release his pheromones.

Ten minutes.

The water is only ankle high at this point but clearly having an effect on troop mobility. Teague and Jade, several yards ahead, have to stomp on the ground with one foot firmly planted to keep the water from freezing their feet in place. This slowed pace means they'll probably not make it to the shuttle at the specified time. This is just fine for Jamie, who cannot express the humiliation of having to keep an arm on Zach's shoulder to stay upright. She only took half of the pill Cella gave her, and it's working but numbing pain and ignoring body mechanics aren't the same thing. The ribs are even more distorted now. She'll need major surgery to realign them. She'll have to survive first though, won't she? So there's only one solution, ignore the pain.

Ten minutes, fifty-five seconds.

Terry admits to himself that he's completely lost. There are so many creatures around his path, and detours. It's near impossible to find out which is the right way. He needs to find a manhole.

To Colt, it seems like triple the number of brogs are in his area, but they are mostly behind him, which is good as it stands, but he has no clue where he's going. He's just keeping to a general northwest direction. He hasn't had the courage to open another pheromone bottle. He's well aware of this cowardice and doesn't give a shit. He'll make up for it when he reaches the plant.

D's being the most careful of everyone and has been going slower naturally. Since he heard the crackle, he's tried his best to only drop specks of pheromone. He should've gotten an analysis of how potent this stuff is per drop, but he was too busy staring at Cella's legs to ask a great question like that. *Still worth it.* The problem is he doesn't know if he's behind Colt and Terry with brogs separating him from the two. Brogs are still hissing, which means they haven't locked in on a target, so he's relatively safe now. The others must be doing a good job.

Bruce is concerned. He's glad there aren't any brogs around him, but he knows well that if brogs have an area covered, there is no sound. The brogs don't like wasting energy. If he's in a trap, he won't know until after he's dead. This thought process has Bruce seeing every step as a threat. He nearly smacks his helmet off as a bead of sweat drips into his ear. He needs to take a breath, then he sees something shift in the shadows.

That's a relative term, but his light goes sixty-five feet at low power and 220 feet at full power. Bruce is at full power and something moved just out of his light's range. It's not a conscious thought, but Bruce doesn't plan on using anymore pheromones until after he reaches the plant.

"Bruce," it whispers.

It takes all of Bruce's self-control to not shoot at the silhouette.

It's a person, and a familiar one.

"Rita," he whispers back.

"I got lost," says Rita.

"Me too. Wanna find our way together?"

She nods, and he walks closer, still glancing side to side for threats.

"This place is crawling with them," says Rita. "Do you think they might be based at the plant?"

"I hope not. They get more aggressive if you're near their young."

Rita doesn't shiver, but she wants too. "How do they look?"

"The kids? I have no idea. I just heard little squeaky sounds, but there was a wall of adults guarding them, so I couldn't see. Then, the girls died."

"What girls?"

Bruce catches himself. He and Colt swore to never talk about that. It was every man for himself.

"How's our time?" asks Bruce.

221

#

"Arraahh," yells Colt, huffing, as the brogs chase him.

There was a shot somewhere just as Colt was about to slip past the last group of brogs. Then, they turned in his direction. Now, he's off tossing mustard gas whenever they're too close. He smiles.

"Yes," says Colt, nearly in tears at the sight of a stepladder.

He leaps onto it with a horde bearing down and releases a pheromone pack as he reaches topside.

#

Terry can't understand why there's no manhole. Did he pass one and not know or is he simply in the wrong place again? Then, a beast grunts behind him. It almost sounds like a shriek, and Terry fires his gun without thinking. The echo bounces off the steel as his suit light finds the beast impaled, its front leg on displaced steel. That's as good as it goes, but the thing is hissing loudly, calling for help. Terry runs, hearing more crackling as he sprints in a general northwest direction.

Terry almost misses it—a manhole. Well, it's the broken rail of a stepladder, but that's where manholes always are. He looks up and makes a laugh that comes out as a yelp. He can't climb up to the manhole, so he tries shimming the rail as the crackling gets closer. He slips, falling hard on his ass. The creatures are about two hundred yards away.

He's certain he'll have a heart attack soon. He pulls out the sonic bomb, priming it for five seconds. He's not sure he properly set the time or just lost track of time, but with the creatures forty yards away, the bomb detonates. Eleven minutes, five seconds.

#

Hank's panicking. It's not that anything's wrong; in fact, they're making good time. However, they've seen no signs of brogs except for white feces everywhere. There should be some crackling, but there's been nothing but humans in this part of the tunnels for too long. It makes Hank think they're walking into an ambush. Maize is near the front, five paces from Teague, and Jaime is feeling much the same.

We're making good time. Let's ride this out.

At their six is a sound like a failing tunnel but more insistent, chaotic, and overwhelming. There can't be that many brogs coming this way; there can't be. Before anyone can turn their guns to aim, the sound wall hits. Eleven minutes, eight seconds.

#

D only observed a sonicbomb once. General showed him one when he was asking for reference as he applied to join the Marine Raiders. D wanted to learn how to assemble and disassemble every type of weapon. General told him that energy never fades but transfers all the time. Each sonicbomb has forty energy syphon chips preloaded with 432 watts. As you click the primer, a minimum of ten chips activate and the chips release their energy in an auditory form, destroying its casing.

D's not thinking of this now. Uglies are closing in on his position. That shot shifted attention. Now, he's running in circles, tossing pheromones randomly away from him, hoping to loop around any excited uglies looking to eat. Then, a vehemence of sound comes screaming through every crevasse, forcing him into unconsciousness.

Colts made a mistake heading topside this early. The wind is incredible. In twenty seconds of walking, he's gone maybe forty feet. Then the sound wall hits.

#

Bruce and Rita see the manhole. Its fifty yards away. Both are smiling as they race for the step ladder. This is when the brogs come. Twenty are crackling behind them, sprinting. Bruce and Rita aren't laughing anymore. They're trying their best to keep a steady balanced run as the crackling gets louder and louder. They're not going to make it. The sound hits, ripping through the tunnel and tearing up the ground. Bruce and Rita can't resist. They stumble into fissures along with the brogs. Their tunnel nearly shatters as rock falls, crushing Bruce, Rita, and the brogs.

Snow is battering off the only structure in the distance and behind him is a wall of lightning and clouds rolling toward Colt. The ground broke open but Colt was quick enough to keep his feet. The waves of sound are almost visible in the storm winds, creating an ionic arch of energy as the sound spreads 360 degrees before stopping a half-mile away. Eleven minutes, twenty-two seconds.

#

The troop and Maize's team are lying atop each other, trying to make their bodies work again.

"What was that?" asks Betty while Saffire pushes off an unconscious Rick.

"Did they get there already?" asks Carlton.

Maize sits, trying to stop a still-vibrating calf. Teague has a smile for the glossy-eyed Jade. If he's judging her expression properly, the bomb has caused an involuntary orgasm. Andrews and Carlton slap Bode awake while finding additional debris crushing twenty-seven creatures behind them. Betty lifts a tearing Saffire, struggling to take her helmet off. She can't hear her squeaking gloves. The dazed pairing of Cella and Jamie help up Hank while Zach needs a moment to control digestive functions.

Twelve minutes, forty-one seconds.

#

D is disgorging the day's meals, before checking the motionless beasts around him. The suit gets congratulations for once again protecting D, but he's lost enhanced vision and one of his pheromone packs opened and spilled all over his jacket. D lifts himself, hoping whatever hasn't left his stomach doesn't bring him back down.

Terry is topside with a nearly destroyed facial plate and shattered right eardrum and two torn quadriceps. He shouldn't have let off the bomb so close to himself. The wind is ferocious and coldness is seeping into cracks in his helmet. He drags himself to the light bobbing in the distance. Fourteen minutes.

#

Hank pulls up Rick as the others check their suits for new openings. Betty can't do anything but wipe trickles of blood from Saffire's ears and put her helmet back on while the young girl slaps her ears.

"You ok?" Jamie asks the teary-eyed Cella.

"I can't stop. I don't understand," says Cella, as her head spins.

"Fifteen minutes. Let's go," says Maize.

#

D is back to full speed while the ferocious uglies take longer to recoup their strength. Colt reaches the recycling plant. It is sixty feet tall with the top five front walls not there. Tubes of piping stand rusted and bent. They were never fully built. He wastes no time setting his charges. Then he sees a light in the distance. Is it Bruce?

Terry yells, willing his body to reach the light. Colt leans over, dragging Terry into the plant. Colt's disappointed it's not Bruce or Rita, but there's still time.

"Did you let off the bomb?" asks Colt.

Terry nods. Colt figured the kid would panic and go to the extreme first. Terry shouldn't even be out here.

"All right," says Colt. "I'm taking all your charges and pheromones. I'm going to set charges on the fourth floor. Wave your light and call the time in fifteen-second intervals. I found a manhole by the back exit. I haven't had time to check if it's open to the tunnel, but the map says it should be a direct line to the shuttle, so if trouble comes, that's our exit, ok? I'll be back."

#

D can't move as fast as he'd like. Some parts of the tunnel are shifting and the uglies are waking up. D finds a step ladder 140 yards ahead, so trots hoping the tunnel won't shift again. At thirty yards, crackling starts on his right, left and back. D runs and stops. The step ladder is a contorted jumble that used to be an opening. If only his suit worked. D doesn't think, just picks a path and goes left then right and left again angling for the plant. The uglies seem very excited to find him. He goes left, right, and left again, throwing more pheromones wherever he can to throw off the scent. His sonic bomb is still in his satchel. He'll only use that if it's a certainty he'll die. Then, he sees it, a real one.

The step ladder's intact, and there's a manhole. D shoots the manhole when thirty feet away. He has to be sure he'll hit the thing. D doesn't just hit the manhole. Six bullets shred the covering, allowing D to hop up the ladder and onto the blustery landscape without a pause. The wind nearly knocks him off his feet, but it's ok. There's a light in the distance. With the wind at his back, D runs for them.

Seventeen minutes.

#

The troop's lugging through shin-high refuse. Teague's heavier male physique and training keeps him ahead of Jade by a body length. The amount of feces is impressive, and the fact that it is white calcium-laced dung balls makes it that much more uncomfortable.

Cella's curious. Does this place operate as a bathroom? The smell may also be hiding them from the brogs. Aside from that, if brogs separate their waste in such a way, this makes their social conventions something she'd like to know more about. Do they designate each other for cleaning and collecting waste? Is there an instinctual knowledge of separating waste from the rest of the horde? The troop pushes ahead as the feces level rises, and Cella takes the chance to collect a feces sample. Her bags are only big enough to collect one ball at a time. She should've prepared better for this possibility.

"Contact," says Rick. "I see four pygmies hopping behind us.

Eighteen minutes, fifty-nine seconds.

#

D is willing out his inner sprinter as he reaches the plant, which is looming large and imposingly with its top walls exposed to the elements. It's clear this place wasn't finished before it was plotted on the map. Someone is waving their flashlight at him from the second floor. A second light is on the fourth floor but turned toward the wall, so D can make out wires from the ambient light. He doesn't see the two other lights as he should. Time to find out who's dead.

Nineteen minutes, forty-four seconds.

#

Rick and Andrews are yelling for everyone to move faster while taking elongated steps as they indiscriminately fire at crackling behind. At the front, Jade resorts to an odd hopping method, to move quicker down the pipeline. Teague starts to copy the move as she passes him. Jamie almost blacks out as Cella and Zach stay on either side to keep her upright. Rick's warning everyone to look out as an explosion sends feces into the air, lathering the walls.

"I think I got 'em," says Rick.

Twenty-one minutes, eleven seconds.

#

D's on the top floor, setting the last wire while Terry continues waving his flashlight. Colt was doing a good job but when he saw D, he was disappointed and distracted. Neither has said anything, but it'll probably be the three of them heading back to the troop.

"I'm setting up two redundant timers," says D, shouting down the steps at Colt, still looking out at the storm wall.

Colt isn't listening; he's waving his light in a back-and-forth motion, same as Terry below him.

Maybe a dead man switch is a good idea too.

D was hoping Colt could keep his wits, but with the kid ripping apart his own legs, D will have to take the lead. It only takes two minutes to make the dead-man switch and synchronize the timers on each floor. They'll have three minutes to get out of dodge as soon as D arms the timer.

"We have to leave now," shouts D.

"We've still got eight minutes," says Colt, waving his light.

"No, we don't. We have eight minutes to reach the shuttle. I'm setting these charges as soon as we hit the first floor. Are you coming or not?"

Colt blinks, turning back to D as Terry steadies his light on something in the distance.

"You'd just leave a man behind?" shouts Colt.

"The mission comes first, and if they were coming, they'd be here already. I have bigger priorities than your friends, and you should know better than to risk the mission with hopes and wishes. We have to leave."

"Oh, it's *we* now. Everyone knows you popped years ago. All that killing broke you. Don't assume we're all like you."

"I'm not getting into some moral debate with a merc. You wanna stay, fine. Take this." D hands him the dead-man switch. "To arm it, press the top button."

Colt frowns at the switch and blinks in shock. He's about to punch D, who's leaning over, eyes tracking Terry's frantically waving light.

"Is it Bruce and Rita?" asks Colt as D rushes for the steps near the back wall.

"Don't be an idiot, Colt. What human runs on four legs?"

Twenty-three minutes, four seconds.

#

Jade is running as hard as possible. At the back Jamie strides with Hank and Maize firing at pygmies. Jade's lights bounces off the seawall, ambient light showing a shuttle doorway. Teague scrambles to open his bag of equipment as the good news relays. Hank tells Rick to help form a horseshoe formation while Jade helps Teague open the shuttle door.

"The pipe's not sealed off," says Bode, aiming his light down the tunnel, leading to the recycling plant.

"Focus on the pygmies, Bode," says Hank.

As the troop is positioning several pygmies launch into them. Hank tries to yank the little freak off as another jumps into Rick's shotgun. Rick fires anyway. There's a popping sound as the pellets rip through the animal flying out to punch into the other pygmies. Jade's up turning to help.

"Hey, keep the light here," says Teague "They're doing this to give us time. Stay here."

The shuttle door blinks as Teague tries his first bypass. It blinks "ACCESS DENIED" in pixilated red.

Twenty-five minutes.

#

D's pulling Terry toward the manhole, while Colt keeps his light on the approaching brogs. They can barely hear each other as Terry yells about his legs. He was trying to shout earlier but neither could hear him over the wind. D's not listening to him now either.

The idiot kid ruptured his own legs to run away. You do something that insane, no one should listen to you.

D lays Terry down as he feels at the manhole. With more time, D would pull out his torch and cut the manhole open. There's no time for that, so he aims his rifle and shoots it, throwing up chips of metal and frozen snow. After five bullets, the thing is open, so he's about to jump down and check if the area is clear of hostiles. Then, he sees a second slab of concrete blocking the main tunnel. This is annoying. The builders must have prepared to reroute water or gas through another pipe by closing this one. D's seen this done on a few construction sites. He should've guessed this might happen and checked how viable this exit was before arming the charges.

Enough wishing, D. Get this bitch open.

"Cover your ears," D yells to Terry before tossing a bomb into the manhole. The concreate slab flips open, as if compelled by an incandescent thumb rippling in the freezing air. The hole is clear, so D jumps in.

Twenty-five minutes, forty-two seconds.

#

The same flashing sign rejects Teague's second attempt. Jade suggests stripping the wiring to expose the underlining circuitry. Wires cut and twist into others as the troop blasts away the pygmies as they creep closer.

"I'm out," says Rick, turning the sixty-caliber into two clubbing instruments while Bode empties his last clip. Twenty-five minutes, fifty-six seconds.

#

Terry aims his light all around himself, listening for crackling as Colt comes into view. He watches Colt scan the ripples fading in the air, then Terry sees a conclusion click into place.

"He left us," says Colt, as if he knew.

Terry blinks. He thought D just went in to check the area. *Did he really leave?*

One minute passes, and D doesn't pop back up. Colt arms the bombs, then drags Terry under the armpits toward the manhole. Colt says nothing but, Terry can feel the anger flowing through him. Terry can't blame him. D claimed to be a decorated officer, and he just leaves a man behind.

This is when the ground rumbles and the wall cracks. Terry and Colt's heads snap to the wall. Both hope it's the storm wall causing the rumble, but wishful thinking doesn't change facts. The wall shakes with more cracks as brogs rush up to the top floor, sniffing. The beasts seem confused. With the wind swirling as it is, smells are harder to track, making it easier for Colt to carry Terry to the manhole without notice.

This doesn't stop a brute from smashing through the wall. Terry fires his rifle, somewhat muted, in the howling winds. Colt stumbles over the cracks by the manhole. And many things happen at once. The brute charges them, followed by a dozen other brogs. The area surrounding the manhole falls. Brogs find several pheromone packs and bite into them, going rabid at the scent.

#

"Pull the blue wire," yells Teague.

Jade yanks it hard as the troop fire in slow bursts to conserve ammo.

"Make a tighter circle," says Hank, as the pygmies close in.

Suddenly, the pygmies squeak and crackle, then hop down the tunnel. Hank orders everyone to stop shooting. They don't have enough ammo to waste.

"Got it," says Teague as the board reads ACCESS GRANTED in wonderful pixilated green.

"Everyone inside," says Teague.

Twenty-six minutes, twenty-three seconds.

#

Most brogs fill the plant while several crackle at Colt and Terry stuck halfway down the manhole. Colt's trying to make room, but Terry's body weight lying atop him gives him no room to maneuver. Suddenly, an iron grip is yanking Colt down. One tug, two, three, and Colt drops to the floor.

D stands there tall as a tower. D steps over him to yank the dangling legs of Terry. He leaps forty-five inches to clasp his ankles. Terry screams, feeling every fiber of his ruptured legs as a brute swipes down at him.

"I need help," says D, dropping down before gearing for another leap.

Colt wraps around D's legs as D tugs on Terry. The kid's screaming his heart out, then jerks and twitches like a dead man on a noose.

"Drop me," says D.

Blood drips off Terry's boots as the body continues twitching. The roof forms more cracks. The men can clearly hear the thumping now. A brute is smashing through Terry's body, searching for what's beneath.

"Let's get out of here," says Colt, pulling out a mustard pack.

Just as Colt's about to release the gas, a pygmy spears him. Several more plow into D, and suddenly both men are trying to claw the little freaks off. Most people that deal with brogs think the brutes are the problem, but there are always more pygmies, and they have six times the strength of humans per pound.

D tries prying off the tendrils. He's only had pygmies swarm him like this a few times, and the trick is moving, not panicking. The pygmies like to latch onto the ground or wall to lock you in place until the brutes come. Pygmies relax when they think the fight's out of you. Then, they use their mouths to chew through any protection to eat you alive. D plays dead, and in moments, the pygmies move to bite through the suit. In a blink, D is up and digging into his bag.

Two pygmies on his arm flick out tendrils to pin his arm to his ribs. With reflexes born from years of combat, the bomb is out, the pin releases, and five seconds later, shrapnel and fire bursts up and engulfs both men.

Three of the pygmies on D are still squeaking, half-melted to his suit. He peels them off with a knife, then turns to see Colt ripping the steaming husks off himself.

"You couldn't warn me?" asks Colt.

"Stop whining."

Twenty-eight minutes.

#

"Shouldn't that plant have blown up by now?" asks Teague as the troop look for lights in the pitch black.

"There's still a couple minutes to go," says Jade, waving her light while periodically looking back out the shuttle.

"There's a switch over here," says Rick.

"What was that?" asks Bode.

"I think it's a pygmy."

227

Someone shoots, and in the flash of light, five pygmies bounce toward the shuttle bay entrance.

"Aim for the doors," says Hank, as an almighty explosion rumbles down the tunnel.

Thirty minutes.

#

"How long have you had that limp?" asks Colt.

"I'm fine," says D, checking his watch. "Can your suit take a blast like what's coming?"

"It's built to take 460 degrees centigrade. Rick and Cella tested them."

D nods, then counts down. "Four, three, two, one."

D curls into a turtle shell, and Colt does the same as fire rolls over them, roaring as the heat penetrates the men's suits. There's a sharp pinch over D's legs. In seconds that felt like minutes, the fire dissipates.

"Fuck," says Colt, pulling off his helmet. "I thought I was gonna bake alive."

Colt takes a deep breath, ignoring the waves of heat rippling in the air and deformations in the pipe. There are pockets of fire and frigid wind. If he stares closely, Colt can see where the cold and hot air battle, making warps in his vision like seeing through a glass of water. He finally notices D still on the ground, squirming. The large slab of stone and metal is lying on his leg. He needs help. They catch each other's eye. D pulls something from his chest pocket. Colt could leave him now, and no one would know.

Colt needs an answer before he decides.

"Were you going to leave us?" asks Colt. "In the plant?"

"If I were, I'd have left already," says D. "I was the one who pulled you down when you got stuck. I didn't have to, but I did."

Colt nods. "Why'd you go down in the first place?"

"I had to check the area before bringing down Terry. How the hell was I supposed to know it was a fourteen-foot drop?"

Colt leans against the slab, lifting it enough for D to move. He wriggles out, his tibia and fibula bent to a K shape. D deactivates the bomb. He lets Colt see him deactivate the bomb, which was set for ten seconds. At this distance, it would have killed both D and Colt. Colt frowns, more uncomfortable with D now than before. He is insane.

D sits on the slab, takes deep breaths, as if psyching himself up for something, then grabs the ankle of his broken leg and snaps the leg straight again. He lets out a shuttering breath, then stands and walks toward the shuttle as if nothing happened. He looks back at Colt, who nods to himself and follows.

"You think they waited?" asks D.

"Would you?" says Colt.

#

"Is everyone ok?" asks Hank.

Luck is the only thing that kept the troop alive. Everyone's suit is seared. If anyone took off their helmet, they wouldn't have a head.

Jade's flexes the arm of her melting suit when she sees bobbing lights through the door.

"It's them," she shouts, while pulling herself up.

Jade nearly trips over herself as she vaults into the arms of Colt. "You took too long," she says, as Colt blinks in shock.

D comes in behind Colt, poking at a lump of burned pygmy. Colt slowed to keep pace with D, which has D feeling surly. He hates pity, and he will not take any pain killers.

"Someone help me shut the door," says Jade.

Chapter 33

The bay, now that everyone has a good look around, is wrecked. Everything is lit in industrial white light. It's capacious. The ceiling is forty feet high with light embedded in a uniform matrix pattern. Twenty feet high is the thick terrace with four exits spaced twenty-five feet apart, all cut into the seawall. A flight of steps leads to each exit. Halfway through the room is an uplifted four-foot thick lip of steel that matches another directly above it. Right in front of that bar is twelve ruined turnstiles and card readers. An arm with a black bracelet hangs on the largest turnstile without a corresponding body.

The limb clues everyone into what may have happened with the five-hundred-plus bodies lying in random spots. The only structures still in their intended shapes are fifteen shuttle cars shaped like bullets with exhaust pipes that filter water at the end of the bay. A control room at the top right of the upper level has smashed-out windows. From here, no one can tell if the control board is damaged.

It's clear what happened. When the bombs hit, these people were going to work. As soon as the nukes were registered, everything was locked down until further notice. The bay never received a signal to reopen, and everyone inside starved to death or ate each other until the human meat became too rotten.

"Shit," says Teague, looking through his tools.

He tosses a bolt past the iron bar, and a wall of steel jumps up from the floor and down from the ceiling, smashing the bolt into a flat disc.

"I'll need to rebuild one of the card readers. It'll take a while," says Teague. "Jade?"

Colt eyes Teague. He doesn't like the way Teague says he's fiancés name.

"Where's Terry?" Maize asks D.

"He's dead. Brute got him before I could drag him into the pipe," says D.

"You have his dog tag?"

"There wasn't any time."

Maize eyes D for a long moment before shaking his head. Colt nods to himself again while the others look between Maize and D.

"What are you doing?" Rick asks Cella.

She's kneeling over the burned body of a pygmy, taking notes. The body is essentially groupings of serrated bone and air sacks with more connective tissue skin. Cella's mesmerized as she takes tweezers from her backpack to lift and turn the subject. The pygmy disintegrates as she fiddles with it.

"No," says Cella, trying to push the pieces back together.

"Goddammit, this is an ugly son of a bitch," says Bode.

"Does anyone have a camera?" she asks while putting pieces into a plastic sample bag.

She scrambles over to another pygmy that has an unburned under belly. She has a pleasant smile as she scoops it into the next sample bag.

"I think when the power came on, a security system reactivated," says Teague, pulling out sheets of schematics. "These things are designed to make sure no one gets in without proper clearance. I can override it."

"Can't we just turn off the lights and walk to the other side?" asks Maize.

"Sir, because we need to have everything on to operate the shuttle, all the circuit breakers and switches are on our side of the room. It's a security feature. The control room can only send ships if the people are cleared by the card reader. If there's a different number on the shuttle half of the room than the card reader, the system shuts down."

"Who the hell thought that was a good idea?"

"I didn't build it, sir."

"So, if we turn the lights off—"

"It resets then registers unauthorized persons and locks itself down."

"Bullshit," snaps Maize. "All right. Do you need anything from us?"

"No, this turnstile looks worse than it is."

The sprinklers come on. Filth and gore drip off the troop, and Maize yells at Teague.

"That was expected," says Teague. "The bombs hit everywhere, so I guess it never had a chance to clean itself. It's fine. Just a maintenance check."

"Thank you," says Bode, letting the excrement wash off.

Cella is not happy. The water is destroying the next sample before she can put it in a bag.

"What's wrong with your leg?" shouts Saffire.

D turns from checking his suit. Those last few explosions didn't help with the self-healing process.

"I'm fine," says D.

"What?" Saffire shouts again.

D looks to Betty for an explanation.

"Whatever you did," says Betty walking over to pull the girl away.

Saffire is desperate to remove her helmet, but no one trusts the air, and the girl might infect herself by touching her face with stained gloves. It's best if she doesn't have that option.

D jerks as if shocked. The suit twitches. He taps his helmet again and the lens goes from near black tint to clear and back again. D keeps cursing, trying to keep the suit from being temperamental.

Jamie walks over, peering at him. "What's wrong with your leg?" she asks.

"I broke it," says D.

"So sad," says Jamie.

D flips her off before continuing to fiddle with his helmet.

"Will you stop it," says Betty, as somehow Saffire gets her helmet off. A colossal stench hits her full in the face.

"Why does it smell like that?" asks Saffire.

"Keep your helmet on next time," says Betty.

D and Jamie, despite their best efforts, start laughing.

"Glad your back," says Zach.

"You didn't volunteer to help with the card reader?" says D.

"No, I didn't. Those guys look like the type that hate when civilians know something they don't."

"If you told them what you could do, I'm sure they'd use your skills."

"Yeah, but what's in it for me?"

D nods. There's good sense in that.

"This is amazing," says Cella.

She sticks part of the serrated bones to the wall and again to her suit. It takes a fair bit of muscle to pull the thing away before she sticks it to a metal frame.

Cella gives notes to a recording device based on her findings. The bones appear to have multiple purposes. The first clear function is the breaking down of food for digestion through expanding and contracting holes at the tips. The next, judging by fine hairs, is for grabbing. Air sacks interconnect with the bone through a series of veins and arteries.

"I need more samples," says Cella.

"Cella, is this crap really important?" asks Bode.

"Yes it is. Get away from me."

The veins and arteries may lead to a single organ at the center of the body. She doesn't believe she can call the serrated bones serrated bones anymore; they are too malleable and work more like tentacles. She can't be sure, if the tentacles are also for language or if they combine with the lungs to produce sounds equal to the crackling of the larger brogs. A more intact subject may solve these questions.

"Your girlfriend's weird," says Jamie.

Cella turns back to roll her eyes at Jamie. D curses, giving up on the helmet and slides down the wall to rest his leg.

"How bad?" asks Jamie. "Scale from one to ten."

"Eleven." D breathes heavily. "I'm ignoring it."

The helmet's back to a deep-brown tint that hides his face, but Jamie knows he's sweating. She'd tell him to take the pain killers, but D hates everything to do with drugs, all of them. Jaime would have to trick him into taking the pills and he's looked worse, so she won't. She just slides down the wall to sit next to him while Teague works.

Teague and Jaime have the card reader exposed now. Jade holds a fiber-optic cable while Teague cuts off the end to solder copper wires from his end to the card reader's mother board. She strips fine wires from the cable and solders those to the screen that reads the card. Maize stands at a distance, watching this, thinking brain surgery might be easier.

Half an hour passes before Teague and Jade smile at each other. Teague passes the black bracelet over the reader then tosses another bolt past the steel lip, and it slides to the other side, unharmed. He throws three more pieces with the same result. Then, he tosses the disembodied arm across the steel lip and nothing happens.

"I've found a way to get us to the other side," says Teague.

"We," says Jade.

"We," Teague apologizes.

"What happened?" asks Maize.

"The system has a passcode feature each card has a key that allows the person with the card to pass. Well, I—we just tricked the reader into thinking everyone has the same passcode."

"Shouldn't the system read that as off?" asks Maize.

"It would if it could access the main database, but it can't because it needs Internet access. So without this, the local system is forced to allow this passcode through."

"How do you know that?" asks Hank.

"Government systems have a uniform way of working, Dad," says Jade. "It's how I got access to the war room data. Anyone with proper access should be able to see its contents. The only way to verify counterfeits is by referring back to the main database, which is offline for the foreseeable future. And even before then, it updated regularly with personnel. The system would never work if it had to shut down every time some new person got clearance."

"Gotta love government red tape," mumbles Hank.

"Ok, who's first?" asks Teague.

Everyone looks around. Maize sniffs, annoyed, then volunteers Carlton. He seems upset but knows better than to argue with Maize.

"Don't stand too long," says Teague. "Otherwise, I'll have to redo the key override."

"If I die," Carlton says to Andrews, "you still owe me fifty watts."

"Prove it, dead man. Walk your punk ass through." says Andrews.

Teague passes the bracelet over the reader again, waiting for Carlton. Carlton, sure he wasn't sweating a moment ago, steps closer to the reader, then sprints to the other side.

"Next," says Teague, as Jade twists a cable, making the screen blink.

Rick will try his hand next; he's through. Hank tells Betty and Saffire to go.

"It has to be one at a time," Teague tells Betty.

She was holding Saffire's hand. Suddenly, Saffire, has a tight grip. Hank takes a firm grip of the girl as Betty goes through. She smiles back at Saffire, who's unsure now. Betty doesn't smile like that unless she's trying to hide something dangerous from Saffire. Saffire wants to hold Hank's hand now. He stares down at her with his riot face on. Well, she doesn't care how serious he is. She's not going past that thing.

"She has to go now," says Teague.

Saffire stands still. Betty is motioning her forward with an annoyed look. Suddenly, a hand sends the girl flying past the turnstile. Hank stands, staring Betty in the eye as they have a silent yelling contest. Bode's next, then Cella, who must be pried away with her new test samples by Colt. Colt's trying to catch Jade's eye, but she keeps staring at the cable a bit too hard to be believable. Next is Hidalgo then Saccarria and the last six of the troop except Hank. He turns to D and Jamie.

"You go," says D.

"I outrank you now. I order you to go first," says Jamie smiling.

She can almost feel the blink of shock in D's helmet. But he gets up and limps past the reader. Jamie quickly follows.

"You go, honey," says Hank.

"Dad, you suck at tech. I got this," says Jade.

Hank's been watching her do and redo the process the entire time. If he weren't able to memorize something this simple, he'd have never made it into the Green Berets. And he doesn't like the way Teague looks at her.

"Sweetie, I'm not going to argue with you about this. The rules were made clear to you before we left. Now, you get your ass up and through that port right now, young lady." shouts Hank.

Jade grinds her teeth, but Hank has that look, so she mumbles some curses then walks past the key reader. Maize was observing the same as Hank. Teague will get them into Three Mile, so he's more important to the mission. He never intended for Teague to be the last through. Teague tries arguing Maize out of it just to have his complaints on the record, then shows him what to do again. Hank and Maize look at each other. Maize holds out a fist, and they play rock, paper, scissors. Loser goes first. Maize wins.

Maize refuses to hide a smile as they prep the reader. Hank walks past the reader a bit wary that Maize might *accidently* kill him, but he's on the other side with no problem. Betty yanks him over, checking him over.

"I'm fine," says Hank.

"Shut up," says Betty checking everywhere.

Maize keeps a straight face as his heart quickly pumps. He's gotten himself into a spot here. Nancy won't be happy if he squashes himself to death. She'll come back and put him back together so he could explain himself. What'll he say then? He laughs at himself then redoes the process and walks past the reader.

Easy.

"There you go, Commander," says Carlton as the seal's cheer.

Teague, happy his commander hasn't killed himself, heads straight for the control room. As best he can tell, the bay shuttle is undamaged. Someone tried repeatedly to destroy the controls but judging by the bent and broken metal pieces scattered around the room, nothing worked. He'll simply tell the shuttle to recommence its duties. It'll take a few moments to run another diagnostic check.

Some of the others stand, looking around. A few try too hard not to notice the bodies. D continues fiddling with his helmet until it opens. D jerks, then wrinkles his nose as the stench hits him. His face is drenched in sweat. All the running he's been doing creates more than enough heat, but with no way for the suit to moderate internal temperature, he's been baking. None of that matters. The smell is unreasonable, so he quickly slaps his jacket and presses his palms to bring back the helmet.

Jamie laughs hard at this, causing others to look at them. D ignores her, turning to Zach.

"What would you have done?" D asks, motioning to the card reader.

"Set up a dummy databank," says Zach. "With uniform systems, they all operate under one command. Soon as I swipe the card, I could tell where the signal wants to go, and I'd create a dummy node to replace the true one. That way, all the info goes to the fake hub. Since it can't verify what's fake, I could use the dummy node to create a master key. I'd turn the bracelet codes into the new master key and tell the reader to give the bracelet unlimited uses. It would trick the control room into thinking an unlimited amount of people had this key, and since it can't verify this command as wrong, everyone could walk right through without resetting the reader every time."

"What would be your dummy node?"

"Any of the other key readers. The local system has no way to tell the difference. It would take longer, but it would have been much safer."

"You've been looking at those scans?"

Zach nods.

"Keep those ideas handy. You might have to brute force a few things."

Zach smiles. Who wouldn't want to crack multiple top-level military systems without the slightest risk of arrest?

"All right," says Teague. "Bay 1 is going to open in three minutes. Shuttle 8B42 is about to load onto track 1. Get in now."

The speakers open with static-filled gibberish. The audio file's too corrupted to tell everyone to load in. A warning light flicks on, showing many maintenance checks needed on tunnels 1–4. Teague tells the computer to ignore it and proceed. He jumps into the shuttle just as its doors close. A moment later, the shuttle is shooting down a tube into a sea of ink. The seats of the shuttle, once smooth white leather, are torn rusty things, barely able to stay in position as the shuttle rattles and bumps down the path. There's groaning as the shuttle reaches 70 miles.

The rattling turns to outright shaking. Grips tighten on arm rests as another dip comes. Bode's seat tears off its hinges. He's suspended in air for a half-second before crashing back into the ground, punching a hole in the floor.

The shuttle rocks harder and more seats loosen from the foundation. There's a jolt, and Saccarria's seat flies off and smashes into the reinforced window. However, it doesn't break, only cracks.

"Keep calm, everyone," says Teague. We're about to hit the Susquehanna lakebed.

The shuttle's bucking like an enraged bull. Cella, Hank, and Andrews nearly collide mid-air as their seats break off. D is nervous, but there's nothing he can do but curl into a ball to protect himself as best he can. Just as every other seat is coming loose, the shuttle doors open to show a domed tunnel resting on the lakebed.

"Ok, we made it," says Teague, leaking with false confidence.

Chapter 34

Everyone glances at the tunnel. Normally, there would be lights along the way, giving a spectacular view of the lake. At night, it would look like steaks of light leading to a great beyond, but without maintenance, the lights fail and crack from along the path, thanks to warps and water pressure. It looks like a black void vomiting wreckage.

"All right, everyone, we made it. Quit looking back," says Hank.

At the end of the hundred-yard entrance is a double door forty-four feet high. There's a governmental seal of the armed forces stamped to the top of the doors. It's too dark to make out the words circling the seal. "Spe," "i-ts," and "m-y" are the only words anyone can make out without better lighting and deep cleaning to clear away the mold.

A panel to its left gives a green salutation. Teague and Jade do the same crisscrossing of wires, and the door opens after he swipes the bracelet. Teague had fake chips ready to make, but having a real card made getting past these defenses much easier. As the system works, getting past the shuttle bay was the hard part. Anyone already in Three Mile has valid access.

The welcoming room is dark and dusty. Fourteen desiccated bodies crowd the entrance. Teague wastes no time stepping over them and looking for security access cards. The rest of the troop and Maize's team pull bodies out of the way. The concierge desk is half-pulverized. The left-hand side is shattered, but the other half is only dented. The rest of the lobby is spacious with 14 barriers that lead further into the compound.

D slaps his helmet in annoyance. Finally, atmosphere readings come back online.

"The air's breathable," D tells Jaime. "It's a comfortable sixty-eight degrees too."

"Don't," says Jamie.

D opens his helmet. The air is stale with a slight taste of rotting meat. The air sampler never takes smell into account, only harmful gases. D needs to talk to a designer about fixing that feature.

Teague is calling Maize to compare system diagrams. This place is supposed to be a massive five-tier complex with countless sections cataloged with containment designations. Level A, section A-1 is their current location. The concierge desk can't tell them anymore then the floor number and sections per floor. The floors past level C are a garbled, unreadable mess.

"Ok," says Maize quietly. "We'll go level by level then. Where's the first lab?"

The diagram shows Teague a color-coded level designation. Level A has fifty-four sections, colored red, code for impassible. Level B is all red except section B-6; all of level C is either unreadable or red, but there's a lab in section C-49. Level D, and E are unreadable but there's some brown color on the screen. Maize asks Hank where his troop plans to go.

Hank didn't have a plan. Anything was better than serving the death sentence inside the bunker.

"We'll follow your lead on this one, commander," says Hank.

Andrews and Carlton are staring at D with scowls, while the troop glance at him, waiting to see if some airborne pathogen makes his face explode. A minute passes before the others begin to take off their helmets, exposing sweating faces and matted hair. It's not the best air, but everyone needs a change from the filtered air of their suits.

Teague's trying to decide to quickest way to get down to Section B. As best he can tell, the only way is to go through barrier 9, which is burned and dented almost as if someone was trying to keep something back. Trying to go through any other routes means heading past a minimum of five red sections; this way leads them past one red section.

"Can the desk tell you why the sections are red?" asks Maize.

"No," says Teague.

After some thinking, Teague types up schematics on the barriers to open them. There's no way to open them remotely. The doors shut manually when the signal comes to lockdown. The desk blinks off exhausting the last of its energy. Teague's out of ideas.

"We just need to get the barrier up?" asks Maize.

"It's not that easy. These doors are built to stop bunker bombs." says Teague.

"Is it any tougher than the doors back home?"

"No, these are a bit thinner actually."

Maize nods to his team, and each of them unveil miniature cranks from their backpacks. They can convert them to gouging instruments to break away the tiles beneath the barrier. While the seals work, Zach comes to D with a question.

"Andrews doesn't like you much," Zach whispers.

"I beat him in a fight without trying," says D. "I wouldn't like me either after that."

"What's making these sections red?"

"I think I know. I think you do too."

Both nod, and Jamie pokes D. She doesn't like being left out.

"Keep your guns ready," says D.

Maize's team digs out foot holdings large enough for proper leverage.

"We still need more manpower. The pulley system for this door is completely broken," says Teague, listening to the barrier rise slightly then fall as Andrews's strength gives out. There should be a clinking noise if the system works properly. There's a screech, clank, then tearing metal.

"Let's get six people to help Andrews," says Maize, looking at Hank.

The entire troop except Betty, Cella, and Saffire go to help. Jamie and Zach leave D to get behind Carlton. No one questions why D is just sitting there. Everyone can see he's useless with his leg the way it is. Cella remembers that she didn't check his leg or even talk to D this entire time. She walks in his direction, but he shifts his weight to aim his rifle at Cella's chest. Betty gives her a firm tug. Men like D are always surly when they're hurt and can't help.

On counts of three, the cranks lights flash, exceeding 4,000 PSI. They get the barrier to waist height before stopping. Carlton's first under the eight-foot-thick barrier. It's pitch black. With everyone passing under, Saffire starts yelling wanting to know where they're going. Betty clamps a hand over the girl's mouth.

The lobby felt dirty, but this other half of the barrier feels disgusting and smells as if the air's tainted. Teague is certain there is a staircase here. Everyone feels around until Colt finds a handrail leading down. As lights pass over the staircase, a thick haze swirls through the light shaft. The air smells burned, soot kicks up with every footstep.

"We're going right," whispers Teague, as they reach the bottom.

At the same time, there's scuffling and banging coming from the left. Mottled pinkish skin and crackling makes everyone turn to see brogs rushing forward at top speed. Teague was sprinting when everyone else stopped to look, so he's already at the lab door as the troop race toward him. Teague types a combination into a nearby number pad. The door opens with D of all people the first through. There's a log jam at the door, as everyone tries to get in at the same time. Saccarria, unfortunately, is last so is first to feel the iron grip of a brute. The beast completely overpowers her, shattering her arm and ripping her intestines open. Blood shoots from her mouth as she screams while being dragged into the horde.

Everyone is in when Saccarria stops screaming. The door shuts with a frenzy of blood, bone, and soot splashing the reinforced door. The crackling is muffled but loud enough to bleed through.

#

Jamie is at the door, looking out at the uglies hissing and grunting as they eat. Flood lights in the lab flick on as she thinks on the unspoken bond with Saccarria. Two women good enough to join a special forces unit.

"She didn't deserve this," says Jamie, quietly.

"There's twelve billion people who didn't deserve this," says D, leaning against the wall. "We're almost there. Stay focused."

Jamie followed D's lead in the hallway. That's why she's in the lab and not with Saccarria now. It's like the people from the ship. She left them and has no way to get back to them. Her being part of the scout party was lucky, and it annoys her. D being right annoys her. All this makes her lash out.

"Will you shut the fuck up right now?" Jamie yells.

D rolls his eyes. He hates when she gets all emotional. It doesn't solve anything, and it makes her look weak in tense moments, like now.

Jamie goes apoplectic at the suffering look he gives her and punches D square on the jaw. He doesn't fall. He was leaning against the wall, but it still hurts his jaw. He keeps his legs sturdy to maintain balance, but the broken leg sends spikes of pain up his body. All this combines to create a very angry D.

Normally, D would mush her into the farthest wall. But he's only got one leg, and Jamie's not above kicking it to win a fight. She can be ruthless when she's angry. Also, D's not having a family fight in front of strangers. He just looks at her.

"Feel better? Did you get it all out?" he asks, then slides down the wall to rest his leg.

Jamie looks at him even more annoyed, but feels bad now. She's a commissioned officer. She should know better than to snap like that.

"That was uncalled for," says Jamie.

D waves it away while rubbing his throbbing leg. The others were expecting something to happen but nothing has. D deescalating a situation is unexpected.

Everyone still has their guns out, waiting for the uglies to tear the door off, but nothing's happening. It is a sturdy door, thick, bulletproof, but these creatures can break through it with a few minutes of effort. For his part, D's sliding away from the door. It's obvious why the uglies aren't breaking through, but a happy trigger finger could mean his head getting blown off.

D's almost at the corner when the normal lights turn on. The flood lights shut off right after, and sprinklers turn on. The lab is a jumble of beakers, chairs, tables, and computers. Cages to the left wall stand twisted and warped with burned pieces of bone and fur layering the bottom. The second exit is facing the front door. It's a strange sight. The lab looks to be melting as the dark gray and black soot rolls down the walls and off the wreckage with beads of water.

When the sprinklers stop, the lab looks more like mounds of grayish ash on white walls.

"Team," says Maize, "see what you can find."

The troop is lost. They obviously had nothing past getting to Three-Mile Island. Seeing brogs here hurts, but Maize definitely came with a goal in mind. Hank and Rick go to the side to discuss how to play this. With brogs here, they can't stay. It doesn't take a genius to see Teague knows this place. Is there another exit from Three-Mile? Can they join Maize's people and return to wherever they're from? Neither buys Maize's story of why his team came here.

"Why don't we just ask?" whispers Betty.

The men blink at her. When did she sneak up on them?

"You might have a point," says Hank. "Is there a way we can help?" he asks Maize.

Maize turns to Hank, thinking. "It couldn't hurt," he says. "Look for any intact documents. Or cylinders. Anything that looks like it's government material."

"I think I can get this back door open," says Teague.

"Make sure there's nothing on the other end before you open it." says Maize.

"Why?" asks Rick, making Maize turn back with annoyance.

"Because I wanna know what's here. Look, I didn't ask you to help. You volunteered. You don't like it, then don't help. Doesn't mean shit to me."

"How'd he know the access code?" asks Rick, motioning to Teague.

"I opened it with the bracelet," says Teague.

"No, you didn't," says Colt. "I saw you type something."

"What the fuck is this?" asks Maize. "You want something? You think you've been wronged in some way? We don't owe you shit. Our deal was to get here. You wanna stay, that's fine by me. We're not going to be interrogated. Keep looking men."

D see's that he's twenty steps from Hank and Rick. Andrews and Carlton are at the other end of the lab with D in their sight line. This won't do. He pulls himself up and walks toward the twisted cages. Jamie and Zach take his cue and follow him.

As Maize and Hank keep up their staring match, Cella heads for the cages. The samples at the bottom are interesting. They look like her bag samples. They're small but solid.

It can't be from pygmies, can it?

Brutes and sniffers have thick bones. Maybe they're from an infant sniffer or brute. Or a fetus cut out before it could be a viable birth. It could be any animal, but her gut is telling her it's from a brog.

"Are you saying there's another way out of here?" asks Hank.

Maize cocks his gun followed by his men.

"Look here, pal. We're not answering any more questions. We're gonna do our job, and you're gonna stay out of our way. Is that clear?"

Hank doesn't like Maize's tone. He's about to make him respect his elders, but he has to think about this. His troop is small now, and one is a child. Another is a civilian woman, and his wife is only four years younger than him. Is an explanation worth this logistical problem?

"Weapons on the ground," says Maize.

Cella's asking herself where all the soot came from. Colt, Bruce, and D have had the most contact with brogs, and each of them says they adapt quickly. She saw a government seal on the door before they walked into Three Mile. There are brogs inside Three Mile. Fire works well on brogs.

Why are the brogs not tearing down the door? Why was everything in the room burned?

Cella looks around the lab, seeing openings behind the cages. She remembers her lab and those test samples. She opens one of her samples.

The backdoor closes. A siren sounds. Lines of fire extend from the walls as the lab lights turn off then back on with red emergency lights. An automated voice sounds, warning all lab employees that the containment protocol is in effect.

"Full containment achieved," says the automated voice.

As the lights return to industrial white, Rick slams Mr. Buckshot's handle into Andrews's face. Bode punches Carlton. Colt gives Teague a hellish right, sending him toppling over Jade who ducks below Teague to make him fall over her. Andrews gut punches Rick. Rick headbutts Andrews. Bode breaks Carlton's orbital bone before Carlton fractures Bode's jaw with a spinning elbow. Jade's kicking a downed Teague while Colt puts him in a sleeper hold.

Hank and Maize are growling while each try tearing off chunks from the other's face. Maize spits in Hank's face. Hank lets go in shock as Maize bites along his scar before Hank starts thumbing Maize's eye. Maize pushes away to charge into a fireman's carry. Hank keeps a tight grip before throwing him through a countertop. Maize, in rage, yells a battle cry as Hank reaches for his rifle. Maize is quick to push the barrel away from his face. Hank simply uses Maize's energy to shove the length of the rifle into his own face. Maize's eyes glaze for an instant as Hank pulls back the rifle to smash Maize's face in. Again, Maize is quicker, taking a piece of the broken countertop to wallop Hank senseless.

Hank falls like a stone as Maize rises, shouting for everyone to stop while aiming the rifle down at Hank. No one hears him. Rick bluffs a punch, then kicks Andrews in the balls, crumpling the sergeant. Bode and Carlton are throwing punches so powerful blood is streaming from each other's face. Teague went unconscious five kicks ago, but Jade and Colt are still stomping away as Maize shoots the ceiling.

Bode lets go of Carlton. Carlton, with his face now a deep shade of velvet, punches Bode again, then takes his gun. Carlton has just volunteered himself as the gun collector, so he punches Bode again before walking to each fight location. Andrews starts cursing Rick, calling him all types of unmanly insults while curling up against the wall, protecting his loins.

Carlton shoves Teague awake as Colt and Jade step back. Teague is furious, so gets up to punch every ounce of air from Colt's body. He turns to Jade, struggling with whether he should or shouldn't. She stares at him with her head held high. Teague takes a breath and a few steps back, grabs a rifle from Carlton, and smacks her in the face. Jade is down in a heartbeat. Colt grunts in outrage but can't move because of Teague's punch.

"Stop fucking moving," yells Maize irascible.

Jamie and Cella stop hovering over a writhing D.

"I didn't think that would happen," whispers Cella.

"I said shut the fuck up," shouts Maize. "You couldn't help?" He looks to Jamie.

"This ain't my fight," says Jamie.

"Sir," says Carlton.

"Shut up, dammit," shouts Maize. "The hell is that smell?"

Carlton is pointing to a heap of smoldering flesh dotted with camouflage. A metal chain sits on top, sizzling the meat. Hidalgo is dead. How did this happen? Maize turns to Cella. She's kneeling over D, asking him to move his hand so she can see his face. Cella looks up, feeling the stares.

"I should kill you," says Maize. "By all rights I can. He had a wife, you fucking bitch. Saccarria worked her ass off to be on this mission. That's three people we've lost because of you."

"Ointment," mumbles D.

Cella starts rummaging through her pack. Carlton leaps forward nearly breaking her wrist as the tube falls into Jamie's hand. She lathers it on his face and the soothing is immediate.

Carlton puts the gun to Jaime's cheek before taking the tube away.

"Sir, what do we do with her?" asks Carlton.

Maize has had to kill women before, but they were combatants. He has a wife. She's not nearly as pretty as Cella, but he's not going to kill a civilian woman no matter how much she deserves it.

"She lives for now," says Maize. "Take her bag and everything on her that looks like it might be dangerous."

The seals disagree but control their reactions. Maize made his decision. Cella keeps knelt, knees are too weak to move.

"We're leaving," says Maize. "Andrews, you're on point."

Teague peels a melted dog tag from the chaos that is Hidalgo's body. Hank takes a slap to the face from Carlton before waking up. Andrews lines the troop into a single file out the backdoor while Teague walks beside Colt and a face-clutching Jade.

"It's not that bad," says Cella to D. "If it hurts, it means the nerves are still working. The salve will keep major scarring away too."

"Get away from him," says Jamie, shoving Cella away.

Andrews turns back for a second to see D's shriveled, twisted left face. His left ear is scrunched and peeling. His face looks like it got dipped into a smelting chamber. Andrews doesn't like D anyway. The new look might humble him.

For his part, D seems to be recovering quickly. He has on a relaxed expression. His face smells like cooking pork and his left eye's blurry. He'll likely need surgery for that also. It'll be all right.

This ointment must have some type of narcotic in it.

"A warning would've been nice," says D.

"I didn't mean for it to hit you like that. Just distract Maize's team," says Cella.

"Well," says Jamie, keeping Cella at arm's length. "At least we know what red means."

Andrews catches Maize's eye as they reach the end of the hallway. D doesn't seem nearly as hurt as a burn victim should. Both thought he was off before but now they need to keep a closer eye on him. Something's loose in this man's head.

#

An elevator stands at the end of the hallway. Carlton and Maize keep guns on the troop as Andrews and Teague use cranks to pry the doors open.

"Why aren't the lights on?" asks Andrews.

"I think they're either blown out or sensors in the hall aren't working," says Teague. "The elevators have a separate power system but with my key card, I can hack the local system and make it take us where we need to go."

"So the sensors won't turn on?" asks Andrews.

"Judging by the reaction inside the lab. If we assume that everywhere the NTs are, they're purged. Then, if the lights come back on, a whole bunch of places are going to be purged if we're there or not. I think it's better the lights stay off for now. Don't you?"

Andrews nods as Teague slides into the elevator. The panel has a key card reader that has to be cleared if you want to enter lower levels. The reader is showing the clearance isn't high enough, so Teague does the same thing he did in the shuttle and compound entrance.

While Teague works, the others scan the blackness. D's thinking about where to go after he finds what he's looking for.

"I'll need to have plastic surgery," D says to Jamie. "You think I can get another nose for my trouble?"

Jamie is quiet for a moment, staring at D.

Did he just make a joke? What is wrong with him?

"Let's get you out of here first and go from there." says Jamie. "Just follow me. I know a place." says D.

The troop is at a loss and the seal team look at D like he's a rabid dog. Andrews sees the burns. No one should be up and talking with burns like that. D's much more dangerous than the seals imagined. They need to do something about him.

The elevator makes an unpleasant squeaking sound as it opens. Maize has Betty at gunpoint before entering to ensure the troop doesn't try anything. Teague is standing over the keypad, which has hundreds of buttons that indicate every level. Lights are highlighting section D-3, D-4, and all of Zone E.

"Which way, sir?" asks Teague.

"The lab on C?" says Maize.

"We can't get there, sir. I tried. I think that section might be ok, but everything surrounding it is unreachable."

"Fine. If we can't find what we need in these other places, we go back through Level C, no matter what's here."

Teague presses for section D-3.

#

Hank hasn't blinked since Maize put the gun to his wife's head; right now, the warmth between Maize and him is somewhere near absolute zero. Rick's keeping a hand ready to stop Hank from doing anything stupid. Cella's in an isolated position. Jamie's not letting her near D and Rick is keeping an eye on Hank.

Cella doesn't know what to do with herself. All she can do is look at D's face. She did not mean to do that. And how is he standing? The salve is good, but it doesn't eliminate all pain.

"Stop poking your face," says Cella. "Let the salve do its work."

"I wouldn't need to if you didn't turn into a fucking pyromaniac," says D. He scowls for a second, then winces. He pokes his face again.

"Stop it," says Cella, moving closer.

Andrews slides in front of Cella, twisting her into an arm bar. D stiffens, and Carlton slams the burned half of his face into the wall. D grunts, and Teague has two guns aimed at Betty and Jade while Maize keeps Betty right beside him while aiming at Hank.

"So, you two fucked, huh," says Andrews, looking into Cella's backpack. "The way she was trying not to look at you clued me in. Is she why you're here now?"

Andrews pulls out a pair of blood-red six-inch heels.

"The hell are you doing with heels?"

"Why, you want some in your size?" asks Cella.

Carlton slams D's head again, causing him to blackout for a heartbeat.

"Stop it," yells Cella.

Andrews and Carlton smile.

"Was it that good?" asks Andrews. "Well, tell you what. You watch that smart fucking mouth, and we'll leave him alone."

Cella looks at D, then puts her head down.

"She's easy to train." says Andrews.

"There's hope for this world yet," says Carlton, smiling.

The elevator doors open to section D-3. Inside is an unadulterated frenzy. The uglies are bloody where their skin isn't mottled with pink lesions. Teague starts tapping for D-4 so hard he nearly breaks the button. The creatures pause from tearing into each other as a new alluring scent fills their nostrils. The creatures hiss then creep towards the elevator. The doors close as the brogs bash the doors.

#

Section D-4 opens with more muffled thumping. This section is about the size of the Level A lobby but denser and with 2 levels. It's mostly smashed computers, storage devices, and lockers separated by a staircase that extends around and down the other side.

"This has promise, sir," Teague says to Maize.

Maize nods before the thumps come again. The elevator shaft shakes visibly for a moment.

"Hurry up, men," says Maize. "Find what we need fast."

Teague gives Maize a look then motions for the troop. It's easy to see what Teague's saying. They need help to find this thing faster. There is good sense in that.

Maize grabs Betty and puts a gun to her head. Hank flinches, almost charging forward before Rick pulls him back.

"Look here, people," says Maize. "You're going to help us find something. There's a lot of storage lockers here but as you can see, no one's cleaned this place in quite a while. We're looking for master keys. Seeing as this is a communication hub and secure holding area, one should be here. If you find anything, one of us will bring it to Teague, and if any of you try to use it as a bargaining chip, I'll break Mrs. Auberon's fingers."

Hank grunts, but Rick holds him back.

"Not smart, not now," whispers Rick.

The seals break the troop into teams of two. Andrews makes it a point to team D with Zach and Jamie with Cella. He moves each to opposite ends so that Jamie and D can't communicate. Everyone else splits the same way more or less with a screaming Saffire as the odd girl out. Carlton is telling her to shut up, but she can't hear anything so continues whaling.

"I can keep her quiet," says Betty.

Carlton gives Maize a look and shoves the girl over to Betty.

Andrews starts pushing D and Zach to the second level.

"Lets go Dr. Jekyll." says Andrews.

"Enjoy it while it lasts," says D.

Andrews drops D with a hit to the small of the back. "Fuck you. Is the pussy that good? Don't answer that. I don't trust a word you say. I'll find out myself."

D gives Andrews a blank stare. It's a stare empty of any human emotion. It makes Andrews step back. Andrews growls ashamed he showed fear, then hits the burned side of D's face. Blood's trickling through cracks in the skin. The salve is wearing off. D can't ignore the pain anymore. He falls to the ground, holding his head.

Zach sees blood curving over pockmarked and blackened flesh and almost vomits.

"Hey, you made your point, all right. You made your point," says Zach.

"You want some, bitch?" says Andrews. "No? Ok, then. Do what I tell you."

This is the second time D's been burned like this. Usually, after any hit, D logs the pain and ignores it next time he feels the same type of pain. He thought it would work this time, but fire is a completely different type of pain. It's coming in waves of needles, and each wave feels worse than the last. He might cry soon if he can't get control of himself.

Andrews starts kicking him. D can't hear a thing past the pain. Nothing matters more right now then this pain. Every heartbeat doubles the throbbing in his face. Andrews has the gun in his face, and D could care less.

As fun as it is to show D he's not as tough as he thinks he is, the mission comes first, and if he kills one, the rest might stop doing as they're told. Killing everyone would be a clusterfuck. And killing civilians is a line you can't uncross.

"Carlton," yells Andrews. "You have that ointment you took from Jamie?"

Andrews catches the tube. He tells Zach to do it. Andrews isn't touching the havoc on D's face. Zach leans over as D snatches the tube and lathers it on his face. Andrews looks on, satisfied.

Across the way, Jamie looks on furious. Cella is several steps away, looking with her jaw tight. Jamie strides over and punches her. Cella drops like a sack of rocks. Not even Rita hit her that hard.

What the hell?

Jamie kicks her stomach, pushing all the air from her body. It's a precision kick. Jamie was aiming for the diaphragm at an upward angle. A strike there ends most fights. Carlton rushes over, pushing Jaime back, but it's already over. Cella's curled in on herself, trying to pull oxygen back into her lungs.

"You deserve worse, bitch," says Jamie.

#

The thumping overhead changes suddenly. It goes one, two, three, four, stop. Again one, two, three, four, stop. Maize doesn't like this. Between the death gaze Hank is giving him and the antics of D and Andrews, no one's paying as much attention to the job as they should. Maize shoots the ground.

"Is everyone done?" yells Maize. "We're here for keys. If you find one, hand them to my team."

"How are they supposed to find this key if they don't know how it looks?" mumbles Betty.

Maize scowls at her. "The keys all look alike. They're all the same damn thing. Now find it."

Zach's doing his best to pretend he's looking, but he doesn't have much will to help these guys. What Andrews did to D is excessive. Jamie and Captain Tiller never allowed this type of treatment. Zach can see now that the military has different qualities of leadership in their ranks also.

"I need something for my face," says D.

The pain's receding quickly. He's on his feet, moving the loose skin on his face; the skin where Andrews hit him is about to fall off. Andrews walks over, looking to hit D again. He stops this time. D's positioned so that Andrews must cross D's face to reach the burned side. Andrews would have to overextend. This would leave his body open for easy hits. Andrews might be able to hit D's shoulder, force him to overcompensate. D will want to keep his face from more damage. That will open up the rest of his body.

Andrews will hit his broken leg, then hit the face again. The problem is, D has that blank stare again. He's leaving the broken leg open for attack. Andrews can see D's already processed what Andrews would do. He's keeping the burns out of reach and leaving the leg open for attack. If D knows where Andrews is going to hit, he can counter easily. Andrews's third option is to go for the uninjured leg. He could sweep low, forcing D to back up, using the broken leg for balance.

Andrews goes for a leg sweep, and D charges in. D falls atop Andrews turning his burned face to Andrews and rubbing the skin and blood on Andrews' face. Andrews yells in shock and disgust. D jumps off holding Andrews' own gun and bag. Across the way, Carlton's aiming his rifle, but Jaime is behind him with a knife, pressing into his lower back.

"Drop it," says Jamie.

Just as Carlton lowers his gun, parts of the roof fall.

"Teague," yells Maize.

244

Teague rushes for the elevator while Maize yanks Betty back as she tries running to Hank. The elevator opens with a ding and Maize moves backward, keeping Hank in sight. Colt is creeping up from behind Maize, but Hank shakes his head. He's not risking Betty.

"Commander?" yells Carlton.

"Hurry up and get down here," says Maize. "We're leaving with or without you."

Jaime runs behind him, holding Carlton's own gun to his back.

There are large, clawed hands slashing down into the room.

"Get up," says D, aiming Andrews's gun down at him.

"Why are we bringing him?" asks Zach.

"You remember what I told you about my mission? We'll need the bodies."

D shoves Andrews down the steps as more of the roof falls.

"Containment breach imminent," says an automated voice.

"Power shutting down. Cleansing procedures to commence." Everyone runs to the elevator after hearing the voice. D's leg prevents him from keeping pace with Andrews so he uses Zach to keep himself at a decent speed. It's pure luck that a slab of concrete falls in front of D. It makes him look up to see Cella crawling down the steps. D tells Zach to get to the elevator. He gives Zach his bag and heads up the steps to grab Cella.

A siren blares, and D acts quickly. He holds the railing five steps up and stretches his long body up the remaining nine steps to jerk Cella's collar. She flies down the steps, landing on her stomach with a hard grunt. She yells again as D throws her at the elevator. She slides to a stop four feet from its doors. She strains to get in the door with no breath.

The lights dim as the door slowly closes. Jamie turns, seeing Cella reaching out and does nothing. Zach is squeezing in next to her, head turned in the opposite direction. The others are fighting to get each other's guns. Cella's heart is about to burst. Is this really how her story ends? The lights turn off. The lights turn back on, and D is there with Andrews's gun lodged between the doors. He drags Cella inside. The lights turn off again with a loud cracking sound. The elevator slams shut with pieces of Andrews's crushed gun littering the floor.

The light of section D-4 blinks off, but no one sees. Everyone is either fighting or trying to get out of the way of the ones fighting. It's a mess in this small space. Hank has Carlton by the throat, threatening to break his neck if Maize doesn't let his wife go. Teague has Saffire under his arm. He's not pointing his gun at her, but the threat is there.

Something large rams the door. Everyone stops fighting. It rams the doors again, bending the metal inward.

"Get us out of here, Teague," says Maize.

Teague presses for zone E, section E-5. The warped metal sticks in place for a moment. After another bang, something loosens, and the elevator falls. The elevator turns sideways, leaning everyone toward the button panel. Maize has Betty in a headlock as the seals press against him and Teague. The elevator turns and tilts the other way, throwing everyone toward D and Cella. D presses into his palms to make the suit helmet come back, but nothing happens.

Jamie slams full into him as the elevator increases to dangerous speeds. There's a loud pop and ripples down the elevator. For a brief moment everyone is weightless as the elevator falls unsupported. Teague can still do something before the inevitable happens. He punches the big red emergency stop button. There's a smashing sound and metal tearing. The elevator stops.

Chapter 35

The elevator is tilted at a thirty-five-degree angle. Maize still has a headlock on Betty, keeping Hank from pulling her away. Teague is squished behind Maize, trying to get free to pull the door open. He wants to know what floor they're on.

"Are you gonna keep staring at me or get the door open?" Maize asks Hank.

"You're outnumbered, you fuck. Give my wife back, and let's settle this one on one like men."

Teague is reaching into his bag as Maize responds.

"You think I'm buying into that bravado shit? I don't trust your people will let me beat the shit out of you again. And I've got bigger priorities then you. My people need what's down here. That comes first, not your pride."

"I'm giving you a chance to not get your skull crushed. You should take it, Commander."

"Fuck you. I've got my own chain of command."

A white light fills the elevator. In these close confines, the impact of the flash multiplies. There's some scuffling and yells. Someone shoots. The glare fades, and the seals are holding their guns again.

"You had flashbangs?" asks Rick, clearing his eyes.

"We couldn't show you all our weapons." says Teague.

D's at the door, trying to open it. He saw Teague squirming behind Maize. Teague's got a knack for crafty moves like the one he just pulled. As Maize and Hank continue their standoff, D uses Andrews's crank to open the door. He thought it would be tougher, but the crank opens the door in a few seconds.

The section door is thankfully there. As best D can tell, the elevator is halfway up on the floor. D cranks this door open also and falls to the floor.

"Hey," yells Andrews. "Sir, D's slipped away."

"Again?" yells Maize.

The fall's harder than D thought it would be. His broken leg is really feeling the pain. D was trying to fall in a way that protected his face but his legs banged into each other as he fell, making the pain radiate up his body. His left arm has a spike of pain, but it fades quickly. He takes deep breaths and stands up.

"D?" says Jamie.

"We're here?" says D. "Zone E, section E-5."

Jamie wiggles herself out and falls to the floor. She rises, pretending her ribs don't hurt, and sees the sign reading "SECTION E-5" above the elevator door.

"Andrews get down there and find out what's going on," says Maize.

"He took my guns, sir," says Andrews.

"You're a trained Navy Seal. Get your ass out there and get 'em back. Then, tell me where we are. Carlton give him one of yours." Andrews pulls himself out and falls to the floor as Jamie presses a knife to his throat.

"Shit," says Andrews.

"What was that, Sergeant?" asks Maize.

"It's Zone E, section E-5, sir."

Jamie looks at D. They could kill Andrews and just wait for the others to crawl out. They have complete control of the battlefield in this position.

"Don't," says D.

"Why not?" says Jamie. "I saw what he was doing to you."

"I may have deserved some of that."

"What?"

"Hey, Maize," D says, yelling into the elevator. "You gonna keep hiding behind an old lady or finish the mission. I think it's here."

Zone E-5 is unaffected by everything except dust mites. There is a circular maze of thick clear walls that stop five feet from the ceiling. There's a fifteen-foot space between the clear partitions and stone walls that lead out to the various exits and hallways. Each of the inner walls separate workspaces. At the center of the maze is the technological heart of the complex. A stupendous mainframe sits there, extending through the ceiling.

"How can I trust you after what you did?" asks Maize.

"Commander, I fucked up, all right. Now please, will you just get out here?"

Jaime is looking at D, eyes wide. It clicks into place.

"D, do you—"

"Not now, Jaime. I'll explain later."

After a moment of silence, Carlton drops to the floor. He's red faced looking at D as if he's a standing pile of garbage. Teague is next, then Maize with Betty tied to him by the wrist. Maize looks at D, stone faced. D stares back handgun aimed at the floor.

"Well, care to explain?" asks Maize.

"I fell asleep," says D. "If I wanted to betray you, why would I have waited till we got the Pennsylvania? Why would I have kept going on with the mission? How does any of that make sense?"

"We lost ten people because of you."

"I know. I'll just have to do better."

Maize's face twists in rage. "What are we going to say to the—"

Maize falls over as Hank spears him from inside the elevator. Rick is out soon after. He doesn't choose a target. He dives at the seals, hoping to catch as many as he can. The rest of the troop is out now, attacking. Jade and Colt swarm Maize with Hank, kicking and punching every inch of the commander.

Zach and Cella are last out. D circles around the fight to collect Zach.

"What do we do?" asks Zach.

D takes his bag back, looking through it for something. He pulls out the box of cubes and the flat-top key with spiral groves to the inside.

"Aren't we gonna make them stop?" asks Jamie.

"Our goal is in that big machine over there. It has to be," says D.

It's as if everyone else disappeared. D's focused on the mainframe and the mainframe only.

"What's in there?" asks Jaime.

"A weapon. It'll give us a chance against the uglies."

D presses the key into the maze entrance wall. It opens a straight path to the mainframe. The troop and the seals stop fighting to stare at D, Jamie, Zach walking through the maze as Cella trails several feet behind.

"Follow the lieutenant," yells Maize, slapping away strikes.

The seals pull away from the troop to run after D; the troop run after the seals. D hobbles into the maze as the others bunch up at the entrance, punching and spitting on each other. D's halfway to the mainframe as the maze shifts its walls randomly.

D snarls in aggravation.

"Zach, you stay with me," says D.

The troop rush at the nearest seals. Maize yanks Betty into a nearby workplace with Teague close by. After fifteen seconds of shifting walls, everyone is scattered around the maze. Andrews is stuck behind Jamie with his gun pointing at Cella. Cella jumps behind a table just as the wall shifts.

D's ignoring everyone except Zach and Jamie. As soon as the shifting allows, he pulls them toward the mainframe. Carlton finds himself running from Jade and Colt while Hank and Rick are tracking Maize and Teague. Zach's heart is pounding as he keeps low while staying within arm's length of D. A shot rings, making everyone stop.

Maize is firing at the reflection of Hank. The bullet bounces off the wall without denting it. Carlton thinks he'll have Rick if the next wall shift works to his favor. It doesn't. The wall in front of Rick opens, letting him reach Hank. The wall behind Carlton opens to show Jade and Colt running at him.

Maize starts firing every time the walls shift. He's only three walls from the mainframe when Hank shoots his calf. The wall shifts before Hank can charge in and take Betty. Maize yells, falling, but there's no blood. He sits up to pull off the bottom of his leg. A bullet is pressed into his prosthetic metal calf, warping it. Maize scowls at Hank before taking the calf off to bang it against a table. The dog tags spill out as the bullet falls out. He misses two wall shifts before the leg goes back on. The mold doesn't fit as it should anymore. Nancy won't be happy. When he gets back home, he'll insist on getting multiple legs. She won't shut up until he takes a promotion to a boring desk job.

Andrews stumbles to a wall right behind Jade and Colt. Carlton is somehow stuck between Jamie and Zach. Andrews is about to side swipe Jade, while Colt is trapped behind Teague. Teague sees Colt eyeing him. He's standing over Maize as he tries making the leg comfortable.

Five seconds later, Maize and Teague are one wall away from the mainframe. Rick shoots at Andrews just as an upside-down check shaped path opens to Teague. The bullet bounces off one wall, hits another, then tumbles into the back of Teague's left hand. The bones in his palm break through the skin. The bullet stops, lodged between his middle and ring finger.

Teague shrieks, clutching his hand. Maize turns to him, seeing the blood. Colt's bearing down on them from the right. Maize yanks Teague through a shifting door but not quickly enough. Teague was holding his left hand, so as the wall shuts, both of his hands shatter with the force of the shift. The last wall to the mainframe opens. Maize does and almighty tug to free Teague, tearing off six of his ten fingers.

They are the first into the center. Six desktop computers bracket the mainframe with three on the west and east. Ten clear walls surround the mainframe. There's ten feet of space between the walls and the computers. The mainframe looks more like a tiered column shaped like two funnels, bottom ends facing each other. It's dark metal three-foot sections stacked atop each other with black circular ports that separate every two feet. The widest at the top and bottom of the mainframe.

Liquid nitrogen leaks from the black circular ports warning that the temperature gauge inside is failing. As Maize steps back to take a good look at this thing, he sees the ports combine to make a contiguous X pattern up and down the mainframe.

Carlton dives in as Bode slams into the wall. Maize turns, about to shoot. Bode just stands there, waiting for the wall to open again.

"Wrap tourniquets around Teague's hands," says Maize, tugging Betty along to the nearest computer.

All of the monitors are off with yellow lights showing that they are on standby.

How am I going to open this mainframe now?

Hank and Rick bang on the walls opposite Bode, eyeing Maize. Hank meets Betty's eyes. Maize doesn't like not being able to understand what type of conversation they're having, so he turns Betty away.

"Sir?" says Carlton, wrapping towels around Teague's hand. "I don't like our position."

"Me neither, Sergeant," says Maize. "Protect Teague."

Carlton slides Teague under a table, cocking his gun, as Rick stands shaking a bottle of mustard gas. Both Rick and Hank have helmets on. Before Maize can call for masks, yellow fog engulfs the clearing. The walls in front of Hank and Rick open, letting him charge in, punching Maize with all the hatred he can muster. Rick cuts Betty loose, letting her helmet come back over her head, then helps Hank stomp on Maize.

An automated voice warns of a noxious gas as vents suck the fog away. Hank is choking Maize as the voice says, "Internal atmospheric integrity now stable."

A bullet kicks up the floor around Hank. Andrews is yelling at Hank to back away. Colt spears Andrews as his wall opens, and Jade is behind him, clawing at Andrews's eyes. Bode flies in, helping Rick stomp Carlton. Jamie and D walk in. She wants in on the fight, but D isn't even looking at them. He loops around everyone to the right-side computers. He blows dust off the first computer and pulls out his diagrams.

Zach is taking in the whole room with a hungry expression. He's never been in a military site this secure. D's punching the computer screen when he reaches them. The computer's been off for some time. It needs a few moments to fully boot up.

"It looks bigger than you said it would," says Zach.

Jamie turns to Zach, eyes wide. She's annoyed D told him something he didn't tell her.

"What the hell is going on, Dice?" demands Jamie.

"This is my mission," says D.

All the computer screens light up with the same pentagon image. Maize sees the images out of the corner of his eye. He tries to pull away from Hank, but the old man has a death grip. Betty's sitting on one of the computer desks, egging him on with bloodlust in her eyes.

D is banging on the keyboard, hoping it'll move faster. It makes Zach wince. You can't do that to a computer. It doesn't help anything. D bangs on the computer again.

"Stop doing that," says Zach.

"The damn thing's taking too long," says D, banging it again.

"Let her breathe," says Zach, pulling the keyboard away.

D stares at the keyboard with murder in his eyes. He digs into his bag and pulls out a laminated card with a series of numbers and dashes on it.

"Password?" asks Zach.

"Yeah," says D, breathing heavy. "Open it up and follow the instructions."

The startup screen shows ninety-nine percent as a dialogue box shows a diagnostics check. D and Zach roll over seat furthest from the fighting. Jamie takes her chair and sits in front of D, insisting on answers. D pulls a cloth from his bag to cover his face and starts talking. While he's doing that, a sound comes from the desktop speaker, welcoming a new guest.

Another dialogue box opens, asking for a password. Right as Zach types in the password, Rick drops headfirst into the table. Carlton elbows Bode's head into the screen.

"Shit, you fucking idiots," yells D, pushing Jamie away to attack Rick and Carlton. "What are you doing?"

The screen isn't off, merely a pixelated jagged mess. Some text is showing, but the screen is too ruined to make out whole words. Zach can see the letters "----mir," but that's it. D's had enough. He pulls out the taser from his bag and shocks Carlton in the neck, then kicks him. He hobbles toward everyone else.

D picks his spots and tasers everyone. The last one is Andrews. D just about punches him in the neck with the taser. Andrews starts convulsing and quivering. D keeps the taser on his neck for longer than needed. Andrews's bowels release. D finally let's go.

He has a relaxed face as he moves away from Andrews.

"The uglies are coming," says D, taking the cloth off his face. "If you want to be here when they break through the elevator, I'll open the maze and let you stand outside. Otherwise, don't fuck with me."

Everyone stares at D as he hobbles back to his chair. Andrews and Colt have a notion, but one look at the burns on D's face, and they stay where they are. Jamie can tell he's showing off the burns to scare people into compliance. She has to admit, it's effective.

"Well played," whispers Jamie.

"I thought that up on the spot," says D.

Zach notices all the computers are damaged. It must have happened before the bombs hit. He leans close to the screen, trying to make out the words. He's unfolded the card D gave him and is just typing in everything as dialogue boxes pop up. It's not the best way to operate, but the bottom right of the screen shows enough of the instructions for Zach to make an educated guess about what should be typed where.

While talking with Jamie, D starts poking his burned face again. She smacks his hand away from his cheek. She can't believe what he's telling her. He's serious though. Jamie looks at the exit on the other end of the section. There's hope. Cella is knocking on the wall, holding Saffire's hand. Jamie turns her head, but D's already up.

"What are you doing?" asks Jamie. "Was the pussy that good?"

"Our job is to protect and serve, not like, Lieutenant," says D.

He slides the key into the wall, and Cella and Saffire rush in. Cella saw Saffire by herself when the fighting started. She turned back to get her before someone else hurt the girl. They were waiting for the fighting to stop before coming closer.

D's moving back to his seat when Cella stops to look at him. He's covered his left face. He's trembling, heavy breathing, overcompensation on the right leg and profuse sweating. He shouldn't be standing right now. He'll need major reconstructive surgery. Some stem cells and a month of skin graphing could fix his face. Cella has no tools here to fix D's injuries. Unless she's very much mistaken, D will go into shock soon.

"You should take a pain killer," says Cella.

Jamie stiffens in her seat. She doesn't like agreeing with Cella.

"Let's not get distracted," says D shrugging her off. "Zach's about to open the mainframe, and if the weapon's inside, we'll go."

"Go where?"

"Go sit Saffire down," says D, motioning toward Betty before walking to his chair.

"Wait." says Cella.

Jamie is up and in Cella's face in under a second. "Do as the lieutenant tells you, civvie."

"I got it," says Zach.

D hobbles to him. The screen's too pixelated for D to tell what he's looking at. Zach's adjusted his vision after five minutes, so he can see the midline of the screen is split. The bottom right shows the middle third of the screen and the top left shows the middle left of the screen. What should be on the bottom left and top left is in the middle. The rest of the screen is too jumbled, but Zach has enough to make out what he should type and where.

"See here?" Zach points to the top left. "That says RV-6693 through RV-7703 is inside." He moves his hand down to the bottom left. "These are the names of each virus. They scroll up to the top right, but if I press "shift" and the down key, the names move to the middle as I scroll. I need a high-ranking voice recognition key to access that. It's not on the card you gave me."

"I wasn't told I needed voice recognition," says D.

"Don't worry about it," says Zach. "This is like every other government system. It'll need to verify a voice with itself and the home databank. I'll just program it to read my voice as the key."

"Could you find the audio file it has on record and just make it play back to itself?" asks D.

Zach looks at D impressed. "I tried. See this part in the middle. It reads '—dio -ile cor---ted.' Whatever the old one was, it doesn't work anymore. So I have to make a new one. I'll just set my voice as the key and open it that way. Not as elegant, but we're on a time limit, right?"

The desktop has a built-in microphone. Zach tells everyone to be quiet and speaks his name. After some more keystrokes and speaking, the mainframe moves; the different sections twist into ports that make straight lines.

"This will take thirty minutes," says Zach.

"Thirty fucking minutes?" snaps D.

"She's been off for a year in a half. Give her some time."

Everyone sits silent for a moment, then they hear the thumping. The uglies are still bashing through the elevator shaft. There are other sounds coming from the exit to the right of the elevator. The uglies are coming from two different directions.

"Zach?" asks D. "Can you pull up the diagnostics again?"

"Sure, what do you need?" asks Zach.

"I wanna know if I can shift these walls on demand."

"I'll check."

"What are you thinking?" asks Jamie.

"I'm setting the battlefield to my liking," says D.

Maize clears his throat. "If I catch your meaning, we'll make it much more effective with some booby traps."

D nods. "You sure you two can keep from killing each other long enough to set the battlefield?"

"The Navy is always professional. The Army's where all the scandals happen."

"The fuck it is, *sailor*." yells Hank with a twist on the last word.

Maize flips him off as Zach pulls up the section maze up. Because of the ruined screen, he has the minimize and shift focus to the middle of the screen to read each part of the maze. D points out spots to give free run to the uglies and where to lay traps. Maize doesn't like taking orders from his junior officer, but D has a long reputation for killing that's only grown since he reached their home.

Zach opens a wall near to them for Maize's team to head in and lay down traps, then another on the opposite end for Hank's team. The thumping is getting progressively louder. Jaime keeps looking at the back exit. She hasn't stopped since D told her his mission.

D is happy. That was much easier than he thought. It should take Maize and Hank's team at most ten minutes to set the field. He'll have to think up something else to keep them busy. And if either or both sides try to start another fight, Zach can keep both sides locked in place. Now there's something else D wants to check.

"Is the media port still ok?" D asks Zach.

"Only one way to find out. What do you want to play?"

D pulls out the four cubes. Zach looks at him.

"You didn't just find that hide out, did you?" says Zach.

"Of course not. It's one of the caches on my map. This place was supposed to have other important tools for beating the uglies, but Nwake had redundant safe houses nearby just in case. You should always plan for the worst." D shrugs.

"Wait," says Jamie. "You just told me—"

"Nwake didn't send us, but he's an informed source. You know I'd never trust just one source of information. But he was vague on a few details. Let's see what's on these cubes."

The image is grainy and jumbled, but Zach shrinks the window and moves it to a clear part of the screen. Words are printed in bold white.

"The following is a skirmish of two equal groups, dated June 26, 2041."

A system of infrared closed-circuit cameras shows a closed arena of hills and some type of animal. They are four legged, with poorly developed facial structures and fur. These creatures aren't uglies. The two groups are slowly circling each other. They make mock charges at each other. Eventually, both groups urinate to scent mark their territories then back away. A voice comes on mid-sentence, narrating the results.

"--
-------------------------------- have learned the value of a numerical advantage."

The cube moves to a second scenario where group 1 has a three-to-one numbers advantage. Group 1 decides who in group 2 to attack before overwhelming them.

Scenario 3 is showing group 2 with a two-to-one numbers advantage. Group 2 does the same as group 1 in the previous scenario and overwhelms them.

Scenario 4 introduces a pride of thirty lions. Lions during the forties were on the endangered species list. In the footage, the creatures of groups 1 and 2 consist of twenty creatures altogether. They join forces and slaughter the petrified felines in fifteen seconds.

Scenario five brings in a hundred wolves to face thirty creatures. The wolves are snarling but keeping a distance before one creature lunges forward, slashing and beheading one of the six alpha wolves. This pack retreats, rushing toward the nearest alpha. The creatures go rabid, chasing after the retreating wolves. The wolves can't outrun them, so they turn back and attack. The creatures back away in shock. They weren't expecting the wolves to attack. The moment passes quickly, then the creatures attack. Seven of them charge, splitting the pack in two. It doesn't last long. This pack is ruined in ten seconds.

The other wolf packs retreat, but the creatures are hungry. The creatures split into two groups of ten and race after the packs. The animals run over the hills. The creatures get tired and try cutting off routes so that the wolves can't double back. However, it's clear to see the creatures heaving. The wolves sense the advantage and attack. Many wolves are being ripped to shreds but four creatures are down. The creatures clack and grunt and suddenly all of them are equally divided atop the hills. They have better tactical position now, and they watch the wolves charge up at them.

In fifteen hours, only five creatures remain with every wolf scattered across the hills. The voice is back, narrating the results.

"Practical experience is the best way to test intelligence and adaptability. We must also improve stamina."

Scenario 6 is time stamped four years later. Two groups of creatures face each other with a few caveats. Group 1 looks severely malnourished, having mottled skin with pink lesions and peeling scabs, and several are supporting broken limbs while group 2 seems perfectly healthy.

Both creatures have the most rudimentary definitions of heads. It looks more like large tumors nudging through shoulder blades and a lipless mouth where the collarbone should be. One creature opens and closes a hole in its back before attacking a hesitant group one all out. Group one in a flash is retreating to hilltops before turning to attack. The image degrades before showing the winner.

Scenario 7, judging by ice crystals at the corners of the cameras, is cold with twelve emaciated creatures that are much closer to the uglies with which D is familiar. At the other end of the field are a dozen polar bears. Sixty feet from them are an equally starved pack of twenty-four wolves.

Neither the polar bears nor the wolves appear willing to attack the creatures but the creatures in two groups of six are swarming out to destroy the alpha wolf and the largest of the polar bears. Two wolves attack a lone creature as the rest of the pack and the creatures claw at each other. The lone creature takes one by the jaw and hind legs before bending the she wolf's spine past its breaking point. The other wolf is biting at the creature's leg as it throws the broken she wolf into the heart of the frenzied fighting. The creature rears back showing a foot long slit in its neck with jagged teeth running down its sides. The creature swoops down on the wolf's neck breaking it in one bite.

A creature in the heart of the fighting lifts a nine-hundred-pound polar bear off its feet to slam it on its head. The bear twitches for a moment then goes limp. The other bears are trying to hold their own but the creatures are as strong and more agile. After fifty seconds, the bears white fur is dark red with blood. The creatures have open wounds but the blood on them clots quickly.

The bears are tiring. They want to retreat but the creatures are cutting off the escape route. The camera pans wide, showing the ice field dyed with blood. It ends with a wolf's dead body flying into the legs of the last polar bear. The force of impact snaps both front legs. The creatures take turns bum rushing the bear from all angles until it falls weak from blood loss. Five creatures remain and the voice returns.

"Strength is improving nicely; this generation has less of a self-preservation instinct. The next will need more protective muscle."

The monitor has a prompt up reading, "No longer able to read the file."

"What did you do?" D asks Zach. "Get it back."

"I'm trying," says Zach, typing furiously. "The cube's too damaged. I don't have the tools to fix it here."

"Forget it. Play this one," says D, handing him cube 2.

"How many files are on that cube?" asks Cella.

Jamie frowns at her. She was about to ask the same question.

"At least seventy," says Zach. "The rest of the cube is too damaged for me to see what else is on it."

"Was that a government water seal I saw on that file?" asks Teague, trembling.

D forgot he was sitting on the ground next to the computer.

"Yes, it was," says D, rolling his chair over to him.

Teague is shaking, skin is paling. He thinks he's about to prop him up to a more comfortable position. He's wrong. D grabs Teague's bag and pulls out empty cubes.

"Zach, use these to copy the files."

Teague looks hurt and frustrated. D never acted as part of the team on their way to Three-Mile Island; why would he be different once inside? Maize is waving from behind the wall. Zach's about to open it, but D tells him to wait. Cella and Betty are confused. Hank and the troop come in from the other side, and then D tells Zach to open the walls.

"What's going on?" Maize asks D before Hank can ask.

"You remember our private conversation?" D asks Maize. "I have some proof to back my feelings."

"You don't have feelings."

"True enough. Play the cube, Zach."

Maize motions D away from the others. Jamie is moving over to act as a shadow, but D waves her back. Zach needs her protection more than him. Hank still has bloodlust in his eyes for Maize, but maybe curiosity will keep him civil.

Maize walks around the other side of the mainframe, blocking everyone else from seeing them. Jamie naturally moves to a position that allows her to keep Zach and D in her line of sight.

"Tell me straight, Lieutenant," begins Maize. "Is Jamie why you came here? It's easy to tell you two are close. Did you hear or see something or cut a deal with that damn Nwake to get on this expedition?"

"No," says D. "My sister being here is a very happy coincidence. To your two other questions, the answer is also no. I had sleeping troubles. You knew that beforehand. I got our team away from plenty of situations before then. The two clusters of uglies by Highway 90 near Cleveland, the chase you fell into by Warren after I strongly suggested you wait for me to find an alternate route."

"There was a storm coming. We couldn't stay top side for an hour while you found another detour. It was the eighth time you'd changed where you were guiding us, by the way."

"I'm a scout. I was born in Ohio. Why didn't you just wait?"

"Because I didn't want a damn ice tornado to kill my team."

"Lake weather's unpredictable. I still got us out, didn't I?"

"Fine. It wasn't Jamie. Was it that other young lady?"

"What?"

"You don't show much, but she tries too hard to pretend she doesn't know who you are. And when she doesn't think anyone's looking, she eye's you like you're her property. Is she some lost love you want to reconnect with?"

"Why can't it be as simple as I fucked up?"

"Don't play that answer my question with a question shit with me, Lieutenant."

"Why's that so hard to believe?"

"Don't take this as a compliment. I do not mean it as one. You are frighteningly efficient at gathering information. You are the best shot I've ever seen, and even before I knew you personally, your records spoke for you. Everyone's capable of making mistakes. I'm not saying that. But by what you're telling me and my opinion of you, you are too good to have made such a simple and monumental mistake."

"I don't know what to tell you, Commander."

Maize looks him in the eye for a long moment. "When we get back home, I'm filing formal charges against you. Manslaughter and negligence in the face of the enemy and striking a fellow officer, depending on how Andrews feels. A few more, once I talk to JAG."

"Ok," D says simply.

"You're not gonna try to argue me out of it?"

"It wouldn't work, and I don't run from my responsibilities."

Maize nods, and they walk back to the group. Hank is cursing loudly. There's a government seal on the screen, and he's demanding to know what's going on.

"Look, I'm just trying to get a grip on this," says Zach, leaning back as Hank looms over him.

"What is this place?" yells Hank.

"The Pennsylvanian Species Reintegration Center," says D, readjusting the cloth on his face.

"I've never heard that name."

"Well before this mission started, I hadn't either. How's about instead of bugging Zach, we let him find out before we leave."

"To go where?" asks Hank.

D ignores the question as he sits. The audio is unintelligible at first, then a voice comes out clear through all six monitors.

"I am fully aware that my attempts to relieve this great gaffe in judgment are for naught. My only hope is that the true account of my work will find the appropriate hands."

This isn't the voice of the first cube. The mainframe is clanking from the inside while the voice degrades, becoming choppy, repeating, then stopping.

"What's the time?" asks Maize.

"Fourteen minutes," says D.

Hank is half-tempted to attack Maize again, but D is sitting between the two while Jamie has everyone's bags. She's looking through Rick's bag and holding up a mustard bomb. He's not putting it past her to knock out everyone to reestablish order. He'll have to be nice to get answers.

"How big is this place you come from?" asks Hank.

D has no intention of answering.

"Just tell them," says Maize. "No point hiding it now."

"Big," says D.

Hank scowls. If he were still in his twenties, he'd take off his shoe and throw it at D. He's too old to do that now, but he's not above head-butting the young asshole.

"That transmission we heard," says Hank slowly. "I thought someone must have been in here. And they reactivated the signal to call people to them. But brogs have taken the house keys for this place. So I'm left with two options; either you sent a signal to the base, hoping this place would still be active, or this place sent in an automated signal when certain conditions occurred. Like if maintenance is needed or something like that. How right am I?"

D looks at him for a long moment then breathes deeply.

"The transmission you heard wasn't meant for you," says D. "It's sent whenever a security breach can't be contained by onsite staff. Now something happened a while back where we're from. Around the same time, this thing beeped. The powers that be were happy to see this site was still active, and it just so happens that it might have what we need to fix our problem back home. So a team was sent to find out. They're dead now, so a second team was sent, and here we are," D says.

"You didn't say a goddamn thing," says Hank.

"You'd have to be there for any of it to make sense. But I will say that what's in the mainframe may be a way to fix the biggest problem we have, the uglies."

"That makes even less sense," says Hank.

D puts more salve on his face and breathes out heavily.

"We're just here to find tools to kill a common problem. How hard is that to understand?"

The voice returns.

"_____

--original purpose was purely humanitarian. The public had been warned time and time again of our duty as chief stewards of the planet --
------------------------------------ aware of a voluntary extinction. I would not allow -------------------------
----
---leading intellects to discuss solutions. --
---unremitting war propaganda ensured that proper funding from our governments would be a fool's errand. We must begin with simple, practical solutions. Success of said solutions would fuel our need for endowments --------------
----
-------------- colleagues felt this approach was a betrayal of our oath to conservation. These members were overruled. --
--- three years of failure our first positive result, portable air purifiers."

"We used the last of our own monies to complete its design and compensate advertising professionals for marketing of the product. The campaign was ingenious, the slogan a masterpiece of human psychology. *Others have caused the problem; you will be the solution.'* Perfection. Using our society's narcissism to bring forth a shared endeavor. The first advertisements aired in 2024. The immediate success brought much needed funding --
--can recollect the day Casamir received his portion of earnings."

"Can you fast forward this shit?" asks D.

"No, I'm not sure the audio will come back if I move anything. This guy sounds bitter though," says Zach.

"This is just to past time, Zach. Hit the side see what happens."

Zach bangs the side to see the cube timescale jumps one hour, forty-two minutes. At this moment, Rick tries darting forward to spear D, but Jaime shoots his broken elbow, and he yells in pain.

"I missed on purpose," says Jamie. "Don't hit him."

"You're a lying piece of shit, D," says Rick.

"What exactly did I lie about?" asks D.

"You said you were by yourself this whole time."

"No, I said I was by myself most of the time. And you were asking in regard to the eighteen months. You should be more specific."

Rick's eyes bulge. D never did give him a direct answer. He still hasn't, and this fact makes Rick even more upset.

"There were eight of you on this team?" asks Rick.

"Seventeen. For each team. My suit came from First Sergeant Dorian Walcott. At least one of them made it all the way here. I couldn't find the others."

The mainframe is clanking again. It opens to show a blast proof glass door with cylinders lined up behind it.

"They are beautiful," says the voice. "--
--- 2031 we now had the investments necessary to focus on our areas of expertise. I naturally went back to biology. ---------------------------
----

started with simple organisms various bacterium and viruses. My plan was to use the findings from my studies to boost the immunizing capabilities for the countless soon to be extinct species and ourselves."

"Fast forward," says D before the cube jumps fifty-seven minutes.

"--- most unintended outcome. --Acquired   Immune   Deficiency Syndrome. ---by 2034, my results would publish. --

Noble Prize, the greatest moment of my life. The acclaim garnered forced me into seclusion. I must admit the limelight was not something I myself was quite prepared for. --- could not fulfill my duties as a scientists while simultaneously growing a celebrity. --after insects came rodents."

"Fast forward," says D. The cube skips twelve minutes.

"---came the primates ---felines, canines, marsupials, and all manner of fish. -- later added the amphibious and avian families."

The cube skips again, then stops, ejecting itself as a message reads, "Unable to read."

"I can't copy all of it," says Zach. "The cubes too damaged." "It's all right," says D, handing him another cube.

Just as the cube plays another, thumps shake the elevator shaft. The uglies are close now. It will be nine minutes before the blast door opens.

Cube 3 is packed with data. Zach's eyes are wide as a dinner plate. He didn't have access to all this confidential information when he was rich. The irony is funny.

"It'll be harder to read this because it's more damaged than the others," says Zach.

D doesn't hear anything Zach says. The cylinders are cycling inside the mainframe.

The cube is showing a wartime map of the world. Land bodies in anti-Coalition areas have an opaque white color with ultra-blue dots at random points. The voice returns midsentence.

"These points will make sense as I continue—" the voice fades as the cubes ejects itself. Zach pushes it back in and opens the desktop to jury rig some of the wires.

The audio is back with the cube jutting ahead sixty minutes. "-- 2039, our first attempt at species reintegration. Marine life seemed the most obvious place to begin seeing as all life originates from --Sharks had sadly passed below their minimum viable population number but we hoped to use our knowledge of their breeding and hunting grounds to help other marine predators occupy the vacating space in time to allow a strong food chain to maintain itself, foolish yes and ---. This is when the first of our moral debates began."

The cube stops with another "Unable to read prompt." Zach gets fed up and punches the hard drive, shooting the cube ahead two hours, thirty-six minutes. Five dots are pulsing in the opaque white over southwest America as the voice returns.

"--- were the sights of our first tests using land-based animals who too proved to be as uncooperative as water-based life forms. Thankfully, our sedatives are equally as tenacious. My colleagues would again protest the ethics of this program but, as we saw it, these wonderful creations were being eradicated through no fault of their own. We as a race played a direct role in the dissention; as such, we are responsible for their continued survival. -------------------------------------- -- -- ----------------standard conservation efforts took too long in our opinion, so we decided on a fresh approach. We would use my bacterial and viral immunology notes to strengthen the genetic code of species most in need of our help. Casamir thought to combine traits distinguishable to one species with others whose environments provide a natural lift. These controlled experiments to evaluate the generous hand given to this maturation process showed a miscalculation on our part. However, the changing genomes brought new possibilities for cures to numerous diseases and congenital malfunctions."

The cube skips three hours, showing a hologram focusing on the bottom third of the United States and Central America.

"In the eight years since our decision to enhance immunity, the subjects have developed unforeseen side effects, increased aggression being the most notable. With the now 471 species under our care, monitoring progress becomes difficult. ----------- -- ------------------facilities with more lax security than our own. An absolute lack of oversight allowed certain species to intermingle and eventually copulate, creating extremely aggressive half-breeds that, though interesting, were sterile."

"These lackluster counterparts, having no sense of security, did manage to log the half-breed's remarkable natural weaponry. A very interesting opportunity became clear to us. ---------------------- -- ---- clear violation of the animal welfare and breeding laws, but I did not."

The voice stops again to make some type of spitting noise that sounds a mix of growling and coughing.

"Please excuse that. The rule as I understood it only applied to non-extinct species. ------------------ -- ---------we would take the DNA of all the unauthorized half-breeds to begin experimentation. --------- -- ------------------ later tests would prove the need for new organisms. In laymen terms, the planet had been scarred beyond the point to where these species could adapt naturally. We would again provide the hand Mother Nature could not. -- ---hyenas, lions, octopi, sea snakes then wolfs, penguins, marlins all in an attempt to take the best of each species and allow a template for survival in all species. -- -- these authorized half-breeds came with the same behavioral issues,

not unexpected but very inconvenient. ---
--- next generation of half-breeds were able to live an entire six days."

"Fast forward," says D. The cube skips forty-seven minutes.

"The funds for our reintegration project were running low following the earthquake on the pacific coast. Seeing our old friends in the clean commitment movement pounce on this news to gain legitimacy was a sad sight to behold. Nwake and his moral certainty disgusted me to no end. ----------
----
----------------- we were at our end when Casamir purposed asking the congress for increased financial assistance. Going through these bureaucratic channels was a hassle I did not want to commit myself. -
----
------------------------- year of wrangling Casamir had persuaded the committee to grant twelve percent of our total funding. I asked my friend how he was able to receive any funding. Casamir stated that certain members of the oversight committee were expressed all the possibilities of our work."

"The next generations of half-breeds would come from our enhanced primates, wolves, and frogs. The stronger immune systems were thought to give these second generations a longer life span; to find it did not was a major setback. --
-- accusations of scientific impropriety threatened to take our funding for a second time. Casamir would again step in to quell concerns of our efforts. For some reason, my friend could always get his way. The potential scandal had caused the congress to assure they would not be seen as part of the reintegration project. It would be renamed and transferred to an unofficial military subsidiary for oversight. This organization had no direct ties to then Lieutenant General Arlington, but I later learned that he had cleared a large funding contract to a friend of one of his former veteran friends. Make of that as you will."

"Arlington's friend I must say, at first was very much against overseeing an animal research project but after a series of meetings with Casamir and an up close viewing of the unalloyed tenacity of the half-breeds there was no more talk of reallocating funding. They'd never admit this, but I could sense the progenies had given our benefactors a fright they never quite lost. It was in the eyes."

"It would be years before I would see Arlington himself. He was heading into politics and a strong firm hand against the coalition was the popular opinion. I can't confirm if he and Casamir ever spoke directly during these years all I can say is that I didn't. Wh--
-- brought more setbacks for some reason we could not extend the half-breed life cycle."

"Casamir purposed adding DNA of other genera during chosen developmental stages. Our first attempt worked to give the half breeds four more days of life. There, it stayed for a year until a most fortuitous solution. One of our many assistants mislabeled strains of DNA that were to be introduced during the third trimester of several enhanced primates' pregnancies. Enhanced octopi, elephant, and mole rat genes were added. By the time the mistake had been found, the process was irreversible. We expected the fetuses to miscarry or be still born, but they survived."

"Miraculously, the offspring would not only live, but live well past four months with what many considered truly disturbing changes. A greatly altered basic mammal body plan. Though they had four limbs, the eyes were not developed, add to this no traditional brain cavity. Nature, even in this controlled circumstance, keeps surprises aplenty. We named this first creature Walter, seeing as our assistant Walter made its existence possible. After death, we performed an autopsy, noting that we could find no brain, only a series of nerve clusters that worked to relay information throughout the

body. --
--------------------------------- four greatly enhanced senses that worked to provide stunningly accurate details of their environment. We would quickly use the same process to grow more. ----------------------
----
------ more soon to be defectors questioning our efforts. They stated that though we meant well, this current situation is not what should have come of it. It was then we severed ties."

"Next, we would decide to focus on creating three more genera from other enhanced animals we felt had the most potential with this method. We were unsuccessful in using all other animal families. There again, a prodigious mistake made by a mundane mislabeling of DNA gave us two new brethren species. Not quite the four-legged original but just as unique. The only thing kept similar by the three, was oddity in body design. I am confident we could have made dozens more -----------------------------
----
another year of research, and we would be able to enhance the nerve clusters into true processing centers. And, thankfully we could breed each animal with the other two. It only took six months and two generations to reconfigure the reproductive systems. Though each one still has its own mating processes and rituals, they could all produce offspring with each other but to date, they still have not progressed."

The voice shouts and growls again before continuing.

"After this progress, we could allow the three to live long enough to produce a third generation of enhanced animals, not with their separate genera, but the fact that they could produce viable offspring at all nearly brought tears to my eyes. Nature had stepped in to provide an ingenious upgrade. The third generations developed additional muscle and sense acuity; lastly, due to all the days of cohabitation, the animals developed gregarious personalities. Animals with large populations tend to have larger brainpower to organize and maintain relationships. We'd grown the nerve centers four-fold in only one generation. I was very proud of our team."

"I struggled to keep up with the progress. Before we could make new animals, we needed to fully understand our success but then there were the east coast floods and having to move the capital to Illinois. Safe to say, our budget decreased, so we were stuck with, for the foreseeable future, only our three enhanced primates. --
-- It would seem having more than one nerve cluster would give the offspring a better chance of reacting and adapting to the changes in its environment. We only allowed these creatures four brains, one a large central one and three smaller ones that run along the spine."

"Some insect species have multiple nerve clusters and can survive weeks after decapitation due to the lack of blood pressure for such tiny bodies. Obviously, our creations are much larger, so that is why, as I mentioned earlier, our need for a failsafe. The one dilemma we could not solve was the hyperaggressive activity. Casamir thought to see what exactly the offspring would do if allowed to rampage. His thinking was if one day these creatures must be released to the wild, they must show an ability to defend themselves. I was adamant in my opposition, but Casamir performed these little tests he thought, without my knowledge. As if I would not know everything being done with my creations. --
---------------------------- When I purposed this idea, an on-off switch as it were, Casamir saw the sense."

"It took experimentation with three more generations before perfecting our control system, molding the body to allow for this one soft spot at the creature's middle where it could easily be put down should the need arise. And after this new triumph, I had my yearly vacation ------------------------------------- --- he sought to bring endangered species from all over to see how the new improved offspring would react. After returning, I would be informed of Casamir's shameful activity and confront him. He admitted his deceit, and I heard no more of these tests."

"Fast forward," says D. The cube jets fifty-one minutes.

"--

----------------------------------imbeciles joined Nwake's clean commitment garbage and threatened to again destroy our reintegration efforts. It was not enough to take their monies with them but to betray colleagues as they planned was not fair."

"This next whistle-blowing exercise would come before the special elections. These turncoats would challenge many officials, so a compromise came. Casamir gave key officials large campaign contributions, and the reintegration sights would move from southern America to Central and South America, away from the outdated environmental guidelines. But our project would continue to be monitored by Arlington who was strangely abreast of our progress. After more salacious accusations and the elections, Arlington would take a firmer hand on our operations in South America."

"I remember how curious it was that the new Amazonian headquarters had a stunning view of the forest formations and was already well known and feared by locals. That night, after a day to take in my new living situation, I had my first meeting with the now General Arlington. Casamir wasn't present. The general commended my work thus far, and he enlightened me on how my dear friend Casamir recently obtained fifty percent of funding through private military outlets, making Arlington's friends equal partners."

"The general's grin made me very uneasy, add to that his knowing of Casamir's unauthorized testing and it became clear what had happened. The general made a very simple offer to me. Either accept that the reintegration project would run under the guidance of the general or the fifty percent funding would reallocate. I was furious; I couldn't speak. This warmonger had come, gun blazing, to destroy my work, and I could do nothing. I came to the realization that my decision didn't matter. Casamir and the others were going to continue the project with or without me. My friend had been running secret tests for years without my knowledge. At least by staying, I would know what exactly was polluting my work, and I cannot deny the unwavering commitment I made to repair the animal kingdom. A commitment is a commitment, and the astounding furtherance made was undeniable."

"The next two years were painstaking and exhilarating. I must admit I found it quite pleasurable watching the defectors and their pathetic Green vs. Grey rallies. I wondered if they knew the history they would not be linked to. Cowards."

The voice stops, growling again.

"My apologies. Then, the fruits of our labor came to flourish. -

----

-------------------------The seventh generation would live for a full year, and we added fleetness of foot to an increasing intellect. Our first four-legged progenies developed tiny smelling orifices running along the back and sides. We had no idea why this happened. The plan was to increase smell sensitivity. We wanted each brain to get signals at roughly the same time from different parts of the body. We had no idea the gestation process would produce this."

"Next, we added additional air sacks and gave primitive speaking apparatus at the shoulder blades more flexibility. This would help to produce more intricate scents through glands and with later generations, sound. The two other genera developed similarly staggering adaptations. We made sure that the animals were still genetically similar enough to breed. That being said, we were curious what these other animals would do if separated. What kind of social groups would they make, and once that was done, what would happen to those groups once all three were combined?"

"For example, the smallest of our three progenies saw no need for limbs after several secret generations of fighting; they could use their entire body to move akin to snakes, forgoing all but two internal organs that were a merging of multiple functions. You should see the things. I thought they were making a heart and brain but not so. The upper organ is cerebral fluid with calcium columns that bend like cartilage. One of my young assistants was guiding this process. He was so curious he didn't try to guide their nerve system evolution. The fool. Still, it was interesting."

"The largest had much the same adaptations as the originals high metabolisms and multiple sets of orifices for breathing and eating at the same time. However, they also liked standing and running on two legs for a short time. My guess is that this is a holdover from their chimp heritage. We still were too worried of the consequences of allowing crossbreeding the actual species with our enhanced versions, so this branch of our research was admittedly held back by our cowardice. Sorry, I'm rambling again. As ---
--------------------------------."

"The general admired the new fearsome appearance and ordered more versions of these animals using more of the traditional predator species. I had to explain to the general that biology is not as simple as he would like. Any species given proper DNA tweaks and a certain environment could be predators. However, I did not want to make him feel stupid so we assured him we'd try our best. ------
----
---."

The monitor shows an assortment of deformed progenies.

"The fool kept insisting on six to twelve new breeds using apex predators. I was satisfied with our three, but Arlington was a man of variety. The general would import bears, African leopards, Asian leopards, wild dogs, Siberian tigers, etcetera, from all over in the following years. We would create forty-nine more fetuses using different animals but none was remotely close to the success of the primate carrier system. I would again have to explain that nature is not orderly."

"Fast forward." says D. The cube zooms ahead one hour, fourteen minutes.

"The ninth generation developed reproductive issues. It was then that our general brought something of scientific value. After reading my notes on other animals, he would suggest mimicking the earthworm reproductive process. Earthworms are hermaphrodites, and this would give the offspring the best of both worlds. It made some sense, having two sets of reproductive organs was worth consideration. ---
--yet another year of almost losing an entire generation, we were able to do as the general asked. Again, nature added its influence by taking away an annual mating cycle, making them behave closer to such mammals as humans and rabbits, which do not need to procreate during arbitrary times of the year."

"The accomplishment would cause an out-of-body experience in all including Casamir and myself. The general now wanted a name for the offspring. Generation 10 didn't roll off the tongue. He wanted something that and I quote *gives a sense of formal militaristic dread.* As always, we tried our best.

The assistants and lead scientists started a friendly competition to find a fitting name. ------------------
----
---------Walter would use an acronym for the offspring, Strategic Operational Urban Land Squads or SOULS. The general loved it.

-----------------------------.” The cube skips thirty-two minutes.

“Economic cutbacks reached the military. Taking a hiatus from military action meant no need for such a large budget, which also meant less places to hide money. The general called in some favors, and the headquarters would move deeper into the Amazon, but our offspring would split between different locations of which I was not allowed to know. I did not agree with this action due to prior lax security, but the general didn’t care. ---

----

eleventh and twelfth generation came roughly seven months apart, each strengthening the communication skills and physical weaknesses of the last.”

“Fast forward.” says D. The cube skips three hours.

“The general seeing the progress of these generations wanted them exposed to real world conditions, such as radiation and extreme cold and heat. The supreme immune systems I had developed would be put to the test. The aggression and stress the environments would bring once exposed was something I watched closely. The Souls performed beautifully and the fourteenth and fifteenth generations would thicken and darken the skin to a blackish-gray quality, most assuredly due to the intense radiation, and develop even more intricate speech patterns to survive the exercises, crackling and such. This was amusing for most people, but I could see the danger matching another unintended side effect, which I felt. The animals had a growing distrust of their keepers.

“Arlington was oblivious to these issues as always. Even Casamir could see it. This is when we started on a small side project. I was of the opinion that the three progenies eventually needed sustained contact with each other. The question was how we would ensure the three could still breed with each other while maintaining their new adaptations. The answer was insectile. In nature, many dimorphic species have wildly different body plans between male and female. In the case of our Souls, they were hermaphrodites, so the solution was in the sperm and eggs.”

“This took some time. The exact details were placed on the fourth cube by Thomas, but essentially, we copied the mating habits of ants and bees. Simple, yes? Ants can make males or female ants depending on the environment. The males and females were based on external forces. What we wanted was stable variation among the three. Our smallest progenies couldn’t do this because it took too long to map out the right process, and Arlington didn’t want it that way. We settled on the original Souls as the queens, if you will. All we had to do was make it so if either of the three genera fell below a certain number, then the original would make more of that genus. Simple.”

“Now to ensure this could be done without artificial assistance, we needed four years and several generations of contact. We manipulated growth rates to ensure full yet short lifecycles of sixteen months to get the needed intel. After destroying those dead ends, we had what we needed. The change we found was all of them had the same skin pigment of dark grey but with a more pronounced pattern of fine hairs and odd skin deformations that look blistered. This worked, but we kept their numbers limited until we could resolve Arlington’s commands.”

“The general wanted to increase communication skills in underwater exercises. This is why the next generations were given another set of lungs, but as evolution teaches, every upgrade has its costs. The impregnable shell of muscle would have to loosen ever more to create more space for the organs to expand. A softer torso allowed the keepers to issue more severe disciplining practices while increasing flexibility and lessening weight for improved speed. Nature can be very annoying sometimes."

"Their protective back orifice membrane would also be able to expand and close as needed, except this adaptation was more nuanced. Prior adaptations would allow these protective skins to expand all communication difficulties in water, meaning the crackle I grew to love could double as an echo locator under water."

The cube skips twenty-two minutes.

"The general, seeing the frightening ease of the Souls, wanted more production. This is when the queen adaptation was fully integrated. Arlington loved it. He thought it as another way to control the beasts. I didn't tell him how wrong he was. More radiation training meant a denser skin. This also meant a more blistered-looking appearance, but we kept the silky smoothness as a dominant trait. --- --- ----------------------The Souls again defeated each, but after one chance session, Walter was attacked and killed. There wasn't enough left for a proper burial. I still cannot forgive Arlington for the lack of safety. --- ------------------------------In light of the killing, the general wanted a new name. ------------------- --- --------was determined not to be bested by my subordinates again. I followed Walter's example, and with Casamir, came up with some acronyms."

"--- ----------------------------name came after a Soul made a gasping sound after being disciplined, 'Asp.' Casamir didn't like it, but I continued to develop a name based on this sound for three days. The name is based on their new abilities as much as their attitude. *Amphibious Strategic Precision Exploration Rampage Squads, ASPERS.* A fitting name, no? My beautiful creatures were perfected with speed, agility, strength, stamina, ravenous, curious and radiation-resistant skin."

The cube skips one hour, thirty-seven minutes.

"After feeling bored by a three-year combat hiatus, the general felt the Aspers had advanced to the point where practical combat experience was needed if they were to reintegrate. The general went ahead with plans to attack aggressive local tribesmen. --- ---."

The voice stops to give way to gagging and shrieking.

"I wouldn't be allowed a glimpse into where the general took my animals, but I am not one to stand by and let the general due as he wishes with my work. With the help of Thomas, my new head assistant, I sneaked from headquarters into local tribal areas --- --- Aspers were very successful. It was complete and utter mutilation. This is when I began to question my loyalties."

"I found what was left of the natives and received eye-opening accounts of numerous attacks. The eldest among these people said they were not pleased with the stone-headed desecration of their land and asked the general to leave. The elder was warned not to, but the decades of torment had not occurred before the start of this Coalition war. Our war had no business near his tribe. ---------------- -- --."

"Should I fast forward?" asks Zach, seeing D move closer.

"No, this is interesting," says D.

"That conversation gave me an unease I have still not been able to shake." The voice continues. "I could now clearly see where the change in behavior first occurred. The Aspers would continue closed session exercises that Thomas would supervise under my orders. The Aspers, with every session, became more difficult to wrangle. They enjoyed the thrill of combat and freedom of fighting. A good rule of thumb is use chemicals to blunt senses. The animals being as social as they are, calm down clump together for easier wrangling."

"Thomas was elevated to an outside mission wrangler for finding that alluring scents worked as well as harmful ones in corralling the Aspers. He would report to me the things being done with my animals. He and the other wranglers would name Arlington's outdoor training missions operation *monthly diplomacy* as a play on the general's coming position of secretary of defense. -------------------------- --- twelve wranglers were attacked on this last diplomatic mission. The Aspers responsible were immediately euthanized. --- --- The Aspers were clearly not as afraid of the staff as they should have been. --- ---Nine of the twelve staff members and nearly four dozen Aspers were quarantined with unspecified illnesses."

"I requested a stop to all diplomacy missions until after a thorough investigation, but my request was denied. The Aspers would recover several days later, but I heard nothing of the staff members. --- --- ----------------------------."

The cube skips thirteen minutes.

"Thomas allowed me access to files on the secretary's missions. They were merely training runs for something else I did not yet know. I returned to the tribe I visited a year ago and was told by the elder speaking to them that they had brought a vengeance.

A demon has come from the dying forest to punish those responsible for its mother's death. It kills with speed and cunning, and what it cannot reach with claws, it takes with its colorless brother.

Its symptoms are skin irritation, cottonmouth, at stage 1. Stage 2 is heightened aggression, accompanied by delusion, and finally, stage 3 brain and heart decay, meaning seizures, strokes, and or heart attacks as the neurons die. Average time of death based on what I could gather was twenty-two days."

"Fast forward," says D. The cube jumps twelve minutes.

"It appears the repeated diplomacy had exposed the Aspers to the rhinovirus, the common cold. The human enterovirus C species has no cure and adapts with every changing season. The Aspers, because of the close confines, caused an outbreak in several hundred of them. The animals would recover, but they were not supposed to be ill at all. Nature can be a very intolerable woman at times. ---------------- --- ------------ the secretary heeded my request and postponed all outdoor training."

The cube skips one hour, fifteen minutes.

"After much congressional discussion, it was decided that war would reconvene. The secretary came to tell us that our budget would upgrade and that preliminary field tests would start soon. Also, we would move to a luxurious Pennsylvanian complex. -- --. The next decade would consist of learning how to best control the Aspers, and for myself, isolating and replicating the antibodies my animals developed for the cold to help other animal's immunity. Later, Thomas would help. He slipped into Casamir's office the day after one of his yearly vacations and found as always, his locked notes in the false bottom of the left side of his desk. I would get detailed medical reports for the nine quarantined staff members infected by an unknown virus and tentative plans for a vaccine based on my research. The problem was this vaccine gave the staff characteristics similar to the Aspers. Some even had slight physical differences."

"When Casamir returned, I confronted him. He attacked me for being short sighted. *'With the progress we'd made, why not cover all bases?'* he said. --- --

--- ---secretary would not answer my phone calls, I had to use Thomas to obtain copies of Arlington's reports to know where and what my Aspers were doing. I was a ghost in the building I had built. But I did not stand still; I had quickly grown cultures for a vaccine to the unnamed virus. I did not recognize my oldest friend anymore, and I was no longer revered or respected. Perhaps, my advanced age was the reason for such disrespect but still none of this would be possible without my work. My position as head scientists was being taken from me, no matter; -------- --- -------------------- these people still could do nothing without my expertise."

"Casamir looked to create a vaccine, but he is not the immunologist I am. The virus is unlike any I have ever seen. Ebola's ease of infection death matched with smallpox is the only comparison that serves. A great challenge. I was all too happy to complete my vaccine in under ten years. My vaccine would not only protect my colleagues but perhaps strengthen their immune systems to the point that this could infect others with the same protection. I called it my own form of herd immunity. The next generation of Aspers, which I believe, would be eighteen-- --. There are others trying to create counteragents for -- --. As a scientist, I am taught to value life but for reasons I will explain later, measures must be taken to ensure the greater good. I tested my vaccine on twenty sta-- -- the inoculation did not go as I had hoped. For some reason, their demeanor changed. I went back to the source to see what I may have overlooked. Everyone knows better than to wake an Asper during its rest period, but I was impatient. It lashed out, looking to protect itself; I was bitten. I scrambled to inject the vaccine. It did not work as hoped. If anything, it increased certain symptoms."

"I called Thomas, who stupidly informed the general. I was given a serum of Casamir's making that I later found was an updated version of the one I had been making. He knew my work was better. I could tell my efforts worked. I could feel my success coursing through my blood. Of course, Casamir in his arrogance, thought this was all his doing. He said my freelancing almost compromised his new failsafe."

"That slug was not satisfied with my original solution, so without my knowledge, for the past eight years, he had been developing a sterilization virus to cull Asper growth rates. My meddling as he deemed it would have resulted in complete genocide. Thereafter, I was quarantined, and my position as head scientist transferred to Casamir, and the man I raised from obscurity, Thomas, would receive the title of lead scientist of the complex. I forgot that Casamir was nearly as smart as me and for some reason, people liked him more than me. No one seemed upset at my disappearance. *Bastards.*"

"I was not feeling like myself anymore. I was not feeling the advanced effects of the disease, at least as I know them to be, but I am changing, physically. --- --- I do report good news. Though being a coconspirator, Thomas was thankfully never suspected since I had many underlings. This allowed him to help me finish the human vaccine. With my help, he took credit for his efforts in helping that disgusting former friend protect ourselves from our creations. I must say, I made it better, but I also must confess it is too late for me in my worsening condition to reap its benefits."

The container now spins a cap at its top, and the blast door opens.

"Thomas has assured me the vaccine will be safeguarded upon completion, but so as not to confuse you, my dear listener, our vaccine does not protect against Casamir's failsafe. This safeguard is meant to stop the Aspers virus. Our vaccine should help to maintain normal brain function for humans. All other animals will die. As for Casamir's failsafe, I'm calling it Casamir strain from now on. That is held in the heart of the Pennsylvanian facility."

That virus is simple. It's only purpose is to kill Aspers when necessary. To do that, it must be able to adapt to every one of the Aspers' protections against disease. In short, this virus kills the reproductive process of all known animals. First chemically, the virus attacks the egg or sperm cells, then it will rupture gonadal tissue from the inside out. Then it works its way up the nervous system shutting down body parts until complete brain death. Casamir, I have to admit, did a very good job here. He had to be sure it would work, you understand."

"Before I explain why I'm telling you this, I must first explain the danger posed by the secretary. After receiving plans via Thomas, I now know Arlington is planning to use my creations on Coalition population centers. He predicts, based on battlefield analysis, that a force of 70,000 Aspers over heavily populated manufacturing areas would decimate any Coalition fighting capability. At the intended time of this operation, five years from the day of this recording, he hopes to have seventeen million Aspers at his disposal, effectively ending the war."

"The secretary is again disregarding nature's power. My creations cannot be allowed to fight in this war. They are meant to help the ecosystem, not the secretary's ego. Arlington will not heed this warning, so I must take matters into my own hands. Thomas and I will release the Casamir strain over the planned attack areas just as Arlington releases the Aspers. This is my record to you, listener, so that you will know why. If we fail, you have the means or the information to find the means to end a nightmare before it starts."

"Because of how smart and intuitive my creations have become, the Casamir strain will have to disperse over a wide area. This will be discussed in cube 4. Now, I must discuss the general's plans to best fend off my creations militarily should the need arise."

A loud crashing sound sends off alerts. The elevator doors are tearing open. Aspers are spewing out, as the automated voice repeats, "Containment breach." The section turns dark with red flood lights dotting the outer walls.

"How much time?" asks D.

"Two minutes, twenty-three seconds and counting," says Zach. "All right. Here they come," says Maize.

Jamie gives the seals and the troop their guns back. Zach gets up, but D frowns at him.

"I need you to copy the next cube," says D.

The last cube inserts then ejects. The seals and the troop stand to separate sides of the mainframe with a wall separating the teams. D sniffs his suit. He still can't smell anything different from what he should.

"Keep the cards," says D to Zach. "You'll need it where you're going."

Zach nods, then accesses the backdoor. These blank cubes are made the same way as the ones he invented.

The government has no imagination.

Zach has worked with these types of mainframes before. They store all information; nothing is deleted, a normal safeguard companies use when a disgruntled ex-employee is looking to blackmail the company. Zach uses this tactic himself. He brings up history files and finds recent files under "unknown." He claps his hands in victory. The computer finds cube 4's files. Success.

In it, he finds 2,500 folders housing 6,021 fighting scenarios as the Aspers slam into the outer walls.

"A lot of these files won't copy," says Zach.

"Just get as much as you can," says D.

The wall is secreting something from inside the edges. The solution is keeping the pygmies from clinging to the walls. It's confusing to the others, so they spread out, trying to find easier ways into the maze. Most are staying near the key port because that is where the scent is strongest. After several seconds, the largest sniffer lets out a plume from its back, and the other Aspers return. The walls don't break at first, but the Aspers keep going. The first large crack starts at the key port and snakes up the wall.

"Shit. Zach, let em in," says D.

Zach was about to suggest the same thing. The key port wall opens, and the Aspers pour into the maze. Zach opens specific walls just as the Aspers reach them. It's hard to see the reaction, but everyone can hear the grunting, hissing, and falling, as pockets of gas overwhelm their senses. Zach opens up more walls that lead in a circle back to the same gas pockets.

"Nice work, Zach," says D.

"I try," says Zach, smugly.

The sniffers crackle and hiss and after six plumes from the largest sniffer, all the Aspers stop and the brutes and sniffers pound on the clear walls as before. Zach opens these walls, but five more sniffers separate themselves and begin throwing up plumes. The brutes and lesser sniffers continue pounding. If D ever did show genuine emotion on a mission, it would be openmouthed befuddlement. As it is, D just frowns in annoyance.

Commander Maize didn't anticipate this either. D did tell him at the beginning of their mission that uglies adjust quickly. This isn't quick; it's smart. That is more concerning than anything else. He'll never admit this, but only a fool ignores D's advice on combat, so he asks now.

"No reason to fight them. We're leaving soon sir." says D.

"Oh, now you decide to show proper deference," says Maize.

"My job's almost done," says D, motioning to the mainframe.

Maize grunts and comes up with a plan as he speaks.

"Did you guys have a plan for getting out of here?" Maize asks the troop.

The troop look at each other before Hank shakes his head.

"I didn't think so." Maize motions to the Aspers. "Our new friends will not stop until they can shake our hands. I say we leave before they go for hugs. How about you?"

The troop looks to Hank. "Where would we be going?" asks Hank.

"Home," says Maize, as if it were obvious. "My wife's waiting on me." Maize stares Hank in the eye. "I say we forget whatever happened before and work together. Can I trust you?"

Hank and Rick look at each other. Rick nods. Behind him, Betty, Jade, Colt, and Bode are nodding as well.

"This home is in Indiana?" asks Hank.

"No, Illinois," says Maize.

"What's behind that wall you've been glancing at this whole time?" asks Hank.

"The diagram says a closed train track. The government used emergency funds to layer it into the building plans of places like this," says Maize.

The Aspers are clumping into smaller groups to aim their combined bulk at the creases between the walls. Zach's fingers are flying over the keyboard as the voice comes out as a garbled mess. Zach's whispering for the cube to play while adjusting the reading lenses.

"This, my friend, is all I could do given the time I have been allotted," says the voice. "I will soon not be able to express coherent thoughts due to my accelerating transmogrification. As I stated in cube 2, the vaccine remains contagious, so neither I nor my fellow subjects will be able to rejoin humanity. And my mind isn't nearly as sharp as I remember. This is a common sentiment among all of us. I'm sorry for how our creations were used. I hope you will use these resources wisely."

The blast wall opens and a hydraulic arm extends a clear composite container. Inside the container is a three-color solution, cold to the touch. Beneath this solution is a layer of frozen nitrogen and inside that is the vaccine. D grabs the cylinder. Maize opens a rucksack, and D carefully places the cylinder in. Maize pulls the string, then puts another bag over that.

"We're done; let's go," says Maize.

Just as Maize says this, a wall shatters. The Aspers are doing a rhythmic grunt now. D frowns at the sound.

Is that laughing? Can uglies do that?

"Zach, time to go. Open a path to the back exit," says D.

In a few strokes, there's a more or less straight line to the exit. Maize and Andrews are lifting Teague off the floor while Carlton stands in front of everyone, ready for Maize to give the word.

More walls shatter, but the sniffers are still frustrated. Walls are moving and breaking, but none of the walls near the mainframe are moving, and the back half of the maze hasn't moved at all. The lead sniffer lets out a series of puffs from its back and a brute climbs the shattered mounds of wall and leaps to the top. It opens its nostrils to hear the walls shifting. After a moment, it has a pattern and pushes off the wall, then the next one and the next one.

"Lead the way, Sergeant," says Maize as the brute leaps into the clearing.

In a flash, it's racing for D. Before he can do anything, the brute is smashing him through the computer. D feels and hears cracks in his body. The explosion of pain forces D into unconsciousness. Jamie screams with anger and fires into the brute. Maize and Andrews drop Teague and fire. In seconds, everyone is shooting the Asper. Seconds later, the brute is a pile of sweet-smelling meat and blood.

Jamie slaps D awake. He's not sure what happened but Hank and Rick are exploding cans of mustard gas over the wall.

"Your left collar bone is broken," says Jamie.

"He has a mild concussion too," adds Cella, kneeling beside her.

"Can you move?" asks Jamie, ignoring Cella.

D looks down at his vest. It's broken. A claw is sticking in the vest but hasn't penetrated. D looks up at Jamie. Her gun is holstered. He winks at her.

"He's fine," says Jamie, smiling. "You're taking a pain killer now," she says firmly.

D tries to fight it, but his body has shut down. It won't allow him to move. Jaime holds D's nostrils so he has to open his mouth and pushes the pain killer down his throat followed by water. It only takes a few seconds.

D's eyes go wide, his pupils dilate, and numbness washes over his body. D gets up while Cella is insisting he stay still. He pushes her away and makes his legs stiffen. Things are fuzzy if he moves too fast, but he can deal with that. This is what he doesn't like about the pills. He can't properly judge limits when this stuff is in him. He's thinking about throwing up the pill, but there's no point now.

"Jamie, pull this thing out of my suit," says D.

Jamie yanks out the claw in three pulls. D grabs his guns and nods.

"What are you still doing here?" asks D.

"I can't control the maze anymore," says Zach.

"Well, then you'll have to get out the hard way then. Where's the salve?" asks D, as Cella stuffs the claw into a sample bag. "You're not coming?" asks Maize.

"No," says D, in an insistent tone. "I spilled some of the pheromones on myself in the tunnels. That's why it came after me instead of all of the people with open, bleeding wounds."

"Makes sense," says Maize. "You're set on this?"

"Yes, I am, Commander."

There's nothing else to say. Maize hands him a few magazines then signals Carlton to lead everyone out. The troop looks at him. D glances back at them, after layering the salve again. Hank and D's eyes meet, and there's a sense of formality. No warmth, no sadness, if anything, D seems annoyed they're still there. Then, D's eye shift to the horde of Aspers. Just as their eyes break, Hank sees Dice, the sharpshooter that controlled entire battlefields and terrified Coalition troops. Something tells him Dice is going to give these brogs quite the time.

As everyone leaves, D finds Jamie still standing there. He looks at Jamie, and she cocks her gun, daring him to say something. He shakes his head and aims up at the cloud of mustard fog. D's wondering if these Aspers are going to use the same tactics to get around the mustard gas. In the red light, the cloud looks blood-orange, swirling over shifting walls.

"We'll be all right," Jamie whispers.

A garbled automated voice comes over one speaker.

"Ten minutes to complete system sterilization."

"What?" asks Jamie.

"Focus, Lieutenant," says D, as a piece of his vest falls off.

"Our bet still on?" asks Jamie.

"I'm at nineteen," says D.

"Eighteen. I killed the last one."

"I shouldn't have started the drag queen rumor."

"I love you too, you piece of shit. Focus."

Another wall shatters. The Aspers are getting more frenzied. In under a minute, the next wall shatters. At this distance, the pheromone scent is so strong the Aspers start attacking each other. Others are confused. The scents so close they ignore the sniffer signals and race around the maze, looking for the scent.

The Aspers reach the last wall. Here, the lead sniffer crouches low and turns its torso so that puffs of mist spray on the walls. As the other Aspers rush past the wall, they stop to pound on the wall. Then, after five seconds, they stop and sniff for the scent again. The lead sniffer runs in a semi-circle, spraying the walls with mist every thirty seconds. After five minutes, the sniffer stops, taking in deep breaths, then sprays again. This time, however, the mist is a thin stream that fades almost as quickly as it is sprayed.

Jamie's been looking to shoot one of the beasts, but they're being chaotic; she doesn't know what to do. She looks back at D sitting in a broken computer chair, gun aimed at the ground, staring at the scene, fascinated.

"Did you know this would happen?" asks Jamie.

"We're buying time for Maize," says D.

"That wasn't my question."

"Look."

The lead sniffer stops, heaving again as it tries to make the others break the last wall. Now, a second sniffer, thinner with more unhealthy pink lesions on its skin, attacks the lead sniffer. It hisses and crackles while clawing at the lead sniffer. Blood pours from slash marks as the lead sniffer slashes back, ripping open long gashes along the upstart's vertical mouth. The upstart lets out three quick puffs and charges, slamming the lead sniffer into the wall. A crack appears in the wall, and blood seeps through, rolling to the ground. Now, D gets up.

"I count five hundred uglies. How many rounds do we have?" asks Jamie.

"I have a sonic bomb." says D.

The lead sniffer keeps tearing at the upstart, opening the gash even more. The roots of the bone slabs are visible through the injury. The upstart's mouth is lopsided, with tooth chips hanging loosely, while its blood clots quickly so that it doesn't bleed out. The lead sniffer hisses long and loud, about to kill the upstart, but then lowers itself to the ground and lets out a huge plume of mist into the lead sniffer's side. It's confused, as the smell is sending a stop signal.

As the lead, only it can send that signal, but in a dominance fight, everything is a weapon, including scent signals. Tired as the lead sniffer is and without a stockpile of water and fluid to make its own signals or resist others, it takes too long to reject the scent. The upstart leaps on its back and tears off the back flap before clawing into the soft spot and ripping out the nerve cluster.

The upstart rumbles a rhythmic grunt, hisses while letting out five small puffs, then eats a chunk of the former lead sniffer. It is the new lead sniffer. It continues eating the dead sniffer while letting out mist. Suddenly, the other Aspers are grabbing pygmies and tearing them open. The ones within ten feet of D and Jamie throw the pygmy skins over their side nostrils and climb each other.

A totem pole of three Aspers pokes over the top of the wall. The dead skin protects from the mustard gas as the brute dives down, or tries to. Soon as Jamie sees its middle, she blasts a hole through it.

#

Maize is telling Carlton to slow down while leading the troop right, left, and left again to the last tunnel path. A large metal door with a thick hatch stands there with an exit sign above it.

"Where are we going?" asks Hank.

"I told you," says Maize. "A little place on the south boarder of Illinois, population 65,000, I hope. They've been waiting for us." Maize hears a hum, then the floor in front of the door opens.

One bullet rips through Maize's mouth, another smashes his jaw, as seven more open his chest. Hank takes a shoulder hit, as an automated sentry in the form of a sixty-caliber automatic machine gun, moves back and forth. Bode watches his knee explode from two bullet shots. He instinctively grabs his knee and because of that, takes three bullets through the skull. Everyone is moving, trying to hide behind natural rock wall grooves.

The sentry fires at anything moving. Rick tosses a rock trying guide the guns fire as he moves but two of Rick's fingers disappear as the sentry is too quick. Andrews jumps involuntarily as one of the fingers hits him in the face. The sentry bullet grazes his skull then the foot sliding out as he tries readjusting. He's spun around as another bullet hits his shoulder. More bullets carve up his lungs as he dies. One of Andrews' flashbangs goes off as its hit by a bullet, blinding everyone. The sentry stops for a moment. Rick was checking how the sentry tracked them. Even with his hand ruined he has the focus to tell what happened. The sentry operates using an external camera.

Everyone better have paid attention.

"Rick." yells Hank squeezing himself against the wall. "There's a lens on top of this thing."

"I figured." yells Rick in a breathy injured voice. "I'm not aiming anything with my hand scrapped. Colt?"

"I've got no line of sight from here." yells Colt near the back.

"Put up some mirrors."

The sentry is firing again, sending bullets at random instead of in a flat arc. Rick takes out his knife and some glue to stick a shaving mirror on. Hank does the same.

"Turn a little more to the right," yells Colt holding his own shaving mirror.

Colt aims and fires his rifle. It hits the base of the sentry's firing platform pinging off harmlessly. The sentry fires a bullet back at the position, as if following a straight line. The bullet misses and Colt has his second shot lined up. The sentry stops to reload and Colt cracks its lens and everyone moves forward. Soon as the sentry reloads it fires even more randomly. The gun is far less accurate but bullets are coming faster. Two crack Rick's forearm bones, and then a third pounds into his face, killing him.

Hank yells in outrage as bullets pepper Rick's body. This is when Colt aims and rips the gun off its platform with two shots. The sentry stops firing. Colt breathes out in relief, while moving forward.

"All right," says Hank, moving toward Rick.

This is when the sentry turns itself right side up, firing exploding armor-piercing rounds. The first bullet flies past Colt's head and leaves a head sized hole in the wall where he was just standing. The sentry continues shooting in that direction at an even faster rate.

Hank and Colt look at each other, hoping the other has a good idea. For now, they'll just squeeze into grooves in the wall as the sentry carves out more pieces.

The humans can't know this, but the sentry is responding to the system sterilization signal to lockdown the site. The best way to do this is by killing all things with a heat signature or collapsing the foundations of the tunnel. Two other sentry units should be here to cut into the inner metal supports. Budget cuts have made only one sentry available to do all the work.

"Maybe we can wait till it runs dry." yells Colt.

"Ok," says Hank.

#

Jamie kills two Aspers trying to climb the wall. On D's end, pygmies are secreting some type of solvent onto the walls.

This is new. Maybe the ones up here were given new fighting traits. Or defensive traits. I need more information.

A brute picks up a pygmy and tosses it over the wall. D shoots it out of the air just as it clears the wall. The brute sends twelve more up at once, and D kills all twelve before they reach the ground.

"I should've yelled pull," says D.

"No one likes a showoff," says Jaime.

The Aspers in Jamie's area are hissing, crackling, and tearing at each other before a brute grunts at the new lead sniffer. The sniffer is still eating the former leader, not really paying attention until the brute shoves it. The sniffer hisses in outrage and claws at the brute. The brute sprays mucus from its nostrils and bows down. The sniffer is still hissing but smells the question. The sniffer grunts and lets out mist. The brute goes back to the other Aspers, and they all pound on the walls again. Cracks are appearing all over the walls, linking to make a cobweb of breaks.

D and Jamie stop shooting, standing side by side as they watch the Aspers crackle and pound. D sets the sonic bomb to thirty seconds for maximum damage. The automated voice is calling out six minutes. The wall is weakening and pieces are falling as the second exit near the elevator rips open.

"Second biological agent has broken its last containment barrier," says the automated voice.

The most heinous and largest of amalgamations roars and stomps into section 5 with broken shackles. It has dotted blond fur from head to shoulder over pinkish red skin, an unreasonably large barrel-shaped torso. A hulking right arm and severely underdeveloped left, supported by a misshaped pelvis, linking to enormous hind limbs bursting with muscle fiber. Aspers follow the titanic beast. Now, there is a proper scale. If the average brute is between nine and eleven feet when standing, then this thing is twenty feet.

"Five minutes," says the automated voice, as the beast rages, smashing down three shifting walls while Aspers claw at him.

Nine more of the titanic beasts charge in. These are only about fifteen feet. They punch and claw at Aspers, roaring as loud as the first beast. The other Aspers turn, hissing and crackling as they charge.

D turns off the sonic bomb while Jamie stares at the new beasts, eyes bulging. The twenty-footer slaps down one brute, snapping its back. A lesser sniffer leaps on its back to slash at its neck. The twenty-footer stands upright and reaches back with the large arm and tears off one of the Asper's front limbs.

D relaxes his face then looks at Jamie.

"What are we doing?" asks Jamie.

"I know your ribs are hurt but, can you climb?"

Jamie stares at him, confused. "There's nothing to climb here. The walls are steep with no handholds. The mainframe is the only— What are you thinking?"

"The startup for the train is supposed to be a minute. The team should've left by now, so we can have some fun," says D, turning to the amalgamation. "We need a name for the big ones," he mutters. "I think the uglies don't care about the pheromone scent on me right now. Get your helmet on. We're going to wreck this whole place before it blows."

Jamie climbs the mainframe, ignoring the spikes of pain in her ribs.

"What should I aim for?" asks Jamie as D keeps an arm under her so she can use both arms.

"Shoot the ass," says D. 'That's gotta piss it off."

Jamie laughs, despite herself. D always gets her in these situations. She slows her heartrate, waiting for the thing to turn its back. She shoots between heartbeats. The bullet pierces its anus. The amalgamation roars, forcing D and Jamie to cover their ears. It starts thrashing, and in a heap of rancor, charges at the bullet source. Jamie jumps down followed by D as the amalgamation shatters the last wall between D, Jamie and It. The thing dents the mainframe with its unnatural fist. A foot barely misses flattening Jamie as D drags her away. An Asper steps within five feet of D and turns, overwhelmed by the scent. D shoots the thing dead while pulling Jamie to the other side of the mainframe.

The amalgamation keeps thrashing, shattering wall after wall.

"Shoot it again," says D.

"That thing almost killed me." says Jamie.

"That's the point."

"I think I enable you too much."

D chuckles. "Shoot it again. We need more room."

Jamie shoots the amalgamation again, this time in the small human-sized arm. The beast roars and stomps toward Jamie and D, then smashes every wall leading to the back exit. Then, in a true show of strength, the amalgamation picks up a brute and slams it against the wall. The wall is reinforced, so it only bulges. However, the amalgamation does it three more times, and another amalgamation charges. Together, they smash several Aspers through the wall.

"Four minutes," says the automated voice, as D synchronizes the time.

D and Jamie keep their heads down as the amalgamations and Aspers tear each other apart. The sharpshooters see the chaos and look at each other positively gleeful. They never get to cause complete destruction for no reason. This is when Jamie hears automatic gunfire. D checks his diagram; that is where Maize should've led everyone. D and Jamie take a few turns and find blood and people lining the walls as something fires high-caliber bullets.

"Go get the big guy," says D.

"Give me your jacket," says Jamie.

D doesn't know what she's thinking, but he releases his helmet and hands the jacket over. Jamie rushes back to the frenzy where the amalgamations and Aspers continue clawing at each other. One of the amalgamations falls, one of its legs broken. The aspers are getting ready to eat. Jamie needs to get their attention.

She pulls out the pheromones the troop gave her and douses the jacket while backing away. The Aspers closest to the scent turn to track it. They smell blood too. They trot nearer to it. The horde crackles in triumph. Two more amalgamations are down. Other Aspers are now looking for the nearest treat. Most attack the remaining amalgamations, but thirty follow the scent.

Jamie releases her last pheromone pack on D's jacket and tosses it into the hallway. The Aspers charge after it, running straight into sentry fire. The Aspers crackle loudly as the sentry blows holes in them. Then, the largest amalgamation follows, roaring. It smells that overpowering stench of the pheromones too, but unlike with the Aspers, he wants to destroy it. The amalgamation swats Aspers, cracking bone while taking high caliber rounds. Then, it charges the sentry, pulverizing the gun. The sentry crashes into the metal doors behind it again and again, warping the doors until its top half folds and breaks open into the room. With the sentry shattered, the amalgamation turns back to find Aspers charging him with renewed tenacity. The amalgamation breaks the front leg of a brute, then a sniffer rips off one of the amalgamations fingers. Other Aspers pile on as the rest of the amalgamations and Aspers continue fighting through the numerous pathways

Chapter 36

"What the hell was that?" asks Colt.

"Helpful," says Jamie.

Colt looks Jamie in the eye and takes a step back. She and D must be related.

"Three minutes, fourteen seconds," says D, rushing to the escape.

"Three minutes, fourteen seconds to what?" asks Hank.

"The building's going to napalm itself to keep the uglies inside," says Jamie as D stops.

The troop is panicking, but D sees Maize is dead, so is Andrews, Bode and Rick. Teague is still moving however. D has to complete the mission. Other people might stop and contemplate what just happened, how the situations changed so quickly, but D has trained since he was nine years old to be reliable in these situations. He takes a second then focuses.

Mission success by any means necessary.

Carlton is staring at his hand in horror. Asper blood is splashed over the gun wound. D kneels over him. Carlton looks at D, then nods. There's a loud boom as Carlton's face explodes. D slings his rifle then takes Carlton's dog tag and the tags of the other seals. D pulls Maize's false leg off and takes the small bag of dog tags, and the rucksack holding the virus.

Hank is helping Betty up, while Jade rushes to Colt. D and Jamie look deranged which has everyone keeping their distance.

Zach is trying to pick up Teague when D finds him.

"Are you hurt?" asks D.

"No," says Zach, maintaining eye contact.

D doesn't look quite as terrifying as when he uncuffed himself. This is what Zach thinks to keep from pissing himself.

Jamie pulls herself up. She feels her injured ribs but doesn't cry out. She's proud of herself for that. Jamie's first through the metal doors. D motions Zach to go before him. Teague can't drive the train with his hands so mangled.

"You were serious about driving trains, right?" asks D.

"Yes," says Zach, dragging Teague.

"Look on the bottom part of the cards I gave you. It should take a minute. Then, don't wait; just drive."

Zach doesn't jump more than falls into the station. Like the shuttle bay, this place is lit by industrial white light. It's a thousand feet across with a dark-silver shuttle sitting there, unmoved for eighteen months. Dust coating everything. Desiccated bodies scatter the area. It's clear everyone in this station suffocated.

D is next in the room. He's replacing the cloth on his face as Zach enters the control room. Zach inputs the emergency code from the card. Flashes pop up, warning of a containment breach in Zone E-5. Zach says his name to the computer, overriding the warnings. Next, all blockades lift. This is usually a five-second procedure, but the screen is saying thirty seconds. Zach notices something as the blocks lift. A map of other blockades around the state corresponds with the dots on maps he marked with D.

The rest of the troop maneuver themselves in. Hank is cursing about why D didn't try helping them. D is down on the tracks, removing debris that fell during the stations dormancy. Jamie is standing outside the control room with her rifle aimed at the door.

The control room is asking which destination Zach wants to go to.

"D. I see seventy stations here. A lot of these active ones are in the southeast," says Zach. "There's no direct route to Illinois. What route should I take?"

"There are seventy? I thought it was only twenty." D shakes his head. "Just pull up the recommended section for the fastest route."

"I found one that takes four hours," says Zach. "Opening the shuttle doors now."

"One minute, fifty-one seconds," says D.

D's on the platform, having removed all the debris he could. All living troop members pile in as a crackle makes everyone stop. D instinctively steps toward the sound, eyes pulsing, wanting to kill.

"Who are you?" asks Colt.

"I'm exactly who I said I was, Mr. Black ops. I'm here because two months ago a bunch of people started rioting because a few people were getting more than others. They smashed things; the lab was one of them. Then, people got sick. Some got euthanized, and that's why we have 65,000 instead of 80,000. That code Zach has will inform Fallout a shuttle is coming, I could explain more, but I don't want too. Get in the train."

An Asper climbs the door. Jamie shoots it dead immediately. Hank picks up Betty by the waist and throws her in the train. Cella and Saffire follow, then six more Aspers leap over the door.

"Zach, set the train to go," says Jamie firing.

"Done," says Zach, rushing behind Jaime as she keeps her rifle between the two of them and the Aspers.

Jamie looks for D. He's rushing to Zach and pulling him towards the conductor controls. He's not going to wait for anyone. This is unfortunate for Jade. She was helping Teague when the Aspers filled the doorway. Now, she's the closest to the animals as they charge.

To her credit, Jade does get off a shot, but the bullet hits the shoulder not the soft spot. The Asper doesn't even stop as it extends its claws. The strike nearly decapitates Jade. The right side of her neck is a pulped mess. She hits the floor with a thump. Colt and Hank scream as they see her flop to the ground, twitching. D's in the train, standing five feet in front of Zach as a dozen more Aspers climb in, with Amalgamations roaring close by.

Jamie is in the train aiming her rifle at the approaching Aspers. D has three civilians in the train, one a child. He's retrieved what he was ordered to collect. That's good enough, right?

"Zach, close the doors," says D.

Hank looks back at the Aspers with tears in his eyes. He looks like a wild animal. He's lifting his rifle to shoot D as Colt lets out a shout from deep in his marrow before shooting the Aspers in a side-to-side shooting pattern before tossing his last mustard gas canister.

"One minute, three seconds," says D.

"Ok, dammit," says Zach.

The Aspers jerk and shutter before stumbling back towards the exit.

"Jade, baby. It's daddy, ok. Stay with me," says Hank, pulling her toward the closing doors while Colt shoots.

D is not letting that infected body inside the train. Jade's still shuddering as Betty gets up, realizing what's wrong. She's trying to get out now. The train doors open again as Betty steps on the ingress. D's cursing his bad luck. Another civilian is out. However, Teague is on the floor curled up coughing in the yellow fog. D runs out to drag Teague into the train.

If Hank and Colt want to be idiots fine. What's he care?

Dammit.

"We have forty-four seconds," says D. "Jamie, grab Betty. Zach get this fucking train moving."

D sprints over. He should let the old bastard die. Colt's younger but Hank's leadership skills will help younger officers when the war begins. This is what D is telling himself to justify getting Hank.

"Look, I know she meant—means a lot to you, but we have to go now." Hank slaps his hand away, trying to stop Jade from convulsing.

"You still have a wife, and where I'm going, I can give you the chance at payback. We know who caused this. You heard it on the cube. Do you want revenge or to burn up in a fucking building?"

Hank looks at D. It's a look D's seen on his own face. He's convinced him.

"Twenty-two seconds," says Jaime.

Jade stops moving. Hank shakes with rage and pulls his daughter into the train. D eyes the blood drops as Colt follows. The door closes and Zach speeds the train out of the station.

Sirens sound as a wave of heat expands from the mainframe through the entire complex. Aspers and amalgamations burn. Zone E-5 carbonizes. The next section and the next and the next ignite. Heat overwhelms even the composite metal foundations, forcing the structure to collapse on itself. Secondary explosions trigger, destroying the elevators and steps leading to upper levels. Then the upper levels burn.

Zach is pushing the train to maximum speed as the flames melt the tracks behind them. The back of the train is warming. Outside, the metal is turning a dark orange. The windows on the back end melt or pop, spontaneously turning to sand. Suddenly, the heat fades.

"We're all right, Zach," says D after two minutes to make sure they're far away from the flames.

D's heart is still pounding. He's not sure why. Are the pain killers doing something? He's refusing to consider the fire itself is why he's panicking.

"Cella, help her. Help her," yells Betty. "Try an adrenaline shot."

Cella is keeping her distance. The disease Aspers carry can survive for two days after death. No one is well protected right now, and no doctor could fix a neck wound like that. There's no more blood pouring out of her body. Jade's been dead for at least a minute. There's no sense wasting medicine on a dead person.

"Do something." Betty screams.

"I can't help her," says Cella, forcing herself to meet Betty's eye. "I'm sorry."

Betty stares back, dumbfounded, then lunges at her. Hank stops her from choking Cella to death.

"Honey, she's gone," says Hank, holding her.

"No she's not. Get off me," says Betty, storming her way to D.

"Turn the train around."

D stares back at Hank, when she kicks his injured leg.

"Owe, lady," he says, slapping her foot away.

"You knew what was in there, didn't you?" she screams.

There's nothing for D to say. Jamie's moving behind Betty. She's protecting Zach from anything Betty might do while she's this emotional and seeing if D wants her to take the old lady out.

"You did, didn't you?" yells Betty.

"Ma'am, please, go back to your seat," says Jamie.

"Get the fuck out of my way," says Betty.

Hank is there again, pulling her away.

Betty again slaps him. "You just let her die? She's your daughter, you fucking coward."

"She's gone, Betty. I'm sorry, but she's gone," says Hank.

The fight leaves Betty, as she shakes her head. Hank holds her tighter, and Betty falls apart with sobs. Hank leads her back to her seat, as D slides his knife back into his sleeve.

The shuttle is silent except for the clanking of loose metal behind the train. Zach slows the trains to 175 miles per hour.

"Dice, your face looks horrible; keep the cloth on," says Jamie.

"Fuck you," says D replacing the cloth.

"What's this place called?"

"We call it Fallout County," he says, putting more salve on his face before covering it.

"65,000 people?" asks Jamie.

"We hope so," says Teague. Cella gave him an adrenaline shot so he could stay awake.

"What's that mean?" asks Jamie.

"There was a riot," says D. "Public trust has declined. That's not the important thing for you. We need to explain what we found out."

Teague nods. "They'll do a full sweep of the train. How do we hide the cubes?"

"You've read the scans of Fallout. We just keep the cubes outside. I can get them at a later time. I've gotten in and out before."

Teague smiles. "I think Wolfgang still has a grudge about that."

"Fuck him. What about our team?"

"I'm not pressing charges on you. Maize was going to, but I think your good outweighs your bad. We wouldn't have gotten out of Ohio without you. I won't call for a court martial."

"That's appreciated, but I think you should have a strong reprimand in your report. Terry lost her kid. She'll want blood. This will distract them from other things we might know."

"How do we explain the NTs inside Three-Mile?"

D thinks for a moment, then in an official voice says, "It's my opinion these creatures did as their name suggests and followed us in. We didn't see the creatures until some minutes after entering Three Mile. The front door was left open. They were tracking us the entire time. It is my opinion that the Night trackers were drawn to this location by our actions alone." he looks at Teague.

"We'll have to work on the wording, but that's good enough for me," says Teague.

They look at Jamie. She doesn't lie on official reports. Even the times when D did questionable things to win the mission, she just left things out. This seems too much like a lie.

"Please?" says D.

"Fine," says Jamie, deflating. "I'm trusting your judgment on this. So how does Fallout County look?"

"You'll see." says D. "Its big; some places look better than others, some people are better than others. The air's clean. I've been a resident there for five months. There's one in Missouri too, a hundred thousand people I heard. They went silent the week we left though. There are other shelters too."

"Seventy apparently," says Teague.

"That's it?" asks Jamie.

"Fuck, lady. I'm not your tour guide," says D.

Jamie gives him a middle finger as they chuckle.

"So how do we get them to go with the official account?" Jamie motions at the troop.

"We have some time. Zach, slow down to 150, will you?" says D. "I have some convincing to do. Teague, you'll back me?"

"Yes." says Teague.

Betty's still sobbing into her hands. Saffire is pushing Cella away while trying to pop earlobes to make the sound come back.

"That's not going to work," says D.

Cella tenses as he comes closer. He tries not to smirk at how pathetic he thinks she's acting, but some of it shows on his face. It makes Cella scowl. His eyes are glossy like one high on pain killers.

"The doctors can fix her ears. She'll be fine," D says. "Or she may not. It all depends on how good everyone's memory is."

He lets his meaning settle on them.

"Go away, please," asks Cella, outraged.

"Now, we're not going to let stupid things like pride ruin good things like shelter," says D, pretending Cella didn't speak.

"None of the stories you told me were true, were they?" says Cella, raising her voice as she stands. *I will not be ignored.*

D would frown if it didn't hurt his face. She's ruining a good presentation. He'll have to go with it.

"I didn't lie," says D.

"Omissions are lies," says Cella.

"You've omitted plenty of things. But if it makes you feel better, we can agree to disagree on that. And you never asked."

"I didn't ask if you were out there eighteen months?"

"You didn't specify where, and I'm not obligated to share my life story."

"I have to ask you to not be a liar?" she says incredulous.

"You're in no position to give moral advice, Priscella."

"My name's not Priscella; it's Chancellor."

"Who names their kid after an office?"

"Who names their kid a stupid letter? What, your parents could only count to four?"

D almost laughs out loud; that was a good one. But this is taking too long.

"I should've expected that attitude from someone like you. Anyone that would do this, isn't big on empathy."

D takes off his cloth to show the burned half of his face. It produces the desired effect. More of the skin is flaking off, making way for new skin, but the raw lower layers of skin still looks like ground beef. Cella flinches while stepping back. Her medical training is the only thing keeping her from vomiting.

Jamie's smiling as D addresses the others. Teague steps to his side, and they tell the troop what they will remember when the Fallout authorities debrief them.

#

The train slows down. Everyone is on guard now. They passed seven stations overrun with Aspers. D dropped off the cubes one mile back in an air pocket when everyone had to get out and clear rubble for the fifth time.

They see the lights. Neon is a change from the white, black, and gray cold everywhere else. The time of arrival to Fallout station is six hours, and thirty-nine minutes. The troop is still upset about going along with D's story, but that's mostly just to be obtuse. They'll follow along; they have no good reason not to follow the story.

"Why didn't we take the segmented tunnels?" asks Zach, guiding the train into the station.

"We did," says D with a glance back at the troop. "Some of them are walkways, and most of them were flooded, remember?"

Zach nods in realization.

Jamie stands to see her new home. The first obvious feature of Fallout is the tremendous heat sending ripples off the platform. The next is the very realistic sky projection on the ceiling a thousand feet above. The station has four other train cars lined in front of them. When Zach stops the train, Jamie sees they are on an elevated platform with confused and excited faces approaching.

"There they are," says one as the crowd erupts.

In moments, military officers coated in hazmat suits push through the crowd. A man holding a bullhorn is telling everyone to move behind the safety line. Soldiers are pulling yellow tape between the crowd and the platform.

"This place is usually a hangout spot for low-sector residents. I'm guessing words out about us." says D to Jamie's unasked question.

The soldiers spray some type of chemical solution over the train.

"Is Commander Maize in there?" asks the man with the bullhorn.

"No," says D. "This is Lieutenant Demetri Peron. Commander Maize died on mission. I have his dog tags and that of the other fifteen officers on our mission. Lieutenant Teague and I are the only surviving members of our party. Be advised we have a dead body likely infected with the NT strain. I have three civilians. One is a child. I also have three military personnel. I can vouch for one but not the other two. Check for a Coronel Henry Auberon, Colt— um, what's your last name?"

"Colt Watkins," says Colt.

"Colt Watkins," says D. "And Dr. Betty Auberon."

"Understood, Lieutenant," says the bullhorn.

The bullhorn instructs them to open the door slowly and back away. This is when a red-haired man walks up to the platform. Everyone makes way for this man. He looks harassed but relieved. He has an easy smile, expensive suit, and thinning hair hurriedly combed over.

Four cameras are here, so the man positions himself and the cameras at an angle that makes him look taller than his five foot ten inches. He has pronounced wrinkles but is fit for a man of his advanced age. Someone is warning him to step back, so they can properly disinfect the train, but he tells them to stand aside.

Jamie sees D and Teague stiffen as they look at this man. A millisecond later, the looks are gone, replaced with professional flat expressions. She follows their lead.

"We're going out in a certain order," says D.

Teague organizes them as D wants, and Zach opens the doors. D stands ramrod straight with his left face covered of course.

Jamie's right next to him. she's squinting to find the edge of Fallout. She can see soft-white streetlights illuminating paved roads, miniature dome shaped apartment buildings pouring out people, trees—actual trees. No insects, but there is a westward blowing wind.

"You ok?" asks D, quietly.

Jamie shakes her head numbly.

"Lieutenant," says the red-haired man.

"Mayor," says D. Then playing to the cameras, he holds up the rucksack. "The mission was a success, sir."

The mayor grins as a wolf would. Hazmat officers take the rucksack before it touches the mayor.

"You're owed a debt, Lieutenant," says the mayor.

This is when Teague lets out the others, with Cella last. Even as untidy as she looks, the woman still gets everyone's attention. The mayor gives D a grin and nod after seeing her. It plays well to the public.

"I'm sorry about the heat," says the mayor. "We have to maintain the unpredictability of weather, helps keep everyone from going crazy, just like the sky up there. It's still summer, you know?"

People are crowding the station entrance as more look on at the public titan screens.

"If we'd known you guys were coming today, we would have set up a better ceremony," says the mayor.

"It's just good to be back home, sir," says D.

"Is this all of them, Lieutenant?"

"I'm afraid so, Mayor. They've gone through a lot. I'd recommend letting them rest after quarantine. And the little one needs surgery on her ears."

D says that loudly enough for the cameras to hear. People love kids. He's thrown the troop a favor. Now, he hopes they'll follow his advice.

The mayor nods, showing real sadness before turning to the troop.

"Excuse me for not properly introducing myself to your friends, Lieutenant. We very much appreciate your arrival at Fallout County. I am Mayor Daniel Casamir. Welcome."

Acknowledgement

To the ones who made me watch monster movies when I was too young to see them. To the ones who showed me the meaning of commitment. To the ones who always supported my wild imagination. To the ones who were always honest with me. To the ones I love more than anyone. To my family.

Printed in Great Britain
by Amazon

30902490R00163